Oystercatchers

ALSO BY SUSAN FLETCHER

Eve Green

Oystercatchers

SUSAN FLETCHER

W. W. NORTON & COMPANY
New York • London

AUG 1 3 2007

For information about permission to reproduce
selections from this book, write to Permissions,
W. W. Norton & Company, Inc.,
500 Fifth Avenue, New York, NY 10110

Manufacturing by R.R. Donnelley, Bloomsburg Division
Book design by Helene Berinsky
Production manager: Julia Druskin

Library of Congress Cataloging-in-Publication Data

Fletcher, Susan, 1979–
    Oystercatchers / Susan Fletcher. — 1st American ed.
        p. cm.
ISBN 978-0-393-06003-4
    1. Sisters—Fiction. 2. Introspection—Fiction.
    3. Domestic fiction.
    I. Title.
PR6106.L48O97 2007
823'.92—dc22

                                        2007007767

W. W. Norton & Company. Inc.
500 Fifth Avenue, New York, N.Y. 10110
www.wwnorton.com

W. W. Norton & Company Ltd.
Castle House, 75/76 Wells Street, London W1T 3QT

1 2 3 4 5 6 7 8 9 0

Contents

For Guy

Oystercatchers

I DREAM OF WATER, EVEN NOW.

I still see its light, and shadows. The wide, dappled wake of a
duck, as it swims. Or I dream, sometimes, of a high tide, and an
evening sea—of the huge, grey rolling backs of my old Atlantic
water, with all its seals and harbours. I see full moons. And stars.
Once, I dreamt of a silvery tail above the waves, and I stood on the
shoreline, squinted. A whale, perhaps, or a mermaid—I also dream
of these things.

Then there is the darker water—wells, riverbeds. I sleep, and I
wade out into my flat, married sea again, with my trousers rolled up,
and my hair untied. I count the fishing boats. Or I turn, and watch
the coastal lights come on. I know that in the marshes the wading
birds are sleeping now—one-legged, with their heads tucked under
their wings—and I know there's salt on them. I smell this, or I think
I can. It is a hard dream to wake from, and I have carried these birds
with me before, in the daytime, in my head.

All my life I've done this. Even before you existed, I paddled or
crab-fished in my sleep. Now, I tend to walk on sand, or sit, but
sometimes, too, I dive in. I still dream of underwater things, of shells
and graves and seaweed, and I dream, too, of hands that brush my

arms, grasp my passing hair, and try to save me. Sometimes I reach for them, and I'm pulled awake. But mostly, I turn away. I don't want to leave my silence, or its greenish light. So I stay. I swim with my eyes open, amongst my quiet anchors and my old, lost shipwrecks. I touch them, as I pass. I think, *I remember you* . . . I sleep amongst their mossy chains, and fishes.

I

Storm Watch

FOUR YEARS, NOW. FOUR—AND HOW MANY MONTHS?

I don't know. Not anymore. I have the years in me, still, but the smaller, paler shapes of time have been lost—the weeks, and days, and the quiet hours within them. They've left me, or maybe my wish to count them has. Once, I did count—the minutes, and your heart sounds; the seconds on my watch. I watched the seasons come—how the trees changed, and the shoots pushed up out of the earth, and the frosts, and I'd see your frail ghost walk out across the ploughed fields. I'd think to myself, *Last year . . .* and imagine it: you, as you were— eating, or in grass. And this, love, is how I measured our lives, at first: by returns, by the slow, silent turning of the world. I counted four pumpkins, four warm Mays. Pine trees, and bank holidays; one leap year. I counted ten thousand tides, Amy. I was the girl with the aba- cus. I did this counting at night.

I was hopeful.

Hopeful, like a bride is, and relieved, at first, for this wasn't a death. I thought it would be. We all did. *She is not dead,* and so, *All will be well*—I told myself this. I sat down, slowed my breath, and imagined futures with you—healthy again, fruit-skinned, with all your scars healed over. Every soft, gentle thing I found was carried to you, laid down on your bed, because I thought you'd miss a world with such things in it—lavender, or eggshells, or the dry, transparent skin of an adder, left on a rock. I'd say, *It's snowing.* Or, *The strawberries are early.* Til sent a postcard, and I read it to you. She wrote of deserts, and huge, cloudless desert skies—and so, for a while, this room was not green-walled, and we were not in an inland town, with your stale smell, and your thin, green heart.

Also, I said: *This, love, is walking.* As I pressed my fist into the balls of your feet, and curled your toes over, cat-like.

And now? Am I still hopeful? For your life, as it was? Perhaps. But hope grows old, as all things do. It loses its shine; it shrinks away. I am older, and I no longer count, or peel oranges in your room to scent it, and I do not bring shells, hold them to your ear. I don't talk of your wise, nut-coloured doctor who stitched you up, saved you, and knows your dark insides. He is lonely, I think. I've seen his eyes.

It's all gone, then—the eggshells, and the songs. Can you blame me? I am only a poor visitor, now, who watches the tree outside, but does not describe it to you. And I am tired—find a stone, feel its weight: I am that heavy. I am that heavy-hearted, and I do not lay a false, lovely world down on your bed anymore, for where was the point? How did it help? Your eyes are still closed, and there may be rabbits in the hospital grounds, and a starry night sky, but the real truths of this world are far darker than that: the falling of towers, diseases. Wars. Bags of nails splitting open on trains. There was a flood in Prague, and the zoo creatures died, or freed themselves—apes on rooftops, a hippo yawning in the town square. In Britain, we burnt our cattle. The house in Stackpole has gone.

Do you even hear this? We are told you can. You sleep—but it isn't the sleep I know. There is little stirring, and no stretching out. Your sleep is half-true and soul-deep, and it is cold, perhaps—a chamber, or a dank room, or it is a wide empty landscape in which you are alone. Or you're under ice, knocking.

Or you are buried. And this is how I've come to think of you the most, in these four years: boxed, soundless. Deep, deep in the earth.

•　•　•

AMY, THESE ARE my words. I want you to know that. They are not from books, or magazines. They are spoken by me—me, whose language was hardly ever in words, like the rest of the world's, but in numbers, symbols, marks on the skin. Bear with me. I know I'll lose myself in this, say things twice, or not at all. I will whisper these words in your wounded ear, or call them out, across the room. But, also, they are in my head. This is my mind's voice, too, which has never been quiet, and these are my thoughts—fast, mackerel-bright. They flash through my brain as I walk, or read. As I kneel on the lawn, planting bulbs. As I close the windows of this room when rain is coming.

I am twenty-seven. Not old—not even slightly; but would you know me, now? I think I look the same, but I know what lies inside me is not as it was. *Nothing changes*—our mother said this, once, which was wrong of her. I've changed a thousand times over; I've shifted my sands more than you have, in so many ways. Once, I walked on the shingle at Cley-next-the-Sea, lonely, and fierce, and crammed full of lies; I carried a brooch with me. Now? I lie in our garden sometimes, watch the clouds moving, and think of my other lives—all the other girls I have been. Thin, vengeful things. Hollow, too, and I have left them behind me, just as I have left the sugar beet fields, and the cloisters, and the stone girl with her feet lost in leaves. Or maybe *left* is wrong—maybe I have not *left* them; but they are locked in me—held down with rocks, pressing their bones against their membrane walls, and sometimes, they stir, as you do. That is, I think, a more truthful way of it. But either way, I threw the brooch into the marshes, as I moved through them for the last time. Heard its neat, music sound as it fell. Walked back to the Blakeney house thinking, *A magpie will find it.* Fall in love with its shine.

So now, I sit. I visit. Pick my fingernails. Watch your heart flinch on a screen.

And this, too: I am the good wife. I'm a dark-haired woman with flesh on her bones and love in my mouth, and stories to tell. My days are spent in a white, west-facing house on an English coast that you have never seen, with Ray, and an attic, and a leafy vegetable patch. I walk barefoot through our rooms, stand by its windows. Or I walk on a campus with my coat buttoned up, books to my chest, spectacles on. I know medical terms, chemicals. I've sat in a dark lecture room. And for a long time after your fall, I'd sit in an airless room with a woman who didn't know me at all, but who, also, did. It was her job to know me, to understand. I cried, confessed. I said your name to her, and other names, and she smiled, noted them down.

As for my evenings?

Sometimes they're with my husband. Chess, or books, or just with each other. Me, alone, in a deep, salted bath.

But also, sometimes I spend them here, with you.

•   •   •

I come to you as the light fades. I drive north, then west. I cross the toll bridge into Wales, follow the last of the sun, and find you lying on your back, as cool as a queen—blue-veined, porous. Shit-smelling. I spend a few hours with you. When it is late, I go home.

Do you remember Cromer pier? How I hit you across the cheek-bone with the side of my hand, and you stumbled backwards, but you did not cry? You stared. And then you came closer to me and took my thumb, as if I was the injured one. Nine years old, and already wise. I knew it—I think we all did. You added poorly; you could not spell; you thought the moon was a night-time sun—and yet, yes, you were wise. As knowing as a priest. And it warmed you, I think, this wisdom—for I stole the blankets off your bed, one winter, hid them away. I secretly opened your window that night, and yet you did not complain. You slept in your clothes, your knees tucked up. Sang to yourself at breakfast.

See? These are the darker truths. I am no saint, Amy, I promise you that. I will turn stones over to prove it. For if I talk of wars, of boundaries, and secrets, and if I talk of the bombers who walk, calmly, into a square, or onto trains, shouldn't I talk of us? Of our war? For it was a war, of sorts. You came. You, the invader, with bubble-gum breath, and I was the hard, stubborn girl who narrowed her eyes, plotted, hungered for armies of her own. I have been called a witch, before now. Imagine that—me, with sparks in my fingertips, spells, and a blistered tongue. All those curses. I cursed you, sometimes. As a baby, you were as pink as a worm. I missed the old world. The old way of things. Amy, I hardened myself.

And did this hardening bring you here? To this hospital bed?

That's the question. I've had it in me for over four years. Of course—for look at my life, and the things I've done. If I had moved, talked, breathed differently, would this bed be empty, now, or slept in by some other girl? Would you be climbing trees, somewhere? Feeding the horses strange things, as you used to—like toast, or unripe plums? I've tried to answer all this. I've worked back, through every part of it, and looked for the moment, the knot in the thread, which brought us here, to this point, this room. There is no such knot. Or rather, there are hundreds of them—slammed doors, lies, my unfaithfulness as a wife, Ray's wife—all on their way to this. To now. This bed in this room.

Guilt. It's in me, all the same, for I have heard of the brain's power—*Imagine,* Til said, *and it can happen that way.* She told me this when I was your age, and facing exams; later, too—when Ray was still a name I dared not say. I never believed her, then. *Stupid,* I thought; I turned away. Yet she told me I should picture myself as a wife, in a house by the coast, shielding my eyes as I looked out across my childhood water, to the ferries and the dipped back of Lundy

Island, where the air shakes with puffin wings, and whether or not there is truth in her way of thinking, or such a thing as Fate, I find myself doing all of this now. I wear a wedding ring. From our bedroom, I see the Atlantic. I am in this sea daily, or so it seems. I tread water, and I look back to our house from the fishing buoy, see myself in the window. I am scared, Amy, that I thought too hard, too clearly, of injuring you.

But I never imagined a fall—nothing so brutal. Believe me: I never did. It was an illness I hoped for, or nightmares, or maybe a deep, yellowing bruise. Once I imagined an adder's bite—for these would be small punishments, small ways of revenge. But not this—not a fall from such a height, with the gulls screaming for you, and the sharp, hard drag of your hands across the rocks, and the crack of your knee, and your brief, huge moment in mid-air, and I never imagined part of your scalp would be lifted up by the rocks, as it was. Nor that, later, the doctor would pluck a mussel out of your skull—glinting, as blue as an eye.

• • •

MOIRA, *we dream what we dream . . .*

This, also, from Til. She wore her rose quartz when she said this; it hung forwards, swayed. And perhaps she's right, it's true—for we can fool our waking hours, and our daytime self, but not the sleeping self at night. I know this. I was tall, solitary; I could raise an eyebrow, as a warrior might. But then, later, I'd dream of old, Atlantic things that undid me, in the dark.

And you? I've often wondered if there are dreams in this strange, dark sleep of yours, and if so, what dreams they might be. Stackpole? If you do dream of it, know this: it does not exist. Or not for us, anymore. The low-slung house in its lane of blackthorn trees and blown sand has gone. Been sold—to a man who knows nothing of tides, or oil spills, and wants the land, not the house on it, so perhaps there are no bricks left at all. Our parents left Stackpole behind them. Packed their boxes and moved inland, to be closer to you. And so the field of horses and the wading birds and the army guns are no longer part of their lives, or yours. Or mine—although I still think of them. I always did. Once, on Freshwater East, I found a dead seagull. I smelt sadness on it, and I still dream of it, two decades on—its open beak, and missing eyes. How its soft, snowy chest feathers parted when the wind came.

Or do you dream of yourself? As you were? The cheerful toddling thing who fell asleep in the wheelbarrow, who left milk out for the hedgehog that lived in the compost heap? Our mother says that, once, you spat cockles into the palm of her hand and wiped them on a stranger's sleeve—and this is the girl she prays for. I have seen her do it. She lays down her embroidery, closes her eyes. *Lord, if . . .* Our father comes, too, at the weekends. And I am here in the evenings— full of confessions, and shadows. Smelling of paint.

Shadows. Many, as if I walk in a cave. I've seen things you never will, and I have done things, too. I've seen a dead frog, dancing. Smelt a whole country on airmail envelopes. I've crossed the tidal creeks at daybreak, seen the low, strange flight of the wading birds, heard them, felt a grief inside me that had no name, no way of expressing it. There are such feelings: deep, and wide. I sit here with them. A man crossed a room just to say to me, *Your husband is lucky. I envy him. Remember I told you that.*

My name, too—written in snow. Lying there, on the hockey fields. How I was punished for it, later: names, and a bed full of grass. I believed those letters, trodden out in snow, were a mistake; I thought, *There are two Moiras. Or a name has been spelt wrong.*

But it was for me, and it wasn't a joke.

"You thought that?" Ray asked me. "A joke?"

•   •   •

I THINK of you all the time.

I do not count the minutes, anymore, and I do not imagine the seasons yet to come that might, perhaps, have you in them. But, still,

I carry you. I feel winds, and bite into fruit on your behalf. Push my hand into a dog's fur. I blow dandelion clocks, as you did, and when I find my husband asleep on his front, with his arms beneath him, it isn't you I think of, at first—I think of him; I say his name, and he stirs. But it all leads to you, in the end.

So we wait, Ray and I. We feel the earth turn. We wake in the mornings and think, *Today?* No—not today. Not tomorrow, even, for my hope has gone, or it almost has, and I am so tired of waiting, now. So tired, and bored, that I think I, too, could sink into this sleep of yours. Or unplug you, tilt your bed over. Or take my thumb and forefinger and seal up your nose, whilst cupping your jaw in my hand. *There*—isn't that another glimpse of the cruelty in me? That it's come to this? That I have such unkind thoughts? That—and other thoughts besides. I've sat in this chair for thousands of evenings, and felt my life drip away at a faster rate than yours, and I've felt the world darken, and the clouds race. I grow older. And at home, in our quiet house, Ray talks to me of jungles, and city heat, elephants, and valley floors; he lists volcanoes, as if they are people he's walked with. And I listen to this, imagine it all. *I will swim in a sound. Stand on the equator.* I long for this. I always have—to walk out into the world with Ray. But we do not go. How can we? Our mother asks me to stay—and she asks this of you, too, when she thinks she's alone. *Stay . . .* She still believes you will survive, somehow. But Amy, I think you will die.

I tell this to no one. Not even Ray. For who would believe it, or want to?

Miracles happen, they say. And also, *You are her sister.*

•   •   •

I sit here, now. Moon-skinned, with my glasses on. There are lilies beside you, dropping their thick pollen onto the tiled floor. I can smell them. I can hear your slow, neat heart.

It is December.

Do you listen? Does this find you, at all?

Atlantic. A word of secrets.

As with most things, this story begins with the sea.

The Field of Horses

HUGE, GREY WATER. RESTLESS WATER, WITH WHITE TIPS TO THE grey waves. There were ferries, and blow-holes. Sea pies, with their orange beaks, standing in their coves. Seals blinked, and the grasses shook, and in the evenings the lighthouse on Caldey Island rolled its slow, pale eye.

It was a coast of foam, and light. And there was a house on this coast that I can still see—weathered, salty. Its blackthorn bushes, and green front door. Furze from the coastal path ran into its garden, and a line of herring gulls hunched on the roof—grey, one-legged. Remember? They clamped their heads beneath their wings, streaked the tiles white. Two fields away there were horses: in stormy weather they'd arch their tails, and flee.

An apple tree, too. A swing.

And I see our parents, there—before they were our parents. George, twirling spanners; Miriam with her curled hair, and her round, hard belly, rolling a chiming ball.

· · ·

THEY CAME to Stackpole because of the sea. They longed for it, as I suppose we all long, sometimes, for a thing we can't name, but feel, inside us. He always said, *The sea . . .*—wistfully, as if it was only a dream he'd had once, as a boy. He'd say, *Smell it?* Tentacles and splintered wood; rope, and glitter, and lobsterpots, and he loved these things, having lived by them in his younger days. And so after their wedding day, before I was born, before I was even two pink cells, they came to Pembrokeshire, hand in hand, to walk across its cliff-tops. To haul in this sea air. To say the word *married* to each other. On low-tide beaches, and in the dark.

For Sale, it said. Outside a house with gulls on the roof.

So they bought the house, cleaned it. Lived there.

Or at least, this is the story they gave to me, as I grew up: all romance, fresh air, sea spray. And I've come back round to imagining it again—to allowing myself to see our parents, newlywed, hearing the caves drip, standing on St Govan's Head for the first time. Finding the chapel, hidden in rocks. Our mother being caught out by the wind, her skirt blowing up on Barafundle.

Stackpole. A sturdy name. A sturdy village, too—sleeping on the south-west coast of Wales. Neat and squat. Its church sat in a hollow, its tearoom steamed, and it had its own, quiet harbour where the fishing buoys bobbed on the tide, and boats rocked themselves. The inn had flowerbeds and chimney smoke, water for dogs, and a rack outside for walker's boots. Sparrows, in its hedges. And cows chewed thoughtfully on the dairy farm; our mother heard them lowing, in the mornings, when she hung the washing out.

She loved it. *Miriam.* She'd lived in a city, till now; but now, she too loved the sea. Maybe not as much as my father loved it—hungrily, instinctively. But she came to love its breath, and its birds. Also, she had her own sea inside her. Walking on evening beaches with a tiny life moored to her, I imagine she thought, *Where's better, than this?* Where else had old castles and harbours? Empty coves? These skies? George didn't know, either. Briny, bearded George—he swam in all weather, picked mussels from rocks, and when they walked together at low tide, the balls of their feet pushed flashes of light into the wet sand.

"One day," he said, "I'll own my own boat." Until then, he twirled spanners like batons, smelt of oil. Bits of cars sat in their garden, under tents of tarpaulin, and their eldest daughter, once she was born, would come to know them—how, in rainstorms, these tents would flap and billow, and she'd creep downstairs to watch them at night, throwing blue shadows on the white kitchen wall. She believed they longed to free themselves. To lift up, like dragons, open their wings, and slip away into the dark.

• • •

IN THEIR first March there, my mother went to Tenby. She often did. But this was different, because I was inside her, and she sucked liquorice as she walked on the seafront, past the pastel-coloured houses. Slipped a coin into a telescope and peered through it, out to sea. And a woman stopped her near the coastguard's house—a woman with stars inked onto her arms, and a mark on her lip. A gypsy, or something like one. She put her hand on my mother's belly and said, *A girl. Dark-eyed.* Blinked, then, and said, *Strange . . .*

Miriam dismissed this. Smiled, stepped backwards, and drove home with songs on the radio, and her windscreen wipers on. She believed in God, not magic. She went to church every Sunday, and said her prayers, and arranged the flowers by the font, sometimes, and she didn't believe in predictions like that, from a woman with an alcohol smell. *How does she know?* She shook her head.

But those words stayed with her. I know that at night, my mother was sleepless. She heard the spring gales, worried the edge of the blanket with her thumb and thought, *A girl.* And also, *Strange?* What was? She did not know what this meant.

Later that night, I was born. On that dark-blue, starless night my mother woke up with a fear inside her—tight, like a fist. She crept out of bed. Stood in the bathroom where blackthorn knocked on the windowpane, held on to the sink, and I slipped out, eel-like, onto the bathroom floor. Ten weeks premature. My parents curled round me, waited. I was mute, small, and in the half-light they clutched hands, made promises—offered up everything if it meant that their early, dark-eyed daughter could stay with them, and survive. *Our money. Our own health.* Nothing, for fourteen minutes. And then, at last, I wailed.

Was that the strange part? That early birth? My father would tell the story, in the years to come. On birthdays, or late at night, he'd retrieve it, polish it up: the blood on the lino, my stare, and how my wet, frail crying made him sink back against the bathtub, say, *Thank God*, over and over. "We wrapped you in a pillowcase," he said, "and you gripped our fingers—like this . . ."

I've often wondered if the herring gulls rose from the roof at the sound of me, their legs dangling, or if the tide had been high—and I've thought of asking my mother these things. But she rarely spoke of my birth, or of the woman with stars on her arms. Only once did she talk of these things: on the telephone, one winter, when I was hateful, and sad, she confessed to me that she'd been afraid that night, and so the happiest moment of her life had not been her wedding, or finding George, or learning of her pregnancy—but lying on the cold bathroom floor one early March night with her nightdress round her waist, and a thin moon outside, and a small, slippery, healthy daughter testing herself. Calling out through the night-time house and altering the shape of it.

• • •

BABY, for a day or so. *Little One.* Because they'd always imagined a boy inside Miriam—a strong, patient, good-hearted boy, not a girl. So they had no girl names, and she was just *Baby*, at first. Small, and white-skinned.

Little One. Baby Girl.

Moira, in the end.

Moira, from Mary—and she existed, then, as much as the sea did, and the clouds, and the headland, and her eyes were so black that all these things were reflected in them—grass, and sky. Miriam said she could see herself, too, sometimes. As she breastfed, or bathed me.

*H*OME. I like the word. I am better with numbers, and facts, for these things don't change, or have different sides. But still, I like *home*. Say it. The breathy *h*; the long, perfect *o*.

It's probably the apple tree, to you. Or the ginger cat at the guest-house that purred, like a bee. What else? The village. The lily-ponds that lay to the west, with their otters and dragonflies. It was Mr Bannister, too, who lived down the lane in a house called Sea View, with a row of fir trees and a trembling wife. He played bowls; he said, *Cheerio!* I think you'd list these things, as might I—but when Ray asks me what home is to me, or was, it isn't the apples or the bowling green that I think of. Not at first, anyway.

It's beaches. *Of course.* You were never a fan of sand between the teeth, or of the black, shiny bladderwrack that popped beneath your heel. But I grew up on these things. I was born in that house as it shook with a storm, and I took my first steps at Freshwater East. Tried my first cockles in its car park—briny, metal-tasting.

Swanlake. Presipe. Barafundle.

I knew their names as well as my own, or better. I knew that fulmars nested at Broad Haven; that orchids grew in the warrens, nearby. The soft boom of guns came from the military range, at Castlemartin, as if they were shutting doors there. I tr ied to eat the tiny pearl-white snails that clung to dune grass at Barafundle, and I brushed my arms with feathers, and I found my dead seagull—sat with it, until evening came, stroking it, and mourning its cold, lonely death. Mussels grew, at Swanlake—a cathedral of them, sighing in their shells. And a thin path of roots and driftwood led down to this beach, its old wire fence sagging, in places. I'd trail my palm along it, when I was older, with spectacles, counting its wooden posts. *One. And two. And . . .* Twenty-five altogether. But later, there'd be fewer, for a fire claimed some, as did the stray, pale-brown dog. It swam there, ran. Slept in its dunes.

Me, and my mother, and beaches. The shape of Lundy Island, and frayed rope, and the small, hard bump of her belly under her swimsuit as I sat on her hip. She paddled. Said, *Look!* This may be my first memory; how can I be sure? But I know I was young, at any rate—three, I think—and we made a sandcastle, so that in the evening I glanced back, and imagined the crabs moving into it— sleeping in their turrets, sliding into the moat. For there were many crabs, there: frail, and translucent, they scuttled across the sand when the tide was out. Tucked up their legs in my fortresses at night, and dreamt their frail crab dreams.

· · ·

"You are a sea baby."

My father said this. Walking back on a Tuesday from crab-fishing at Stackpole Quay. We passed the ginger cat on its wall, and the dairy farm, and he said, "That's what you are. If you're born on the coast, you become it. You slide into its rhythms—the tides, the breezes." He smiled. "Trust me, Moira—you'll never sleep soundly inland."

And I did trust him. I trusted him like I trusted the sky to stay above my head, and the kettle to sing, and everything he ever told me was true, because why should I doubt him? He, who could make a piece of grass sing? I believed that starfish could grow new limbs, and gannets swam like white fishes, and mermaids were real, and babies were gifts, and pirates sailed in splintery boats, and that moonlight survived in a jar. Sometimes we sailed to Skomer Island together, the two of us: a sky of underbellies, and a draught of wings. I saw gannets, shags, and fulmars; black-backed gulls and cor-morants. Seals slapped themselves on rocks, and kittiwakes called out their names, and there were puffins. I liked them best of all: I liked their busy wings and clumsy landings, and their big, crayoned bills. Sometimes I gripped the rope so tightly my palms would be sore, in bed, that night.

I'd lie, then, beneath my patchwork rug. Warm as a teacake. Hear the handclap of birds as they dived into the water, and the burr of puffin flight.

. . .

A NOVEMBER of storms when I was four years old. He sensed it. Felt it in his bones, perhaps, or he knew from the moon's colour, or the wind's changes, or the sea. Some gales passed by, in the night. Others knocked against the house, and set the swing creaking, and with these storms we'd file up to the attic room in our dressing gowns to hear the rain on the skylight, to see the trees, and watch the storm move in, over the house.

The winds span the church's weathervane, round and round. A tree came down in Lamphey, on top of a letterbox; the horses kicked, flashed into the dark. One night the waves were so high that they picked off some of Stackpole Head—lying in bed, I heard it. I thought it was thunder, at first, and waited for more. But in the morning, my father and I braved the wind to walk to the beach, where we found huge breakers, and a new shape to the cliff.

Rain, for days, too, and mud. A cable was blown down on the main road so that our house fell into darkness. My mother said, "What about the Bannisters?" For they were old people. Mr Bannister walked stiffly, had a white moustache, and his wife had an illness that made her shake and stumble, and her words fluttered out like a moth. And so my mother carried soup, matches and candles down the lane, to Sea View. Past the fir trees. And she was gone for so long that my father said, "Wait here," and pulled on his coat, and went out to find her. She'd fallen, slipped in the mud. She fell on her belly, on the hard bump, so that an ambulance came to the field of horses, and I saw its blue light through the blackthorn bushes. My mother left blood on her skirt, and candles in the lane. She said, *It's all right,* over and over.

It was not all right. Not quite. She slept in the daytime, for a while, after that. Ate less.

This is all I knew at four years old, and nothing more. How could I? Know more? I was young, and mute, or as good as; I wandered the house with a sea bean in my hand, that the storm had left on Freshwater East for me. A small, smooth seed, from a foreign land. *South America*, my father told me. I held it, in the well of my palm.

I knew nothing of losses. I only knew the different types of gull; that I could live without blinking for over a minute; that if I squinted, trees became clearer; that Mrs Bannister, our neighbour, was dying slowly, and there were two of her, maybe. Or so it seemed, because when she talked of her old life, before she shook, she said, *She was so pretty* . . . As if that person had never been her.

I knew the sea mist, too. Was standing in it, in my anorak, and my black Wellington boots, when a red car came, bumped up the lane.

A dent in the driver's door. The door opened, and there was a woman in a purple coat, with purple gloves, who smiled and said, "Moira?"

This was Til—who I did not remember, or maybe I half did. Maybe I remembered her buckled shoes, as I sat on the carpet, years before, with my mussel shell that clacked, like a mouth, and my coloured shapes. But I might have made that up. The buckled shoes could have been my mother's. Or somebody else's.

*T*wins," said my father. He explained to me what twins were—"made and born at the same time, in the same place . . ." But how were these two alike? They weren't. I watched them: my mother was short, quiet, butter-haired; Aunt Til had wooden bracelets, and red shoes, and she wore long, patterned skirts that she lifted a little, when she walked, in the lane. Said, *Golly* . . . My mother did not say *Golly*. Knickers appeared on radiators, and wild, loopy handwriting found its way onto the telephone pad. "I know," she said. "No one can read it. But I do try . . ."

Not twins, either, because the younger sister lived in a house in Stackpole, with gulls on the roof and a green front door, with a daughter who wanted to be a sea bean when she grew up—and Til was from London. Not by the sea. She said, "It's true. I live in the city. In a flat above a bakery. I think the owner loves me, or wants to, because he gives me free cakes and pastries." She winked. "And doughnuts with real jam!"

. . .

She was beautiful. She had long dark hair that she threw back in an arc, and a silver ring on her thumb. She sang. Beckoned to me, said, "Come here . . ."—holding out a small glass bottle with a yellow liquid in it. She dabbed this, on my wrists and ears. "There." Smelling of oranges.

Aunt Til unpacked her suitcase in the spare room that overlooked the furze bushes. She hung up floor-length skirts. Placed glass jars and powder on the dressing table, and crystals, so that the room smelt different, and reflected the winter light. She had a wooden jewellery box, which she showed to me, because I squinted at it. She said, "Open it . . . Go on!" I did, with my nose touching the wood, and a doll was inside it—pink, small. It danced on its tiptoes to music. Sank into a silence, when I closed the lid again.

"Do you remember me? You might not."

She was here, she said, to help my mother—"comfort her." I blinked at that, let it go. In the evening, as my parents and Til uncorked wine and settled into the kitchen, I padded across the landing to peep into the spare room. I went up to a jar of thick, white cream. Heard Til, downstairs, say, *She's all eyes!* And I did not open the jewellery box, but imagined the ballerina in there—dancing, upside down, or on her side, in her own private dark.

· · ·

I SEE Til as a wind. She felt like one: a warm wind from a southerly place—scented, with a high laugh. She blew the quietness away, and the storm clouds, and the mud dried up in the lane. My mother climbed out of bed, blew her nose. Wrapped herself around the woman with the purple coat. Said, "Hello, Til," every morning. And they linked arms in the wintery lane. Held their mugs of tea with both hands.

Til wore a pink stone around her neck, on a chain. She ran deep, scented baths for her sister, and dropped pale syrups into water glasses with a small, brown dropper. Talked of London places. *Hammersmith. The Strand.*

"Your birthday soon. Isn't it?"

It was. I nodded.

"You are *such* a March birth."

She knew about these things—birthdays, and stars. Not that stars could be seen in London, she said, because of the lights, and the taxi fumes. But as my parents washed the plates one night, she took me outside, and we stood on the lawn in our slippers, looked up. Lots of stars. Blurry, to me, but I could still see them. Til said, "I believe there's a purpose to things."

And she believed in crystals, and oils, and positive thought, and in a red embroidery handbag that she wore across herself, with picture cards inside it. She believed in the lines on palms. In the four elements, which were in all of us. "And we are each one, more than most, you know." In that handbag, I found a silvery pen, and tissues, and a little turquoise mirror that closed up, like a clam. Three lipsticks. A ticket— for the train which ran, Til said, underneath London's streets. "Mice live down there. I've seen them, at stations—peeping over the tracks."

In return, I took hold of Til's little finger, and led her to all my own favourite places—to the horses, and the badger set. To Stackpole Quay with its fishing buoys. And Til said, "Golly . . ." to all these things—but she loved the lily-ponds, above all else. Not because of the lilies, or the swans that glided on them. Til paused, saw a robin eyeing her. Returned the next day with a bag of breadcrumbs and raisins, and by the Grassy Bridge, a robin hovered, and perched for a moment on Til's silvered thumb—its splayed legs, and eggshell weight. It lifted a crust out of her hand, flew away.

• • •

ELEMENTS? Crystals? So Til should have met the gypsy at Tenby, five years before, not her twin. They'd have liked each other—talked about burdock root or retrograde moons, or of all the things there are in this world to believe in. Love. Medicine. Families.

Did I like her because she made things better? Because she was wise? Or maybe I hoped my hair was like hers, or would be, in time— thick, and bright, like a wing. She was violet eyes, and cream cakes. She was wooden bracelets that clinked when she coiled her hair up, and then let it go.

"I'll come back," she said. Crouching in front of me.

• • •

I WAS safe in that house; I was loved. I knew my place in the world, and who I was, and I did not yet mind my reflection. When the seagulls laughed down the chimneypot, I thought they might be talking to me, so I'd stand by the fireplace, talk back. The house did feel a little empty, once Aunt Til had gone—the spare room was bare again, save for the cot in the corner, and its pink quilt. But I returned to colouring-in, and holding my breath in the bath. To counting the waves. To my parents, and car parts, and weed.

*S*CHOOL WAS A FAT, whitewashed building with a snake chalked out in the playground, and a shady sycamore tree. A cloak-room with pipes that creaked in the winter. The classroom itself had the alphabet, green paper towels, and a globe at the back of the room that Mrs Mole span with a painted nail. *The world*. And I sat on the tip of a small country, cross-legged, on carpet tiles.

Twenty other children, in the class. They chanted, and listened, or they stretched their arms u p, flapped like the dragons in the garden, at night. I looked sideways at them—at the loose jaws, the crusty noses. But I could not see the blackboard, or much of the world. The alpha-bet made no sense, and the carpet tiles scratched my legs, and I was more silent than ever, in there. Did not smile, or cry. Only raised my hand to leave the room to wash my hands, or blow my nose, and then it was my turn to be looked at—slyly, for a little too long.

An arched eyebrow, from Mrs Mole. "Is there anybody in there?" she asked on a Thursday, leaning over, rapping on my head with the hard part of her hand. And when my eyes began to hurt, I wondered, at first, if this was Mrs Mole's fault—if she had damaged my head, somehow. I frowned. Walked home, down the lane, and didn't see the stray dog lifting its leg in the fir trees, so when it barked, I was scared, and fell over.

Not Mrs Mole's fault, in the end. My head was not split from her knuckles, or her wedding ring.

Instead, on my sixth birthday, I was taken to Tenby, where a pair of red plastic spectacles were lowered onto my nose. After this, I could see the foam on the sea, and the pinkish buds of the trees. The blackboard made sense.

Gold stars, now, from Mrs Mole.

Well done, written in felt-tipped pen.

· · ·

So the seasons passed. And for the first time in a while, I could see their passing; I could see the smallest parts of them because I had two thick glass lenses perched before my eyes. Like the veins in the leaves of the apple tree. The freckles on the apples.

"Those glasses look lovely on you."

I wasn't very sure. But the men in G. Stone Autos, where my father worked, all said so. In their blue shed, with its metal tubes and wires and a fringe of raindrops over the door, they nodded. Wiped their hands on rags and said, "What can you see now?"

Fledglings. Daffodils. Scones, sold at the quay, with hundreds of seeds in its pots of strawberry jam. The five dots every month on my mother's calendar. And I could see every sum on the board, every tick in red pen. And I could see the fishing buoys, and the numbers marked on them, and I saw the nails in the shoes of the white horse that broke free from its field, in the autumn. It bucked by the school, clattered down the road. Scattered the traffic cones.

Frogspawn, too. I'd never seen it before. But in the following spring, when I was nearly seven years old, and my hands and feet were growing faster than the rest of me, I sat by the lily-ponds. Frogspawn was thick, soft, gluey-blue, and I scooped it into a jar. Carried it home to keep.

My mother crouched beside me in her apron, said, "Wouldn't they rather be free? Back in the pond where you found them? It would be kinder . . ." She said she didn't like cages—wire ones, or glass ones. She liked things to grow.

So I took them back down to the pond. Lowered the jar into the water, and let their blunt heads and little brown tails swim away from me. I felt sad. Missed them for a while. I'd whispered secrets to them; fed them on ham and mottled corned beef that was meant for my father's packed lunch.

But there are some things that even I couldn't see—of course. I was stung in the summer, on Lydstep beach, with my parents, and a tartan picnic rug, and a flask of coffee. Hot, white-sun weather. I wore a hat, and a bathing suit with a frilled white skirt, and as I placed my left foot down, into the wet sand, I felt it: a knife, or a fire, into my heel. A fast, deep pain, and my father carried me back, up to the dunes, calling, *Weaver fish!* Coffee was poured on my foot. Me, Moira, on my back, or her back, with her leg in the air, and the seagulls flying close to the ground, and the clouds sailing above her.

I could see me, lying there. A girl who was hurt.

Later, I said it had not hurt at all. But it had. It'd made my whole foot red, and sore, and it throbbed that night, under my patchwork rug. Still, my father had lifted me up, and carried me, and I dreamt of it. Dreamt of the weaver fish sinking back down into the sand, afterwards.

· · ·

THE WEAVER fish must have been in 1984, because my glasses were no longer new, really, and I was quick as a fish at long division by then. My mother rubbed cream onto her stomach, and squirrels nested in the roof of The Stackpole Inn, ran on the telephone wires.

Aunt Til, I thought, would like my spectacles. Cherry-red, plastic frames, that made a red dent on my nose. She hadn't come back, yet, but I knew she would, and I sat on Barafundle and wished her to. I chewed on weed, thought, *Come back.* And she did, soon enough. In the months after the weaver fish had punctured my foot, like that, my mother sat down on the supermarket floor, prayed, said, *No no no,* and there was a watery sound. George arrived from the garage with oil on his face. A second ambulance came, too, and that was that.

And in came Aunt Til, soon after. Blown in on an easterly wind. Heeled boots and bottles and a soft pigeon-coo in her as she hugged my mother and said, "I'm so sorry," and I thought she looked even lovelier than before, with coppery streaks in her hair.

So. AMY. Do you know any of this? That there were half-formed babies between you and me? Whose globes leaked, or broke, and so they dropped out or drifted free of their moorings? I guess not. Because if I was not told, why should you be? You were the trickier sister, in some ways: noisier, and full of smiles, but far less sensible. Less practical, in that you trusted too much, and stamped your foot, and blamed our parents on rainy days. I doubt, then, they ever told you. For what would you have done? How would you have seen it? You never understood road kill, or the purpose of a lie.

I understand them. Yes. After Ray and I came to live on this coast, and after your fall, I chose to study, to go back to books and the echo of shoes in a corridor, and chalk dust. I was right to. And I've lowered my head and studied the threads and chemicals inside us. I've cut open a real person, in a bleached room, on a city campus not so far from here—where I wear a white overall, as I did in school. I think of Mr Hodge, sometimes. How happy he'd be—to know I was doing such things. And I think of you, when we talk of the limbic system in the brain, or use the word *traumatic*. And *coma*, of course. It's a beckoning word, and it's yours.

And I've thought of our mother, at times. Not that she knows it. Such losses happen: we are wrong, Amy, to ever think that making and keeping a life is an easy thing, and at your age, I thought it. But the body can break—as well you know. I think, sometimes, of the Stackpole house, and how the Bannisters always blamed themselves for the death of that first baby. *If we weren't so frail . . .* For their frailty led our mother into the lane, with rugs and candles, and slippery shoes. Such was their thinking. That they were at fault; that they caused that loss.

So they always remembered my birthday; sent me cards at boarding school, out of sadness, and guilt.

• • •

AN EARLY summer. The lilies were out. The thrift bloomed on the cliff-tops—pink, tidy flowers, and the chiffchaffs chirped in them.

I was older and wiser, than before. Taller, too, and my aunt no longer crouched beside me, or watched me colouring-in. She said, instead, "Miss Stone, shall we go walking?" Tying a silk scarf on her head.

So the twin from London who ate free pastries clambered over stiles with her niece, tested plum-coloured lipsticks on the back of her hand in the chemist, or tore sugar packets with her white teeth, tapped them into her peppermint tea. Caught her skirt on the wire at Swanlake Bay, said a new word. Blushed. "Don't repeat that," she said.

Til—for Matilda. "An old lady's name." Not old—but the older twin by nine, brief minutes, born in a London hospital three decades before. A hospital she'd walk past, sometimes, on the way to the theatres where she worked—as a warm powdered actress, with lines in her mouth, and spotlights, and dust. "I don't suppose it's changed very much," she said. "Hospitals don't."

We walked. I'd find Til at the school gates, arms folded, leaning against the fence, and she'd take my schoolbag, widen her eyes at the gold stars, then throw it into her car. "Where to, then?" To Tenby, with its tearooms. Or the pub at Bosherston. Or Angle Bay, by the oil refineries. To the wild, thundering surf at Freshwater West, where my eyes watered behind their lenses, and the telegraph wires sang in the gales. We heard this—how their thin, mournful music blew over our heads, and inland.

She said, "Such space . . ." Because there wasn't much of it in London. All taxis, tourists, litter, and alleyways. Neon lights, and she said she lay in the parks, sometimes. Or went to the zoo. "Or I sit by the stone lions in Trafalgar Square. Lots and lots of pigeons."

And the underground mice?

"Still there."

All these things. Til's stories—like the man who juggled with sticks on fire, and her nosebleed on a bus. She saw a man propose on a tube train, and the girl said *yes!* And they got off at Hyde Park Corner.

I walked with her on beaches, heard the soft boom of army guns, and a great-tit took a raisin from the palm of my hand, and yet all I could think of in bed that night was London, and London things: lights, puddles, red theatre seats. My aunt swaying, as a tube train stopped.

She was so pretty. I could see, with my spectacles, the down on her earlobes, and the pale-green powder swept round her eyes.

• • •

I REMEMBER, too, how we stood together—Til and I—on Stackpole Head, with bottles in our hands. Empty lemonade bottles. We'd written secret notes in crayon, pushed these notes inside. A blustery day. And we threw them, and Til stood on her tiptoes, waving, saying *Goodbye! Good luck!*

Why do I remember that? Talk of it? I've always thought of it—of my message, in my bottle, bobbing in the Atlantic, knocking against boats and grey dorsal fins. Sometimes, I longed to be like that. In time, when I was a woman, or almost one, I'd read airmail letters, and think of tropical seas. But back then, in Stackpole, I was happy enough to let it go, to return to the house with the green front door, drink milk from a mug in the kitchen. To have a bristled bedtime kiss from my father.

• • •

TIL LEFT, again—sounding her horn as she drove down the lane, so that Mr Bannister, maybe, spilt his wife's soup at the sound. And the horses flinched in their field, and the stray dog that lived in the dunes might have barked at it, ears up.

*T*en *out of ten*—written in my Maths book. I showed it to my mother, who rubbed her hand on my back. Said, "That deserves a treacle sponge with custard." Which we ate, with big spoons.

Ten out of ten, and *Top of the class*, and other words—written in neat, red pen. Maybe it was my age. Or it was because my lenses had been strengthened further, so that I could see the lines on gulls' feet, and a pale-yellow balloon drifting over Tenby's roofs on a Sunday afternoon. A clammy hand had let it go. It bumped against an aerial, and squeaked through an oak tree, before moving on—over the monastery, and Tenby's bowling green.

Either way, I thought, *There is something*. I didn't know what. I didn't know why I felt it, but I could feel secrets, or half-truths—in my bones, like bad weather. My mother went to bed again—said, *Indigestion*. But a doctor came, and flowers, and I sat on the swing, looked at my feet. There was *something*—like the seal that had looked at me, on the blistered boat, blinked, and then closed up its nostrils and slunk down, beneath the waves. I'd known it was there; knew that if I had longer, stronger arms I could dip my hand into the sea, and stroke it. But as it was, I couldn't. All I could do was imagine it. Its flippers, applauding me.

And I did—imagine. In bed, at night, with the sea's breath, and the sound of my parents' bed, squeaking.

• • •

CLEVER GIRL. We never think we are. What was clever in the tadpole jar, or knowing about decimals? Or in the Thursday morning, at break-time, when I dropped my lunch money into a puddle and knelt down, sifted through shoes and mud to find it? I didn't know the word *scholarship*. So I did not think I was very clever, at all; just different. With glasses that made my eyes look even bigger.

But, one day, there was this question:

"Have you thought of life after Stackpole School?"

My mother asked me this, in the kitchen, as she sieved the peas at teatime. My father was not home, yet, and my fringe had been cut with the dressmaking scissors, and I was nearly eleven years old.

I'd never thought of *after*; I'd never been asked about it. I just thought I would live in Stackpole. With the sea bean. Go to another school nearby, with the same carpet tiles. My mother said "Never mind, my lovely," and let it go.

A Friday afternoon, at four o'clock. My parents—both of them— met me at the school gate, and led me back inside. I sat in the cloakroom with a bottle of cola, which had leaked in my bag, so that my diary and pens were sticky to touch, and my shoelace was undone, and down the corridor, my parents knocked on Mrs Mole's door. A long way from the cloakroom, but I still heard all of it: Mrs Mole's voice was like the army guns. Also, she'd left her door open.

My parents said, *Yes*, and *Really?* They talked of schools, and of me. Of inland places. And the local school in Tenby was nothing special, Mrs Mole said. "She's exceptionally bright, you know. I urge you . . ."

My hands were sticky, and there were thirty-two coat-pegs in the cloakroom, and my mother replied, "You do? Well . . . we can't afford . . ."

Scholarship. There it was. Mrs Mole whispered it—a magician's hat, or a pulling back of a cloth. "Isn't it worth trying for?"

A pie, for tea, that evening. It steamed, and my father rubbed his hands, but I did not eat much of it. I felt hard, in my stomach. I sat with my knife and fork in my hand, and later, I pulled the dictionary off the shelf in the hallway, looked up the word.

My mother climbed into bed with me, under the rug, and said, "Don't be afraid, Moira. Nothing will change—I promise you that."

• • •

NOTHING? Believe me—she said that. She said it, and I believed it, because didn't I believe everything? Why should I have frowned at that, thought, *No*?

My mother said *Nothing will change*, whilst knowing it would. And this is what I would unwrap in the dark, at Locke: *She lied.*

Anyway.

I did as I was told. In April, I took three exams. I stayed in the classroom after school—sat on my own, with the clock and my pencils, and Mrs Mole reading a women's magazine. The furze was blooming. I smelt it. Did sums. Listed capital cities. Chewed my fingernails.

And one of my pens broke, on the paper—I'd chewed through it, so that I returned home with colourful hands, and a bright-blue tongue, and I sank into a salty bath.

My last exam was the hardest. It was as I walked back, past the field of horses, that Mr Bannister waved to me, said, "How are the exams? I've heard all about them."

I shrugged, I think. Blushed, probably.

He also asked, "How's your mother? We're praying for her and the baby. Will you tell her? That we send our love?"

Well. There you have it. I learnt of your existence in my school uniform, after a scholarship exam from a man with a moustache who played bowls on a Sunday. Afterwards, he said, *Cheerio!*

• • •

CAN YOU BLAME ME? Are you really surprised? It would be like the trees being taken from you, or the grass changing colour, and nobody telling you why. Hadn't the gypsy called me strange? I knew the story, by then. My mother had told me, on my birthday.

I don't think I had ever been angry before. But I became it. I was fierce. I stared at my mother in the evening, stared at her body. I stood in the lane with fists, and a scowl, and I did not eat, and I did not sleep, and I thought, *Betrayal! Betrayal!* And who else had known, before me? I felt everything did. The stray dog. Lundy. The herring gulls on the roof.

Three exams, for three schools. Three offers of a place, for free. Miriam said, "This one, love? Look—it's nearby. We could drive you, every day!"

Or there was an old convent on the Welsh borders.

Or there was a boarding school on the far side of the country, in Norfolk, where Mrs Mole had been a pupil herself, and she'd said, "I'd recommend it. I liked it there." And on her desk she unrolled a map, showed me Norfolk, and where Locke School was: a forearm's length on the map. A whole country lay between it and the house at Stackpole, with its apple tree, and car parts.

George rubbed his beard with the heel of his hand. Said, "Love, it's so far . . ."

Miriam was tearful. She said that she'd never wanted that school, anyway, and that I shouldn't have ever sat its exam, because how many miles away was it? "*Hundreds,* George!" But Mrs Mole had been persistent. Mrs Mole, with her huge engagement ring and her beady eyes. And George and Miriam were not fighters. They nodded too quickly. Gave in. Said, *OK.*

Til, though, was not surprised. She nodded, sagely, when she next came to stay. She looked at the lines on my palms. Talked of hardness, and water, and full moons—whatever these things meant.

· · ·

DON'T UNDERESTIMATE the stubbornness of an eleven-year-old. There's a truth. Maybe we are more alike than I think, you and I. You fell: I jumped. Both of us had love, of one kind or another, in our blood, at the time.

Nothing will change.

A wonderful lie. As dark and huge as a lie can be. Everything changed, and I chose Locke because what else was there, when it was all gone? All that I knew? And I was so angry. Flashing my fins.

S o YOU WERE THE FIFTH LIFE to grow beneath our mother's skin. At least, I think you were the fifth: I was the first, and three more followed me, who all slipped their anchors or sank away. The lane, the supermarket, and a miscarriage, I think, in the bathroom where I was born, for one evening I heard them both crying in there. Perhaps there were more. But who ever asks of these things?

They did tell me themselves about you, in time. Two weeks before I left for Locke, when your sticky foetus was five months old, and out of danger, or almost, and when there was a firm swelling underneath her blue cotton sundress, Miriam said, "We've good news, Moira..." Believing I'd be happy at this.

I hoped you wouldn't make it. I hoped you'd drop out, or break free, or wither away like an old, brown fruit. I hope there'd be another blue, flashing light, and more blood—in the lane, or on a tiled floor, or in bed. Anywhere. So that it would just be us, again. Just three sets of footprints in the wet sand.

But you didn't. You hung on.

I walked out into the lane. On my own. Hating them, and you.

• • •

TELL ME ABOUT YOU, back then.

Ray asked this once—Christmas, the year before we were married. I knew what he wanted: the emotions, the hopes and fears of me, as a child. Stories, as ever. He wanted the story I gave you, just now, but I wasn't ready for that. So I scowled. Considered him for a moment, shrugged. *Like I am now. But smaller.*

Oh, my answers: so often sharp, like that. Said with a raised eyebrow, or over my shoulder, as I walked away. I was known for that, at one time. Still, he was right to ask it, I think—for she has gone, who-ever she is.

Moira, with her crab-lines. Moira who'd been happy gave way to the Moira with the suitcase, the anger in her, and the commas in the palm of her hands that were made by her fingernails. Who sealed herself up.

She did not go back to the lily-ponds or the bowling green for years.

Rocks

LET ME TELL YOU ABOUT YOUR WOUNDS. LET ME TELL YOU HOW THEY were, at first, for they're mostly healed now. Just the white, thicker skin where you bled. The new bone shapes.

I'll start with your feet. Neat and small. They sleep beneath these blankets with their crooked toes, and their one missing nail. Pink feet, now, as feet should be—but in the beginning, they were split open, and red, and black, too, from the weed that grows on Church Rock. *She slipped, Mrs Cole. There are marks* . . . On your soles. Three broken toes. A deep graze on your left heel, which, later, they washed the salt from.

Your legs? Doctors pulled the sheet aside to show a huge, ink-coloured bruise on your thigh, like a hand, from your fall. It changed colour, over the weeks. And a swollen left knee—*patella*—because you broke it when you fell. The doctor described it to me—his fist against the tabletop. He said, *Crack!* So this is the sound I believe your knee made. It shattered, and they replaced it with a plastic knee, so there are scars on your left leg, now—a puckering of skin, and a smooth, false dome.

On to your body, Amy. Your trunk; *abdomen*. And these are sly, quiet wounds. Harder to see, for it was under the skin that the damage was done, not on it. Four broken ribs—three false, one vertebrosternal. They were pushed deeper, towards your organs, and no punctured lungs, but there was damage inside you. *Internal bruising,* they called it. I haven't seen this, yet, but I've imagined it a thousand times—a bluish bloom on a kidney, or a liver's yellowy eye.

Other fractures, too. There was a crack to your collarbone. The place where a pendant might lie, where a silk scarf might be knotted—that bone, the *clavicle,* beneath that stretch of skin—was broken. They drugged you, and laid you out. Pinned you. So you have a strange inward dip there, now. A thumb's groove. A boy might have fallen in love with that, if you'd woken, by now. Called it *beautiful.*

Then there are the long, freckled arms that used to dangle from trees, and bear your weight in handstands. A torn muscle—the *deltoid,* up by your shoulder. Made, perhaps, from a desperate lunge, for your hands were raw, at first—burnt by the blue nylon rope I'd tied there. You must have grabbed at everything—rocks, plants, air. Weed and gull droppings under your nails.

And to your head, skull, *cranium,* and this is the part of you, and the damage to it, that leaves you here, sleeping. Three smacks, they think. *Left, right*—as if your head ricocheted. Quick, blunt bangs above your ears. The third wound was larger. You landed on your front, on a slab of rock that cracked your collarbone, chipped your teeth, but the worst wound came just before this—for you caught your head on an edge that sheared it, lifted the scalp. A flap of skin. Sticky hair. Here, they found the mussel, twisted it out.

I don't know how you didn't bleed to death, on Church Rock, for you did bleed. So much blood. The gulls screamed at it. The walker on the cliffs saw this redness, first—in the water, spreading. He thought it was a cloth, of some kind.

So. That was you. All you have of these injuries, now, is their scars, their ghost versions, and your white, wrapped crown. The chipped tooth, which I see if I pull your lower lip down. The tooth, and the bluish veins in your gums.

Still. *Your sister is lucky.* I hear that a lot—or I used to. Because your neck and back were not broken. And because you fell as the tide was low—a hard, sharp landing place, but if the sea had been high, it would have taken you with it, filled your lungs and cavities with salt, and sand, and fish scales, and left you in the shallows a day or so later—bloated, plucked at by crabs.

Lucky? I'm not so sure. I'd have chosen the wild, bloody, watery death. Far better, I think—to have been a legend, in South Wales, with flowers left on the beach for me. A plaque, even. Or a bench with my name, up on the cliffs, and a southerly view.

But then, we are different creatures, you and I. And you chose to come here, and sleep. Deep in the earth. In a hospital room.

I sit back from you.

· · ·

THERE WERE NO last walks. No tears. Nor did George and Miriam say, *No. You can't go.* Their daughter thought they might. Half expected it when he came towards her, one afternoon, with his hands deep in his dungarees. But he said, instead, "Tea?"

A damp, colourless September. Tourists billowed on the coastal path; the horses hung their wet heads under the trees. Moira pulled up her hood, sat on the swing in their garden, and spied Lundy through the mist. She stood by the fir trees, smelt them. But she did not go very far.

She spent her last days indoors. Amongst the books and peacock feathers. An old, leather trunk was pulled down from the attic—G.S. marked on it, in black—and laid on her bed. It had faded straps, and a red silk lining. It rained in the lane, on the beaches. She folded her clothes. Tied her shoes together by their laces.

And as she folded, she wondered if she'd be forgotten by the things here, like the horses, and the blackthorn trees. If she'd come back to find her rock pools gone, or that the halyards didn't sing any-more. Or the sea might have lost the shape of her. Her weight, or her sideways kick.

Maybe the seagulls will shout at me because they won't know who I am, when I come back.

In her room, that night, she considered this. If things had mem-ories, or not. She thought, *not*—but then, a tree had rings inside it to show its age, and birds knew where their nests were. Bulbs woke up in the spring, and so maybe, actually, they did have memories, and better ones than she did, so the sea, like her parents, might miss her, after all.

• • •

MIRIAM SAID, "I want you to be happy." She leant against the bath-room door as she said this—a towel in her arms, her hair tied back. "That's all mothers ever want, you know. For their children to be happy."

Moira was brushing her teeth. She emptied her mouth, rinsed. In her bedroom, she wrote *toothbrush* on her pad, to remind her to take it with her.

• • •

SAY SORRY. And, *Don't have the baby.* Moira thought this, grinding her teeth.

Aunt Til came, in the last few days. She walked up the drive with an umbrella and a fistful of blue hydrangeas, wrapped in tin foil, that she'd picked from a front garden, at night. Drank her peppermint tea. Sat cross-legged on Moira's bed and watched this careful folding of things.

"Very neat," she said. Impressed.

She did not say, *How are you feeling?* Nor did she say, *Are you sure? It is so far away . . .*—which Moira had heard five times, now, from five different mouths. Mr Bannister has said, "Why so far? Heavens!" And her mother had said, "There are nearer places . . . There's one in Cardiff that said yes, to you . . ." Moira expected this from Til, too— or something like it.

But instead, Til wound her thick, waist-length hair up into a knot, hooked silver rings into her ears, and said, "Come with me." Put down her tea. Steered Moira down the stairs, and out into the lane, and the August rain.

Two hours in The Stackpole Inn. A hot, steaming room, where fabric flowers sat in jugs, and a wet dog slept by the door. Til drank a pint of stout. A thick, black, magic drink, and she raised her glass, said, "To you. To new things." Wiped the froth from her top lip.

And Aunt Til talked of London, as ever. Of backstage, and the hot, electric second before stepping out into view—laced-up, wet-palmed. "Far worse," she said, "in the wings, waiting, than out in a spotlight on my own." She talked of prompts, and backdrops. Of opening nights, and the pink rose that was thrown on stage for her, once. Pink as a shell's lip. She dried its petals, filled a wine glass with them.

As for Norfolk, she'd heard it was flat, and beautiful, and that birds wintered there. "And it's windy, I think. Lots of windmills."

Moira nodded. She had read this, too. Windmills, and round church towers. And you could pick flint out of the ground as you walked. Lavender. A big-looking sea.

"Listen," Til said. Leaning forwards. "It isn't a question of love. You know that?"

Til, with her silver earrings. In The Stackpole Inn.

• • •

MOIRA CLOSED the trunk's lid. She'd packed coat-hangers, her pyjamas, her spare spectacles. A plastic compass. Her smooth sea bean.

She packed, too, the cool, hard gift that Til had pressed into her

hand, as they'd walked back from the inn. Her aunt had said, *Here* . . .
A silver brooch. Two fishes, swimming—one upwards, one down.
They had scales, and fins, and two glass eyes.

"Pisces," Til said. "From a shop in Camden Market. I saw it and
thought of you . . ."

This is what Moira looked at, as they drove away from the house
with the green front door: at their neat, open mouths. Their tails. She
felt the sharp tip of its pin.

She didn't look back. But still, Moira knew how the house must
look behind her, that it had not changed—its tarpaulin, and windows, and foxgloves that drooped in the rain. The orange crab-lines,
sitting in the porch. The line of herring gulls.

 𝒆 AST, AND EAST. Through the mountains. Into England, and east—past cities, airports, factories. On motorways. Lunch in a gateway of thistles and fumes, and a thermos of coffee that leaked in the car. Into the seats.

East, to the flatter land. Onto a road that crept through dark, low, marshy fields where cows stood up to their knees in mud, and a church sailed to the left of her. Past windmills. Past a scarecrow in a hedge with a cloth cap, and George said, "Not long now. All right in the back?"

She'd remember this from the journey: a lay-by, in the Fens. Her mother, bent over, holding back her hair. Hard, animal noises. Moira watched from the car as a thin, milky liquid spilt out of her mother's mouth. The gust from a lorry caught it. Strings hung from Miriam's lip, and she wiped it on her sleeve.

There was a sourness when Miriam climbed back in. They drove on in silence. Moira thought of it—the glutting, meaty worm. This was its smell: sharp, sly. It belched inside her mother, fattened her ankles, made her breath foul. Left its white, slimy mark on her sleeve.

4

East

Locke Hall Residential School for Girls. 1 mile. Gold letters on a dark-blue board, whose paint blistered in her third summer there. Tied to a telegraph pole, so that they drove through the village of Lockham Thorpe, and saw it. "One mile," said George.

Late afternoon. A day of sickness, the backs of heads. Stiff legs, and no air in the car, and, at last, they turned off the road onto a gravel driveway. Through a gateway with stone urns. They crunched under trees, and Locke Hall was made of grey bricks, and dark climbing plants, and windows. A flagpole, with a damp flag. "Well," said George. He exhaled, kettle-like. Switched the engine off.

• • •

Hard Moira. As hard as a pebble. And cross, too. But also, she was uneasy, and she found the edges of her teeth with her tongue as she stood on the gravel, looked at the school.

The headmistress was slim, firm as a wire. She pressed Moira's knuckles together, when she shook her hand and said, *Welcome*. A voice like scissors, snipping. She talked of the journey, and scholarships. Offered them all tea.

Miss Burke—in a tight, deep-purple jacket with silver buttons, and a purple skirt that reached down to her calves. Large, clipped earrings. Magpie-coloured hair, crunched into a ball at the nape of neck, and held there with nets, and needles. As if her hair had a temper, or a slyness to it, and needed to be held back.

Into a square room with armchairs, and a disused fireplace, and a view of a walnut tree. "Tea," she said, "in here." The ceilings were huge. Miriam and George sat gingerly. Tea in real china, which clinked against their wedding rings. They were all offered cakes—perfect, small white-iced cakes with a red cherry, and a sugary smell. Moira picked at hers, tasted it. Knew that cherries would taste of this, now: Locke, and car journeys.

She chewed. And whilst Miss Burke talked of grades, courtesy, and sportsmanship, Miriam looked sadly out at the walnut tree, and the sparrows in it, and George nodded too much in his bright-red tie, with crumbs on it, said, *Yes, yes, of course.*

• • •

CURIE. She was given this word, pocketed it.

An older girl with metal teeth took Moira and her parents away from the main house, and the china cups. A watery sun on the brickwork. Her smile glinted, and there were elastic bands in her mouth, too, which stretched as she talked of netball, and French lessons. She said, "It's this way." Down a gravel path, beside a long, brick building with sash windows. A privet hedge to the right of them, with archways cut into it. A sundial. Wet leaves sticking to the soles of Moira's shoes.

Four boarding houses. All named after women who'd changed the world, walked down their own gravel paths with their heads held high, their skirts rustling.

Curie. The last of them.

Moira pushed her spectacles up her nose. It overlooked a tennis court, and a wooden bench, and a dark, empty stretch of hockey fields.

• • •

LATER, MIRIAM CRIED—stiffly, with a hard jaw. She said it wasn't hormones. She sat on a chair, blew her nose. Was sick again, in the bathroom, at the end of the corridor.

Twelve beds, in this room. Six pairs. A cream-walled, quiet room with ivy on the windowpanes, so that the light was strange. A wooden floor. Moira had a bed, a desk, a wardrobe, and an angle-poise lamp with a red-ink drawing on its bulb. Other beds were marked out— with cushions or clothes, or shapes beneath the blankets. But the room was empty of people. Just Moira, and her parents, and the sucking worm.

And so Miriam cried. And her tears were black, and her breath was sharp as she said goodbye.

Moira let them go. She did not wave, or watch their car grow smaller. Instead, she stayed there, by her bed. Her parents crept down the stairs, down the drive, and away to their guesthouse in Holt, ten miles away, where Miriam would cry all night into a lace pillowcase, and Moira remained in her new bedroom, unpacking her leather case. There were shafts of light, and dust motes. Cherries in her mouth.

I am here, now.

She took the silver fishes and placed them in her bedside drawer.

*T*HIS WAS THE BEGINNING. And in her beginning in the eastern side of England, in a building without seagulls or feathers in vases, she did not sleep. She tried. But she spent her first night there in a bed that creaked, in a shared room, in a building called Curie. She lay on her back, wide-eyed. She looked at her nearest sleeper—a girl whose hair was plum-coloured, and slept with a grey cotton rag in her hand.

It was the sounds, maybe. Above all else, it was the sounds, for there were many new sounds, at night. She listed them, in her head: the breathing, and the clocks; the heating pipes. A noise in the dark, outside. Far away, on a floor above, she heard a door close.

No sea. No owl in the lane.

She wrote them down, in pencil. Her round, small words. But also, there were new daytime noises—the bell that rang for breakfast, and feet in the stairwell, and the knock of a metal ladle of porridge against her metal tray. The suck of Curie's main door, when she pushed it. And chair legs scraped on the floor, and Miss Bailey was a plump, blonde-haired housemistress with red cheeks and a red nose who clapped her hands, said, "All new girls to the tennis court, please!" So Moira heard a dozen feet crunch on the gravel path, then.

There was an orientation tour. Or so it was called. Three older girls with holes in their tights led Moira and five others with fists for hands through the school. Corridors, and classrooms. The changing rooms. The music hut. The assembly hall. The gym with its polished floor, and the science laboratories, and the small, chemical indoor pool which smelt fierce, and whose water was a bright turquoise-blue. Her glasses steamed. They dripped on the floor. She wiped them, saw her reflection—black hair, and dark-blue clothes.

The girls had talked of which library books had sex in them, which teachers drank too much. And "See that? The bell-tower? A pupil hung herself in it, years back, and they say you can hear her swinging there . . ."

More and more sounds. The next day she heard hockey boots, being smacked against walls, to remove their mud and clotted grass, and the electric snag of bands being pulled through hair, and the sound of a distant piano. The thin scratch of an ink pen on paper. The flagpole on top of the main house clinked in breezy weather, and she paused by the privet hedge, listened to it.

And silence? Was that, too, a noise? Never a silent moment on the coast, by an army range. Never had a time without the sea's breathing, in and out. Now? Now, she had a huge, dark silence that came into the dormitories at midnight, when the generator shut down, and lay itself down next to her, as a person might, pressed against her ears.

•   •   •

STACKPOLE *is gone.* It was Locke, now, with its lawn as green as bottle glass, and squirrels that stole walnuts from the walnut tree, buried them all over the grounds. She saw them do this.

Slowly, lessons began. Two long, high buildings joined the back of Locke Hall—these were the teaching blocks. Flat-roofed, so that rainwater turned green on them. She sat neatly, pencil in hand. No words to her, or from her, but she watched every teacher—Mrs Maynard's clackety shoes; the bump on the nose of Miss Kearney. Blackboards, and protractors; the gluey smell of textbooks. She did her work, because what else could she do? But she looked out of windows, too, sometimes, for the rooms were high up, and their northerly views were of sugar beet fields, and pylons, and the distant grey roof of a chicken farm. To the south, Moira saw the church in Lockham Thorpe, and a row of poplar trees that swayed in high winds, and whispered to themselves. And beneath it all was the courtyard—its moss, and litter, and an archway. An old, forgotten fountain sat in it. *It is sad,* she thought—a stone girl with a stone jug, not pouring water. The girl was meant to—but there was nothing. Her feet were hidden by dead leaves, and her hands were copper-stained, and all she was poured was a cobweb and cold, blustery Norfolk air. One afternoon, a week after her parents had brought her there, Moira decided that the dark mouth of the stone jug might be a good hiding place, one day—for a note, or a nesting bird.

Also, she noticed the cracked windowpane in the History room. The black damp on the French room's wall. She could hear the wire fence by the tennis courts whistling, sometimes, and in the evenings, she read quietly in her room. Came to like the red-inked monkey on her angle-poise light. It watched her do her homework; it wore a small red hat. She spoke to it, once, when nobody was there, told it her name—*Moira Stone*—and this was her first friend at Locke, for it did not call her *Swot,* or *Bubble Eyes,* or whisper behind her back. A felt-tipped monkey, on a light bulb.

•   •   •

THIS HAPPENED:

On a Monday, she fell. There was mud—out by the hockey field. She'd been walking alone at lunchtime, with her sea bean in her hand, and slipped over. Onto her side with a thump, and as she tried to stand up, she fell over again. Seen, by girls in the Maths room. Laughing at her.

She scrambled back to Curie. Locked herself in the bathroom at the end of the corridor. Pulled off her school skirt and ran it under the tap, scrubbing it with a bar of cracked, grey soap which left an oily mark, and did not foam. The bath filled with mud. She got it on her hands, and the floor, and she had made it all worse, and she was standing in her knickers when there was a knock on the door.

"Hello-ee?"

Miss Bailey. She'd heard the taps, and the locked door. She knocked again, and on finding Moira, she bustled like a collared-dove, and took the dirty skirt away—"Leave it to me . . . Poor old you." Returned with one that was two sizes too big, but clean—it had lain in lost property for a year, unclaimed, and so she'd washed it, kept it for just such moments as this.

Moira hated that soap. She hated the taps, and the scratchy toilet paper, and the soreness that came up on her bottom, later, from falling. She'd lost her sea bean, out in the mud; it was gone. But her skirt came back, as good as new.

"These things happen," Miss Bailey said.

·   ·   ·

MOIRA ALMOST forgot about it. If you try hard to forget a thing, you almost can, so she busied herself with verbs, and multiplication. But outside the dining hall, a girl with long, pale-brown hair that curled at its ends said to her, "I saw it. You. Falling over." She smiled. "Is it Moira? Is that your name?"

Moira watched her name being tested, shaped in this mouth. *Moy-rah.*

This, in turn, was Heather—the plant that grew in craggy places. Heather, who thought that the two worst things in the world were thick, plastic glasses and scholarships.

*O*N THE PIGEONHOLE for *S*, she found a pink envelope, with an inky address. Her name had run in the rain.

The letter said this:

> *My dearest M,*
>
> *How are you? It is the afternoon, Dad is at work, so I thought I would sit down at the table and write. It's a windy day. The sea is white-tipped, and this is real cliff-top weather, so I'm thinking of you. Do you remember when we walked to Manorbier, and saw the dolphin? You were only little, so perhaps you don't.*
>
> *Life goes on here. Your father had a bad cold last week, and was sniffling all over the house. I avoided it—vitamins, I think! The inn has new hanging baskets with winter pansies in them, which look beautiful, but I doubt they'll last the month. We've been forecast gales. We'll light the fire and stay indoors for the next week or so.*
>
> *The Bannisters send their love. Their oak tree is dropping branches and so might have to be taken down. If so, the lane will feel strange without it. And the baby is growing daily. It kicks, and wakes me up sometimes, and it sends its love with this letter.*
>
> *Moira—there are days when I miss you very much. Today is one of those days. I was in your room, and I saw all your books on the shelf. I hope you're happy, and that everything is right.*
>
> *It will be so lovely to see you at Christmas.*
>
> *Who are your friends, at school? Tell me all about them. Maybe they can visit us in the holidays, if you'd like them to?*
>
> *Write if you can.*
>
> *With lots of love*
>
> *Mum xxx*

Moira took this letter, folded it.

• • •

PERHAPS SHE would have liked Locke Hall a little better if she'd been alone. No other girls at all. Just her—and the monkey, and maybe Miss Bailey. And the fish tank in the Biology room.

But there were hundreds of girls. Hundreds of plaits, and purses on strings. It took her a long time, but, slowly, she learnt a few names. The girl who slept in the nearest bed, with the grey cloth in her hand, was Annie, for Annabel. She never untied the laces on her shoes—just pushed her heels down into them, so that the leather softened and became a paler tan. She lay in bed, said to Moira, "You *won* a place here? You *applied*?" Annie hadn't—she'd been dumped at Locke, she said, by her parents who hadn't the time or effort for her. "They were divorcing—or they said they were." That was three years ago, and Annie said she'd divorce them herself when she was old enough—"because you can do that now." Smelt of talcum powder. Tied elastic bands around her fingers when she was bored, so that their tips darkened and swelled up, like fruit.

Jo played hockey, and sat next to Heather in the dining hall. Vee (her real name? Or short for something else? Moira wasn't sure, and didn't ask her) had dozens of plaits, which she pinned against her dark scalp, and there was Geraldine—whale-like, slow, with cracked skin on her hands and eyelids, and she scratched herself in bed, at night. Nails on skin.

"Shut *up* . . ." Heather said, turning over in the dark.

Also, Moira knew who the Knox cousins were. Small, and quick, and they pressed their thumbs into Curie's fire alarms, knew all the worst words. In a Biology class, on a Tuesday, Mr Hodge asked the class to grow mustard cress on a wet paper towel—"to show the importance of light to growth," he said—and as Moira leant down to place her seeds in a neat, straight line, the Knox girls fought. Threw their wet paper towels at each other, across the room.

Mr Hodge said, *"Please . . ."* One hit the ceiling, stuck there. Hardened, and stayed above their heads.

Also, they fought in church. Sunday mornings, they all filed down to the church in Lockham Thorpe, and sat in its half-darkness. Miss Burke read a lesson, and Moira looked at the kneelers, and the sad people in the glass windows, and a single shriek filled the church on a Sunday in October, when one Knox girl pulled another's hair.

The head girl hauled them outside. Her name? Moira didn't know it. But she was eighteen years old, and graceful, but then, all the Sixth Formers were—living on the top floor of Curie, beyond a strawberry-pink door, which said, in round, happy handwriting in black pen, *Keep Out!*

And those mustard cress seeds grew tall and proud on the windowsill, turning their little green heads towards the autumn light, and the sugar beet fields. The seeds placed in the darkness of the storeroom did not grow as well. She made a note of this. How they were white, and died.

• • •

BUBBLE EYES. This came with the autumn. So did thick, blue-coloured frosts, and as she walked back from church, she passed a field of pumpkins—laid out on the ground. Orange, and swollen, with their thick, grooved rinds. She'd never seen this before.

And she had never known an inland autumn. Its leaves blew into doorways, and over feet; the caretaker and his workers raked them into tall, copper piles and burnt them. She watched them do this, from the gravel path. The smell drifted over the school, filled stairwells, and caught itself on her clothing, and there was a smell, too, from the radiators—of dust, or heat itself. Odd, big radiators. Too hot to touch, and yet they didn't heat the rooms at all. The girls picked the paint off them. Pressed their socked feet to the pipes.

And in these evenings, she walked. *Bubble Eyes*, or *Brains*—and so if she didn't have homework to do, she left the red-inked monkey and the dormitory and the people, and she slipped outside. She probably wasn't meant to. The other girls read, or took showers, or sat with their chins on their knees in the television room, but Moira went outdoors instead. Wore her blue cardigan with its sleeves pulled over her hands. Stepped over puddles in her buckled shoes.

East. She held her plastic compass. Or she just walked, on her own—viewing the school from all its secret angles. From the tennis courts, and the driveway, and from the back of the kitchen where the huge metal bins were, and the blue flytrap, and the old vegetable smell. She crouched against the infirmary, and saw the starched bed sheets, and the row of white sinks. The nurse was a soft, rolling woman with circular glasses, whose neck swayed when she shook the thermometer down. Moira learnt this from her evening walks. Also, that the nurse liked snow-globes—for she had five of them on her desk—pinkish, heavy, made of glass.

I am here now, and that's that. And once, she stood by the walnut tree and watched the light in the hall's west wing. Miss Burke's home— where she slept, and read. Where she must file her nails, and wash her magpie hair. Moira stood by the tree, imagining this, and as she did, she saw another girl out at this time—by the dining hall, smoking slowly, one arm wrapped around her for warmth, breathing the smoke out through her nose. Old and wise. No spectacles.

Moira hid herself. Moira the detective, in a blue cardigan.

It was only in those evenings, as she stood by the stone fountain, or crunched over frost, or crept round the games shed where the hurdles and netballs were kept, that she let herself think of Stackpole, and her parents with their bed-socks on. *Nothing changes.* Everything does, and had, and yet she knew from her mother's letters that the patch-work rug was still folded over, at the end of her bed. *We light the fire, and . . .* Still with apple wood, and with the porch light on.

• • •

SHE DREAMT, soon enough, of the sea.

She dreamt of the wake of a boat, slapping against the limestone quay. The gill of a fish. She saw the dimpled water when it rained, off Barafundle. One night, she was a gull on a black rock, and when she woke up the next morning, she had to blink the dream away. Sleet, outside. She scuttled down the gravel path with her woollen hat on, and after breakfast, a thought came to her.

In the library, she found a map of the Norfolk coast and opened it up on a smooth mahogany table, cleaned the sleet off her glasses, and took off her hat. A big sea. A better one, surely—for it was the *North Sea*, which sounded cold, and choppy, with big waves and foam, and better gulls; to stand on its shore would be much better, she felt, than any Stackpole beach. All spume and pirate coves. And hers.

She told the red monkey about it. *Did you know . . . ?* He didn't. He listened to her, with wide felt-tipped eyes. She imagined this wild North Sea, too, on her evening walks, or in church, or standing on the netball court with mottled hands. Or at night, when the generator shut down and the silence came, she'd think of this new water, curl her toes, and imagine burying them into wet, cold sand. Who needed old things? She didn't. She didn't need anything, really, and her stomach hurt a little less, at night, as the term moved on, as the North Sea became stronger, and knocked at her dormitory door.

• • •

ANNIE SAID, "At last," when December came in. She stood in the entrance hall of the main house, span a silver bauble on the Christmas tree with her hand. Fox tracks, too, out by the privet hedge. A carol service in the church with the round tower.

One night, as Moira slept, somebody touched her.

She flinched. Hit out.

A hand was on her shoulder, and at first she thought of water, but her dream skittered away. She fumbled for her glasses. Thought, *Moy-rah!* But it was not Heather.

"Moira? Are you awake? I know it's late, but . . ."

So Moira rubbed her eyes, and followed Miss Bailey. She tiptoed out of the dormitory and found herself standing in the stairwell of Curie House in her dressing gown, at nearly eleven o'clock at night, in December '89, with the telephone in her left hand. She heard the words *girl*, and *healthy*. She imagined her mother's face, and George beside her. Stickiness.

She hung up.

She went back to bed, stayed in her dressing gown because she was cold. She thought she could hear it, for a moment—the bleating. The hungry mouth that was in the world, now—far out in the school grounds. Trembling the surface of the ditch's water.

Moira turned onto her right-hand side, slept.

5

The Fish Pin

LOVE: AS I DROVE HERE TONIGHT, OVER THE DARK RIVER, I THOUGHT OF the tidal creeks and reed beds, and the old sea wall. This is their weather—or I think it is. I have seen them in every season, and all weathers, and they shine in the summer months. Ice creams and sunsets, and sea lavender. There is a beauty in it. But I know I preferred my slow, wintery walks on the Norfolk coast—the sideways wind, and the grey sky. The mud. It was the turning back, too, as I walked, that I liked—to see the coastal lights come on, and the beacon in the smaller of the two church towers, and I'd see it all with a fisherman's eye, after a day at sea. *Fires, and beer. A steaming pie.* I'd think of my husband, waiting. And the birds would fly slowly, their thin legs reflected in the waterways.

If we have a season, then, it is mine. Winter. There is something to love—or to need, even—in the long nights, and the short days. I'm sure you don't agree with this. You were the girl with the Frisbee, and the daisy chain. But I padded over ploughed fields, blowing my hands, and I'd sooner have space and cold weather than share Blakeney Quay or Titchwell Reserve or any beach in the sunshine. Maybe I get this from our father—because hasn't he always loved the bleaker weather? Or I am a miser, or a hermit, of sorts. The pale crab, seeking a quiet room in the weed, where it can snap its claws. Til probably saw this coming, too, or at least saw sense in it: *she likes the rainy weather . . .*

And this is a good winter. Some rain. But there have been frosts, mostly, and clear skies, and I had my old, familiar dream of ice in the waves last night. Our house is warm. I was worried, at first, that it might not be, for its windows are huge, and the floors are more wooden than not. But we have lived through several winters in it, before this one, and we know how it is there, now—where the warmest places are. The landing; the attic room, where he paints; the kitchen, of course. It matters—for if I'm to walk out in the cold, by a wintery sea, I want to return to a house of heat, and kettles, and radio songs. A bath to run. It's all part of it. Don't we all have our secret things?

Cold, then. A slow gritting lorry flashed its orange globe at me as I came here. I see our parents have left a glass jar of pot-pourri with you—fir cones in it, cinnamon sticks. A dried, golden pear. I don't know what its scent is—spice, but also a musk, of some kind. Frankincense? Nor do I know very much of how love is shown, for I so rarely showed it. But these are the gestures people remember, or kneel at, I know that much. It isn't the big declarations. No brass bands playing. It's cinnamon sticks, or a drawing of a sleeping dog. Or the gift of a stone moved with the sea for so many years that its rolled into a smooth, round ball.

So. You are born.

And in another world a stronger, darker Moira sees you exactly—fruit-skinned, so loud that the glass in the science laboratories seem to rattle with your cries for milk, or for being held.

• • •

THE LABORATORIES were on the top floor of the southerly teaching block. Long, glassy rooms—smelling of chalk dust and green paper towels, and a sourness—chemicals, and the rubber tubes on gas burners. The walls were all cabinets. Filled with jars, phials, wooden clamps, test tubes, litmus paper, a pickled organ of some kind—small, orange-coloured. There were fish, too. A tank of five goldfish sat at the back—bubbling quietly, with a blue light and a sign amongst the weed and fish that said *No Fishing!* Her skin felt dry in there. Once, she dared herself to place a small drop of hydrochloric acid onto her wrist, to see what happened. Nothing, really. No redness. Yet she noticed that it ate into her white science overall and, later, that her skin itched there.

She sat at a bench with Anne-Marie—a girl whose arms were so big that her own overall was tight, and its elastic cuffs left their mark on her. Moira saw this when she looked up from her exercise book—dark, and deep, like teeth marks. Moira wrote equations. The properties of gases. The seven characteristics of all living things. Mr Hodge slipped through the room like an anxious creature—buck-toothed, with busy hands. He peered into test tubes and, sometimes, leapt with his arms outstretched towards an accident—a tall flame, or a new, strange smell. His phrase was, *Didn't you listen?* He said this a lot. And he'd take his left hand, run it repeatedly over his balding head, from back to front, as if calming himself. His wedding ring shone against his white scalp. The rumours were that his wife was much older than him.

Movement. Respiration. Sensitivity. Growth. Reproduction. Excretion. Nutrition.

Also, in the Biology room, a plastic skeleton hung by the blackboard, and it moved a little every time the door was opened, or shut. Clinked, like a wind chime. It was old—"It's been here as long as I have," Mr Hodge told her. He found her there, at the end of the day. Not touching the skeleton, but next to it, her head tilted, reading the names of its thin yellow bones. She had these bones in her, too. *Sternum. Fibula.*

"There are," he said, as he put his coat on, "stories about this chap. He's been taken, in the last weeks of term. Hidden—as a joke,

Hung up in the bell-tower. I found him sitting cross-legged in Maths room, once." He paused, looked at her. "Do you want to stay here a little longer? I can leave it unlocked for an hour, or so."

Yes. She did. So Moira came to know the Biology lab. All the chemicals were shut away, but there were still many things to look at. And so she walked through the room on her own, that afternoon— pressing her face against cabinets, studying posters, eyeing a Venus flytrap, leaving her thumbprints on the tank of goldfish who mouthed their stories at her. She lifted the hands of the skeleton. Told Mr Hodge, later, she thought that perhaps there was a metatarsal missing.

"Is there? There *is* . . ."

No other girls in there. The bell rang, and they left, and only Moira stayed in there. No one to tease her for wearing goggles on top of her glasses, so that they left red marks on her cheekbones. Small, sore indentations at the side of her face, by her ears.

• • •

HAIL BLEW around her ankles as she made her way to the library. Past the stone fountain.

Inside, Moira whispered to the librarian, *Science books*. She was led to the final row—twice her height, dusty. And on the long mahogany tables she opened up books with rainbows in them, and formulae, and a map of the human eye. $E = O$ *is the Big Bang*—and Moira was not quite sure what this meant yet.

Ventricles. Lymph nodes.

On her pink library card, the names of books were written down. *A Guide to the Human Body* and *The Periodic Table* would, she decided, be taken back to Stackpole with her, opened up in her old bedroom. If she couldn't take the goldfish or the walnut tree with her, these would do. She would smell Locke Hall on their pages. The glue in their spines.

The books were carried back to the dormitory in her arms, against her chest, back through the hail. She startled a crow, which rose up, shouting.

• • •

MISS KEARNEY PLAYED the piano in the last assembly of term, and Miss Burke wore a wooden bracelet that knocked against the lectern. She talked of the gift of giving, and faith. Coughed into a handkerchief during "Good King Wenceslas."

In Curie, Miss Bailey wore a paper hat and checked the rooms—that the windows were shut, the chairs were upturned on desks, and the linen was folded. "See you next year," she called.

Three months had gone by.

The caretaker drove fifteen girls to Norwich, in the school minibus. Past the cathedral, and the river. A very grey city, and at the railway station, Moira wedged her hands under her arms for warmth. Her father had written each train down—its times, numbers. *And we will all be there to meet you at Haverfordwest!*

Nearly eight hours. Three changes, in all—three times she stood on an icy platform with her suitcase between her legs, and her woollen hat pulled down over her fringe, to her glasses. The trains themselves weren't much better. They smelt of bodies. There were smears on the glass, like handprints, where someone's head had been.

She half slept. Half watched the Midlands roll by, and the first glimpse of the Welsh hills. By mid-afternoon, all she could see when she looked out of the window was her own reflection, so she stared at it. Her big glasses. Her small mouth.

• • •

THE TRAIN ARRIVED at Haverfordwest late in the evening. No stars, but as she climbed down from the train with her suitcase, she smelt the sea instantly—it rushed at her, with fish in it, and crabs, and weed, and puffin wings, and the wet wood of boats, and mussels, and its lengths of old, frayed rope, and maybe even Lundy Island—and she saw her parents standing under the awning in their anoraks. Her mother with a white scarf, and she waved with a white glove. Her father, with his bristly beard. There was a navy-blue pram with them.

Miriam knelt down, and hugged Moira. She kissed her shoulders, and her forehead. "You're thinner," she said.

In the porch of End House there was a piece of white cloth pinned with *Welcome Home* painted on it.

*E*ND HOUSE WAS THE SAME, at first. The same curtains, and the peacock feathers, and the same rusty stains in the bath. Still the furze, and the swing. Her bedroom, too, was exactly the same— small, and warm, with the squeaky floorboard, and the postcards of Pembrokeshire, and the toy puffin on her bed. The same books. And she heard the old pipe noises at night, she padded across to the window, opened it, heard the Atlantic in the dark.

It could have been a dream. Locke could have never happened at all, except that she had the science books with the school's name stamped in them, and the brooch of fishes with its cool, sharp pin. She could smell chalk dust on her jumper, so she knew Locke existed. But Stackpole was just the same, in many ways, and if there were changes, perhaps they were in Moira. Not in the house at all.

She almost believed this. *It's me that's different.* But as she sat by the window in her pyjamas, looked over the night-time garden, a shrill, piercing noise came to her. It stopped. Then it came to her again, and there were footsteps, and a light came on, and this, she knew, was the change in End House. A baby. Screaming at night. Screaming in the daytime, too. A horrible smell to it, and pale-brown cloths soaking in a bucket by the back door, which Miriam poked with a wooden spoon. A new noise in Miriam, too—*sshh* . . . Over and over. She tested milk on her elbow. Smelt of cream. Unbuttoned her blouse, so that Moira left the room.

George said, "Well? What do you think of your sister?"

She went outside. She pulled doors behind her. On the third afternoon, without telling her parents, she put her arms into her duffle coat and made her way down the lane. Past the Bannisters. Past the horses, who steamed by the gate, and she stopped there for a while, looking at them. Then she walked through the wood smoke of

The Stackpole Inn, and down the road to the quay. The dairy farm was quiet. The guesthouse said *No Vacancies*, and no ginger cat sprawled there. Too cold for it. Or it was dead. Her nose felt pink.

Moira sat on the limestone jetty, and looked down at the water, at the brown fronds of weed that grew on the stones beneath the water line, and that wafted with the waves. She counted the fishing buoys. *Five.* A black-headed gull stood on one, and it bobbed on the tide, and in the distance, Manorbier twinkled. It was quiet there. The sea slopped. Too icy to swim in it, she thought, and she knew of hypothermia now, from her book, and frostbite. *Ice crystals can form in the tissues; flesh hardens, and sensation is lost.* But she felt, perhaps, the sea did remember her, after all. Maybe the gull did, too, because it cleaned its feathers, and did not fly away when she blew her nose.

The uphill walk home. And she scuffed through the sand in the lane towards the porch light, and the green front door, and Miriam blinked, put her hands up on her cheekbones. "I thought you were reading in your room," she said. Shocked. Cross, later.

• • •

MOIRA IGNORED the baby for five days. No sideways glances. She turned her head when the bundle was offered to her.

But on Christmas Eve, they all sat in Stackpole church, amongst its candles and bat droppings. The same pulpit, and pews, and the worm filled its lungs up, screeched out mid-prayer. Wailed and wailed, and a thick smell came, so that Moira turned, looked into the wide, wet mouth of it, and Miriam hurried outside like a thief, and George glanced over his shoulder, again and again. Moira stared ahead. She thought of the red-inked monkey, and the pumpkins. She thought there might be two Moiras, now, in two different worlds. It felt that way.

Midnight. She lifted the blankets up. Crept out of bed, across the landing. The baby slept in the spare room, in its cot, and Moira stood beside it, peered in. A fat face. Dimply, and its eyes were squished together, as if made of dough. The baby lay on its back, with its arms up by its head, and if it had woken up it would have seen a dark fringe, and dark eyes, and maybe its own fat face reflected in the spectacles. *This is what it looks like.* She knew, now.

Ugly. Small and fat.

She went back to bed.

• • •

MOIRA WAS GIVEN a writing set for Christmas that year. Pink and blue paper, with envelopes; an address book; a real fountain pen. The Bannisters sent her a five-pound note. Til's card had glitter on it, and the words *I'll see you soon!*

Miriam asked, "What are you favourite lessons? Who are your friends?"

This, in the kitchen. Moira stood with a tea towel in her hand. She made a few, small answers, and spent the rest of Christmas Day upstairs, on her bed, with *A Guide to the Human Body,* which smelt of dust and cleverness, and Locke, and she read it as the baby's bawling shook the light bulb, and Moira's tympanic membrane.

The house was not the same anymore, and she was not the same, and nothing was. Lost, as lots of things were.

*S*OMETIMES, AT LOCKE, in the night-time, I would stand in the white-tiled bathroom of the boarding house, and open up my hands. A map of skin rivers. Red lines or colourless, running over my palms. I'd bend back my fingers, until each crease darkened, opened up for me. Like valleys. I'd stare at them, under the bare light bulb. Then close up my hands, go back to bed.

• • •

THE SPRING TERM at Locke Hall was cream-coloured, freshly painted. The corridors smelt of it. Annie found a sign—*Wet Paint*—and did not believe it. She touched it, dotted cream fingerprints onto a dark-glossed door.

So it went. Moira returned to the scratchy toilet paper, and the thin toast for breakfast in the dining hall. The dinner ladies no longer wore their flashing Christmas earrings, and the tinsel in Curie's stair-well had gone, and the dormitory air was thick with disinfectant for a week or so—so that the girls complained of it, grew headaches, wheezed. "Every new term it's like this," Geraldine said, scratching at her hands. The webbing between her thumb and forefinger was red.

Heather smiled. "And how was Christmas, Moira?" She wore a silver heart on a chain, and played with it, and when she saw Moira's ink pen and pink writing paper she widened her eyes, delighted. Said, "Lucky *you* . . ."

A bluish light on the hockey pitch, in the afternoons. The crack of stick and ball—and in the changing rooms afterwards, the same sour, vinegar smell of feet, and aerosol sprays. Lost socks. She had to take her glasses off when she peeled her sweatshirt over her head, and so for ten seconds or so, she'd see nothing at all.

She played a lot of hockey that month. Not that she was very good at it—but the four boarding houses played each other, and Moira shivered at the back of the pitch as Jo hit the white board at the back of the goal with the ball. Austen House shivered, too. She stood beside a redheaded girl with spots on her forehead who said, "It's *freezing* . . ." and stamped her boots. Miss Bailey, with her whistle. The bare poplar trees.

In the match against Nightingale, the ball was hit into a shinbone, so that even Moira at the end of the field heard the cracking sound. A grey sky overhead. Gunshots, far away, in the woods where the pheasants were. She watched the crowd gather around the girl who was crying, and clutching her leg. There was snow in the air. Moira held out her hand for it. Her blue, cold hand.

An ambulance was called to Locke. It rolled over the gravel, brought faces to the windows of the classrooms, and Miss Bailey shook her head, shook her hands, said, "Where were your bloody shin pads?" The ambulance doors shut, and rocked away, down the drive.

"Ouch," Annie said, knowingly.

Only a bruised bone, in the end, but the girl wore a bandage there. Hobbled a bit. Took her time on the stairs. Nightingale won the rematch, and she mended.

• • •

THE SKELETON had not run away at Christmas. Mr Hodge said it was a nice surprise, to find it still hanging there, slack-jawed. And the fish shimmied up by the glass when Moira approached with a pinch of food in her hand. She noticed this.

He said to her, on a Friday afternoon, "Moira, how are you? In yourself?" Worried, maybe, that a girl should choose to spend her spare time alone, in a classroom of fish and false bones. He looked over his half-moon glasses.

And maybe he spoke to Miss Bailey, or maybe Miss Bailey was smart enough on her own—either way, she found Moira by the pigeonholes in February, and whispered, "How's things?" Things were fine. Things would be better if people stopped asking her that, but she didn't say this. Moira just nodded. Turned back to the pigeonholes that had lots of red envelopes in them. No Valentine's cards for her, but Heather had three, and Geraldine had one, but it was from her parents, so it didn't really count, and she hid it, knowing how Heather would be if she saw it. *Love Mum and Dad.*

"Don't tell?" she pleaded. Her big, damp face.

Moira lay down on her bed with the silver fishes, and thought of the horses, in windy weather. She opened the clip, closed it.

• • •

THERE WERE ENVELOPES, though in time. Three weeks later, on a day of wind, Moira turned twelve years old. Crocuses grew by the sundial. She combed her fringe, buttoned up her cardigan, and found three birthday cards with her name on them.

Two from Stackpole—from her parents, and a seascape from the Bannisters which read, *May your coming year be full of joy.* A card, too, from the grandmother in Scotland she'd never met. Moira's birthday present was a pale-blue lambswool jumper.

"*Very* smart. Look at *you.*"

She looked in the pigeonhole again, at lunchtime. Just in case. She looked for anything with a London postmark on it, but there was nothing.

She was twelve, now. It sounded a lot older, really, than eleven.

• • •

THE WEEKENDS at Locke were strange—empty, shapeless hours that Moira wasn't sure of. How to use them, or see them. She worked, mostly. Sat in the library, on a high-backed chair, licking the pad of her finger as she turned a page. Or she walked around the school grounds. Watched the caretaker mending the boundary fence where the foxes got in. She went to the infirmary once, with a headache, or at least saying she did. Spent two hours sleeping there, in a silent room, on a starched bed. The snow-globes shining, and the nurse's fleshy ankles spilling over her tan shoes.

Some of the girls didn't stay. The weekends could be a freedom—those who lived close enough to their homes could go back to them, on the Friday nights. Sink into a bath. Use softer loo roll. Have mugs of tea in a room with a television in it. Also, there were daytrips: the older girls who slept behind the strawberry-pink door walked down the driveway, their hair blowing, to catch the bus into Holt, where they'd drink coffee or buy clothes, or shampoo. And parents came, sometimes—parked on the gravel by the walnut tree, greeted their daughters, and took them away to cities, or restaurants, or to shops, or to the seaside. Moira saw this, from her room. She sat on her bed, hands in her lap. Once, her mother had written, *When Amy is bigger, we'd love to drive over . . .* But it was many hours in the car. And anyway, she didn't want that—had thought, *Don't bother.* Didn't want George's blue tie, her mother, vomiting, or the baby with its doughy face, and smell.

So she studied, or walked. Or fed the goldfish.

And she did not understand when, on the Saturday that followed, Miss Bailey said to her, "Visitor for you. In the main house." Moira was standing by the sundial. In her duffle coat, with her head tilted, trying to read the time. But the sunlight was pale, watery. She used her wristwatch, in the end.

A visitor?

"Hurry up!" Miss Bailey said. Vanished.

She thought, *Who?*

Then, *It's a mistake.*

But as she walked to the main house, she saw it: a red car, with a dent in its door. And a woman in heeled boots and black fur collar was leaning against it, powdering her nose.

Aunt Til looked up. Put her fingers in her mouth, and whistled.

• • •

TIL, FOR MATILDA, who was as luminous and scented as ever she was—with hair as thick as it had been in Stackpole, on the cliff-top, and her eyelashes were black and curled, and she said, "Surprise!" Bent down, to embrace Moira. Warm Aunt Til, and she wore the silver ring on her thumb, and a belt with a huge buckle that reflected things—birds in flight; the light on the school windows. When Til signed her name in the visitors' book, it was with a wild, inky flourish. Her name as a loop, a tail.

She said, "I know, I know. I should have told you. But I wanted to surprise you! You don't mind?"

Moira didn't mind. She hurried back to Curie to find her woollen hat and gloves, so that Heather asked, "Where are *you* going?" And Moira thought the red car might have gone, when she got back. But Til was still there. Hands in her pockets, twisting her heel.

"Well," she said, considering her, "you look older. And skinnier—why's that?"

Til of the citrus smell. Til of the moon-shaped scar and the underground mice, who had driven from London just to see her—and would have come sooner, but she'd been so busy, and anyway, this was a birthday lunch. "Tea and cake is in order, I think. *Golly*—twelve years old! I remember . . ." She talked of the dark-blue, starless night when her sister had called, said, *It's a girl!* And Til talked, too, as she drove, of the theatre she'd been working in, how it was haunted, how an understudy had been pushed, mysteriously, from behind. "A jealous spook . . ." Til said. "Imagine that. I'll let you know if I see it, of course."

Away from Locke. North, away from the village, and the poplar trees, and the sign that said *Locke Hall Residential School for Girls. 1 mile.* The car rattled. Til muttered at the gearbox, leant forwards as she drove. Wiped the windscreen with her sleeve. And Moira wound the window down, rested her chin on the door, and saw the cobbled walls, the hedgerows, the drains, the stubbly fields. When they pulled into a passing place, she saw the veins in a leaf, or the rust on a gate.

Happy. Or as close to it as she had been for a while, now.

"Ah, Moira . . . Smell that. *Countryside.*" Pronounced the names of villages, or tried to. *Letheringsett. Field Dalling.*

Til didn't ask of Amy, or Locke, or parents. She did not say a word of those things—only of theatres, and the churches with round towers. Pressed her horn at a pheasant, shouted, "Watch out!" And she turned to Moira with her violet eyes and said, "Well, then. Where do you think I'm taking you?"

The sea.

She knew this.

• • •

DON'T THINK that Moira always dreamt of water, there. Don't think that.

Sometimes, in her dormitory bed, in the hush that came when the generator died, she'd think of other things—like science, or the damp school flag. Or she'd think of the clot of hair she'd pulled out of the plughole in the shower, once—eel-slick, snapping on things.

But Til smiled, at this. "You dream what you dream . . . How can you help it?"

And Moira knew she was right. No walls in sleep; locks came undone. For some nights, she'd imagine how the North Sea would be when, at last, she saw it—how its might rock boats, or burst over rocks, and splatter back down into itself. All the fish. The wrecks in it. The grey waves, like backs. If she tried to dream of other things, this still came to her. She couldn't stop herself. She'd wake from it with salt in her mouth, sand in her hair, and eyes.

There will be surf. There will be cliffs with fulmars on them.

Or a jetty. A pirate ship. Or the huge lifting up of a tail.

Til parked at Wells-next-the-Sea. Said, "Ready?"

No cliffs. No pirates.

Moira would remember this. There was salty air, and gulls—but it was a flat, dark beach. A straight coast. No rocks, or rock pools. No cliffs at all. No whales, or fulmars, and if there are moments in life when our heart drops down, and sadness feels like a watery thing creeping inside us, she had such a moment then, as she stood in her duffle coat, arms at her side, and the sea was far, far away—brown, and slow-moving, and the sky, too, was brown, and there was no sea spray, or white, hissing water. Just a beach. And Til. Two sea pies at the end of the beach, digging for cockles.

Her aunt said, "Oh." Seeing this, too.

And Moira felt sad. Sad, and stupid—for thinking that all seas were the same, with the same waves. *Stupid Moira.*

They climbed back into the car, and Aunt Til never took Moira to Wells again. It was Titchwell, next time—a bird reserve, with marshes. Reed-beds and wooden hides, and this was a safer place, because she had no other reed-beds to compare it to. And it was Titchwell, for every visit after this—its avocets, and wind sounds, and the east-facing benches they'd sit on, thinking of their lives, and the spaces in them.

•   •   •

She wrapped her arm around her niece's neck, and kissed her head. Walking into a tearoom in Holt, in the afternoon. A day of empty sea and empty sky, and Til ordered two slices of sponge cake with lemon-yellow icing, eyed Moira, leant over the tablecloth and said, "Would you like your present, now?"

A birthday card with a feathered handbag on it. And a parcel wrapped in tissue paper, and a bow, which Moira slowly unpicked. Inside it, lay a nightdress: pale-green, with a ribbon, and a green lace hem, and it was soft, and cottony, and Til said, "Do you like it? I saw it, and thought, *I know who might like that . . .*"

Yes, she did like it. It was lovely, and pretty, and it smelt clean, and she folded it back into the tissue paper. Sat it on her knees, as they drove back. Held it, as she stood on the gravel, and watched Til leave Locke Hall—her tail-lights growing smaller. Til tooted the horn. A hand with a silver ring on its thumb waved through the car window, just before it turned onto the road, and then she was gone.

• • •

BUT MOIRA didn't wear it. She couldn't. It was so pretty.

She lay in bed, instead, with the nightdress, on her side, facing the wall. And she thought of the world beyond this wall, beyond the plastering and brickwork. Out there. Past the sugar beet fields and the pylons, and the tearoom. She thought of the black-and-white birds, and the foxes, and of all the people she knew, and she wondered what they were doing at that moment, right now, at nine-forty on a Saturday night in March. She imagined it. Her father, perhaps, in his striped apron, a saucepan in his hand; her mother's knees in bath foam; the worm asleep; Aunt Til, back in London, standing on the platform of an underground station, with her eyes closed, feeling the soft buffet of air on her face as a train comes nearer. She imagined Mr Bannister lying in a bed with his wife, and the bed trembling.

Some days, the world can feel so big that it's too much to take. It steals away all the safe things. We feel as small as a seed, or sand on a beach, and Moira knew of the Big Bang, now—that the universe came from a sole, minute dot of matter that exploded, expanded, and threw out stars and planets and gases and all the atoms that make life. All the trees, and plants, and herring gulls. She picked at the flaking plaster, marked her own skin with a brooch, and thought of this. $E = 0$, and an inflationary universe. So a dot could still matter? Still have magic in it.

6

In Shadows

You grew.

You won't remember any of it, for how old were you? Six months. Smiling, but not talking, or crawling very much. You sucked things. You ate. Slept. Made stenches. That was all you did, then.

And I'm not sure when we have a memory, as such—they say three years old. I've heard that the brain, the cerebral cortex, and all its paths and small trapdoors, are not able to keep hold of memories until that age. Maybe it's true. But I have met people who say otherwise. And perhaps I was younger than three when my mother placed me on her hip and walked out into the sea off Barafundle with me. I remember that. Her blue swimsuit. The white broken water curling round her knees. I think she said, *This, love, is the sea*—or something like that. But I've added this part, and it is not a true memory, as the sunhat and her hipbones are.

Your first? Memory? I never asked. I'd make a guess of furze, or molehills. A happy, earthy thing, at any rate, but I don't know for sure, and probably won't, now. Another lost thing. Another space in my stories of you.

• • •

THE SUMMER OF '90. Moira climbed down off the train at Haverfordwest to see a larger creature. Restless, fat-handed. As squat as a bomb.

A hot, white-coloured summer. The lane was filled with mallow, and the blown sand was warm, from sun. Crayon-yellow furze, and towering, so that George called it *glorious*. He loved its smell. Said it meant summer, for him. And Mr Bannister pegged out his washing on the line, hauled it up in a wooden prop, so that Moira could see their clothes and bed sheets from her bedroom window. White sails. A blue-patterned skirt.

End House creaked with the heat. Its drainpipes shifted, and Moira spent afternoons in the garden, at first—reading, or sitting on the swing. She sat, mute, watching a butterfly unfold its tongue. *I want to walk on my own*, but her mother said, "Too young. I'm sorry— but you are." She could only walk to the inn, at the end of the lane, but what was there, for her? She didn't want to go inside. She didn't want to hold apples out, for the horses.

On a Saturday, Amy was wedged into a strange, metal chair that fixed itself on George's back, and they walked through Tenby—all four of them. A day out. A family trip—but Tenby was busy with tourists, and the tide was high, so they could not walk to the rock in the bay, and Moira kept behind her parents. Five steps behind them. They wandered past the coloured houses, and the lifeboat slip, and the telescopes glinting on the promenade. They made their way up to the castle ruins, above the town. Sat there. And the baby drank, and George sighed, and they sat on a bench in a line, looking down at the sea and the rooftops, and the sky. The statue of Prince Albert, behind them. Wearing a herring gull as a hat.

"This is lovely," Miriam said. "Isn't it?"

No. The baby ruined the day. A fist in Moira's ice cream—lunging for it, pushing it, so that it plopped onto the grass.

Moira thought, too, *There are warning signs.* She learnt them—the baby's stiffening, the bracing of itself. Then the mouth opened, and the screams came. Huge and rhythmic. Startling a dog and the sparrows in a bush, and Miriam bounced her baby up against her chest, cooed, said, "There, now. Amy, love. Baby girl."

• • •

TWELVE. She could make the word sound hard, and nasty. She practised it, scowling. Making her lips as tight as a clam.

In the dunes, at Freshwater East. Only three of them—since George was working inland, in the shed with the fringe of raindrops, and the oil. A tartan rug was spread out on the sand. Moira wore a long-sleeved shirt. Not wanting to burn.

The baby crushed a colourless crab with her thumb, that day, and cried at sand, and Moira tied her glasses onto her head with string, walked down to the sea, and its weed, and she waded out, in her swimsuit and white long-sleeved shirt. Stayed out for an hour. It seemed a long time since she last swam in this sea. Since she last filled her ears with its noises, and snagged her toes on hidden weed. She lolled in it, star-shaped. Held her breath, sank under, and rubbed her eyes under her glasses with her fingertips. *Stone the Bone.* Her mother and Amy looked tiny, from there.

A long time, too, since she last tasted salt on her skin, later. A whole year. But also, it felt a lot longer than that.

• • •

I HAVE A PHOTOGRAPH of this. Not of my swim, or licking the salt from my hands, as the horses did. But of Tenby. Taken by a stranger, I think—for we are all in it. You know the shot. You've seen it. The bench, and the grass, and our mother wears a headscarf with roses on it. And you were appalled at the picture, because of the rolls of fat under your chin, and on your legs, and you are squirming, in it. Pushing against her lap. I am not smiling. I look suspicious, I think. Sullen—but then, I always looked that.

No, not sullen, said Ray, when I showed this to him. *But serious . . .* As if I am contemplating world peace, or a cure for diseases. As if I am a well, full of deep, cool secrets, and he smiled at this photograph, raised his eyebrows as if it was a confirmation of what he suspected, from our first words.

This was not long ago. It took me a thousand years, I think, to give Stackpole to him. To share it—its lily-ponds, and chimney smoke. The lone, lost striped glove that was placed on a fencepost one winter, and stayed there for months, so that I thought it was raised in greeting, waving, saying *hello* to me. A friend, as the red-inked monkey was. As the sea bean had been. I don't think Ray knows that part, yet, but he will, in time.

*S*EPTEMBER WAS RED, with crisp leaves from a summer of sun. Also, it was the month of new dormitories. Everyone shifted like chess pieces—left, up, sideways. Rooms were taken over. Names on headboards were scratched out with a compass point; beds were tested by new weights. It was a noisy process. Always complaints. Always a slammed door, and in the brief cold silence that followed she'd hear a bird singing, or the lawn mower, or the church bell in Lockham Thorpe. She left the monkey with its fez behind.

· · ·

MISS BAILEY SAID, "Dormitory Ten, Miss Stone"—pointing at the list pinned on the notice board. Moira found her name, and, with her finger, she traced the other names. Twelve beds had become six. Her new room-mates. Five names, and she stepped away from it.

Annie was already there, in the room. She said, "Hey"—gum in her mouth, one leg outstretched on the bed with her foot bare, her toenails berry red. "Can't escape each other. You know who else?"

Moira shook her head.

"Jo—short hair, plays hockey. Orlaith. Heather." She squinted, then. "Can't remember the fourth. Someone, anyway."

Moira sat down on her bed in the corner, looked out of the window. This was the new view: Nightingale House, and the back of the dining hall. She could see the walnut tree, too, or part of it—its squirrels, and its long afternoon shadow out across the lawn.

New sounds, again, of course. Orlaith's nose was a smooth white quadrant, and she snored—a flap of skin in her nostril, it seemed, fluttering in the dark. No ivy on the windows, so no tapping of leaves on the glass. No scratching of skin, from Geraldine, but Moira could hear the food scraps dropping into the metal bins, in the evenings, and the slow yellow lorry that came, on Tuesdays, to take this food away. Also, this was new: as she left the Biology room on a Thursday afternoon, to go to Maths class, Mr Hodge beckoned to her and said, "I thought you'd like to know." He'd returned from his summer of vegetable-growing and crosswords to find an empty space behind the door. He searched the whole school and, in the end, he found the skeleton sitting in the music room, at Miss Kearney's piano, his fingers on the keys and the manuscript for "Für Elise" laid out on the music stand.

• • •

MOIRA CONSULTED a book called *Common Complaints*, and in it she learnt that snoring was caused by a constriction of the airways during sleep—from mucus, or tissue. That it could be lessened with sprays, or by opening the airways with tape, of some kind. Or taking the pressure off the body by turning over. By lying on her front, or her side. She said nothing to Orlaith, because Orlaith could be sharp-tongued, and had made Heather laugh, so that they were friends— but Moira left *Common Complaints* in the dormitory, open on this page. Hoped that Orlaith might see it. Take the hint. Sleep on her front in the future so that Moira could get some rest, and not be tired in the mornings, with a bluishness under the eyes.

• • •

So lovely to see you, as always, dear Moira. Only a year gone, and you're so grown up now! Amy enjoyed you being here, too. She is trying to talk—at nine months!—and she seems to know her own mind. She is in love with the cat at the guesthouse, but is yet to understand that cats do not like being grappled. So I keep her away from it. You can imagine the tantrums at that . . .

Your father works hard, as ever. There is talk of another garage opening on the Lamphey road. We must hope it doesn't happen. As for the Bannisters, they send their love. And Aunt Matilda has been given a main role in her play! She's

*been upgraded! The actress who fell off the stage, and broke her leg? Til has taken
over for good! She talks of Fate, of course.*

*We wondered if you'd been given a new dormitory this year. Have you? I'd
love to know what it's like, so that I can see you there. How many of you? The
view?*

Write to us, my love
Love
M, D, and A x

Moira didn't write. Instead, she described the view to herself, in her
head—the roof, the dining hall, the walnut tree. But from her desk,
she saw none of this, because her desk faced the wall, so that all she
had was a crack in the paint, and a brown-coloured splattering, as if
someone had thrown a cup of tea. Also, it meant she sat with her
back to the rest of the room. Didn't like this. Knew faces were pulled,
behind her. Heather laughed, once. When Moira turned round,
Heather widened her eyes and said, "And?"

No red monkey, either, so in her second year at Locke Hall,
Moira did all her homework in the library instead. On the mahogany
tables, and under a green desk lamp with tassels, on its shade. A very
quiet room. Mrs Duff, the librarian, took off her shoes when she
walked, in there—tiptoeing, in her tights. It was all whispers. And
Moira liked the chair in the very back corner, where the dictionaries
were. From there, she had a view of the room, and of the courtyard
with its fountain, filled with last year's dead leaves.

• • •

SHE SOLVED EQUATIONS. Listed the different types of rock in the
world, and how they were made. And in History class, they copied
down the Tudor family tree in their books with a sharpened HB pencil and rulers.

"Homework," they were told, "is this."

They had to pick one of Henry VIII's six queens and pretend to be her. To write a diary, as she might have done. To imagine the skirts on the dormitory floor, and the pearls in the ears. Six queens, and Moira sat in the library at eight o'clock in the evening, pretending to be the fourth wife, the German one, who wasn't his wife for very long. *I am Anne of Cleves,* she wrote. *I have ladies-in-waiting, and a high fore-head.* She bit her fingernails, read her textbook, and wrote, *And the king isn't clean.* Cruel, too, because he called her names, and Moira wrote in her neatest, blue-inked writing, *I am a far better person than him.*

"Goodness," said Miss McPherson, with her thinning hair. "What a strong lady! And she was, you know."

An *A* grade for Moira, and a fact to think of, in bed, sometimes: that Anne of Cleves survived them all—Henry, and all the other younger, prettier wives. She wore a white ruff, arched a black eyebrow, and was rich, and proud, and the king *was* unclean, too. He died of a very grubby disease, in the end—or so Miss McPherson said.

Moira liked this. Said the word *grubby* in her head, when Heather—or someone, but probably her—had filled her canvas shoes with wet clots of loo roll, so that she spent her lunch break scooping it all out, shaking it off her fingers, and leaving her shoes on the radiator, upside down, to dry.

• • •

THE WIND changed direction. It blew in from the west, and brought the smell of chickens, and earth, and machines rumbled over the sugar beet fields. It also blew in Aunt Matilda, with her lipstick, a green felt hat with matching gloves, and a dark-blue thickness of eyeliner. It was a Sunday. "A day off!" she said, exhaling. "So. How are you?"

They spent the afternoon at Titchwell Reserve—west, along the coast road. Amongst the wading birds and the reed-beds. They wandered on the boardwalks, and sat on a bench to look out across the marshes, and the sky, and the church towers.

"Did your mother tell you? About the play?"

Til eyed her niece, and said she fully believed in ghosts, now. How could she not? Now she was a real actress, she said. "Not an understudy, or just a *member of the company* . . . I am allowed to take a bow all on my own, at the end! Just me! Mind you, the tarot cards saw all of this . . ."

Moira wasn't sure. She didn't really know what she believed. Ghosts? Perhaps. But there were definitely birds—avocets, said Til, and lapwing, and curlews, and redshanks with their skinny, pinkish legs. Three big grey swans, creaking over their heads. She saw all these things with her aunt, from a wooden hide—binoculars and metal flasks of tea. *Matilda.*

"Tell me about school, love. Lessons. The people in it."

Moira did, a little. She pulled her jumper over her hands, and talked about science, and Anne of Cleves, and rock formation, but not about the brooch of fishes, or the names they used for her, instead of *Moira.*

Til said, later, "You are very special. Do you know that?" Then she hurried back to London, and *Hedda Gabler,* and she left her niece in the library with these words in her head, and the sound of the flying swans, and a strange, cold feeling. She thought she might dream of ghosts, that night. But she saw herring gulls, heads under wings.

• • •

So: THE AUNT was treading the boards at a London theatre with a view of St Paul's Cathedral, and, in the news, the Berlin Wall was knocked down. Moira saw it, in the television room—all hands raised up, and the sky had stars.

I remember this, too: Miss Burke, in an emerald suit with platform shoes, talked of Bonfire Night—of having one, at Locke, for the first time. Perhaps out of a strange good will. Perhaps to raise funds for the roof of the drama room, which was leaking in wet weather, so that the costume cupboard smelt of damp, and in the school play there was wheezing.

She announced it in assembly. "With a firework display!"

The room shifted itself. On the walk back to the dormitory, Vee with the plaited hair said to Moira, "I'll believe it when I see it." She pouted her lips when she shrugged. Moira noticed this—it seemed a grown-up thing.

But it did happen. Miss Burke didn't lie. As Moira stood on the hockey field, with her stick in her hand, she watched the caretaker pile broken chairs and wooden shelves by the running track. And as the days grew shorter, and the leaves fell, a rope was tied around these chairs to keep the wind from taking them. The caretaker smacked his hands of dust, and wood shavings.

"It'll be nice," said Geraldine. Scratching her chin.

Maybe. Moira couldn't be sure. She walked out on a Saturday night, with her duffle coat on, and the red woollen hat. The fire was huge. It lit up the grounds, so that she could see the poplar trees, and the windows of the laboratories were lit up, red as eyes. There were crowds—mulled wine in their hands, collars turned up. Half-lit faces of parents. Miss Burke wore a fur hat, as if she were Russian, and her cheeks were red, with the cold. Moira circled the fire. No stars, because of the wood smoke. She took a tissue from her pocket, wiped her nose.

Miss Bailey appeared beside her. She carried a tray of toffee apples, and said, "Help stop the drama room mould. Fifty pence each." So Moira bought one.

As for the other girls, they stood in clusters, stamping their feet, calling to each other. The youngest—the seven-year-olds—had lined up by the equipment shed, with ear muffs, and sparklers in their hands, and teachers guarding them. Eyes upturned, waiting for the firework display. But the others wandered. Sat on the bench by the tennis courts. Or led each other by the wrist to different people, and told stories, and Moira walked through all of this. She looked for Heather, or Annie. Someone.

As she walked nearer the boundary fence, where the ground was soft, she heard low, different voices. And there was laughter, and she thought, *Boys*, and she felt tearful. Heard *odd-looking* . . . So she dropped her toffee apple, left.

She felt lonely. The fireworks burst open on her spectacles.

Then Moira headed back, climbed the stairs to her dormitory, and watched the fire die down from the end of her bed.

A fire alarm that night. Two in the morning. A firework—not, said Miss Burke, one of the school's—was set off secretly by the sports shed. It was a spark, or maybe the rocket itself. Either way, the walls began smoking, and Moira awoke to a shrill, hammering bell that hurt her ears, and Orlaith's, too, so that she clamped her hands over them as she passed through the corridor. Down the stairs. Miss Bailey in a pink tracksuit, saying, *No running* . . . Wild-haired.

For thirty-two minutes the whole school shivered in the November night air, on the front lawn. A flock of them—pale, hunched. And then they were all lit up in blue, as the fire engines came. Their lights rolling over the brick of Locke Hall.

The fire engines drove across the hockey pitch. They had to. The next day the grass was churned up, ruined, and no match could be played on it, for a time. The caretaker would lay down new turf, then. Kneel, with the blackbirds singing.

As for the sports shed, it was a black mark on the grass, in the end. The hurdles, tennis nets, javelins, and beanbags were all charred, or gone, and so the money raised by the bonfire was spent on new versions of these things, instead. No more firework displays, and the grey bloom of dampness in the drama room did not go away.

●   ●   ●

THAT, THEN, was a disruption. But in the spring term, another came: a wild, sudden head-lice infestation. Nobody knew who the source was—which girl had returned from holiday with a colony of legs and teeth in her hair. But suddenly, everyone was scratching. There was the sound of fingernails drawn across the scalp, the shaking loose of hair. Moira noticed this. She turned round in assembly, counted the number of active hands. Within two weeks, every girl in the school was sent to the nurse. Moira was summoned during Geography. She made her way down the infirmary, sat in a chair, removed her glasses, and felt the metal comb and the busy fingers scrape their way across her skin. She shut her eyes. It was quiet in that room, and cool, and she felt her body loosen.

"You're fine," the nurse said. "But anything—any itching, any sign of eggs—come back. And brush you hair as often as you can. It breaks their legs, kills them."

She did keep an eye out, for this. For eggs, or a tickling up in her scalp. But there was nothing, and she wasn't surprised, because wasn't head lice caught from piggybacks and pillow fights, and sharing hairbrushes? No legs to break. She didn't feel the metal comb in her hair again.

• • •

I CARRY it in me. Bonfire Night. How it was to stand on a soft, midnight lawn in my old striped pyjamas and dressing gown. Lace-up school shoes.

You had head lice, once. I was—how old? I was married, at least. And as you sat in a tearoom at Sheringham you tore out your hair tie, dropped it in a saucer, grabbed your hair, and tugged it. Bellowed out, over the teapot. I remember it. And I washed all your sheets, pushed you over the bathroom sink, and scrubbed a thick, pink, chemical lotion into your raw scalp.

You cried. But what sympathy did I have? None. I thought, instead, of the day that no lotion or breaking of legs would stop the lice. Because things adapt. Things resist what, at first, hurt them, and they grow stronger, and I thought then—as now—that if head lice took over the world, it would be a sore, terrible place to be. A world of nails drawn over skin, and baldness, and suicides.

7

Needles

I AM LATE, TONIGHT, I KNOW. BUT IT'S BEEN A DAY OF STRANGENESS in our white house. This hasn't a name, but I'm tired, quiet, so I may not stay long with you, tonight. An hour, perhaps. Then I'll go.

I know how it is—that Ray's most difficult days are those that follow a painting, and the selling of it. Months of tending it, and then it's sold. A mourning follows. He misses *Evening, North Devon*—the easel is bare without it, and he spends his time quietly, as if a friend has gone. There's an absence that I can't ignore, or fill. So Ray was withdrawn, today, and I understood it, yet I also carried a weight beneath my chest like homesickness, or envy, or fear. All known things, to me. But it was none of them, in the end.

I spent my day in the kitchen, revising for a test on musculature. *Dr Cole.* Me—a doctor. Imagine that—a long way from it, but I walk, now, on that road. I study medicine at a university with sculptures in its grounds, and a lecture theatre with wooden smells, and I wonder if Mr Hodge would be proud of me—that I know joints, and hormones. And I sat, today, at the kitchen table, with my textbooks, the fridge's hum, and the old, dripping tap. *Latissimus dorsi, quadriceps femoris,* and I only saw my husband when he came downstairs for coffee—unshaven, tired-eyed. I laid down my pen, rose. We touched each other for a while, as we might touch trees—cautiously, with the flats of our hands. We half smiled. But we didn't say much.

Does this surprise you? That we are not always the calm river, flowing? At least, not always. He still looks at me, often, and says, *You are* . . . But there have been storms within this marriage, Amy—mud brought into the house, or a lost note, or pride. Or my old hardness has come back. I've thrown back my hair, slammed doors. Left the house for hours to prove a point. As for Ray, he is loving and tolerant but even he can lose his patience—put his hands up into the air, his palms facing me, and say, *Fine* . . . But we return. We examine our fingers as they lock with each other's. I do not believe there is such a thing as perfection—whatever lies nearest to it, is in this. We have never slept on an argument, Ray and I. We have small, honest, shy apologies, which can lead elsewhere, and in these moments, I see him all over again. *Him.* Who wrote letters; who lingered by the boundary fence at Locke, looking for me. Show me a better way of it, Amy; show me the couple who talk unblinkingly of a perfect marriage and I will ask Til to deal out the cards, to see where their shadows are, and what lies ahead. There will be swords, and towers, I'm certain of that. This is as close as we can come to it. And I tell you this because there is a good chance, tonight, that you will never know an arm's weight across your hips in the dark, or a gold wedding ring.

It is past ten. Late.

I will tell you, then, about being a teenager—how it is, for you became one in this coma. All you know of your teen years is the back of your eyelids, and the smell of this room. So I'll tell you how it was, for me. And then I will leave you, go back to him.

• • •

THERE WERE FROSTS on frosts in the new year. Crusts that held their footprints for days, and to draw back the dormitory curtain was to find pools of water on the windowsill, and birds at the back of the dining room—picking at the bacon rinds, and toast crumbs. From the science rooms Moira saw the empty, ploughed sugar beet fields, and the geese on them.

It was an echoing school. There were chilblains, and a cold sore like a berry on Jo's lip—dark, at first; then it browned like a loaf, and she picked it. Sleeves were pulled down over hands. Outside class it was the common room they all flocked to—its carpets, curtains, and the long green radiator, and the tables with coffee rings.

Clouds of breath in the courtyard, as they crossed it. The stone fountain grew whiter, and on one February morning, as she walked to History, Moira found a thin clear icicle hanging from the stone jug's lip. So it had, for a moment, poured water. When she was lying in bed, last night.

For the first time, too, she used the hot water bottle she had taken from Stackpole over a year before. Miss Bailey filled it for her, wearing gloves.

• • •

IT WENT on and on. Hockey boots did not need banging against the brick wall because there was no mud to clog them—all the mud was frozen, still. It was hard, to play on such grass. Ankles shifted. Girls returned with dry, scarlet wounds to their knees and elbows, and in the changing rooms, Moira's hands would be too blue and stiff to button up her shirt. Fat, useless fingers. She'd sit in the corner, suck them. Hold them under her armpits, between her legs.

"This weather," Jo said, "hurts my knees." Slinging her bag onto the floor. "I want the sun, now. Warmth . . ." Moira also felt this. And the closest she could get to warmth was not the radiator, or even her bed. She eyed the indoor pool, for a while. Shivered outside it, looking through the glass. All steam and chemicals, and noise, and she saw no fun in it. But when the glass door opened she felt its warmth. Imagined it, like a bath.

So she braved its chlorine and discarded plasters, and the sting to her eyes, and the smell to her hair. She found her old muscles again. She pulled through it, with her arms. She bent at the waist and ducked underwater, eyes open, her belly skimming the white tiles. Not the same. But she surfaced feeling stronger. As she walked back to Curie House one evening, wet-haired, she looked at her fingertips, at their puckering. "Oh *God* . . . Is this ever going to end?" said Annie, lying under her blankets. No limbs showing.

One day, perhaps. But not yet. There were colds—blocked noses, wet upper lips, and medicinal smells in the corridors. Menthol, wintergreen. Lemons, in the infirmary because the nurse handed out sour lemon tea with an aspirin in it. Moira drank it herself—for she felt a pin drawn down inside her throat, warning her. "This, and an early night," the nurse said. She obeyed, and it worked. Although she did not sleep well, for Orlaith snored, and coughed loosely, wearily, into her pillow in the dark.

• • •

To HER AUNT, Moira wrote, *We are still having very cold weather here. Hard frosts, and there's a lot of sneezing. The school smells of menthol and lemons.*

She didn't hear back from Til for weeks, but she knew she was busy in London. Theatres, and basement bars. A different type of cold down there—cracked puddles, and a sharp rain. She imagined her aunt tucked up, holding tea, looking out of the window onto Camden Market, in her flat above the bakery.

• • •

MOIRA SAID to herself, as she stood in the bathroom one morning, slowly brushing her teeth, *This is not the only coldness.* She felt grown-up in saying this. But it was true. Things were different. Heather had a new, oval-shaped bottle of scent, which she kept in her bedside drawer. She'd tilt it, onto her fingertip, and then dab it onto her neck. The dip between her new breasts. *No* . . . She'd say this, hold it away, above her head, when anyone asked for it.

Thirteen years old, now. Cards from Stackpole, and the Bannisters. The parcel that came from Til had blue nail varnish in it, and a bottle of blue, marbled liquid—a mermaid colour, and she came out of the shower mermaid-scented. She liked this. She stored it away, held the bottle up to the light sometimes. All other colours were in it. Petrol, and rainbows. She had never had something like this before.

She thought to herself, *Thirteen.*

"Teenagers," said Annie, looking at her own blue-painted toes. "I feel the same. What does it mean, anyway? Spots and stuff. Mood swings."

Also, it meant that Moira flushed sometimes. Never before—but just before Easter, she felt a fire move over her skin, almost heard her skin hiss. What was this? She wondered if this was diabetes, or heatstroke, or mitral valve syndrome. Hodgkin's disease, even. She waited. A quick, fierce reddening of the skin.

But it was not these things. Maybe the moon was in ascent, or Saturn was turning, or Venus was at her lowest for years—Til would know, or claim to. But there were other girls who changed in those few months. Moira, with her spectacles, noticed this. She was not alone in this new, quiet unwrapping in the dark.

If you would like to talk to the nurse about this . . . As if anyone would. As if there was a single girl who would knock on the infirmary door with questions. It was a secret. It was stored away in silence—like shower gel, or a teddy bear, or Annie's grey cotton rag, or a bag of food that had been swallowed down and brought back up in the dormitory, whilst everyone was at class. Moira suspected such things like this happened, because there were a few skinnier girls than her—although they never got prodded in queues and called *Bones.* Or maybe they did. Either way, they were thin. Lost underneath their cardigans. But Moira had no proof of anything.

· · ·

THERE WAS A telephone call to the house in Stackpole. And three days later, a letter arrived from there.

Love, are you really sure about this? It's been three months since we saw you last. If it's the train journey you don't like, your father can drive. We'd make sure your room was nice and quiet, if that's what you want. What does the school say about this? How many others spend Easter there?

Not much news, of course. We aren't as cold over here as you are, I think. Have you used the hot water bottle? Amy's voice is finding itself—it's deep! Like a bear.

Also, her mother wrote, *What have you discovered this term?*

In her head, Moira made a list: that meandering rivers form an ox-bow lake; the shape of a sonnet; how to use litmus paper. How Annie began French horn lessons in a room with no windows in Austen House, and came back red-cheeked, light-headed.

She'd discovered, too, that it was possible to pierce the skin and yet not bleed. In a Textile lesson, she took a needle and pushed it through the skin on her fingertips. The white, hard skin. And there was no blood. She was surprised at this. So this was dead skin? A rind? She hadn't known that before. She sat by the window in the most southerly of the classrooms, with needles pushed through the tips of three fingers, turning her hand over so that the needles caught the light.

• • •

SHE DECIDED to stay at Locke Hall for Easter because she didn't want to sit on a train for eight hours, and she didn't want to have three weeks of baby smells and noises, and she wanted to have the dormitory to herself—to hear its true silence, and to wake when she chose to.

So the term ended; the girls left. "Enjoy . . ." said Heather, putting her arms through a backpack. Glancing Moira up and down.

And the weather changed, slowly. As if sensing the school was emptier, the north-easterly wind quietened itself, and moved, so that the air that shook the poplar trees no longer came from Russia, with its geese, but from the sea itself. Water, not ice—but it was still cold. So for the three weeks of holiday, Moira slept in an empty dormitory. Five empty beds, and her own. She sat against her pillows with a book, her blankets pulled up to her chest, and looked at the spaces. Imagined where they all might be. Or she lay in the dark at night—no snoring, no turning over. Curie House was truly, deeply silent for the first time, in those nights. No lungs or distant doors, or footsteps. *Just me.* And, sometimes, Miss Bailey—for she stayed, too. With her radio, and Morris Minor car, and essays to mark.

Mr Hodge had bestowed on her the solemn duty of feeding the five goldfish. She did this at eight o'clock, and four-thirty. A pinch of coloured flakes that the fish plucked off the surface with their neat, round mouths. Like the mouths, she thought, of her own silver fish, that she kept in her pockets, or bedside drawer. She watched the goldfish feeding—bent down, hands on her knees.

And she wore three jumpers and her duffle coat in the library, because its radiators had been turned off. Ate her food in the dining hall, with the few remaining others. The overseas girls. The studious ones. And she'd stand in the silent stairwells, hold her breath.

Just me. Or nearly.

It was also this Easter that Moira began to run. She'd never really run before. But in the afternoons, she'd tie up her shoes and set off across the hockey fields—over white lines and fox droppings. The school lying to her right, red-bricked and empty. She ran with her thumbs tucked into her palms, and her elbows out, and with her own thoughts in her head. *In, in, in. Out, out . . .* The jolt of her knees on the netball courts, when she crossed it. Once, as she passed the old fence by the icehouse, she slowed—believing she had seen a shadow move beside it. More than a bird in there. Perhaps for a moment, two people were holding their breath. But she saw nothing else. She ran on. *Out, out . . .*

A good runner. It was her thinness, maybe. All muscle and bone, and she jumped a fallen log by the boundary fence, so that somebody said, "Nice jump."

Moira turned.

An older girl stood, bent over, hands on hips. Breathing hard, and with tea-coloured skin, and a plait that hung down over her shoulder, tied with a black bow. *Rita.* More than that, really—but Rita was a shorter, easier name.

• • •

RITA—who spoke with a pearl in her mouth, or it sounded that way—very neatly, with her lips together, as if keeping the pearl in. She was fifteen years old, and in Pankhurst House, and Rita came from Sri Lanka, where there were elephants, and monsoons, and freedom fighters, and Ceylon tea, and two hundred different species of frog. "We have cockroaches as big as my hand," she said, "and Nil Mahanel flowers, which are purple, and grow in streams, like stars." Too far to go home, in the holidays, so here she was. Still at Locke.

Moira blinked. Saw the elephants. Saw the flowers, unfurling.

"And you? Why are you still here?"

Moira mentioned the baby. Said its name, so that it was real, for the first time.

Amy.

"Noisy." Rita nodded. The youngest of six. She talked of families and missing them, smiled, and rose, later, from the table, walked away like a nurse might, or a nun, even—quickly, neatly, with her head dipped and her hands clasped behind.

• • •

A THURSDAY AFTERNOON—Moira left the school grounds without telling Miss Bailey, or Rita. She had never done such a thing as this. No rules broken, till now. With ten pounds from her savings in her hand, she caught the bus heading north from outside The Plough Inn in Lockham Thorpe, past barley fields, past the cows, and into Holt. The bus hissed, and Moira stepped down onto the pavement. Sun on the shop windows. People here, and traffic. Smells of coffee and diesel, and aftershave. Ivy growing on the boys' school, and antique shops, and a war memorial, and Moira bought a carton of orange juice which she drank through its straw, as she waited for a second bus. Near the cake shop where Til, once, had taken her.

This second bus took her on to the coast. To Sheringham, where she hadn't been yet—but still, she knew how the sea would be. Brown, without caves. A low sea. No big waves, or foam, and she sat on concrete benches, picked at a cone of chips that the gulls stalked her for. Still flat water. No whales, and she posted twenty-pence pieces into the metal telescopes, to make sure. Undid her shoes, and sprinkled cold sand onto her toes.

Caught the bus back, at four.

An empty school, she thought, was strange. As strange as a sea with no spray, or paper skeleton, and it was almost too much for her, at night; she almost ran to Miss Bailey's door, knocked on it. But then, it had advantages. For three weeks, Moira did not have to brace herself outside the dormitory—did not have to hide her spectacles, or her silver brooch, or feel words prick the back of her neck. She could sit on Heather's bed, if she dared herself to.

This is what it's like to be her.

This was all new, and she hardened all the more, and what we have, and who we are, we must cope with. Otherwise, what?

• • •

THE EXPLORER in me, that—my trip to Sheringham. Sitting on four buses with my purse and long, black fringe that fell into my eyes. Finding that if I pressed my head against the bus window, my vision blurred, because of the engine, shaking. Who'd have imagined a girl like that—mute, scientific, who lined up her pencils on her desk, in order of size—would have gone there, like that, and broken the rules? I think even I was surprised. I looked in the mirror as I brushed my teeth, that night.

Perhaps that was the start. My first breaking of rules, and when Miss Bailey said, later, *Where were you, yesterday? I looked for you . . .* I told my first real, considered lie. Talked of the swimming pool. Or maybe it was the infirmary.

I wrote, too, to Aunt Til.

On a Friday, I sat in the library and wrote in real blue ink. I asked if I could come to London—to see her on stage, beautiful, powdery, with flecks of her spit glinting under the lights as she shouted her lines. To eat her free pastries. To sit in a basement bar with a lemonade. Sit on a lion. To stand on one of the London streets I'd read about, in newspapers, and I used words like *please; different; lovely*. I wanted this. I wanted to lie in the dark, hear the noises outside her London flat.

"No. I don't think so . . ." This was her answer. On the telephone. She dismissed it, maybe waved her hand at it, said, "So—how is school?"

No. How do you think that felt? To me? When I heard the telephone line go dead, and replaced the receiver, walked back through the empty school? I thought Til was different. I thought she'd have said yes, and we'd have ridden the London buses, and seen a show, but then, I told myself that she was like a wind, and winds were not things to rely upon.

We are such different animals, you and I. But we both have fists. Have both narrowed our eyes.

I've guessed, since, at her reasons. I was a difficult age. I was a difficult girl to be with, perhaps. Or maybe she was not the woman of backstage flowers and floor-length skirts she knew I thought her to be. Or she had no friends. Or there were weeks without work where she slept, smoked, did not wash. Or her flat was too small. Or her heart was newly broken, or newly lit up. Something.

Anyway. I learnt a lesson, and it's one I don't think you've learnt yourself yet, or will live to, but it's this: we carry on. We have ourselves, and we carry on—in spite of our losses, and mistakes, and women, I think, have more than most. We are good secret-keepers. We can tie weights to our guilt and passions, and hatred, and deceitfulness, and let them sink down, so that you'd never know they existed at all. But we know. I can count all mine.

She's forgiven, now. I suppose that all women—even you, nearly sixteen; even the happy, married, mothering women who think that their choices were easy, and wise—must have their dark places. Lies. They must all look out of a window, once in a while, and imagine them, their other lives.

Although I wish, even now, she'd said *yes*. I'd have loved to have walked through Green Park with her. Or seen a palace.

But she didn't say *yes*, and that's that.

*R*AIN ON THE WINDOWS, as quick as silverfish. Miss Burke did not stand on her own, on the school stage. A hymn, and a prayer, and then she stretched out her hand towards a man in a navy-blue jacket, and a white shirt unbuttoned at the neck. Fair hair. Youngish. His early thirties.

"This, girls," she said, in her snipping voice, "is Mr Partridge."

The new Geography teacher.

Annie leant over, gave a soft, slow whistle. She returned to the dormitory, lay on her bed with her head and arms hanging over the side, watching Orlaith brush her hair. Annie repeated his name. *Mr Partridge* . . . Sleepy-eyed, she laid her cheek against her Geography book, sighing like a queen, smiling at herself.

The bell rang, then. Shook the plastering, and they went to class.

•   •   •

HE WAS NOT TALL. This was what Moira noticed when she passed him in the corridors, and stepped back against walls to let him pass. He'd say, *Thank you*. Or if he walked ahead of her, he'd keep a door open for her, with his fingertips. He smelt of something. Fruit. Soap.

No, not too tall. A few inches taller than her, maybe—although Moira herself was tall, for her age. Ducking under the clematis, now, that grew over Curie's door; leaving a far, clear mark in the long-jump pit. Her feet, too, had grown. Hands like trowels, or so she was told.

"He is . . ." said Annie. *Super. Wonderful.* She was lovesick. She'd leave her Geography lessons with her arms up, her book somewhere behind her head. "I don't know what he is . . ."

"The only male teacher under fifty," said Jo. "That's what he is. Get over it."

As for Orlaith, she called him old, and short. And Heather raised her eyebrows, scoffed—but she brushed perfume through her hair, which she had never done before.

So Annie tuned to Moira, if there was any turning at all—which didn't make much sense. What did Moira know, of such things? Maybe that was why: she couldn't retort, or disprove, or answer back. Or tease her. Moira was teased, and did not do the teasing, so she walked, for a time, with Annie. Stood beside her in the queue for her tuberculosis vaccination, and listened.

He holds open doors for me.

When he says, Good morning, he has this look . . .

Mr Partridge. His office was on the top floor of Locke Hall, with a view of the roof of the swimming pool, and the running track.

•   •   •

THE VACCINATION came on a dark, thundery Friday. They all lined up outside the infirmary. Slouched against walls. Bit their nails. Slowly rolled up their left sleeves.

Some cried. Some grew restless in the queue, and said too much, or said nothing at all. As for Moira, she watched each girl who came out of the nurse's room—their faces, and the ball of cotton wool pressed against their arm. She looked for their blood. Some girls were pale, and she thought they might buckle at the knees, fall down. But none did. They returned, one by one, to Physics—to their white overalls and circuit boards.

It didn't hurt. Moira kept her arms to her side, sat in the plastic chair, and looked out of the window. Past the snow-globes to the courtyard. The sky. A slow, warm, overcast afternoon. She felt the needle pierce her skin, sink inside her, and then she felt the cool, thin serum rush into her, fill her arm. She was, briefly, on Lydstep. She smelt coffee, saw a tartan rug, felt her left foot aching. Then the nurse spoke to her. She came back to Norfolk, was given her own cotton wool, and she rose, walked out of the room.

Still, her arm bled. She threw away the cotton wool too soon:

blood soaked through onto the sleeve of her Physics overall—a neat, red dot.

Crescent-shaped now. *Tuberculosis,* I tell them. *I was thirteen.* Sunlight makes it freckled, and there are days when I wear cotton sleeves over the scar, or sunblock. Nights, when it's smoothed by the pad of his thumb.

· · ·

YOU HAVE SEEN this scar, too, and others. Later, as I leant on the white railings at Blakeney in a thin blouse, you saw my white, full-moon scar through the cloth, prodded it, with a jammy fingertip. Said, *What's that, then?* And I told you of needles, puncturing arms, and the blood that comes, and the pain of it, and that you'd have it yourself, one day.

Did you? Even get that far?

It isn't high, on my arm. I said my sleeve could only go so far. And the nurse with the fleshy legs sat beside me, said, *There, there,* as if she thought I might cry, or fight her, because Annie had, before me. Annie had seen the needle, broken free, and run. So a second nurse grasped my arm so tightly, she left her own marks on it—fingerprints, as well as that dot of blood.

· · ·

WE ALL SAW Annie run. Bursting through the infirmary door, and outside. Having learnt that she actually hated needles, was terrified of them, and the small squirt they made before coming towards her, glinting. So she pushed the nurse, and kicked at the door, and was gone—hoping, perhaps, to be saved by the dashing Mr Partridge, or to find an empty room and hide in it. She clambered through the school in her white overall. She told Moira this, later—chalk-pale, and breathless. Goggles still pushed up onto her head.

Nobody saw her for hours. An empty desk in the Physics room, and then a space on the tennis courts. The caretaker was looking for her, with a radio transmitter that crackled with Miss Burke's voice.

Such a strange, purple-coloured afternoon. A headache, in Moira. The Norfolk sky was heavy, and it was as she looked up at it later, her tennis racket in her hand, that she saw Annie, standing there. On the roof of a teaching block. She'd crawled out of a loo window, and had, now, a view of the lawn, and the sugar beet fields, and of Curie, Austen, Pankhurst, and Nightingale's roofs. And of the tennis courts, and the Lockham Thorpe, and maybe even the church in Holt. She stood up there, in her overall—white, against the dark sky.

Annie. Star-shaped, with her arms held out. A queen, of some kind, for a moment or two.

Heather said, "What the . . . ?"

And Annie sat cross-legged on the flat school roof until the rain came, and the caretaker joined her, beckoned. And she stood then, slipped. Fell—not all the way down, which would have killed her, but back onto the tar roof, which might not have hurt her at all— except it did. She said she heard the crack of a bone. Like a hockey stick on a ball.

"What were you thinking?" Miss Bailey went with Annie in the ambulance, still in her tennis whites.

Annie's right arm was broken in two places, in the end. A clean break in her ulna; a hairline fracture in her radius. She wore a plaster for five months—no Sports Day for her, that year. She wrote left-handed, in a scrawl. She had no choice but to sleep on her back, sit on the sidelines, and she wore a bin bag over her cast in the shower. Later, her skin was lily-white, beneath it. In all the following years at school, she had to flex her arm in lessons. She couldn't fully rotate it, and her cartwheeling days were gone.

Also, in the hospital, as she'd been picking tentatively at her new, yellow plaster-cast, a nurse came beside her, and jabbed tuberculosis into her left arm. Annie yelled, smacked the bed. So it had all been pointless, or nearly.

"But it was good, up there," she said. Remembering it. A stormy summer sky, and a view from a flat tar roof.

And Mr Partridge signed her cast, as other teachers did—a green sweep, by her elbow. She was thrilled, pained. Said this meant love, for sure.

Love . . .

So the word was free, now. Out there.

• • •

I CAN TELL YOU that time may fade some colours, but not all. Fourteen years ago, now—but I can still see it: there she is, standing there. In her white overall. She is on your skin, or she is against the hospital wall. I can see her wherever I look, if I choose to. Odd, what we save in our heads, like that. But Annie's tuberculosis escapade was wild, and different, and I can see the quick, green scribble of a man who didn't love a thirteen-year-old girl at all. Of course not. Probably couldn't even remember her name.

Annie served underarm, in tennis, after this. I think of her, like that.

But, Amy, if I talk of tennis, then I should talk, too, of Miss Bailey, who wound down the nets in the autumn, and wound them back up in the summer term. Her plump tennis calves. The white sunvisor she wore on her head, when she served.

She always watched the Wimbledon championships on the television in her room. Every June and July. Asked me to watch it, too—a green court with two white players. Sunshine, and polite applause, and a crisp old-fashioned wave of Englishness came out into the room, filled it with fruit scents and laziness. Pollen in the air. Round, neat accents.

So she, for me, is tennis. Wimbledon is the sound of Locke, and her, and of my middle life—not the Stackpole one, or my grown-up life—although I'd also hear this tennis later, when I was in love, or trying not to be. I'd drift with the sound of it—away, far from exams, across the playing fields. To foreign places. Where there was no tennis, but there were trade winds, and ink for currency, and birds that skimmed the surface of pale swimming pools.

8

Church Rock

FIVE DAYS NOW, SINCE I LAST CAME TO YOU. MAYBE YOU KNOW this; maybe not. And this is the longest time since your accident in which I have not come. Four years—more than that, now.

Sorry, then. But it wasn't my fault—and maybe you didn't even notice I was gone. I've had to work hard, and for long hours. I've had the test on muscles, and an essay to finish on the hypothalamus in the brain, of all things. I could talk of appetite and hormones. Draw a picture with my finger on the palm of your hand, to show you where it lies.

Did I tell you that *Evening, North Devon* sold for twice the asking price? I can't remember. But it did. He doesn't understand it—he has never understood that he is gifted, and has a magic in him. But I think it's the beach he chose, too, and not just how he chose to paint it. Barricane Bay—where all its shells have been washed there from the southern hemisphere. That is the Gulf Stream for you. Stronger than any human, or all of them together. We owe our mildness to it—did you know that? Even that cold, punishing winter at Locke, where I swam in chlorine, watched the sparrows line up in the edge of the metal kitchen bins, was milder than it could have been, because of it.

So—he painted a pinkish, evening beach, with the sun on its easterly cliffs, and it has sold for more than he thought. It was a good painting—but it wasn't my favourite. I liked *Rialto*, and *Cley Mill at Dusk*. But there is value, and then there is worth—they are different things, and I value his flamingos more than all his art together. Pencil on paper—that was all. But they were a different world to me. They were fresh, shrimp-scented, free, equatorial, and they flew with their legs dangling, over my dormitory bed.

So we were busy, Ray and I—paintings, and the brain. But we are not now. The hypothalamus and Barricane Bay are far from us, at last, existing on their own. And we were tired, and for the first time in four years we have bought a real, pine Christmas tree, which sits in the bay window, away from the sea. Silver lights are in it. Last weekend, we spent two nights inland, in a thatched hotel, where the soap was wrapped in thin, pink paper, as neatly as a bud. And how our Aunt Til would have loved this: *Happy New Year*, written across the balconies, and so our room was lit up by the words. And in the morning I pushed the curtains back to see mist in the fields, and frost, and cows eating hay.

Anyway.

I am back now, in this room. And I can't remember where I reached. How old am I? Fourteen? I've briefly had a friend in Rita, with the deer-eyes and the pearl in her mouth. I think Annie has stood on the roof with her arms outstretched, and been pumped with tuberculosis, all the same. I think half the school is in love with the Geography teacher, with his hair that was slightly too long, and his Scottish accent. Did I tell you that part? From the Highlands, he said. And I heard the older girls talk of kilts, after that—*Imagine it . . .* Jo was right, I think: he was liked because he was rare, and young to us—that's all. No wedding ring.

A long time ago. Yet I can still see, exactly, the green rubber feet on the music stands, and the mark they left on the polished hall floor, if you dragged them.

Terms fell into terms. They always did. I'd blink, and be a year older. At one point, I burnt my hair in a Bunsen burner, and the smell filled the corridor. I'd meant to do it. I'd leant forwards, lowered my fringe. But I don't think this has happened yet.

· · ·

WIMBLEDON, AND NEEDLES, and a man not much taller than Moira. And a Sports Day of heat. One, lone day of it—the school creaked, and the parents sat under umbrellas for shade, and Miss Burke crossed her nylon legs. Moira daubed herself with cream. She ran, then drank her water by the poplar trees. But she saw blistered shoulders that afternoon, noses that peeled off into strips, like snakeskin.

Wooden chairs, and bunting. The girls in navy-blue shorts. Moira ran in four races, and won them. Running through clouds of midges, a plaster on her upper arm. Five red ribbons were pinned onto her— for she threw the javelin, too. She was tall, with long arms, and in the far field, near the swimming pool, she hauled it high, high in the air, watched its journey, and turned before it had landed, knowing it was good. Rubbing her hands free of chalk.

A tractor in the distance. An easterly breeze, and parents applauding.

"Look at *you*. With all your *ribbons* . . ." Heather said this. "Aren't *you* the runner?"

Later, in the toilets, Moira found Anne-Marie by the sink. Sweating in the heat. Her running shorts showed all the flesh on her legs, and she shifted, cried, did not speak. Moira stood, unsure. In the end, she gave a red ribbon to her. Let Anne-Marie take it, surprised. Then Moira walked away.

· · ·

RITA LEFT, in July. At lunchtime, she knocked on the door of Dormitory Ten. Moira was rolling a ball of her own skin, which she'd peeled off the side of her thumb. Heard the knock, and looked up.

"Goodbye," she said.

For she was sixteen, and Locke was over, for her. She was going back to an island with saffron in it, and brown rivers, and the monsoon rains brought insects out of the ground. Rita laid a piece of paper on the bed.

"My address. If you're ever out there."

After this, Moira sat by the open window, watched Rita walk along the gravel path. Blue-black hair. Past the privet hedge, out of sight.

Moira kept her address—although when would she ever use it? When would she be in Sri Lanka, at all? It was a gesture, only. Politeness. Or pity, for the girl with glasses and big feet and hands.

Still, she pressed it into her *Dictionary of Scientific Terms*, just in case.

Moira left, too. Headed west on the train to Stackpole, where her father spent the summer with his head beneath the bonnet of an old green car. "An Aston Martin," he said. Proud.

And Amy was two years old, which was enough to know who her sister was, and to follow her, say a gurgled version of her name, and she had a wilder, murderous scream that came with a closed door, or bedtime, or when Moira walked too quickly for stumbling legs to match. She left Amy behind, in the garden. Heard her bawling, frightening the gulls.

And Miriam stared at her eldest daughter a lot, or she seemed to. She'd stepped back at the sight of Moira, climbing down from the train, and said, frowning, "You've grown . . ." Which was the truth—for her skirt no longer met her knees, but fell above them, and she felt new bones in her. An older-looking Moira, now. Hands she could tighten up into a real fist. So she was allowed, this summer, to walk alone—down towards Bosherston, and through the wood. Or out onto the coastal path, where the sun caught her spectacles, so that the fulmars flew away, calling *fire!* Their greying wings stretched out.

The sea. As she'd wanted the North Sea, and all seas, to be. *Stupid thing.* She knew so much more, now. She was not jealous of the paddlers, or angry with the tourists who strayed from the path and trod on thrift. *Not home anymore.* She told herself this.

At Broad Haven, she climbed down through the rocks, onto the sand. Late afternoon, and the beach was quieter. She squinted, shielded her eyes—but there was nobody out there that she knew.

So Moira tied her spectacles onto her head with string. She peeled off her shirt, and stepped out of her shorts. Beneath it, she wore her red two-piece swimsuit, that made her skin milk-white and blue-veined, and she waded out into the sea. It bit. It rose up against her, and her toes knocked against old rocks. A tightening of the skin on her hipbones. She let her hands skim the surface of this water.

Moira thought, *I will swim to the rock.* The big, black sea stack that she knew the shape of, but not the touch, or the view from. She'd never wanted to swim to it before; but she was a different Moira now, and it was there, in front of her, and so she ducked under. The salt filled her, and she surfaced with her hair flattened back. And then she swam out towards Church Rock—front-crawl, face underwater, bending at the waist and kicking down when the larger waves came in. Imagined the depths beneath her.

Fifteen minutes, to reach it. She arrived breathless. The base of the rock was mossy with weed, and mussels grew there. She felt them with her palm.

Moira did not climb Church Rock that afternoon. She bobbed, against it. Anchored by her fingernails, and feeling her bones bump the rock. She'd climb it one day, when she was older. She decided this.

George said, "The Bannisters would love to see you, sometime."

Or Mr Bannister would. Not his rickety wife, and Moira did not want to knock on his rickety door. She eyed their fir trees. Saw her flesh-coloured underwear rising and falling on their line.

May your coming year be full of joy. She caught the bus to Tenby on a Saturday afternoon without telling her parents, or Amy, and walked past the city walls towards the bowling green. The lawn shone. She stood by the gate, held its bars. He was there—kneeling, his white hat tilted over one eye. Standing back up slowly, and maybe she should have waved at him, but she didn't. She left him, instead. Sat on a bench, by Prince Albert's statue, and looked at the evening sky, and the lifeboats, and felt a sadness inside her. Like a mouth, or a cave.

Miriam weeping, when she got home.

"Where did you go? Where *were* you?" Mourning her lost daughter, whilst her other one tried to stand on her head in the corner, naked, save for a shoe.

• • •

MOIRA MARKED herself off against the board of head girls' names, outside the main hall—in January, she had barely reached the board at all; now, she was three names higher. She seemed to have grown up faster than her hair had grown down—although that, too, altered. Her fringe fell right over her glasses. In the shower, when her hair was wet, she could feel it against her spine, beneath her shoulder blades. Also, she felt her pelvis under her skirt.

Annie said, "You're taller than me." She turned Moira round, stood behind her, back to back. "By"—she held out the thumb and forefinger of her pale, newly mended arm—"*that* much."

And taller than Mademoiselle Lac, in her fuchsia jacket, and taller than the girl in Austen who played netball for the county, and who did not have to jump for goals. But the skeleton in the Biology room still looked down on her. His chin could rest on the top of her head.

Perhaps it was this. Or some other reason. But Moira slept for most of the autumn, or so it seemed to her. *Rise and shine . . .* Miss Bailey said. But Moira slept in the daytime—with her books beside her, her knees to her chest, and a hand over her eyes. Too much light. Too many voices calling outside. She wanted darkness, and silences. She stood on the hockey fields and longed for winter, and the shortening days. For a deep, slow sleep.

Her waking hours were strange. She saw blackboards and clocks as if through a veil, and when she was spoken to, she watched their mouths—how they moved, how pale the skin was, where their lips met. The stained-glass windows in church, or the pheasants that slunk beneath the boundary fence—such things drew her, made her stare. The cracked skin on Geraldine's hands. Mr Hodge's knitted tie.

Back to the science room, for her. To the fish tank, and the petri dishes stacked in the corner with initials on them, in marker pen.

"*So* weird," Heather called her. Passing her, in the corridor.

I am, she thought. *Yes.*

And she wanted to sleep. And to dream of small, safe things, like the badger she'd seen, snuffling by the sundial, or the shape of Lundy Island, or the pole star.

•   •   •

GLAD OF TIL. No longer angry at her refusal, her *I don't think so.* She walked, and Aunt Matilda curled a strand of hair behind her ear and said, "Look at you . . ."

A girl of ball-and-socket joints, and her violet-eyed aunt. Autumn at Titchwell Reserve, and they trod down the boardwalk, through the reed-beds, towards the sea. Sandpipers, to their right—so Til said. A wide, cold sky.

"How long has it been, since I saw you, Moira?" She shook her head. "You are . . ."—Moira waited. She had her names—*Bones; Chicken tits*—". . . graceful." Til beamed. She seemed proud of this word, for she said it twice, and linked their arms.

Til looked away as she spoke. Across the marshes, and skyward. She talked of strange things—a busker who knew her name; a leaf that followed her all the way down Oxford Street, avoiding the buses and feet. "I've met someone," she said.

Moira did not understand, at first. Til met people.

"A man. Well, actually—*Hamlet*. He spilt his rum and coke on me in the theatre bar. Asked me out." She turned, embarrassed. "He's ten years younger! Don't tell your mother . . . Not yet."

Moira looked at the wire on the boardwalk, listened to this. How he'd picked up the ice cubes, in case she fell on them. His square, capable hands. "And he's a wonderful Hamlet . . ." Til fingered the rose quartz on her necklace, sat down on a bench to watch the birds. Squeezed Moira's arm.

And something felt lost, as if the marsh of birds was lifting up, or a single, different bird was joining them. Something. And Moira was tired, and she unhooked her arms from Aunt Til's.

"And you? How are you?"

But Til said it as if she knew anyway, and her thoughts were on an actor, Moira knew that. As they walked past the reed-beds at Titchwell, with their coats buttoned up to their chins.

• • •

CHICKEN TITS. Because that's what she had. That's what she looked like, to all of them.

Also, Jo threw bread rolls at her, at lunch, and said, "Juggle!" Because of her big hands and feet. Like a clown, with glasses on.

And *Bubble Eyes*, still. Which was old, and boring, and not very imaginative, and had lost its bite, on the whole.

• • •

SHE HAD DREAMS of Church Rock—she didn't know why. No water dreams had come to Moira for a while, now, and yet one night in November, she saw the rock and its mussels—midnight-dark, petrol-blue—at its base. In the changing rooms, amongst the mud, and the underwear, and the fast changing of clothes with her back to them all, she tried to think what its view might be, from the top. All the beaches? Not Freshwater West. But the others, perhaps. A view of the Gower peninsular or, on a crisp, wintery day, she might see Devon from there.

She dreamt she could smell it. Hear the mussels breathe.

. . .

IN THE MATHS ROOM, Mrs Maynard stood with a white chalk in her hand, eyeing the girls. Said, "Moira will do."

And she wrote MOIRA STONE on the board, in tall white letters, and talked of symmetry. Mirror images. And hands went up, and lines were drawn down through these letters, through her name. The *M*, the *I. E.* And the two round, hollow *O*'s in her name were endless, full of symmetry, and could have lines drawn through them forever, and ever, so that they lost their shape, and filled with chalk.

"And that," she said, "is today's lesson."

So Moira left the room with her name crossed out.

. . .

SHE LOOKED AT her own mirror image, in the evening. The girl with the oil-black hair. The veins that were knotted under wrists, and down her side. In her neck, too. Lifting her arms, and her ribs were there, under her skin, like rope.

Long, white feet, which she had swum like a fish with, and jumped with. But no pretty shoes, for Moira. She'd bought a larger pair of tennis shoes from the clothing shop, in Holt, and lived in them, now. Would learn, in time, how canvas shoes weren't warm, and they leaked in the rain.

She walked back from the bathroom to find them all asleep, save for Heather. Heather, who said nothing. She was brushing her hair— her head down, so that her neck and shoulders were lying there, pink, beneath the bare light bulb. Her face hidden, by hair. And as she brushed, Moira watched, and saw a strange bruise there. On her neck—purple as a grape. Neat. Too small for a tennis ball, or a hand; too big for a thumb. On the side of her neck, beneath her ear, so that when Heather threw her hair back, and said, "Yes? Can I help you?" the bruise was gone.

It took two days. Two. Then Moira realised. She sickened, and curled up a little tighter in her bed. A *mouth*? A mouth on the neck, an inward kiss. She'd heard of this. Heard in the shower and the walk down to church. This was a boy's mark, and it was far beyond her, out of reach. *So much is lost.* She knew it. A weaker girl would have cried, in the dark, at this.

· · ·

O's WERE INFINITELY SYMMETRICAL, and a boy had sucked at Heather's neck, and Aunt Til was in love, and Miss Bailey beckoned to her in November, or maybe December, and said, "Your grades are not quite their usual selves, this term. How are you, Moira? Not ill?"

Not ill. Strong and thick-skinned, so that sometimes there were only dry, white lines on her, no red. Geraldine was ill, though, and the Knox cousins had fought in the dining hall, so that one of them had a bitten lip that swelled up, and Annie sat in Geography lessons with shining eyes and her chin cupped in her hands. Heather was marked, secretly. But Moira was not; she was not ill.

Miss Bailey pursed her lips at this. Narrowed an eye, suspicious. She said, "Well . . ." And let Moira go. Perhaps she read people as if they were books, or perhaps she saw flashes of her younger self, in this tall, thin girl. Moira considered this. But then, she saw Miss Bailey leading the warm-ups on the hockey pitch—star jumps, and standing one-legged with her knee to her chest, and shouting through her hands—and it seemed very hard to believe a person as real and pink-cheeked as this, and who hummed to her radio, could, once, have had a crocodile clip fastened to the back of her jumper in class, and not know it, and so had walked to lunch, and on to a History lesson with a plastic tail, swinging. Moira only found hers because the nurse plucked it off, as she passed by. "You girls . . ." she said, tutting. As if Moira had been part of this, and had known, for six hours. Worn it on purpose. Been in on the joke.

Still, there was the brooch of silver fishes, and the four red ribbons. The pins they were attached to, and their sharpness, and the silent lock of the bathroom door. A card from Stackpole. Amy, at playschool, had dipped her fat hands into orange paint, and pressed them onto the card, like autumn leaves. *To Moira.* Written in an adult hand, and then copied, in a crayon scrawl.

· · ·

"She's talking in sentences now," said Miriam. "She asks for things. She is very good at saying *no*."

She was. Her third birthday, in December—a pink-iced cake, and a balloon tied to the tree outside. At bedtime she screamed, "No! I don't want to!" So Miriam relented, and Amy pushed another fistful of cake into her mouth. A westerly wind came in off the sea for three days, so that, on Christmas Eve, the balloon was untied and carried away, down the lane, inland. George ran after it, for a time. Miriam and Moira watched this, from the kitchen, side by side. But it was lost near East Trewent—above the roofs and pylons.

Yes, I am.

A new coat, for Christmas—dark-green, too big for her, with a fur-lined hood. She watched Amy grapple with her own present—a set of fairy wings, and a wand. She struggled to put the wings on. Damp eyelashes, frustrated, so that she wailed, held out her arms.

Ice, out in the waves. Dark water, and grey foam, and the gulls bobbed out at sea, heads tucked beneath their wings. She left Amy behind. Breathed in the air, which had needles in it, and her ears hurt beneath the fur hood.

She stepped out of her tennis shoes, unpeeled her socks. Unbuckled her trousers. Church Rock was bluish, with mussels, and weed, and old gull droppings, and bluer, still, in the winter afternoon light. It rose up from the sea. A long gull sat on it.

There are some coldnesses that have no words for them, because they are so cold that words don't come at all. The body forgets how to work, or it feels that way. All it knows is the cold; all it thinks is, *how to be warm.* And so it was, for Moira, like a death, or a huge, fierce moment of life, and her skin shrank on her bones. The water rose up, gnawed her, and her breath was gone, and she closed her eyes, lifted her arms above her head. Dived. Swam—under a wave, and up. Ears were numb, and she was noisy—rasping breath, and her jaw was shaking so that her teeth knocked against themselves. She swam to the rock, but could not feel it. Tried to pull herself up, but her hands were stiff, and she slipped. Grazed her skin.

People have died this way. She made her way back, and on the beach, she looked at herself. Purple-mottled, and shaking. Ink-coloured, white-fingered, and she was slow, to dress herself. Stumbled back home. Locked the bathroom door.

The wound on her body was small. A mussel had pushed at her skin, lifted it. A pale, thin flap hung there, and she took it off, that night, by twisting the skin until it broke.

I DID CLIMB IT. You know that.

I climbed it for the first time in the Easter that followed, when the first Gulf War was on the horizon, and the Hamlet who had spilt rum on Til's sleeve had left her a note, saying, *Sorry, but I'm just too young for this* . . . Left her. Cowardly, of him. Til threw herself into a small, cheap television role, and drank too much, and said, "What he meant was, I'm too *old* . . ." But she mended herself. Dropped flower tinctures under her tongue, moved on, or claimed to.

And you were the girl who always asked, *Why?* Questions, everywhere. Why was the sky blue? My hair black? Why did the three-legged dog that you saw tied up, outside the inn, not fall over? You tugged on my sleeve all year, so it seemed.

Also, *Why does the sea make me sick?* For it did. A trip to Skomer was a bad event, because you turned green, and the wind blew your thick spit back at you. Our father told us this. Sick for hours afterwards, he said, and I was glad of it, as it happens. If truth be told.

• • •

MOIRA—AS TALL AS she'd ever be, now. Muscular arms from terms of throwing the discus, and javelin, and she'd run, too—every afternoon, along the edge of the school grounds and, sometimes, down into the village and through the churchyard. Hard legs, then.

So in April, she pulled herself up onto Church Rock. Pushed, gently, against the mussels with the balls of her feet. Held the rock with her fingernails, and found her footholds in the crags of it. Twice, she slipped. Once, she swore, for she had such words in her now. Mid-teens, and fierce. She kept her body close to the rock, did not look down.

And the view? Everything. Manorbier, and the lighthouse. Lundy Island, sleeping. Behind her, if she turned carefully on her rock, she could see the English coast where she'd live, one day, with a husband. Not that she knew it. Did not even hope.

I don't know what we need, or what our souls crave when we aren't happy, but I sat on the top of Church Rock, with the air, and the space, and a lone black-headed gull hovering, next to me. And then I jumped. A wet, bright moment in mid-air. Limbs and hair. Spectacles tied onto my head and weed under my nails, later.

I did this at fourteen, and fifteen, and sixteen years old. Came to know the footholds. Tied a length of blue nylon rope to the rock, to pull myself up by.

Me before Ray, and Blakeney.

He saw Church Rock and said, *You climbed this?* Called me his Sherpa, his mountain goat; a wife like a salmon, swimming upstream.

9

The Tower Card

HAVE I, OR OUR PARENTS, EVER TOLD YOU ABOUT THE CLEANER?
I pass a man in the corridor, most nights—no hair, blue plastic glasses
that seem tight against his temples. I guess he's in his fifties, although
he may be older than that. He mops. This is his job—to mop the
blue-and-beige-tiled floors of this place. In his overalls, he pushes it
back and forth, squeezes it dry. I tiptoe past him, because his floor is
clean, and I wear Ray's old, dirty shoes most of the time—shoes that
I run in, or wear on low-tide beaches. I say *sorry*, for leaving my footprints there. And he says, *Never mind!* Or *Don't you worry, now.*

We know each other these days, of course. How could I not?
Four years of stepping round him. We say *Good evening* to each other,
and *Good night*, and he has never asked me who I'm here to see—perhaps he is not allowed to. There are so many rules. But he knows, all
the same. Tonight, just now, as I passed him, he said, "Your sister
moved her hand tonight." Then nodded, and returned to his mop.

I know nothing about him—not really. But I feel he deserves better than a life of mopping hospital floors—of cleaning up mud, and
vomit, and blood, and other things. He gives your flowers fresh water,
and he dusts your table, and he is more hopeful about you, I think,
than I am. Perhaps he believes in God, or in Fate, as Til did, or still

does, and I haven't the heart to tell him your hand has flinched many times before, that it's nothing to hold on to. Involuntary muscle movement, that's all. You make them. We all do.

So he's a stranger, really. But I've always felt that he's probably a good man. Maybe that's stupid or hasty of me, but I think of Mr Hodge with his bald patch, and how my husband towels himself dry, and so maybe we do, actually, recognise the good people when we see them. Or our hidden self notices them. Look at Miss Bailey: cheeks like cricket balls when she blew the half-time whistle. I felt her kindness from my first day at Locke. And he whistles to himself, this cleaner. He seems happy to be here, late at night, a mop in hand, and it's strange to come here, in the dark, and to find the floor wet, and the air full of sour disinfectant smells, and no trace of him. To have just missed him. And I'll miss him, when you've gone, and I no longer drive west to come here, in Ray's old shoes.

He whistled "Jingle Bells," tonight. It's Christmas Eve. The light shined off his smooth, pink scalp.

• • •

WELL. CAN YOU SEE ME? In a blue cardigan? Or in a coat with a fur-lined hood which I pulled up, over my school uniform, as I walked down to church in the winter months? Stick-like, with a hood, big feet, and spectacles. And in the summer, I stopped wearing the red swimsuit. Far too small for me. Til placed a new one on a picnic table for me, when I turned fifteen—plum-coloured, and a black trim. And I did wear it, later, when I was alone.

The other girls caught me up, of course. I was not the tallest girl in the year for long, nor the thinnest. At first, I was a beanpole, a *skinny cow. What's the weather like up there?* But by fifteen, I only looked older because of the frown line between my eyes, and because I had a coolness in me, a dark stare which seemed womanly, and I don't think I ever snapped gum between my teeth, like they did. Jo with her off-white peppermint mouth.

During that summer, after my fifteenth birthday, my hair was at its longest—nearly to the waist, although I rarely wore it down. I twisted it instead, pinned it back—so that it surprised even me, sometimes, when I shook it out, combed it. I'd forget its length. Stand in the shower, eyes open, and let it fill up with water.

Love? Annie had released the word two years before—let it go, like a bird, that had knocked against the windowpane, left its feathered mark on it. We'd all heard it. It hadn't beaten its wings since, but it had perched nearby. On Curie's roof. Inside us. I knew, at some point, it would come back down, and be said again. Over and over. And so it did, when I was fifteen.

And if my hair was long and mermaid-like at that age, Annie's was not. She'd sliced it, over a holiday. A foul, furious row with her mother, she said—and this was the punishment. Her crowning glory, gone. Dyed orange, and spiked. "She didn't like it one bit," she said. Victorious.

Maybe Annie liked it, for its own sake, for a little while. I don't know. But she came to hate it, by the end, in June, when Mr Partridge left the school quietly, at night. I couldn't sleep. I padded to the bathroom for water and paused, in the corridor, by an open window. Saw him. Carrying boxes, and a pot plant. Miss Burke watching him, arms folded.

He did more than tutor a Sixth Form student, in the end. Or so I heard. That was the rumour, and I wondered how this had happened, if it were true—and mostly, I supposed it was a dark, unrequited thing. A girl, like Annie, with a heart pulled wide; who'd been refused by him, and so lied, and been devious, and cruel. Because wasn't that possible? This was old enough. Or maybe, it was different, to that. Once or twice, I imagined it to have been a real, proper love, like ones in books. The touch of their hands as the girl passed an essay over to him, the glances over rows of heads. The timid knock on his door.

Either way, Annie cried. Blamed her hair. Said it might have all worked out if she hadn't been so stupid. "Look at the state of me!" Tugging what was left of her hair, and the lips that were cracked from her French horn exam. "No wonder he left . . ."

What could Moira say to that?

Not much.

So. A different dormitory, facing the boundary fence, and trees. A dark room. Jo hated it—had to sit on the windowsill to cover her spots with make-up, or to paint Paris in Spring onto her toes.

· · ·

WIND, IN JANUARY—days of it, against the window, biting Moira's wrists and ears as she made her way across the courtyard, or down the gravel path to the dining hall. They wore their tights, in this weather. Her hands reddened, and the school flag tugged at its line. It brought with it a sideways rain, for a time, so that Moira would look out of classroom windows and only see the tennis courts, and a bench. In the rain, she lost the poplar trees.

Also, there were frogs. Not outside, in the fields, but inside—on Thursday morning they filed into the Biology lab to find them laid out on the dark wooden counters. On their backs, limbs splayed, with their white speckled bellies uppermost. Moira stared, appalled. She lost her breath. She leant in, saw their tiny, bulbous fingers. She lifted each elegant leg, the delicate shape of the throat where, once, it croaked.

Mr Hodge said, "You will find scalpels . . ."

Heather refused to do this. She was noisy, repulsed, claimed that she could smell them. She sat at the back of the room, arms crossed. "This is *disgusting* . . ." Some girls joined her. Moira could feel their eyes on her back, or believed she could.

But she dissected her frog. She was careful, full of whispers. Its skin opened up, and inside it she found its air sacs, the hair-thin bones, its tiny heart. Beautiful things, which she had to lift out, and lay down on a white tile. Slowly, the frog softened. It lost its shape. Only its head remained the same—stretched back with its eyes shut, mouth slightly open. She thought, *I'm sorry.*

"How *can* she? It's sick . . ."

She discovered, too, that if certain pink, thin ligaments were pulled inside the dead frog, it moved. Its legs twitched—trying to swim across the wooden worktop, out of the classroom, back to its shady pond. The bell rang, and the class was dismissed, but Moira stayed a little longer. In her white coat, with her goggles over her glasses, and her white-bellied frog, dancing.

• • •

THIS NEW DORMITORY was a quieter place. The coming exams, perhaps—there were textbooks and revision notes on desks, and under beds. But also there was a change in the others, of some kind, so that as Moira sat on her bed with a book she'd glance over the top of it to see Jo's hand held in the air, as she examined her fingernails— bitten, her left thumb blackened from a hockey ball. Geraldine was larger, now. With looser arms, and a drop of flesh under her chin that shook when she coughed. Heather had seen this, too. Smiled. But she hadn't said anything.

Heather, too, was different. Once, she'd have spent the evenings in the dormitory, working gum, loving the weight or poor grammar or accents of the other girls in there. *Don't you care that you are . . . ?* Legs like a deer. A frail, blondish down on them. Once, innocent-eyed, she'd said to Anne-Marie, whose overall bit into her fleshy arms, *Don't your knees hurt? With that body?* And it stung—for Anne-Marie was ill after that, and couldn't swim, or eat. But Heather did not say such things, now. She didn't say, *Freak.* But as she lay on her front on the bed, at eight in the evening, twisting a strand of fair hair, reading a magazine, she still eyed Moira. She folded over the tips of pages which had glittered dresses on them. She plucked at her split ends.

No scorn. No lazy, knowing smile at Moira, or at Moira's lace-up shoes. One evening she kept a door open for Moira, using her heel—and this was enough for Moira to be wary. She didn't trust this. In the evenings, in the dormitory, she listened to her wristwatch and Jo's nail file. She looked at her book. Or she saw her own reflection in the night-time window, and thought of all the world's water, and the pale frog heart.

. . .

SHE STUDIED in the library until late. Sat at a corner table, under a green desk lamp, with its pool of yellow light the only bright thing in the room. It was all shadows, and dark words on pages. She read about osmosis, and pronouns, pathogens. She underlined the dates of wars, in red. *1793–1815. 1939–45.* Found, in her old, small hand-writing from her first year at Locke, a list of the twelve disciples.

She wiped her glasses on the hem of her skirt.

In her pigeonhole, she found this:

You'll be fine, my love. We all know it. You have the brains, and you've put in all the hard work. We're thinking of you! Here, we've had a stomach bug, or rather, Amy has. Horrible—she was in bed for three days.

She read this, and looked up. From the library window, she saw the church at Lockham Thorpe, and the poplar trees. Eight pylons, in the distance. And builders, too, on the swimming pool roof: four of them, this May—bare-backed, straining, middle-aged. A green-and-yellow football scarf on the bonnet of their van.

She walked beneath them, sometimes. Had to—for in the evenings, she'd swim. Eyes open underwater, so that the chlorine pricked them, and they'd itch in bed, at night. Her hair became thick and dry. Snapped, when she combed it.

. . .

IMAGINE IT. Use all your strength, and imagine it exactly. And it will happen that way.

All she wanted to do was study. But Til came, in an orange sun-dress worn over her jeans. Orange sandals, and a sequinned bag. On their bench at Titchwell she eyed the birds through her binoculars, sucked a peppermint, and said, "You have never worried about school before. You don't need to start. Advice from your old Aunt Matilda: imagine it. All the questions are easy ones. Imagine the grades . . . Use all your strength, and imagine it exactly. And it will happen this way."

Moira wore her cardigan. Picked at the loose wool on the left sleeve.

· · ·

WAS TIL RIGHT? Moira didn't know if the brain worked that way, or if pink quartz helped a heart, or if lines on the palm of her hand spoke of her future. All she knew was that the gymnasium, in late June and early July, smelt of floor polish, and splintered wood. Moira sat at the small, foldable table with her paper before her, and the tick-ing clock, and a plastic cup of water. And she wrote down her answers, and imagined the grade A on the wall in mid-August.

Miss Kearney walked the room, in rubber shoes, looking for cheats, or giving out more paper. Her shoes squeaked, and a girl from Pankhurst with asthma was carried out of a Maths exam. Moira looked at all the backs of heads in the room—the knots, and the combs, and the clasps of silver necklaces, and the tiny backs of ear-rings, the freckles, and the scars. And the brains burning inside their skins. The clock-face was grey, with a red second hand, and however long three hours seemed, it always came. Always. And Miss Kearney always said to the room, *Pens down.*

Some of the girls left, then. Sixteen years old—and on a bright, silent summer morning, they left for other colleges, or because divorces were over, or money had gone, or because they were tired of the place. Many reasons. In the final assembly, Miss Burke talked of the future—"Courage, faith, and good manners."

Life, then. Moira watched them go. Sat beside the sundial, and thought of all their future things. Jobs and husbands. Babies.

She walked to the infirmary for a plaster, for her hand, and found the nurse shaking her head, baffled. "Look!" she said. Ushered her through the small bedroom with the starched beds. The skeleton lay there, on its back, a thermometer in its mouth.

*F*IVE FOOT ELEVEN, with black-rimmed glasses. A thick fringe, and two thin lips which I pressed together, and bit the insides of with my teeth. I still do that, I think. I still have paddles for hands, and webbed feet.

And clumsy. I hadn't been, till then, but I became it—knocking my hips against door handles, banging my skull on an open cupboard door. Miss Bailey heard the noise, followed it. She leant into the room and said, *Ow!* Huge-eyed. As if she also felt it, and was light-headed, later.

A girl, then, of hinges. No elegance, or manicures. No sense at all in how, as she walked out of the swimming pool building, an hour before she left Locke for the summer, she heard it: swift, shrill. She was drying her hair with a towel as she walked. Glasses in her pocket, laces undone. She stopped at the noise. Not water in her ears; not a bird. She glanced around, and then it came again—two high-pitched notes swinging through the air to her, coming from between the fingers in a builder's mouth, on the swimming pool roof.

Moira walked a little faster. Pressed herself into the stairwell, her towel in her hand, smelling of chlorine, and scared from the wolf-whistle.

Heard the sound of it over and over, on her train back to Stackpole. It rang out. She spent eight hours looking for all the different jokes in it, the puns.

• • •

SHE HAD SALTY HAIR, in the summer—up on her scalp, so that at night she'd push her fingers into the roots and feel it there. Sticky. Half-warm, like spit.

Amy was four. She, too, was growing. Her waist was widening, further, and she rattled with neat milk-teeth. Her feet were lengthening faster than anything else—two pink, hard-heeled additions which slapped over the kitchen floor, scuffed through sand. "Flippers," said George. "She'll be tall, like you, in the end." Moira drank, watched—how Amy slid in her bed-socks, dropped orange peel over her shoulder. Wrote her name, its three small letters, into Barafundle sand with a stick.

"Moira? Will you colour-in with me?" Or sing. Or somersault. Or look for unicorns.

No. She never did. She read books, any books she could find—atlases, *Wuthering Heights*, the Highway Code, sea poems, *Topsy & Tim*, the Bible, Miriam's recipe books. She stayed in her room, in the mornings, and then pulled on her trainers and ran down the lane, to Stackpole Quay, and along the cliff-tops. On a Friday, she ran eastwards towards Manorbier, and arrived there mid-afternoon—hot, wet-clothed. She went down to the water and dipped her head down into it, felt the cold sea, and scooped her hair back in an arc. Tied it up. The quick, true way to cool down. So her father had showed her, once. And she lay there until her hair was dry, and her clothes had lightened again.

Here, too, she skimmed her stones. The red sandstone cliffs of Manorbier, and the airy walls of the castle, and she'd spend the late afternoons there—pebbles in hand, knees bent. In August, as she counted the skips of a single throw, a man said to her, "Fourteen? I've never managed that. Twelve is my record." Hands in his pockets, and an unshaven jaw. She didn't stay, or answer him.

She held out her thumb on the Lamphey road, and hitched to Tenby. Drank a pint of stout in The Ship Inn, and she paddled up to her knees—or past her knees, for her summer skirt got wet. Sat on the old bench by Prince Albert. *I need no one. Nothing at all.* Under a split sky.

Also, she took herself down to the lily-ponds on a quiet evening, with gnats above the water, and swallows dipping down for them. And here, as she sat on the Grassy Bridge, floating leaves on the pond's surface, she saw the Bannisters. He was tall, as ever. A white clipped moustache and ironed trousers, and in his hands were two grey, rubber handles that led to a metal wheelchair. He rocked his wife over the path. Over tree roots, and past the furze, and Moira looked at her: Mrs Bannister had never been in a wheelchair before. Hands on her lap, and her white hair streaming over her shoulders. There was, too, a brief, light kiss—from Mr Bannister, onto his wife's thin head. And Moira heard his voice across the water, but not his words, and still heard his voice once they were out of sight. And that was all she ever saw of Mrs Bannister—for she died, in the autumn. Trembled in her bed for the last time.

• • •

ANOTHER CHANGE IS COMING.

If Moira didn't say these words, as such, she thought them. Felt them, inside her. It was her age, perhaps, or something more. The strange dreams that had come to her, in her small, quiet Stackpole room. *Something.* Like an offshore wind, or a full moon. Or the headache she had felt, on the tennis court, when thunder and Annie's broken arm was near. When an envelope came with her exam results in, her parents said, "Well?" Ten A's. Of course. Miriam cried, and George pushed a cork out of a bottle of real champagne; Amy tried to catch the cork, missed. It fell in the furze somewhere.

Yet Moira still felt a change. Was coming.

It was only on Church Rock that she could leave it, and not be Moira with the ten A-grades, or the scholarship, or any of it. *My rock,* now. For she'd lifted a coil of blue nylon rope out of the garage, on the Lamphey road, and swum with it against herself, looped over her shoulder, and round her waist. Out to the rock, where she'd tied the rope around the spire of it—testing the knot by holding the rope, leaning back. Tied more knots.

Salt, and wind, and the pop of mussel breath.

And she jumped down, into the water, swam ashore, and went back across the headland to Stackpole—where Amy was wearing socks on her hands, and George was sleeping. She walked into the kitchen to find the kettle whistling.

•   •   •

A DREAM OF A BELL, ringing. Of Heather leaning over her, chanting her name. *Moy-rah* . . .

"Moira?"

She opened her eyes. Followed her mother downstairs, picked up the telephone. It was Aunt Til—sitting, in her London flat, smoking, wistful, watching the shopkeeper opposite pull down his metal grille, for the night. All the graffiti on it.

"I'm going away," she said.

What? Where to?

Not for a play. Not with a man—or with anyone. She was tired. She wanted sun, and space, and a holiday, to lie on a towel, to watch pelicans come in to land, and to not have to learn any lines, or to risk seeing Hamlet on the underground.

"So I bought the tickets. To Florida. For Christmas-time. And now? Guess what. Guess which card I turned over, last night."

Death? The Magician?

"The Tower card," she said. "I had to tell *you*, of course." Her niece—the only person who didn't roll her eyes at this: this worrying card. This card of upheavals.

How were they twins? Her mother, and this woman who smoked on the telephone, talked of tarot cards, and did not believe in a single god? Who longed to see a bittern at Titchwell Reserve? Who did not want a cold, gloomy Christmas in London, and so would look for a better life and a happier, calmer self in the Everglades, on beaches? With dollar bills and pelicans and *mojito* cocktails, and white tiles on the bedroom floor, and no old ghosts, no Hamlet, no traffic to keep her awake at night. Just cicadas. Just Til, on her own, and the night-time movement of palm trees with dusty undersides to their leaves.

10

Snow

OUR AUNT AND HER CARDS. THEIR SHELL-PINK BACKS BENEATH her fingers. I watched her, once, as she spread them out on a sticky pub table, and say to me, *Choose one* . . . I chose eleven. And she peeled them back, clicked her tongue. As if she was surprised by them.

Of course, I don't know what she saw in her own reading, when she turned the Tower card over, or if what she saw was the truth, or just coincidence. An upheaval, she said. *Life-changing*. But what? I doubt it was Florida. Or Lady Macbeth. Perhaps it was what would happen to her, on the aeroplane, or it was my life she saw, instead, for didn't I have several dark, vast moments of my own, to come? Nor did she say when—and this matters. How far ahead did she claim to see? A week? A decade?

Did she see you? That's the question, really—and it's knocked at me, for more than four years, like a bottle at sea, as I sit alone. Did Aunt Til—silver-thumbed, citrus-scented—look in the cards one day and see this? Wires, and a white band on your wrist, with your name? The mussel? Or maybe she saw the fall itself—the rope, and the gulls. Your small, bloodied cat's-mouth opening, in a mewl.

If she did see these things, she said nothing of it. She did not take

my hand. Til kept it to herself, hidden in a box with her pink ballerina and tiger's eye.

Or maybe she didn't know what it was, that she'd seen. Thought,
Seaweed?

Or maybe she saw nothing at all.

• • •

SIXTEEN. It glinted. All summer, Moira held the age up to the light,
as if it were glass, and she saw the colours in it. It was here, now.
When she was twelve, she'd imagined it, and had watched the older
girls walk with their hips, and how they'd curled their hair behind
their ears. She never thought it would come to her. *Sixteen.* Like a gift
of some kind, and she had it now. She stared at it, in her hands.

They all did. They tried out the words *Sixth Formers.* And on the
first day of the new term Moira carried her suitcase up, up, through
the strawberry-pink-painted door with *Keep Out!* on it, and onto the
top floor of Curie House. A smell of polish and aerosols. Skylights
in the corridor with moss on them, bird droppings, and black marks
from sitting rain. So that the floor was dappled with light. As if
under water, or trees.

Miss Bailey was freckled, straw-haired. Clipboard in hand, she
read it and said, *Room One.* So Moira walked the corridor, moving
round the girls, reading the numbers on the dormitory doors. *Five,
four* . . . Past a single bathroom. She pushed the last door open. Jo was
lying on her back, on a bed by the wall—her legs up against it. She
lowered her book. Disappointed. Said, "Hey."

• • •

SO IT WAS. Moira unpacked her clothes, laid her pyjamas under the
pillow of the bed nearest the window. A wide, green view of the
hockey fields—and of the poplar trees, and the sugar beet fields
beyond it. The round church tower, and a few slate roofs. High up.

High, like on a cliff. She pushed up the window, smelt the air. Not salt, but metal—a sour, metallic smell, because a fire escape ran down the side of the room. Cobwebs on it. Pigeon signs.

She thought this was the best view yet. South-facing, and high. It felt familiar, although she wasn't sure why. She was sitting on her bed when Heather arrived—Italian tan, whitishness to her hair. A raised brow. Later, she would lift up her blouse to show a small gold hoop through her navel. Later still, this would bleed.

As for the last bed, it remained empty for three days. Annie filled it, in the end—tonsillitis had sealed her up, reddened her. She smelt of disinfectant and menthol, and she slept in the bed by the door. A hump under the blankets. Her breathing was ragged at night.

• • •

THE POPLAR TREES by the boundary fence swayed when the wind came, so that Moira would hear their sound from her bed when the window was open—a slow, watery rush, and she saw how the poplar leaves turned themselves to show their white undersides. She'd heard their sound on the hockey fields, before. But she'd never listened to it—she'd been too busy, or her eyes had been on the sky, or the school. Now she did. The rustle of twenty poplar trees. It came to her as she studied, or opened another envelope with an x on the back of it, in her mother's hand.

We are so proud of you, Moira. Such grades! I have no idea how your father and I managed to make you . . . So: how is Sixth Form life?

How was it? Different. There was a new common room for them, on the top floor of Curie, with half-split patterned armchairs, and a television on wheels. Magazine racks, and a kettle. Its single window looked across to Austen, and the dining hall, so that this room often smelt of boiled carrots, or steam, and only the cooks could see them up there. Up on the gravelled roof. Girls climbed out onto it, sat with their backs to the brickwork, and smoked. The tug of the gold paper. Legs straight in front of them. Talking with their eyes shut, and their elbows in their hands. They ran their cigarette ends under taps and hid them in the bin, or they dropped them into the gutter, which blocked in her second autumn up there, with all the ends and leaf mulch. The caretaker had to follow them, through the window, out onto the roof.

Classes, too, had changed. Moira no longer studied languages, or History. She had left them behind her, as she had left Stackpole, and the red-inked monkey on its bulb. She walked into the Maths room and the laboratories only. She wore her white overall most days, and her goggles, and she'd return to her dormitory in the evenings with an acid smell, and chalk dust in her hair. She experimented with a slice of cow's liver. Drew proteins. She set fire to her hair, briefly, so that the room filled with the smell of it. She could pass her bare finger through the yellow part of a flame, and Mr Hodge was unwell for all of that autumn, sneezing into handkerchiefs. His sneezes were high-pitched, boyish. When he said, "Good, Moira," his voice was thick. His nose became as pink as a plum.

• • •

MISS BAILEY, pinning up lists on Curie's notice board, believed that sixteen was a responsible age, and that the girls could go walk to the village on a weekday, if they wanted to. Not to Holt, or Norwich— unless she granted it. But they could write their names in a blue exercise book with the chewed pencil tied to it, leave the school behind them, walk down to Lockham Thorpe. "Back for dinner, though."

A freedom, then, of sorts. A kettle, a blocked gutter, no more French oral exams, and a view of clouds and sugar beet leaves—but, also, Moira could walk away from it all. The autumn afternoons were crisp, misty, and she'd tread down the lane in her hooded coat. Stepping over the old leaves. Skirting a dead pheasant that sank, slowly, into the grass. Stopping outside The Plough Inn to breathe its ale, and flowerbeds. Moira took her time, and saw it all—the dung, the cobbled walls, a box of marrows for sale. The row of almshouses. She'd walk through the churchyard, sit in the porch of the squat, round tower of All Saints, with its handwritten note, faded from sun: *Quiet please: swallows nesting*. A different church, when Locke Hall's pupils were not in it. Quieter.

She'd feel tired, walking back. Up the lane, towards the gold lettering that she'd driven beneath with her parents, five years ago, and the concrete urns by the gate. And later, in the evenings, she'd find a different scent on her skin—the moss of the churchyard, maybe, or wood smoke. Ale. Something, at least.

In October, as Miss Bailey folded up the tennis net, she beckoned to Moira, said, "You must know the village well, by now. I see your name in the book."

Not a reprimand. Moira thought it might be. But Miss Bailey looked up, smiled, gave a slow pursing of the lips. "There isn't a boy—is there?"

Moira folded the net, too. Carried the end of it, following Miss Bailey's wide, hard legs over the grass to the sports shed. Miss Bailey talked of winter things—netball, frosts, a new tarpaulin over the long-jump pit. How she wished for spring. They tucked the net into a dark space, between the relay batons and the wall. Moira thought, *A boy?* She pushed her glasses up her nose.

"Moira," Miss Bailey said, crouching, locking the shed door, "you know where my office is. Don't you?"

Whatever that meant.

•   •   •

A SOUTH-WESTERLY wind, bringing dust from the Brecklands, and a sour, thin smell from the battery farms. She wrote,

The liver is the largest internal organ. Its roles include bile production, mineral storage, heat generation, detoxification. It is a deep red colour.

Her neat, small handwriting. No wild loops, like Til, or circles for dots over her *i*'s, like Mrs Duff. She underlined *liver* with a ruler, in blue. She drew it carefully, with a sharpened lead.

Heather said, "It's Saturday night? And you're working? *Please . . .*"

She left the room. Moira stared at the space she'd left behind, considered this.

I am sixteen, now.

And after this, after dark, Moira would, sometimes, sit in the common room instead, or walk down to the television room to watch a film, or she'd walk the grounds, as she used to. Sit on the edge of the stone fountain, watching the frost come down. What else was there to do? She did not smoke. Annie was now styling her hair the way Heather suggested, said Heather's words. Aunt Til was silent, in her north London flat, counting the hours till her Florida trip.

So in the dormitory, in her yellow pool of lamplight, she wrote, *The liver has two blood supplies . . .*

• • •

PERHAPS IT WAS her fault, then—weren't most things?—that one night she dreamt of a dark, wet world again, in which she could hear her own heartbeat, and in which each thing she touched stuck to her, like a red glue. Wading through it, as if it were mud. Arms up above her head.

And in this dream, she carried a spear in her hand. Or a javelin. But she held it high, so her arm hurt, and the thick, wet redness rose around her, in waves. Waist-deep. She saw something—a shape in it, like a fish, or fishes. So she threw down the spear, piercing the water, and an arc of red, and it pinned the creature down. But it was not a fish. She lifted the spear to find Mrs Bannister squirming, on the end of it—her tongue squealing, wild-eyed.

Moira woke. Dry-mouthed.

A noise like a saw, back and forth. Her breathing.

She lay herself back down. The red water slid back into her head, and away. Mrs Bannister was only a pale, silent woman.

But there was still a noise like a saw. Back and forth. Moira fumbled for her glasses on the table, put them on. Blinked. And she saw, then, that Heather's bed was empty, that the window was open, and its thin, cream curtains were stirring in, and out.

Maybe it was also part of the dream. It didn't happen at all. It was possible. For she had such solemn dreams that she had woken with sand in her eyes, before. Moira had dreamt of her teeth falling into her palm, like pearls, and the next day, her gums had hurt in the laboratory. Ached. Her heartbeat was in them. So perhaps Heather had slept all night— bed-socks on, lip balm—and Moira had been wrong.

A dream. That's all.

Yet it worried her. She watched Heather's small, girlish jump as she pulled her rucksack on. A sign? No. Nor, in the afternoon, when Moira drew her eyes down level with the windowsill, looking for footprints, did she find any proof. *I dreamt it.* She felt ashamed. Sat back at her desk with her Biology, or Maths. Where would Heather have gone, anyway? Why would somebody creep out so late—at midnight, or later—when it was getting so cold, and there were only ditches out there, poplar trees, and the dark, soft fields—empty of crops, now?

• • •

She called Stackpole in the evening. George answered. He said that the weather was strange there, unsettled, and their fire was lit. She leant against the wall, saw it. The stone hearth. Flat October beaches.

Amy, too, had news. "Guess what I have! Guess!" Her mouth was noisy—with spit, or food—and she said, *Guess, Moira!*

Moira was tired. Thought, *What?*

A pet. A hamster, of all things. Five weeks of pleading, with her grey, brimming eyes, and her parents had relented. A fat, gingery, useless, bustling thing. A rodent. Who ate slices of cucumber in his hands. Who fell asleep in his food bowl, and swung from the roof of his cage, monkey-like. Moira imagined it all. Miriam came to the phone, said, "Amy's been asking for months, now . . ."

A new thing to haunt me. In its cage.

It was, too. Moira cocked her head in the library, believing she'd heard a scurry, or a quiet gnawing amongst the books. She heard the tiny patter of hamster feet on her bed.

So for a time—a week or two—she forgot her dream of Heather, and the curtains, breathing in and out. She could only think of the skirting boards at Stackpole, and its wires. Its new sawdust smell.

She worked, too. Diagrams, equations. A return to photosynthesis, and she sharpened all her pencils with the point of her compass.

"Get a life, Moira. *Honestly . . .*"

And three days before Halloween, she woke to find an empty bed, and the window was open again.

*A*MY, IT BEGAN. Twice, or three times a week, when Moira was lying in the dark, with her glasses on, she'd hear a sound before the generator switched off, and the silence came in. A lifting of blankets. A slow zip, and the push of a heel into a shoe. Then the window was lifted, and there was cold air, and Heather was gone.

Moira waited. She counted the ticks of her wristwatch. She pushed herself up onto her elbows, found her glasses, put them on. Stared at Heather's bed to make sure she wasn't there. An hour came in. Sometimes, two. Once she heard the birds, and Heather's bed was still empty. And Annie and Jo slept on, or seemed to—on their fronts, under their blankets. Maybe they knew, secretly, that Heather was leaving, like this. But if so, they said nothing of it. They cleaned their teeth in the mornings. They yawned, fastened their hair.

Where do you go? Moira wanted to know. There were moments, in the daytime, when she looked for shadows under Heather's eyes, or for a hidden smile. Some kind of knowing look. But there was none—so that Moira, briefly, doubted it all over again. A dream? She still asked herself this, until, as she dressed on a Thursday, with rain outside, and a morning of Maths ahead of her, she saw Heather's plimsolls under her bed—damp, with grass on the toes.

• • •

IT WAS SLY. It was silent, and slow, and if Moira lay on her side, with her glasses on, she saw it all. The mirror, in which Heather lined her eyes. The bracelets that clinked. The jumper that she pulled down, smoothed over, and the thick, dark scent that she sprayed on her wrists and into her hair before she left. She passed Moira, who tasted this in her mouth, like spices.

It made Moira think of her aunt, and she didn't know why. In these nights. So in the days, she pushed a coin into the payphone in the hall, and dialled her number. Wanting the curious *Hello?* But Til didn't answer. She was acting, or sleeping, Moira supposed. Re-reading Hamlet's note. Or sitting by the huge, stone lions in Trafalgar Square, gazing over pigeons, imagining the avenues and the warm beach towel she'd lie herself down on, soon three thousand miles away.

· · ·

DAMP WEATHER. All the berries had gone. The ploughed fields moved with flocks of geese—bean, and pink-footed—who had come inland for shelter, and on the quieter days, in the quieter rooms, she'd hear them. Murmuring to each other. She saw them cleaning under their wings.

The cobwebs on the fire escape were beautiful in the mornings, but the rest of the world began to sink into mud and clotted leaves, and the caretaker pulled a sheet of tarpaulin over the pile of broken chairs and desks behind the dining hall. He weighed its corners down with bricks. But with winds, it still tugged to be free.

And the winds themselves grew stronger. The weathervane on All Saints shifted itself, so the cockerel faced south, and the wind had ice in it. Sharp, new, arctic air, which had blown over black water and fjords and oil rigs and whales. Over the marshes. She breathed it. She walked to Lockham Thorpe, with these thoughts in her. *An onshore wind. A new-phase moon.*

In the laboratories, she heard it. The wind called out. It cornered the building, moved through the telegraph wires. Moira, in her white overall, with a test tube in her hand, turned her head to see this. Mr Hodge worried for the beech tree near his home. He said it was rotten. He thought it might fall down on his car, or his vegetable patch.

"Moira," he asked, at four in the afternoon, as he was clearing the blackboard of chalk. "Have you thought of life after this? After Locke?"

He meant university. He meant, *Will you be a doctor? A vet? A scientist? A professor? A teacher in a boarding school? A bio-chemist? A naturalist?* He made this list. And she blinked. She hadn't thought of it. She'd never thought of a life beyond Stackpole until she'd sat in the cloakroom with her leaking drink, and she hadn't imagined a life after here, after Locke. Not really—not yet. She supposed she'd go somewhere. But she didn't know where, or what lay ahead of her.

· · ·

STILL HEATHER LEFT, at night. The crackle of hair, as she brushed it. Moira picked at her nails in class, and thought of talking to Miss Bailey—of walking out beside her along the gravel path, or finding her, in the changing rooms. But she didn't.

· · ·

THE NEXT MORNING. Or maybe it was the morning after that.

Heather, in assembly, talking behind her hand. Into Jo's ear. Jo's eyes were wide, and her mouth was half-open.

A matter of time, maybe. Moira wasn't surprised, as such, when it happened—when she lifted her head, squinted, and saw three white shapes in the room, which were the sheets of their three empty beds, and three silences, and she was in the room on her own.

*A*RE YOU THINKING, *Poor Moira?* Don't. It was her doing. Solemn, and scientific, and freakish, and she should have got contact lenses sooner. Shouldn't have had such staring eyes, or such bones, or a fur-lined hood to hide in, as they walked down to church. She heard nothing, inside that hood. Just her, when she swallowed. Her own heart.

I don't know. It was a long time ago. But don't be fooled, Amy— I may have lain in a dormitory at night, and felt the wide, cold distances, and thought of you, and home, and of the pied birds that stood in a neat, quiet black-and-white line on water's edge at Manorbier, but you, of all people, know of the harder parts in me. Flint heart, and flint eyes. A girl of walls. Flicking her mermaid's tail.

I passed the infirmary at some point during this time, and the nurse caught me—caught my elbow, as a warden would. She said I looked exhausted. *Care-worn*—a strange phrase. She took my pulse. Talked of sleep, and eating. And as I was leaving she said to me, *Hop on the scales? Whilst you're here?* I have talked of slyness, Amy—of how those girls crept out of the room at night, like thieves. Testing my depth of sleep by whispering my name, or running a pencil's point over my toes. I did not expect it from Annie, but then, the best slyness is never foreseen. I stood on those scales. Hands in my pockets. The nurse was surprised, I think, for she pouted a little, wrote something down. *Slightly underweight, but . . .* I imagine the caretaker was surprised, too, when he was clearing the school fountain of leaves and litter in the spring, and found a snow-globe in it. Heavy, and pocket-sized. Perhaps he felt its weight in his hand, ball-like. Heavy as a rock, and I'd taken it, used it, dropped it into stone jug of the fountain as I'd passed by. *Job done.* See? Slyness. I had it in me, too.

And I wanted to know where they went, what they did, who they met when they left me behind in bed. So I tiptoed and held my breath by doors. I feigned sleep. I lifted my legs up, as I sat in a toilet cubicle, so they'd think the room was empty, and I heard Jo say, *I'm tired today . . .*

Worth it, though?

Yes.

Eyes, too. I spied. I watched them, how they moved. Jo would take hold of Heather's wrist as she whispered to her. Annie, with her orange hair, was always one or two steps behind.

• • •

THE HOURS. The long, lonely hours in an empty room.

The bedside clock, and the sound of her dry heels moving over the sheets. Or the air from the open window would come to her, fall on her hands, or face—and she'd smell it, testing it, as all night-time creatures do. She heard, once or twice, a strange sound behind the wall she slept by—a scraping, or a brushing past. And she'd imagine bats, in the wall. Stretching out their dark, veined wings. Opening their tiny mouths, bleating.

She always heard them leave. Or in the beginning, she did. Lying in the dark, with her glasses on, she'd hear the slow movement of a zip, or the quick, rough sound of laces being tied. Heather saying, *Right.* Or *Ready?* And the pop of a mascara, or a clink of jewellery. And then Moira let them leave—lift the window, step out onto the fire escape. Tread down it, in their heeled boots, and away.

Sometimes, she watched. Crouched by the curtain. The first time, there were no stars, and she saw nothing at all out there. But then, afterwards, there was a wild, galleon sky, and a moon, and she saw them—all three of them. In a line. Ghostly, and mercury-quick. Slipping under the boundary fence, and gone.

She wondered how she'd look, if they glanced back. A second moon. Her pale face—round, shadowy, waxy, gazing out over the grounds.

Where do they go? Moira could only guess. In the daytime, as she moved through her lessons with shadows under her eyes, she'd picture how they could have been a few hours before—skirting mud, catching their sleeves on wire. She didn't know where they went, but she imagined trees. A copse, beyond the sugar beet fields—low, twisted trees that grew close together, where there were toadstools, and cobwebs, and maybe an owl somewhere. Moss under fingernails. Snapped twigs. And then what? Then what took place?

Hours and hours. Only herself, and the silence and the hard light from the moon. She'd pluck her toes. She'd feel her fingernails and search for the silver brooch with two swimming fish on it. There were spaces between stars, and the lines on a map, and the depths of things.

She thought, *I don't even have a best friend.*

Moira discovered the tenderness of her inside lip, and probably slept less than they did, those nights, in the end.

• • •

THIS, AT LAST, from Aunt Matilda:

> *I sleep a lot, and I read children's books in the bakery downstairs. And I'm packing already—skirts, dresses, shoes, and a sunhat (which is a hard thing to fit in a suitcase). I will lie on a sun-lounger for three weeks, and I will love it.*
>
> *Have you talked to your mother lately? Amy is in trouble for hiding behind a curtain at school, and missing all the lessons. At least it's imaginative.*
>
> *I'll call you before I leave—I promise. And I shall think of you out there, Moira. Look after your precious self.*

Precious. She ran her thumb over it. She thought of Til, sitting against a painted wall, with a coffee, and a pastry. Lost in a book. She folded up the note.

• • •

A FROST, AND A FIRE DRILL, and a bird flew into the window of the swimming pool as Moira surfaced, broke its neck, and she stood in the doorway of the main hall, listened to the soft, high voices of the choir who practised their Christmas carols in there. Two Knox girls fought in the corridor, saying, *Bitch. Take it back.* In the television room, Moira learnt the Hubble telescope had found some of the smallest stars, and that too many people for her to fathom had died, in an African war.

And, in the dormitory, Heather threw her hair forwards to brush it, so that Moira saw her neck, and a second strange mark on it—a soft apple-bruise, a penny of skin.

And George caught his hand in the door of his workshop, needed stitches for it. And the hamster liked breadcrumbs, and mild cheddar cheese, and Amy had learnt the word *cool*. It was her answer to all things, now. Serious, and slow. *Cool . . .*

And also, in the lunch queue, amongst the smell of peas and old meat, and the steam, and the noise, and the cutlery, Moira stood with her tray in her hand, and listened to Heather, talking. Woollen hats, and *the usual place*, and cider with blackcurrant cordial in it. "Midnight tonight. OK?" Heather glanced behind her, saw Moira, raised an eyebrow.

It was in the dining hall, on a Friday—fish and chips, treacle sponge—when Moira first heard the word *Ray*. She didn't think it was a boy's name. She thought it was a flat, grey creature that skimmed the sea floor, with a barb in its tail; or a light, that showed up her bones. Or sunshine, in a column.

This was all *Ray* meant to her, then.

*I*T CAME TO THIS:

She knew of ox-bow lakes and French verbs, pi and the world wars, and she had plucked the tendons of a dead frog and watched, as it danced on its own. She'd written a letter as Anne of Cleves, had designed a cloak for Prospero, and she knew about iambic pentameters, vignettes, sonnets, odes, that Socrates drank hemlock, and Hemingway shot himself. She'd folded over the tips of pages in her *Aeneid* and *Metamorphoses*. She knew the diamond wealth of Africa, the migratory routes of the humpback whale, that Thales invented geometry, that the skin was the largest organ, that the Aztecs believed in thirteen heavens and sirens sang men to their deaths on rocks. Aphrodite walked out of sea foam. Marie Curie won two Nobel Prizes. Aristotle taught in a garden, and Kansas was the Sunflower State, and it was a *murmuration* of starlings. Lymph nodes were bean-shaped. Ice caps were melting. Emily Dickinson labelled jam jars, and only one American president had never had a wife.

She knew these things, and more. That Annie still slept with a grey cotton rag.

But there were things Moira knew nothing of. There were, she thought, two educations, and what did she know of a life away from books, and science rooms? The real things? The lessons that a fire escape led to? She was left behind; she was lost. She'd lie in her bed and see herself—bones, and veins, and striped pyjamas. She only dreamt of things that were gone, or would never come to her, and Moira was empty of all the important lessons and truths, because how could Prospero's cloak help, now? With its silver thread? How did it ever? *I don't want to know about that.* She wanted to know of marks on a girl's neck, of cider, of midnights, of a thing called Ray. Of how the school looked, in moonlight.

Fists, sometimes, in the darkness. Fists, and the silver fishes, and her upper arms, and a whole world moving outside that she wasn't in—not even a little. Couldn't even reach out for it. Moira knew nothing at all. Only osmosis, and how a frog worked. That pipistrelle bats were roosting behind the dormitory wall.

• • •

HER MOTHER, on the telephone, said, "You don't sound the same."

What do you say, to such a thing? *So?* Or, *I think I do, actually.* Moira felt the telephone cord with her fingers. Thought of words. *I'm left alone at night. They climb outside with perfume on.* But why would she tell her mother that? Of all people?

The wintery, cliff-top, molehill world of Stackpole was all inside her mother's voice, as she talked. Church Rock stood, in a rough sea. The squill and furze would shake on the headland. Miriam said the Bannister house was for sale, now, because Mrs Bannister had passed away, and how could he live there, anymore? "All those memories"— and the army guns were dropping away, east of them.

"Moira," said George, when he came to the phone, "you sound different to me."

Moira wanted to kick the wall. Or throw the chair. A real, physical thing. Slam the phone down on all four of them.

• • •

The average heart weighs three hundred grams, and is the size of a grapefruit. It expels blood into the aorta and the pulmonary artery.

They returned, one night, at three o'clock, with their hands over their mouths, saying, *Sshh* . . . A shoelace caught on the window-frame—quick, smothered laughter. Moira kept her eyes closed, and one of them came up to her bed, held their breath, retreated. *She is asleep!* And there was a new smell, too, in the room. Sweet, like old fruit.

She did think, for a time, of knocking softly on Miss Bailey's door—or Miss Burke's even, with its woodcarvings and iron latch—and informing them. This thought came to her in class. Or, more innocently, of waking in the night, calling out, worried by the empty beds. Or she thought of pushing the end of a pencil through a fire alarm at midnight, so in the frosty line-up, their names would ring out, unclaimed. She imagined shutting the window completely. Locking it. Closing the curtains. Lying in bed, hearing them scratch at the glass, and plead, *Moira . . . ?* Saying nice, false things to her.

Moira did think of all this, as she swam in the hot, chemical pool, or underlined answers. It would stop them. It would make her a violent, red-eyed queen, with power, and they might view her differently, and they might sleep in their beds again. And she wouldn't have to lie there, with the world racing outside her, the clouds flying, the bats peeling out across a dark Norfolk, catching gnats, skirting trees, before filing into their roost again. She hated it. More than anything else. She hated the small raft of her bed, and she hated the clammy marks behind her ears that her glasses made, and she hated the fire escape, and their breath on her, blowing to see if she was asleep, Jo's whispered, mocking, *Bye, then . . .* And she hated all the old names which still slunk in the corners—good old *Bubble Eyes*—and their slow, wise talk of boys, whose smell they came back wearing. Outside the Maths room, Heather saw that Moira was in earshot, that her head was tilted. So she turned, smiled—a dazzling, triumphant smile, of white teeth, and gloss. One hand on hip. "Yes, Moira?"

He told me he loves me, she whispered later, and winked, as if they were friends.

• • •

I DISCOVERED THAT if I stood in the bathroom, took my hips in my hands, and pulled the skin, tightly, I could see my pelvic bone perfectly. The *ilium, ischium,* and *pubis.* Like a face, through my skin.

Also, I could move my knee-caps with the well of my hand, shifting them till they clicked, stopped.

And I spoke to my aunt, in December, who still talked of the Tower card, and how she looked for its truth every day. Of her longing for sun. *To feel . . .* What? Alive again? Beautiful? Full of possibilities? "I'll send you a postcard," she said. Leaving an icy London. A picture of herself in her passport, copper-haired, eight years before. A smile at the shallow edges of her voice.

• • •

SO THERE WAS DECEMBER, and with it came a dry, dusty smell of heat, hanging in the corridors. Miss Bailey pinned the same red tinsel above Curie's door.

Moira looked at her watch, and thought of Aunt Til's aeroplane, lifting up, into the sky above Heathrow. Til's eyes closed.

Imagine it, and it will be that way. And Mrs Bannister was dead, now, and she unscrewed Jo's strange bottle of shampoo that was not shampoo at all, but a clear, sharp liquid, and she tried some. Drank it.

She thought, *I could go with them.*

I could. If a ghost could push a woman off stage, and a bird believe a sheet of glass is lawn, and sky, what couldn't happen? She could ask. She did.

And Heather stood, expressionless. Her hair was twisted back, held in place by a single tortoiseshell grip. Arms folded. She blinked then, frowned, said, "I misheard, I think. Ask me that again."

To go, too.

"What?"

But Heather knew it—that Moira could slide a note beneath a teacher's door. Seal the window. End it all. She stared at Moira—at the glasses, and the big hands, and the long hair.

She stood, waited.

Heather said *"Fine,* then." Left the room.

. . .

THERE ARE MANY THINGS I've done which mattered, and ran on, elsewhere—the blue nylon rope, or a lift home on a cold night. But this, I think, was the most important thing I've done, in my whole life—this asking. Because where would I be, otherwise? I drank vodka from a shampoo bottle, and asked to go, too. And if I hadn't, what then? And what now? Which Moira would have walked, in my place?

No Cley-next-the-Sea, and no sapphire on a ring. Perhaps I'd be sleeping here, not you.

*Y*OU'D HAVE DONE THE SAME, I think. You'd have done it ear-
lier, perhaps—but yes, I think you too would've asked Heather, or
told her, even. Or followed them all, without asking. Just tapped on
their shoulders, out in the dark by the boundary fence or the icehouse, and said, *Boo.*

I can only think this because of the stories our parents have told
me, since you fell from Church Rock. From the few, fierce moments
I have seen with my own eyes: the stamping of feet; how you removed
a wobbly tooth. *Amy the brave*—even at eight or nine years old. Brave
to have swum out to the rock, like that, when you didn't like water.
Brave, or foolish. I know it's a thin line.

Do you think we were planned? Raymond asked me this, once. In barley, somewhere near Salthouse church. There is only one answer to a
question like that: *I don't know.* For how can we know? It all came
down to one small choice I made, in December, when I was sixteen.
A spun coin. A thrown dice. Perhaps we were planned; or perhaps
not. That's all I have now, as ever.

If I hadn't . . . But I did, Amy. I wore my hooded coat, and my tennis shoes. Flattened down my fringe.

•   •   •

MOIRA SAW EVERYTHING. She noted the shadows, and the sounds.
Half-lit faces. The shudder of the window, pushed up. How Annie
pushed her finger into a pot of wax, rubbed it over her lips. Pulled
on her fingerless gloves.

It was cold. No wind, but the air stung. Moira's shoes made a
quiet, metallic sound on the fire escape. She pushed her glasses up her
nose, and followed them down—past other sleepers, and bricks. She

held her breath. Heather's bracelet knocked against the rail. There
was no moon at all.

Sshh . . .

The midnight air. Smelling of water—*no, of ice*. Or metal. And
they crept east. They filed along the boundary fence, with its splintered
wood under her palm, and its moss smells. Past the dip that the foxes
made. Heather's hair shone in front, and Moira thought, *I am here. I am
out here, and it's night-time.* She was not in bed, staring. She wasn't left
behind, this time—she was here, and cold, and she glanced back at
the school, at its wet flag, and the porch lights. She imagined her
empty bed, still warm from her. She imagined her old self in the dormitory, to the north—moon-faced, stranded. Pale-blue-striped
pyjamas.

Over the fence. Onto a plank that spanned a ditch. Behind the
line of poplar trees, which were silent, and white-barked, and tall—
Moira looked up at them.

Annie waited for her. Shoulders hunched in the cold.

"Come *on . . .*"

Over the sugar beet field. Clotted earth under her shoes. And they
came to darker trees, and a pyramid of bricks. The icehouse. Torchlight. A smell of moss.

I am here, she thought. Inside her hood.

A hiss of a struck match, and she was lit up, seen.

· · ·

THERE ARE BIRDS *by the lily-ponds who will fly down, take seed from your hands.*
Nobody said, *This is Moira Stone.* There were no other logs or
upturned crates, so she sat on the ground. Its coldness bit her. Wet,
too—she felt her trousers stick to her. *Mud.* But she had nowhere else
to sit. A beer was pressed into her hand, and she tried it.

Boys. Three, maybe. She wasn't sure, because she didn't really
look, but she knew that they all sat on the far side of the fire—twigs,

and newspaper, and she could smell fumes. They laughed. Jokes she didn't get. Boys next to Heather and Jo. One said, "Is that the best you can do?" And there were elbows, and fists, and Jo knocked over her beer and she laughed out, shook her hair.

There are fulmars that roost at Broad Haven.

Moira was cold. She had no gloves, and the fire was small, and too far away. She blew on her fingers. Bit them, to waken them. Then she untied her laces, pressed her hands down into her tennis shoes. She thought, *I know what I am*: glasses, white skin, height, bones. Black hair. A padded coat. She was nameless, and she was wrong for believing anything else. She retrieved a hand, drained her beer.

Her hood fell back as she drank. She felt this. Heard this:

"Your friend's thirsty." A boy's voice.

Heather scoffed. "She isn't my friend."

The white correction fluid daubed on her spare spectacles, or the water in her bed, or the glances, or the names, maybe—*Chicken tits; Six Eyes; Stone the Bone.* Or just the tone in her—hard to explain it, but for five years Heather had dipped her shoulder when she spoke, smiled, found every corner of the word *scholarship.* Moira had had all of this. Had never worn the nightdress from Til, with the green lace, because of the words that would have come out, or the scissors or the marker pen, and now it was all too late, for the nightdress was too small for her, although she still had it. Wrapped up, in the dark.

Other things. Like checking all the loos before using one in case Heather was in there, waiting, because things could be thrown over loo walls.

Or the day Moira had fallen, lost her sea bean.

Or the crocodile clip, on her jumper.

She looked up. Over the fire, to where Heather sat on a log, beside a blond boy—so blond his hair was almost white. Heather, in a cream wool jumper. Beautiful. With earrings, and her tight, dry smile. Moira met her stare, and maybe it was the beer in her, or the cold, or the currents inside her, or the Tower card, or something else entirely, like an outward anger, at last, and vengeance, but Moira didn't look away. Not for ten whole seconds. She counted them, and for the first time, Moira stared—her cold, black, flint-hard stare, so that Heather's smile lessened, and, later, years later, this blond boy beside her would try to capture that stare again, and draw it down. He'd call Moira *witch-like*. He'd say, *You were like a cave, I think.*

She hated being there. Hated the fire, and her cold hands.

So she rose, tugged up her hood. She tucked her hair into it, blew her fringe out of her eyes, brushed down her trousers. Took one quick look at all of them. All six faces.

Then she walked back to Curie on her own. Across the sugar beet fields, where the pink-footed geese were murmuring. She slipped through the window. Undressed.

Found her bed was still warm from the body she had before this one, which had beer in it, now, and a smell, and a wisdom she wished she didn't have, after all.

• • •

A DREAM OF OLD WATER, in the night that followed. Of deep, known Atlantic waves that rocked her, and she sank into them, and she dreamt of Lydstep beach with one, standing gull. The pearl-white snails in the dune grass, and the bump beneath her mother's bathing suit. Sun on the water. Sun, so it glinted. Warm, and bright, and she narrowed her eyes, in her dream.

She was haunted by this. The quick, dappled flashing of sunlight on water. She walked with it, through a wintery school. She thought, *I said nothing. To anybody. I didn't even say a single, tiny word.*

• • •

THE FINAL WEEK OF TERM. Outside, it sleeted. Inside, the class-rooms steamed with radiators and breath, and drying clothes. Drowsy indoor hours. She sat with a pen in her hand. She watched Mrs Maynard strain in her skirt, press words onto the blackboard, cough. Moira, slouching, with her left cheek in her hand. Or, later, she sat in the library and closed her eyes. Even she was too tired to want this. Lessons. Work. It was mid-December, and she had beaches in her head, and a need for sleep.

Only Miss Bailey had life in her. Moira heard her radio—Christmas songs, which she sang to. Pinned mistletoe in the hallway, which seemed odd. Who was there to kiss? Mr Hodge. The caretaker.

"I know, I know . . . But what's wrong with cheering this place up?"

True. Moira watched this, with her thumbs pushed through the holes in her sleeves. She felt sick inside herself, and vomited, later—in the shower, without warning, so that she panicked, rinsed the tiles more than herself, and ate toothpaste, and worried about it. Worried that somebody heard, or knew.

Another night-time leaving. Wednesday—fiercely cold. All day she had worn her scarf, so that walking across the courtyard or over to the dining hall didn't hurt her. The Arctic, she thought. Blowing down to Locke, and running round its brickwork. Shivering the stone girl. The flag was wet, flapping, and in the afternoons she could see the small, hard snowflakes falling in the glow from the lights above the gravel path. A circular falling. Icy on the cheeks, and blurred on her spectacles. She'd take out her cloth, wipe them.

So at night, she did not expect it. Did not look for it. Too cold, surely, for a ducking out of windows. She believed it would not happen again, and yet, she was always awake, at midnight. Not even dozing, and she lay wide-eyed as they dressed around her, whispering. A zip, and the push of a heel into a shoe. Someone came close to her, leant over her bed, checking. *No. She's asleep.* Jo's voice. Jo's rosebud smell.

And Moira was back there again—back being the sleeper, the sole breath in a dark room, and she reasoned, again, that she could pad after them, as a spy might, or a traveller. Crept down the metal stairs. Pulled her collar up. But why? She said this word out loud. *Why bother?* Beer, and a log. Heather's hands and mouth on a blond-haired boy.

So Moira stayed there, let them go.

And that night, for the first time, her sleep had fire in it. She dreamt of burning—felt heat and smoke. Her fingertips were flaming, and Moira saw the fire in the woods, at first. Then, another kind—glass bursting, a roof falling into itself. Or the pile of broken desks that the caretaker lit, stepped back from, so that suddenly she could see faces, and eyes in the shadows, and the flames coiled upwards. The fire in the dining hall. How to make a soufflé—and the bells rang, and the fire engines came, but the men who piled out of them were crooked, and serious, and the fire didn't stop. They shook hands with each other, admiring it. Wood snapped. And Moira wanted to throw water on it, to douse it. But there was no water there.

She didn't hear them return. Instead, she woke early, with her fists up against herself. They were sleeping, and she turned her head, looked up at the window. Grey sky. A frost, maybe.

She brushed her teeth till her gums bled.

• • •

I WANT TO GO HOME.

Imagined a hamster walking across her homework. She heard its feet, saw it empty its pouches onto the textbook—sunflower seeds, a dried pea.

In the Biology room, she could not see the blackboard, as if her sight had gone, and she could not understand it. She found herself, face down. Forehead against the desktop, with her pen in her hand. Mr Hodge leant down, said, "Moira?" Put his hand on her shoulder.

Home. Or in Florida. Or sitting like a mussel on top of Church Rock.

• • •

TUESDAY MORNING. Four days before the end of term. A few, small snowflakes in the air, dying on the glass. Heather in her dressing gown and sheepskin slippers, queuing for the shower. Heather combing her wet hair, dipping her hand into a pot of cream and smoothing it onto her shins and elbows and hips. Buttoning up her shirt. Taking a wand of black mascara and bending down to the mirror— mouth open, a tilt of the chin. Stepping into her black shoes. Jumper. A pin in her hair.

The same as every morning? Moira thought so. No difference in her. The same—of course, the same.

Until Heather turned round to her in the dormitory, and said, "What? Fucking, *what?*" She threw her hairbrush across the room at her.

And Moira thought, *That is new.*

• • •

THERE IS SO MUCH you don't know.

And this, Amy, is the next part of it: that Moira walked to Lockham Thorpe, hollow, but also brimming over. Her breath clouded, and she passed the almshouses, and the pumpkin field. She sat in the church porch. Listened to a tractor in the distance. And she dug into her skin with a red sports ribbon, thought of things on the stone bench—you, and the skeleton, and the bottle she'd thrown, once, full of words.

A low red sun, as she walked back. Glinting on the windows.

The boy was standing by the boundary fence. Hair so blond it was almost white. A green coat, and jeans.

She stopped. Stumbled sideways, behind the games shed. Pressed herself against its wood. Thought, *I'll stay here.* Out of sight. Until her feet grew numb, and it darkened, and he'd have gone.

So she did. She stood behind the games shed. Nervous, and thinking of peering round the edge of it, to see, but not brave enough.

A minute passed. Two.

Five minutes.

In the end, she thought, *He must have gone.* She moved slowly to the end of the shed, and looked round. The poplar trees swayed. No one stood beneath them, and she softened, was ready to walk away.

"Hey."

Jumped. Fell against the shed, lost her footing. Two choices, when somebody frightens you, like that: to scream, and lash out—to push at them, and be the angry girl with the sharp tongue, as I've been before now, and would be again; or to put your fist against your own beating chest, breathe. To nod, dismiss it with a hand. And I chose this, by the games shed. I swallowed air, nearly smiled.

"I saw your feet," he said, pointing. "And your breath."

He has blue eyes. He has pale eyelashes. Needs a shave.

"It's Moira, isn't it?"

·   ·   ·

We walked. He and I. The boy I'd seen over the fire, who'd said, *Your friend's thirsty.* Not far—just to the back of the gymnasium, where the netball courts were. Hands in our pockets. And my hood was down but my hair was, too, so I hid behind it. Viewed him through it. The frost crunched, and the sun dipped.

He said, "You didn't stay long." He talked of Heather, and how she'd been—rude, and bitter, and had drunk too much. Came out with spiteful things, later. "About you," he said. "I thought you should know."

He was my height. And older—not sixteen, like I was. Nineteen, maybe. Still in his teens but broader than boys were meant to be, at that age. Or so I thought. But what did I know? A crooked tooth in his mouth, when he smiled. He blew on his hands, and said, "So. Is she always like that?"

Pretty much. For she was. Beautiful, and cruel.

And I can tell you, too, that we talked of the weather, as all nervous people do—of Norfolk winters, and icy winds that come down from the Russian tundra, and I told him about the pink-footed geese, and he said yes, he'd seen them. Lapwings, too, wintered in fields. And he asked what I liked, what I wanted to be. *A scientist, maybe.* And he sucked his teeth, shook his head. "Brains, then . . ." As other people had done. So that I thought he was disappointed—of course. A dull reply, from a girl with brains.

· · ·

IT WASN'T MUCH. Ten minutes of this, maybe. But the world can change in seconds only—look at you, and at bombs, and the speed of a virus, and he said, later, that he knew. *Knew what?* I asked. And he'd smiled. *I don't know. Something.*

"I thought you might come back to the icehouse," he said. And he didn't touch me at all, save for the kiss, which was small, and strange, and I think I must have frowned at him, as if he was crazy, or dangerous. I stepped back.

· · ·

DO YOU KNOW what it was? Why he was there? Not to see how I was, or to tell me how Heather had stamped her foot, slapped him, when he told her how it was over, and it had never been love. Nor how, when my hood fell back, the fire seemed to burn on it, and that I stared like a witch, he said, or a warrior, and that the other girls were blonde, and powdered, and smiled too much, and then there was me: silent. As dark as a cave. He didn't say this—not then. Although, one day, he would lean back in a car and tell me all of it.

"I'm saying goodbye," he said. Leaving. Pulling a backpack on, and travelling the world for a year. A whole rotation.

Twelve full moons.

Of course.

I nodded, turned.

Curie House was dry-heated, smelling of dust.

Moira heard the door shut behind her. Stood for a while in its stairwell, on her own.

I'VE NEVER TOLD ANYONE before. The kiss, or the way of it. Heather's hairbrush had caught me, when she threw it—cut my left cheek, and he'd questioned it there, by the netball courts, but with his eyes, not with words.

Is it romantic? Well. As with all stories, I think it depends on the telling of it. I could make it cool, and coincidental. Or an embarrassment—he saw my breath rising from behind the shed, and my toes sticking out, clown-like, and knew I was hiding there. Or I can make it flame with all sorts of things—destiny, intellect, tragedy, spirituality, love.

It's late, but know this: it snowed overnight.

Jo opened the curtains. She looked young in her dressing gown. She said, *Moira?* My name was trodden out, laid down beneath the window, on the whitened hockey fields. Not neatly, or clearly, but it was there. I thought, *It is a lie.*

So I turned from the window, and dressed. It scared me. I was scared, and confused. But I stored it, Amy—it had melted by elevenses, and my name was gone, yet I can still see it, exactly as it was. It is here, in this room. It is here, on your bed. The dot of the *i* in my name, and the huge, empty, symmetrical whiteness of the *o*.

II

Ray

HAVE YOU SEEN AN EVENING SEA, AT HIGH TIDE, AS SNOW IS COMING? Stood on a cliff with that strange, slow light and the gulls that wheel, but do not call, as if they sense it, too, and have you looked down to the sea, where the waves are ghostly-looking, with an Arctic blueness to them, and the cove is full of white, hissing water, and their foam scuds on beaches, and you can smell it—the snow? You feel aware. You know the sea's power, and your own, on an evening like this. And the light fades, so you walk home—feeling wise but with no words for it. It is in you, then. It is part of you, and in rooms, or on a wintery walk in the future, you'll say, *I've been on the coast as it snows. Once.* And the listener will tilt their head, say, *You have?* Try to see it themselves.

The blueness, and the silent gulls.

· · ·

MOIRA RETURNED TO THIS. To a grey, restless Atlantic. No snow at Stackpole—but the sea's foam was blown over the beaches, over her feet. The waves were high. Gulls hung above them, and all the caves, arches, and blow-holes on this coastline hissed with the rough water. A north-westerly wind. It shook the blackthorn bushes, raced across the black rocks and dunes at Freshwater West.

She walked the coastal paths of Pembrokeshire every day, in that winter, after him. Every afternoon, she put on her coat and left them behind her—set out across the cliffs to Manorbier, with its pub and ivied castle; or to the lily-ponds; or further still, to the tiny secret chapel hidden in the rocks, by St Govan's Head. She found herself sheltering there. A sharp sleet caught her; she sat on the stone floor, with her knees tucked up. The chapel smelt of salt, fish, and urine, and through its single window the Atlantic rose and fell. She watched it. It was cold, and she was far from home.

Or, once, she walked eastwards, to Presipe Bay, which vanished when the tide was high, and where men stood in huge boots, fishing for bass. She sat above it, listened to its spray, hoped the bass knew better. *Swim.* She hoped for this. And she returned home after dark to find her mother angry, talking of mists and accidents, of cliff falls. "It's late!" she explained. "Where *were* you?"

And she peeled off her clothes on Broad Haven as she had done a hundred times before. Inched down to the shore, waded up to her knees. *Go,* she said. Not to climb Church Rock, but to swim to it, that was all. To swim in this blue, iceberg water, and she counted the three. But Moira couldn't do it—for the first time, she couldn't quite bring herself to push with her toes, to dive underwater. She feared it. The bite. The tightness. *Go!* But she couldn't quite.

Angry, in the evening. Moira ran a bath. She undressed quickly, not looking down. A hot, neck-deep bath, and she held her breath, listened to her heartbeat. She imagined the sea bass, or the chapel, or Biology, and looked for Moira, or the Moira she thought she had been, and wasn't now.

. . .

AMY WAS ALL HEADSTANDS and dungarees, in love with a yellow tape recorder. For a whole week, she wore a badge that read, *I am five!* She splayed out her hand, to show this. "One, two . . ." She counted many things. Spoons, buttons, molehills in the garden. How many times

George yawned. She walked into Moira's bedroom, counted all her pencils, and all her books, and laid them all out on the floor. She was proud of this. She beamed, expectant.

"Will you play . . . ?" This request, and others. A tug on the sleeve, or a tap on the door. She'd plead, one-legged, holding her socked foot in her hand. *Please?* No. Moira had work to do—of one kind, or another. So she'd shut the door, turn her back. Wait till Amy had pattered away.

Mostly, she'd patter to her own bedroom. For in the corner, sat a tall, wire cage with tubes, and a sour smell. She kept her heart in it. In this house of sawdust was her favourite of all things. At night, Amy sat cross-legged beside the cage, and talked to the small dumpling of fur that washed itself inside it. *Moira says . . .* Or, *I am five!* Moira overheard this. So did her parents, who secretly adored all of it—this child's cheerfulness, her solemn promises. The fact that they now had a daughter who wore pink, and who skipped, and spoke to a hamster, and who lifted the skirts of dolls to check for clean, white knickers.

Or at least, Moira supposed they felt this way. After all, she'd seen their glances. And she thought of this, too, when she walked on her cliff-tops—her chattering, and upturned dolls. Of wax crayons and fairy-lights. *I was dark and silent.*

A sea baby.

She did not think of Ray.

• • •

A POSTCARD SAT on the doorstep in the morning. It had pelicans on it, and a pier, and a long sand beach with the words *Sunny Florida* printed across it. Moira turned it over. She found that Til had written:

Sun; sea; red snapper; red flowers; traffic lights that hang off wires; air conditioning; Mexican beer with lime in the neck; lights in the trees; French fries; good coffee . . .

Merry Christmas to G, M, M, A—and Mr Pouch.
Love from T x

A long way from Stackpole. Moira sat on the swing in their garden with the postcard in her hand. She imagined her aunt at that exact moment, sun-tanned and happy, walking down an avenue of white-barked trees.

Then she rose from the swing, moved indoors.

• • •

RAY. NOT A LIGHT. Not a grey sea creature.

Later, on the train back to boarding school, she thought: *You move on. You pretend something isn't there, until it isn't anymore.* A form of self-hypnosis. She had always believed it was possible to do this, and she had tried it, almost made it. It was discipline, resolve, and she had fought homesickness, so she would fight this, too—say, *I don't even know him.* For what was her other choice?

No hanging around for her, then, behind the school gym, moon-eyed. No walking by the games shed.

January again, with snowdrops in the same places as last year, and the year before, and pheasants creeping out in the lane. The same words from the headmistress—*endeavour,* and *reliance.* "New challenges for the new year!" She always said this. Every year, for six years.

Dead water lying on the Curie roof from a winter of slow rain, and the dining hall door still caught itself on the concrete path so it scraped, shook, when you pushed it. And Annie's hair was still tangerine-coloured, and the only difference that Moira could tell in the whole school lay in the tiny French teacher, Mademoiselle Lac, who'd returned to school as Mrs Brown, with a gold ring on her left hand, and a softer accent. She beamed. Wrote her name on the black-board over and over—so Geraldine said. *Mrs Brown! Mrs Brown!*

"Mon Dieu," said Heather. Scornful.

And the fish still mouthed through the glass at Moira. And the dry stone fountain was still arm-deep with leaves. And the only thing to make her feel safe, or calm, for the briefest moment was Mr Hodge—sighing, and rubbing the bridge of his nose because the skeleton had gone again. The whole school was searched. Moira dreamt of it, one night—rung up on the flagpole, clinking in the wind.

"Stolen," said Mr Hodge. Defeated by it.

But the skeleton was found, by the second week—in the male changing room of the swimming pool, where nobody went. Cross-legged with a towel on its arm. It smelt of chlorine after that.

• • •

THIS: *I AM somewhere in Italy.*

She read these five words, folded the letter up, and took it to the bathroom. Locked the door. Nervous. She sat on the edge of the bath.

I am somewhere in Italy. I'm on the night train, from Nice to Rome, and I'm writing to you from the top bunk, by torchlight. There are six of us in here. It's too hot in here to sleep, and I'm so close to the ceiling I can touch it by lifting my head up.

She'd never had an airmail letter. Not once.

Only letters from Stackpole, or a postcard from Florida in Til's loopy hand. Nothing like this. No letters ever came for her from other countries.

It was crisp and feather-light. A foreign postmark, and large, untidy handwriting. He hadn't known her surname, so had written on the envelope: *Moira (dark hair, glasses, Lower Sixth Form).*

He apologised in it—for leaving. He said perhaps he shouldn't have met her by the games shed, after all—but then, he wasn't sorry that he did. Which meant?

Moira tried not to think of it. In her uniform or tracksuit or her pyjamas, she tried not to think of the rock of the train, the slow sounds of the brakes as it pulled into a dark station. She hid the letter. It confused her. It felt dangerous, and she did not want Heather to see it, to read it, or throw it away.

• • •

IT'S A JOKE. Or a single gesture. An apology. Clearing his conscience. Or it is a dare.

All such things were likely. She numbered them, wrote them down in the margin of her textbook, sat by the window with the book on her lap.

Miss Bailey summoned her. Moira found her perched on the edge of her desk with a mug of tea, and an African violet that she watered with a milk jug.

She said, "Tea?"

No tea for Moira. She lowered herself onto a wooden chair, chewing her fingernails. Wondering what this was—a request? A telling-off?

It's a joke, Moira. The airmail letter? But Miss Bailey didn't say that.

"You must know," Miss Bailey said, both hands around her mug, "that you are a very able student. And soon enough, you'll be free of this place . . ." Swept her eyes around her room.

And Miss Bailey talked of universities. Oxford. Cambridge. Laid them down, like parcels with bows. "You have it in you," she said. "You are gifted." She talked of talent. Of wasting it. Of the secret slice carved out of a stone ball on Clare Bridge, in Cambridge, which she'd felt with an ex-boyfriend of hers. "Think of it, Moira, at least," she said. "Won't you?"

She did. She knew, by now, how one small event, one conversation, could shrink a place. Change the brickwork, and the sound a tree made, so that it all felt thin, older. Church Rock, too, had seemed smaller. She knew who was to blame: she had his letter. His hand-writing shaken by the night-time train.

•   •   •

HE WILL NOT write again.

She believed this. There was rain, blowing itself in from the north, ploughing up the seedlings in the fields, and the bats fluttered in the wall cavity, and where was he? Somewhere warm. Italy, or further. She took her face up to the mirror, so that her nose was touching it. Seeing how she was, close up.

I am writing to you from the top bunk, by torchlight. She tried to let it go. She held it over the bin in the dormitory, took it to the kitchen's back door. She scrubbed her hair, as if trying to take the kiss away, to watch it twirl down the plughole, with the foam, and the old Moira might have managed this. The Moira who burnt her fringe in the Bunsen burner and had never written a letter to her parents—not even once.

Easier, really, if he had never written. No proof of him, then. The other girls still dipped out of windows at night, but did not mention Ray at all.

As it was, she looked at the Italian postmark. When she returned from dinner and opened her top drawer of clothes—vests, under-wear, socks—to find water in it, slopping against the wood, and her socks floating like tongues, she knelt under her bed, grappled for the envelope. Found it—dry, intact.

Nothing was said, by anyone. But Annie knew about the water poured into Moira's drawer, so that her socks and knickers were sodden, and cold, and took hours to dry. She had witnessed it—Heather, with a tooth-mug carried back and forth. "Sorry," she said. Gave Moira a bunched, tired smile.

*M*OIRA,

These are some things I've seen since I've been here, in Egypt:

- *Birds drinking and washing themselves in the overspill of water from the hostel's swimming pool*
- *A man walking on his hands*
- *Sheesha—tobacco, apple-flavoured, smoked through water*
- *A herd of goats asleep on the pavement*
- *An advertisement for skin-whitening cream*
- *The Pyramids (of course)*
- *Hibiscus tea—it's bitter, and purple, and it comes in glasses with no handles, so you have to use your hands, and the tea is so hot I have to keep putting the glass down. Why not mugs? Something heat-proof?*

Also, I get woken by calls to prayer, which I know is a cliché. And so are stray cats, I think—but they're here in their thousands, with their knobbly spines.

I hope you don't mind me writing to you. Not sure why I am (are you a witch??)

R

A witch. And what did that mean? Old and crooked? Or just dark-eyed? Or mysterious, or was it her hands, which she knew were strange, with their bony fingers that could reach over an octave on the piano, or so Miss Kearney said, and with all the lines on her palms? Til had sucked in her cheeks at the sight of those lines. *Golly . . .* Teasing her. But now?

A witch.

She sat on her bed, cross-legged, with minarets singing over Cairo's baked, flat evening roofs, and its stray cats licking their paws, and her Maths book resting against her left knee.

• • •

A WEEK PASSED. Then two.

February came in with wetter weather. It kept them indoors. No hockey or netball, no cross-country running. It was the weather for sleep, for reading, and she'd read in the chair by the window whilst the others were in the common room, drinking tea or filing their nails. She had noticed this—the new interest in hands. The dormitory smelt of acetone, now.

Lessons were slow, as if they had water in them. Rooms became bluish, and lights did not seem enough. Sometimes the rain on the window was so loud that they would all pause, look out at it as if such a sound had a message in it. The boundary ditches flooded. On Wednesday, mid-month, the rain was too painful to walk through bare-headed and they ran between buildings, with books over their heads. It leapt off the ground, stung them.

Rain on the window of the science laboratory. Then, a knock on the classroom door.

They looked up. A secretary who lurked in the main house came in. Nervous, like a shrew. She whispered to Mr Hodge, who said, "Moira?"

Emergency. She was given the word. She followed the shrew down the stairs, outside, where the wind caught her hair. It made her think of cars. Of a windscreen wiper still flinching over wet glass. A hospital, and a machine that filled up and emptied, like a lung.

"That's all I know," the secretary said. Hurrying.

Or an arm with a needle in it. Sawdust being laid on the road. An ambulance's blue eye, flickering.

In the reception, she saw Til.

Til alive. Til in a red, belted raincoat, and with darker skin. Blonde streaks in her hair. Moira thought, *A plane crash. Til has crashed into the sea, or into Greenland, and is dead.* But it wasn't that. Because Til was here, back off the plane.

"I'm stealing you away," she said. Half-smiling.

No emergency, then. Nothing was wrong, as such. "Everyone is alive, and well," she said. Til told the lie because she'd been passing this way, had wanted to see her niece, and she knew very well you couldn't just take a girl out of school on a weekday. For a pub lunch, to catch up. It didn't work like that. "So I made it up, Moira." A sideways glance. "It scared you?"

They drove north-west, to Titchwell, in Til's dented car. Moira's knees against the dashboard, now. Rain, on the windows. She wore an old pink jumper of Til's over her school uniform, so that only the grey skirt showed. Was she angry? Til asked her this. No, Moira thought—hard to be cross with her aunt, with her rose quartz necklace, and her sunburnt nose. Her bad driving.

In the café at the bird reserve they drank hot chocolate in pottery mugs.

"Florida was fine," she said. "I sunbathed, swam. It was . . ."

Moira waited. For whatever it was that had brought Til here, midweek, with an edge in her. Something had. Moira thought, *There is no witchcraft, or there is plenty.* For she sensed a new man, was sure of it. Saw him, even. Tall. Sandy-haired.

Hamlet, Til said, was long gone. Instead, in the departure lounge at Heathrow, there was a man in a pilot's uniform, with a leather bag, and an accent, who sat beside her, smiled. Talked of small, insignificant things—a packet of butter, a flight number, Til's broken chair. Not much. "But he looked back at me three times, Moira—*three*—as he walked towards our plane."

She paused. Sipped.

His voice on the tannoy. The rest of him, thirty feet away.

And?

"He lives in London. He flies the Miami route. And he gave me his hotel's number at baggage claim, Moira. And then? Guess what?" She grimaced. "I lost it."

Lost it?

They walked on the marshes, that afternoon. In Florida, Til had been a creature of fists, and self-hatred, and regret—tugging her fingers, unable to eat. Turning her pockets inside out. Calling the Miami airport, pleading for the name of the pilot on *flight number* . . . Then she called a hundred hotels, described him to them. "But how could I find him?" she said. For she had no name to ask for—no name to look up in telephone books, because he'd written down a number, only. Ten digits, and a room number. Had said, *Here you go . . . If you like* . . . On a square of pale-yellow paper.

"So . . ."

Avocets, as always, dabbling through the mud. A marsh harrier, too.

This, perhaps, was the Tower card in her. Making her see a meaning in things—in a pilot, and a ten-hour flight, and a lost piece of paper. Still, Moira thought of touching her aunt's hand, for a moment. Sitting in the wooden hide, she thought of this.

• • •

LOCKE WAS SPLIT OPEN. Its walls were long gone. Moira lay in bed, and thought of it—not of the pilot, or his leather bag. But of the crescent moons Til's nails had made on her skin, and the lines on her forehead.

She turned onto her side. Wondered who her aunt would become, in time. But she thought, too, of her own life. Of what might lie ahead of her. Of night trains; of birds dipping to drink from a pool.

She brought her knees up to her chest. Did not sleep.

ORTNIGHTLY, SOMETIMES MORE, Ray sent her words that she plucked like fruit off the page—hibiscus, lorikeet, *tor-ti-lla*. She wrote these words down, in margins. Saw them lying out on the lawn. In her mouth, she felt the shape of *sheesha* and thought, *He has also said this.*

She studied, in the day. She was the good pupil, still. But in the evenings, she left the dormitory and trawled the library for books on tropical illnesses, insects that could bite. Spiders, which could jump across rooms, land on a face like a hairy, brown hand. There was no homework, as such. Instead, the atlas creaked itself open, and she followed its maps with her fingertips, saw their colourings. Ray told her that in Zambia, he could use ballpoint pens as currency. *They want biros*, he wrote, in a letter, and she was angry at this, or jealous, or both. She didn't know.

He wrote, once, *The wind is so warm here that I can't feel it. It's just a soft noise, past my ears.* And that, then, was anger. She seized on it: decided, *He is arrogant, and proud.* She screwed the letter into a ball, only to smooth it out, later. She was here: her life was a science room, and a vaccination mark, and fire drills, and cigarette butts were placed in her pencil case as she showered, so that all her pens and protractors smelt, and felt gritty, and she would hold his envelopes in bed, after dark, wondering where they were written. In a *taverna*, or on his lap in a bus. On a balcony with geraniums, overlooking a pool where a woman swam underwater, surfacing in silence, her hair as bright as glass.

She had no way of writing back. She had no address, and was relieved. What would she write to him of? The weather? Sugar beet? Would she write to say, *Why are you writing? Where is the joke?* Sometimes she resented his letters so that she'd see them in her pigeonhole and leave them there. *Who cares?* He was probably making most of his stories up anyway. But in the end, she'd read them. She'd bring her knees up to her chest and pick through his handwriting, looking for hints in the words, or the spaces between them. For traces of other travellers, of women he might ask to dance in a Thai nightclub, or invite back to his room.

· · ·

SEVENTEEN CAME. She looked at herself in the shower room mirror, as if expecting a difference there—a new line, or different glasses. She felt the year had been a long one, and must have marked her somehow.

At lunchtime, with books in her arms, she wandered past her pigeonhole to find three birthday cards in it. Til sent a seascape, and a jewelled spectacles case. Her parents had written, *To our darling Moira*, and she found a cheque in their envelope, and a photograph of the three of them—in their Stackpole garden, Amy with huge plasters on her knees. Amy had sent her own card. It was mainly glue, with the odd patch of glitter, and when Moira opened it up she found her name written in luminous pink, the *i* dotted with a flower.

She put them between two books. But as she turned to go she saw a bluish corner underneath a parcel, and when she pulled it, it became an airmail envelope for a girl with no surname.

She took it to the bathroom, locked the door.

It's the driving that might kill me. It's crazy. They ignore red lights, and we skidded on the side of a mountain yesterday. Never mind gun crime or lions or malaria—I'll die in an African car crash, and no one will know about it for weeks . . . I'll just be buried by the side of the road, forgotten about. I can see you out here, Moira . . . The only white-skinned thing, laying flowers down.

Go out? Lay flowers down by the grave of a man who had kissed her once? He had no idea who she was. He thought she was a witch, but she was half-Welsh, bony, and bad with words—she didn't even know how to pronounce *tortilla*. His Moira was, surely, not this one, leaning against white bathroom tiles.

She looked into the envelope again, later. She had missed it at first. But, inside, there was a small piece of paper. A pencil drawing, neatly done: flamingos, in water. She brought it right up to her glasses. *He draws.* And these birds had strange, backward knees, and hooked beaks, and she knew their feathers were bright, shrimp-coloured, and she could imagine those birds, then—lifting up at one, small sound, like a handclap, or a biro's click, and flying into the corridor, smelling of fish, and leaving their footprints in the river's mud.

• • •

I'M BECOMING A different person. She felt it. Sometimes she felt she was walking on an edge, barefoot, with her arms out. In the bathroom in the evenings she stared at herself. She wondered if there was any sort of beauty at all in white skin and black eyes, and a serious fringe. In her muscular arms. If it was at all possible for these letters to be real, and not a dare. But she thought not, for she had glasses. And she had said to him, *A scientist, maybe,* and he was an artist—so where was the sense? The common ground?

She was certain of the answer. *He's tricking me.* Yet she pretended, too—she couldn't help it. Even her, with all her shortcomings, found herself *hoping*—for a knock on the glass of the dormitory window, or a pebble, thrown. She slipped soundlessly into these thoughts, at night. Of what lay ahead. What might come. She often imagined Ray in his own bed, in a humid country, with insect noises and a ceiling fan. Hoped he was thinking of her. She'd let herself pretend this, briefly—see him with one arm up behind his head. And then she'd be angry that she had.

In the daylight, she was fierce. She snapped a word at Jo. She dropped her eyes down into textbooks, as she always had done—into Maths, cubic equations, and she picked at her nails again. She tore off curves. Once, this way, she bled. She had to leave the Maths lesson to go to the infirmary, find a plaster, clean her hand. Over the sink, rinsing the blood, she stumbled. She thought, *Look.* She had removed most of her thumbnail. The skin beneath was shell-pink, raw. She examined it under the light. There were vessels in it, pin-heads of blood. She turned on the cold tap and held it under there.

Til knew. No one else seemed to at all. But Til glanced across at her niece when she next came to Locke. She said, "You're different . . ." Moira ignored that. She asked, instead, about London—theatres, bars, Danish pastries, and mice. The pilot, of course. Til's dreams. She blamed the heavy library door for her bandaged thumb.

"You know where I am, Moira . . ." Til's parting words. Maybe she'd seen it in the stars—that all Pisces would flail this month. Flap on the shore, gulping. She kissed her niece on the forehead when she left. Also, she glanced back in her rear-view mirror—round, grey eyes, curled eyelashes.

On with the days. On with the pulling back of curtains each morning to see the same empty running track, and the fences, and the sugar beet fields.

• • •

MISS BAILEY put her fingers in her mouth, whistled. Moira turned at this, saw her—standing by the pigeonholes, cloud-haired, with a letter in her hand. Dog-eared, airmail paper. "For you," she said. "Look at the stamps . . ."

Later, she'd say on the stairwell that Moira should take good care of them. These letters. "When you're old and grey, you'll be glad of it." A dozen softened envelopes, tied with a piece of string.

• • •

HE ALSO SAID,

In northern Thailand there is a shrine to the elephant. The Thai king was passing through the region when his childhood elephant died there, and he built it, in its honour. It's a wishing well, of sorts. You leave flowers and incense, make a wish. And the shrine is surrounded with small elephant statues, because if your wish comes true you have to say thank you—by bringing another elephant here. A friend for the dead one, maybe? Anyway, it's peaceful. I've sketched it. And of course, I made a wish.

She read this, and looked out over the lawn. No elephant shrine here. Only the athletics track being marked out in lime by the caretaker. A blackbird in the walnut tree, singing.

Yes—it's all true. If you doubt me, feel this—here, on your arm. That? It's his letter. His Thai one. I've bought it here tonight, for you, as proof, in case you also think it's all lies, as some people did. *There.* Breathe it in, as I did, hunting for the scent of the place, of Bangkok, or rice, or frangipani, or Ray's sweat, or the sweat of the man who'd put this letter on the aeroplane. The dirt on his hands. Breathe it, and see. Perhaps it's there, and we smell it, but we think it is the ink. Perhaps Thailand smells of airmail paper.

July. Wimbledon was over, and the usual people won.

*T*AP TAP. Late at night.

Moira opened her eyes. A knock on the glass? She sat up. She waited for the sound again. It was quicker, this time. The knocking did not come from the window. It was in the room. Near her. To her left. She pushed back her blankets.

A rapid, light knocking. And then, in the darkness, there was a new sound—thick, clotted. An animal sound. She couldn't place it. A growling? Words? She didn't know. Then, suddenly, she thought, *choking. It is choking.* She was sure. It was exactly that, and she lunged for her bedside lamp, found it, switched it on.

Annie. Annie, on her back—or rather, on her shoulders, for her back was arched up, off the mattress, and her arms were stiff, and her whole bed was shaking, knocking against the wall. Annie was stuttering like gunfire. She seemed awake, for her eyes were open, but there were no green irises there—just white—and when Moira bent over her she could see the vessels in her eyeballs, and how her eyeballs shook. There was saliva, on Annie's chin. Blood, too. Blood on the pillow, and Moira thought, *She is dying.*

Jo cried, "What . . . ?"

Miss Bailey came—wrapped in a pink dressing gown, with a first aid kit, and a smell of lavender. She moved them all aside. She said, "OK, stand back," and she sat on Annie's bed, tilted her over onto her right side, and placed the edge of the duvet between Annie's teeth. Then she waited. She stroked Annie's hair. She cooed, motherly, as legs kicked out against her. Heather and Jo stood with their backs to the wall.

The seizure did not last long. A minute, perhaps. Annie did not wake from it, but she quietened. Her body slowly softened back down onto the bed. Miss Bailey took a tissue, dabbed Annie's mouth. Spit. More blood.

She turned, then, left the room, and returned with three mugs of cocoa on a tray, as if they had been ill, not Annie.

In the morning, Annie woke, gripped her head. She could barely walk with the pain of it. She mumbled, stared at the lines of blood on her bed.

She was taken to the nurse, and to hospital. She was gone for two days, whilst they inched her through machines, read her brainwaves with suckers and gel. Moira thought of her constantly. In classes, she was distracted. She recalled the stiff, arched back; the *tap tap*. She looked out at the grey Norfolk sky and thought of the brain, of the diagrams she had seen of it—its electrical signals, its lobes and hemispheres. In the margins of her exercise books, she drew new shapes, and remembered the moon-white eyes.

When Annie returned, she said little. Embarrassment, thought Moira. Embarrassed to have made such noises, and to have been watched like that—for Heather recounted it all, electric-eyed. *You were drooling. There was blood . . . You wet yourself, you know.* The indignity of it silenced Annie, perhaps—the loss of control. But this was only half-true.

At the end of the week, she confided. On the floor of the changing rooms, when everyone else had gone out onto the hockey fields, Moira lowered herself next to Annie, and her orange hair, and waited. Amongst the mud and deodorant cans.

"I bit into my tongue, Moira. I bit right into it."

And she cried. She pressed her eyes against her knees, hugged her shins, and cried. She had not spoken, because it hurt her to. Her tongue was too sore. Still swollen.

• • •

IF MOIRA HAD HAD an address for Raymond, she would have written to him about this. Not about Annie—she did not want to name her. But she'd have put pen to paper and told him what she had learnt, from seeing a fit. That a human body is a charged thing. It is huge, dark—full of unknowable shadows. She had seen a girl's body attack itself. She had never seen that before.

If she'd had an address, Moira would have told Ray about the blood, and the mugs of cocoa, and that he could talk about all the world's countries and flowers, if he wanted to, but no one really knew what their body was capable of.

*I*T'S AMAZING. *I wish I could tell you that I am disappointed with it, and that it's not as good as I thought it would be. But I'm not, and it is . . . Everything is red—the rocks, the kangaroos. Even red tree sap. And it's so hot here. This is my best moment so far—sitting here on a rock, in the Red Centre, writing to you. I have just eaten an apple; there is one cloud. I wish I could write down exactly what it's like.*

He had it; he could write. He knew words, and how to use them, and she couldn't help but marvel at that. Didn't stop to think he might not know the chemical symbols, or how to find the pineal gland.

He is better than me. Much more.

She wandered the Pembrokeshire coastline that summer, her sleeves rolled to her elbow. Moved the palm of her hand over the yellow furze. *Everything is red.* But here, it was a blue, calm sea with blue mussels growing on the wetter rocks. Millions of them on Swanlake. A cathedral of them—in shadows they were midnight-blue; in the afternoon light they were bleached, brittle-looking. She played them like piano keys. She drew her fingers down them, heard them click against her nails.

She tried so hard to think of other things—of Amy, who could sleep in a tree, sloth-like, or of Mrs Bannister's small plaque where her ashes were buried, at Stackpole church. Or of cakes, for Miriam baked a lot. She had a strange need to, that summer, and so she opened the windows and worked in the kitchen, making sponges, tarts, a strawberry flan—gelatinous things that Amy tucked into, humming, armed with a spoon.

"Crab-fishing?" George asked. Hopeful.

Crabs that could crack a human bone, in South-East Asia. Grasshoppers sang in wicker cages, and she saw them. Saw cold beer glasses clinking high above tablecloths, and a full moon, and maybe he lay, sometimes, on beaches which turtles laid their eggs on, their flippers pushing the sand.

At the top of Church Rock, with her sore palms, and her glasses tied on with kitchen string, she thought, *He has a missing tooth, at the back of his mouth. His hair is white-blond.* The ministry guns boomed softly to the west of her. Lundy slept. And she thought of those grasshopper legs protruding from their wicker homes, and his pencil sketch of a dog, sleeping, in an alleyway.

· · ·

ANGRY WITH HERSELF. She drank alone in The Stackpole Inn. She studied in the beer garden, with a pint of stout, and her shoes kicked off. She drew lines and cubes in *Biology—Higher Level*, and, back in Locke Hall in the following spring, she'd open this book to find a small, dead insect in it. Stuck to the pages, in a dried reddish stain. A Stackpole bug—she eyed it. Saw the crisped wings, and, beneath a reading lamp in Locke's library, she remembered who she had been, that summer.

Angry with Miss Bailey, who forwarded any mail to her. So that in her old bedroom, with its patchwork rug and stuffed puffin that sang if you squeezed it, she lifted up new words. *Paua shells. Raratonga.* She smelt sweat, and dung, and believed that she, too, had been gnawed by mosquitoes up her left arm. They itched at night. She imagined her nails catching the bites, making them bleed.

She thought, *Words are powerful.* Moira spoke in equations, scientific terms; she had no real art in her, like he did.

In an old letter, Ray had written in a red ink, *Always a dog barking in Europe.* And after that, she'd hear it—in the stairwell at Locke, or by the poplar trees. She can hear it here, now, in your hospital room, if she is quiet enough.

• • •

THIS, TOO. Late August.

There was trouble last night. I was walking back from the bar, and I saw a man crying. He was on the ground, and he'd been robbed of his camera, his wallet, his wristwatch. All at knifepoint. So I called the police and sat with him. He was British—he came from Southend-on-Sea.

So I am miserable with the world today. Here I am, amongst boutiques and Hollywood things, and I'm fed up with it all. I think I've been naïve.

I take a risk in writing these letters. I have no idea what you might think of me. You could be throwing these away. Are you embarrassed? Irritated? You might see these in your pigeonhole and ignore them, even. Perhaps these letters are just unread. In which case, there is no risk at all.

I have an address, here in L.A. Either way, I'd like to hear from you.

*M*OIRA RETURNED to school two days early, and found the dormitory airless after six weeks of being shut up. She opened all the windows. There was the scent of cut grass, and she could hear a lawnmower in the far distance. As she stood by them, hands on hips, Miss Bailey found her. "Did you get them? The letters? I sent them all on!"

• • •

I SEE HER, saying that. Maybe in her tennis whites, I'm not sure—but definitely in white, because her teeth, too, were white, and you could say I have a romantic view of her, since I wouldn't see her again. That she'd die, within days. *Become an angel*, as you said, on the telephone.

Miss Bailey died at the end of the month. Was found early one morning in the Curie House stairwell, her head pointing downwards and her skirt folded back on itself. A terrible, ungainly death. Worse, still, in that a Sixth Former found her. As Moira was washing her face in the bathroom, a single, short scream rang out. A bird's alarm call, maybe. But when she went to the top of the stairs and looked down, she saw the awkward angle of a pale left arm, and the flung skirt.

The rumour was alcohol. Then it was suicide. For two days it was guesswork, until they were called to assembly, and they learnt of blood clots that inch towards the brain.

Miss Bailey had been thirty-six. Her room was emptied. Her mugs and pot plants and cushions and radio were all carried out in cardboard boxes, taken down the stairs. Annie watched this, with me. She said, "I don't understand where she's gone to." I thought of her mistletoe, and whistle on its string. Wimbledon, her dialect.

• • •

A BENCH WAS set up in her memory. And, later, after I had left the place, a willow tree was planted, out by the tennis courts. I never saw it, but I imagined it a thousand times. Tennis balls got lost in its boughs; the younger girls sat beneath it, feeling homesick, making daisy chains. Boys might have waited there, as Ray waited by the sundial. And no one will really know who Miss Bailey was, beyond what the plaque on her bench told them. The tinsel, and the lollipop she gave to every Curie girl on their birthdays—me included. Did I ever tell you that? Swirled, red-and-white. These things have gone, and will not be remembered for long. A generation keeps such things alive. But who will know these things, in a century's time? Who knows them now?

I see no fairness in her death. None.

A service was held in All Saints church, but she was buried in Yorkshire, by her own sea, her own childhood places.

· · ·

THIS:

Ray,

Our housemistress died last week. She had a blood clot. It was a lonely, undignified death and she deserved better. She was only thirty-six, and she told me I should keep all of your letters, because when I'm old I'll hardly ever believe I was sent them at all. I'll remember her for lots of things, but that's one of them.

So no—I haven't thrown your letters away. I read them. I'm angry with you, sometimes, and I am confused, because why do you write them? But I read them.

Life goes on here. Exams, essays. I don't know what you're expecting when you get back here, but I think you've imagined me to be someone I'm not—just so you know.

Have you seen Hollywood? The sign?

Moira. (Stone)

She sealed the envelope, sent it.

*W*HAT WOULD YOU like to know? What doesn't make sense? I know what it seems—that we only met twice, or once, even. Not much, either way. Opposites, too. I know what they say about opposites, but there is a limit—there always is. And surely here, there was one.

I questioned it, too. Don't think I didn't. I questioned every inked word on his pages, and every comma, and each full stop, and I narrowed my eyes, looked for the lie. Was Heather part of this? The thought came to me. I felt nothing was beneath her—nothing. *It is an act. They are in it together.*

I knew. He'd say this, later. That he was sure.

Well, know this: I didn't. Not me. I have never been Til, with her tarot and tinctures, nor my parents, who prayed on pink kneelers for Mrs Bannister's soul. I've never had a faith, like that, and I probably intended to creep through my life as a single, hard-hearted girl who clinked with test tubes, and put salts in her bath. No, I didn't know. I saw him as I saw the fire itself, by the icehouse—real enough. And bright, and warm, and I wanted to look at it, and it seemed to be on the backs of my eyes afterwards, and who doesn't turn their head to look at fire? But flames die. They don't last, and I thought this. I'd marry Ray, thinking this.

Still. I move too fast.

Your room is fierce with bleach, tonight. Too much of it. Our cleaner with the baldness has certainly been in here, or maybe another cleaner has. I caught our parents in the hall, who said they'd opened your window. *Don't let her get cold,* they said. Perhaps I'd have asked you, years before, to blink twice if you did feel cold, or three times for too

warm—something like that. But I'll just watch your arms, instead. It's
the easiest way—goose-bumps, the raising of hairs.

• • •

SEVENTEEN YEARS and nine months old. A year had gone by.

She carried her books in her arms, crossed the courtyard, past the
stone girl. Sleet in the air. Biting her ankles, her ears.

Her eyes were down, on the gravel, and her head was full of algebra, and so she did not see the hand, or hear it—she only felt it, on
her back, and it shocked her, so that she snapped herself round, sharp-
tongued, with her arm raised and her hair blown forwards. She was
wild-looking. Warrior-like. She instantly knew this. *I am wild-looking.*

Ray flinched. He stepped back from the raised hand, frowned.
This was his instinct. She saw the hair—pale, fistfuls of it. She saw
the browner skin, the lines around his eyes. Broader.

Later, in the spring, he'd say to Moira, *You looked the same. A few more
grey hairs, perhaps, but . . .*

Instead, she was fierce. She was angry with him. She said she
could have lost her breath, dropped her books, fallen. Called him
mad. A trespasser. She had revision to do. And Moira turned away
from him, with her books and knotted hair.

Only at the front door of Curie House, by the ivy, did she look
back. Quickly, afraid. Over her shoulder.

He smiled.

• • •

AND I REMEMBER THAT—his wide, unbothered, easy smile. He says,
too, that he remembers mine. If I hear a song, or hear a complicated
joke, my smile is slow, widening, and he says, *That's it! That's how it was.*
In the courtyard, ten years ago.

12

Cley-next-the-Sea

RAYMOND.

He confessed this to her—sheepish, believing the name sounded old. They stood outside, and he wore a heavy dark-green military coat, a black scarf. She looked at him, imagined his name written out in full, on paper. She disagreed with Ray—said that if he thought his name was dusty, and old-fashioned, what about hers? *Moira?* Grandmotherly. A name like a book, or an attic map. She said, *Try living with that.*

• • •

THE FIRST TIME that Ray came to visit her at Locke Hall—the first time after his travels—he'd met her in the courtyard as she carried Maths books in her arms. He'd crept onto the school grounds in daylight, and waited behind the kitchen bins until he heard the school bell.

The second time, Mrs Duff knocked on the dormitory door on a Saturday afternoon and told Moira she had a visitor. Down in the entrance hall. Moira put down her book. She did not comb her hair or brush her teeth, because she thought it was Til who'd be standing there. Til, whose last visit had been as the Bewick swans migrated, so that Titchwell had winked with lenses, smelt of waxed jackets. *It goes on*, she'd said, *life*—shrugging at the pilot's shadow. And Moira expected to see her again—a new London story in her, pacing the wooden floor in her knee-high boots. She imagined this and nothing else, so she pulled on her cardigan slowly. Felt tired. Made her way down the Curie stairs, rubbing her eyes under her glasses, out onto the gravel path.

He sat as if waiting for a train—neatly, thoughtful, hands pressed between his knees. She saw him through the glass door. She thought, *I could walk away now*. Back to her dormitory. And then what?

But she pushed the door, and Ray looked up, and they walked into the room of tapestries and the unlit fireplace, where, once, a smaller version of Moira ate a cherry cake. They sat opposite each other on the upright velvet chairs. He asked about exams, and the weather, and if she minded the letters he'd sent to her—"I know it was weird to have written like that, but I . . ." He cracked his knuckles. He scratched deep into his thatch of hair with his thumb. Perhaps he'd just wanted to write to *someone*. Mark it all down. "I think it does strange things to you—travelling . . ." He asked, "Does this make sense?"

Sort of.

Ray tilted his head. "And I'm sorry about your housemistress."

She took him to see the bench with Miss Bailey's name on it. They did not sit on it, but they looked at its plaque, and the view from there—the hockey fields, the tennis courts with their missing nets. They talked of names. Arms folded. He said he was *Raymond*—an old-fashioned name.

He did not say if he'd come back. But she watched how he moved his hand through his hair, in circles, when thinking—and thought, *He won't come back*.

• • •

HEAVY RAIN HAMMERED against the windows of the science room, so that they all glanced up from their desks to hear it. A cool blue light in the school. The ditches swelled up, the seedlings drowned, and water trickled into Pankhurst's attic, so that the electrics blew, and a string of girls she'd never seen before used Curie's hot water that night. A queue of them, with towels on their arms. Comparing the paint, and the notice board. *Have you seen . . . ?* They laughed at the trophy cabinet, for Pankhurst's was full—they ran well, won prizes on Sports Day.

Three days. Four days. A week. *How is the weather with you?* wrote Miriam. *The television says it's rainy. Stay dry! Here, the weather is . . .*

She didn't care. She didn't want to know how Stackpole was, if it was raining there or not, or how a rat-like thing was faring. She was almost eighteen. She had her final exams this year. She stepped into the shower in the mornings, drew the curtains, and glanced down at the new body she stood in—its tough, narrow hipbones, and its knees. It was impossible, at times, to believe it—that she was in this, that it was hers—and she watched the bones in her feet move when she flexed her toes on the shower floor. Saw her whiteness, and her darker places. She could imagine her spine.

In the corridor, Heather said, *Bitch.*

Moira did not mishear this. It was a known word. Had heard it before, but not like this—hard, spat-out.

•   •   •

AND A WEEK became nine days, nine days became a fortnight, and she thought, *I am right*—and she nearly took all his letters that he'd written to her, all their stamps and dirt and words, and dropped them into the huge metal kitchen bins, where the vegetable scraps and eggshells went. She nearly did this. Held them over the edge, counted to three. But returned to the dormitory with them, still, in her hand.

But on the fifteenth day after he had told her his full name, there was a tap on the window of the dormitory. She looked up. A black scarf, and a beckoning.

On the landing of the fire escape, late in the afternoon, she unwrapped a parcel from him. White paper, with a blue ribbon. Inside it she found a string of shells. Not mussel shells, or cockles. They were small shells, speckled and brown-lipped. A bracelet. With a silver clasp. She lifted it up, closed her palm around it so that the shells twisted against themselves.

He said, "It's from Thailand." She nodded, placed it back inside its white tissue paper.

Later, though, she did wear it. She fastened the bracelet, studied it on her. She wanted to know what these shells were, what their name was, and which creatures had once lived inside them. She'd find out. There would be a book, somewhere. Her arm had a new, cool weight. Music, in her few gestures.

• • •

HER LAST MONTHS at Locke Hall were not of school at all, but of him—this boy, or a man, perhaps, because he was twenty, now. Brown skin, and sun-whitened hair. Freckles on the backs of his hands.

So he'd come. Ray with the sketchbook and pencils in a canvas bag, and a small orange car that he'd park under the walnut tree. On Saturday afternoons they'd walk around the school grounds in their coats, cautious, aware of each other and the space between their hands. She rarely talked. Instead, he did—of many things. Of the scent of eucalyptus trees, and the traffic in Los Angeles, and how, in New Zealand, they cooked their meat by burying it with hot coals, underground. He said, "I met a man who'd been stung by a jellyfish, too. He had scars. All up his leg. He nearly died."

She knew this. She had read of jellyfish. How they had no hearts at all. When they caught themselves over mooring ropes, the tide left them behind, so she'd crouch down, touch them. Look at their transparency.

But she did not know that Uluru was a woman's place—where the aboriginal women met and told their daughters about the world, and their bodies, and what to expect from them. There were paintings.

They had painted these things around the rock's base, in its caves. He'd seen them—full, heavy women in ochre, on the walls. He'd walked round the rock at sunrise, sunburnt from the day before. "As red as the rock itself," he said. He'd blistered. Peeled his skin off. Shreds of epidermis on the grass.

She chewed a nail, said, *you wrote of* . . . And she'd list things she wanted to hear more of, or which she'd not quite fathomed. The elephant shrine. Or the ballpoint pens. She'd ask for more, and bend into these stories, try to remember them later. *America? Did it have . . . ?* Bison? Trailer parks?

His stories took her away from Locke. But there were other times, too, when she had nothing to say to him, and did not know how she should act around him, who was full of sights and different smells. She felt sullen. Distrustful, still—because it had no sense in it at all. She hid behind her black hair. What did she have? What journeys? She could only talk of weaver fish, or the mice on the underground she hadn't even seen.

Moira turned the pages of his sketchbook, in his car. Leaves. A building with turrets, and archways.

"What is it?" Ray asked.

But she didn't say. She only knew that Locke didn't matter to her, not even a little, and nor did exams, or universities, and he was to blame. *His fault.* Because he had all these stories in him, which made her hungry—for a life elsewhere. His pyramids, and wombats. And on Miss Bailey's bench Ray talked of pink lightning, which he'd watched on his own on a broken deck-chair by a night-time swimming pool. "I liked it," he said. A pink electrical storm. Palm trees swaying, and a wet-earth smell. But, also, he confessed, it had made him feel alone.

• • •

HE IS HANDSOME. She couldn't help but think it, because he was. Which part? Just his face? Or perhaps it was another reason that made her think it—his sideways glance at her. Or perhaps he was not handsome at all—rather, she was just foolish. *Foolish Moira.* A fool, just because he happened to notice her.

One evening, she was meant to meet him at the sundial but did not. Refused. Lay on her bed, instead, with one leg hanging, so that her toes touched the wooden floor. Six o'clock became seven. Then eight.

Nothing from him, for three more days. She sat in classrooms, considering it—him, holding up his hands to Heather and saying, *She's worked us out.* Or she imagined him in his dark-green jacket, waiting by the sundial, and maybe he hadn't been tricking her; maybe there was a chance that he was decent, after all, and that he hadn't written, or said, or acted out lies. Pigs could fly, and moons could be blue, and somebody could like Moira's face, and her shape, and more besides. Believable? She kicked a stone on the gravel path so that it hit the front door of Nightingale House, dented it. She didn't know. She never knew what to believe, anymore.

. . .

STILL, HE CAME. Climbed up the fire escape, knocked on the glass twice. Heather saw him, and turned onto her front.

Moira climbed out of the window. And she could smell him— clean, and warm, even though it was frosty. He looked down the metal stairs. Said, "If you don't want this, Moira, just say."

But she picked at her fingernails, and didn't say.

. . .

SOMETIMES RAY DROVE to the school, parked, and wrote his name in the visitors' book—like he was meant to. Walked with her in the school grounds, or down to The Plough Inn.

But also, sometimes, he met her after dark, which was not allowed. He hung in the shadows, gave a soft whistle, or he caught her wrist as she stood by Curie's door, unlocking it. *Moira?* A quick whisper, and a beckoning.

It was not all about him. Perhaps, in the first few weeks, it was—
for his skin was still settling from all that foreign heat, and he was a
good talker. Spoke as if he was confiding in her. Confessing things.
In L.A. . . .

But also, he'd say, *Tell me about* . . . Her. Moira Stone. This girl in
the tennis shoes, with the firm, solid mouth. In the car, or on the
bench, or as they sat in The Plough, with its warm, damp smell, he'd
say, *What about* . . . Boarding school. Or family. Or home—wherever
home was, for her. Or he asked about the scientific mind of hers,
because Ray's was not like that—no science in him whatsoever. And
Moira would bite her bottom lip, thinking of answers.

The school gave out scholarships.

*The heart pumps out nine thousand litres of blood a day; blue eyes are a reces-
sive gene; there are seven noble gases.*

She told him, too, about the dead frog. How it danced for her.
And she glanced across, then, at him—fearing he may laugh at her,
because what kind of strange story was that? But he didn't. He
watched her. And maybe he could see it, too—the splayed frog,
gluey-eyed, trying to swim upside down over the worktop, away from
the scalpel and back into its pond.

She thought *plop*.

With his back against the games shed, where he'd first kissed her,
he said, "Tell me about Stackpole, then." He smoked. She didn't
know he smoked, and watched him do it. His face was pink from the
cold weather, and, against the shed, he asked what she was like, in her
toddling days. "Go on." To which she exhaled, rolled her eyes, even.
Said, *Like I am now. But smaller.*

He gave her stories in return, of course—of the blond-haired boy
with his teeth braces. Who stole his brother's Beano comic. How he
spent one whole summer in the pine forest at Holkham with his
metal detector—finding tin cans, jewellery, a half-shilling piece. The

story of his father's cricket ball. Two brothers, jumping off a pier. Raymond, aged eight, in his scruffy Cub uniform.

•   •   •

So MOIRA FOUND herself being this: sharp-tongued, with her high walls. But she still listened to him, eyed him from behind her hair. Was still there to be kissed—although, once, she pushed him away from her, didn't say why, and he held his hands up, exhaled, backed away. And she tore beer-mats, and was angry when he tried to help her climb over the boundary fence by putting his left hand on her inner arm. He could have been offended by this. But he laughed, instead—openly, unashamed. "So *stubborn!*"

And she had dreams, too. For two months, she had many—and all of water, or watery things. Of puffins with eels in their beaks, and a seal's eye. A beached whale, too—its skin cracking in the sun, calling out for its pod, and for cold, green depths. And she was sitting on Church Rock, but the tide was rising—above the mussels, and the blue rope, and it crept up round her neck so that she hauled in her breath, slipped under. Sun, too, on water. So bright she had to close her eyes.

These dreams stayed with her, all day.

A slap from Heather, so that she stumbled. This, too, was a dream. But she woke with a sore face, and she walked through the corridors with fists, which made her think, *I'd have struck her back, if it had happened.* Made her pay for new glasses.

•   •   •

A RED ENVELOPE in her pigeonhole, in February. Her name on it.

She opened it in the bathroom. His name was not inside, but she knew—because who else would have sent it? She felt the soft parts of the card. Felt worried, and tender in the stomach. No Valentine's card, to give Ray. She'd decided against it; felt it was for the best.

Thought of his slightly crooked tooth, in the evening. The hand he'd placed at the back of her head, under her hair. Heather's small, fruit-bruise on her neck—long gone, now; years had passed. But she thought of it, and tucked up her legs.

Raymond.

Said his name, in her head.

• • •

THE NEXT DAY. Fifteenth February 1996.

You should know the date, Amy Stone. Who doesn't, from Stackpole? Or from Wales at all? Maybe all nations have a date that they mark in their heads, if nowhere else.

I know it, and I was four hundred miles away, cutting a thin, hidden chunk of hair from my head—as long as my forearm. Black, and sea-soft. I wrapped it in paper, put it in the kitchen bins.

I didn't hear the news until the next morning. George rang, and he sounded as if the air had left his body—breathless, weak. I saw it on the news, too. I sat in the common room, by the television, and there were birds with strings of oil stretching between their beaks when they opened them. No flight in them. Stumbling, instead, onto rocks which were also covered in it. And the fish were dead. And seals surfaced into it. And the gulls lay on blackened beaches, their wings clamped together, as if held in a hand.

The *Sea Empress* tanker spilled over seventy thousand tonnes of crude oil into the sea where I—we—had grown up, and onto our beaches, and I squatted on the common room floor in the morning afterwards, almost eighteen, with my thumb between my teeth, and I cried, and I thought, *Many things have gone.* And maybe I should have learnt, then, and remembered, that it is wrong to think anything—a place, or a feeling, or a person, or fish, or a memory, even—will not change. That my mother was so hugely, incredibly wrong, seven years before, to say that nothing alters, and that you can treat something as you chose to, and return to it later.

Nothing will change.

Cormorants floated. The tanker ran aground three times.

George said, "We're trying to help. We're cleaning them with newspaper and rags."

• • •

IT WAS RAY I went to. Sat in his orange car.

No walls, then. Not as oil floated on water. I couldn't doubt him anymore—I wanted to believe him, his every word, and every glance he gave me. I wanted honesty. To not be left. And he took my hands, which were big, and ungainly, and he could have walked away, then, from this dark-haired girl who wiped her nose on his coat sleeve, and whose sadness was a rock inside her, but he didn't. He stayed. Said no words at all. He gave me his handkerchief.

I WILL NEVER GO *back there again.*

She was certain. It was gone—truly, wholly. And she lay beside Ray in a field and mourned it. A death. A hundred thousand deaths. George's anger, and the church bells that rang along the coast, in the evenings.

Ray said to her, "Life recovers. It does."

The old Moira would have fought that. Turned away. But this Moira chose to believe in it, in all of it—in the rolling back of a dolphin, and in Ray, and to think that there were other beaches for her, now. Another life.

•   •   •

SHE MET RAY on the gravel path, in her overall. Left her school bag and books in the privet hedge and walked with him—under the poplar trees, through the sugar beet fields, to a gateway near Lockham Thorpe where he'd left his car. Late afternoon. Daffodils, and he drove her to a pub near the coast called The Rising Sun, where she drank a pint of Woodthorpe beer, and she watched how his mouth was, how he talked, and how his face creased, so that she could guess where his lines would form, when he was older than twenty. Lines by his mouth. Up on his forehead. *I am eighteen*—old enough for most things. She drank too much, and told him, whispered to him that she used to ride out to Skomer Island in a boat, with her father—puffin flight, and his beard, and how he tied her glasses on with string; that the caves had had music; that there were gulls that had perched on their roof, and where were they now? These gulls?

This was all done, now.

He moved closer, in the car. Lifted those glasses off her nose.

•

A new Moira, then. Or so it felt, to her. There was the old, creeping Moira who'd talked to a red-inked monkey on a light bulb, and who'd lain in the dark, with bats in the walls. Who'd had a choppy Atlantic in her, not a black one.

Now this girl. Or this woman, or this hybrid of both—a Moira who turned the pages of Ray's sketchbook and saw herself drawn down in it: a shoulder blade, and her turned head. Who no longer cared about Heather, or school. Who knew how Ray's knees cracked when he stood back up, how his father was dead, and how he— Ray—had jumped off a seal boat on its way out to Blakeney Point, once, when he was seven, because he'd wanted to swim with the seals. Lifebelts, and an anxious mother, calling *My boy! My boy!* Ray winced, smiling at this.

She knew how he stretched. That his feet smelt in hot weather.

The curfews were gone. Or rather, she ignored them entirely. Moira would leave the others sleeping—or half-sleeping—and climb out of the fire escape on her own, now, to find him down by the boundary fence. Hands in his pockets. And she'd return later and later. Midnight, or one. It was his car she knew the inside of—not textbooks anymore, or the nitrogen cycle. Once, she lifted the windowpane at three-thirty, as the sky was lightening and a blackbird was singing on Miss Bailey's bench. The hour of milk-floats, of foxes coming home. Her arms smelt grassy as she climbed into bed, and her hair was damp, and she only slept lightly. She dreamt of herself, turned over. She could tell, as she lay there, that the dormitory was listening, and not really asleep.

How many Moiras, now?

Miss Burke summoned her. Moira knocked on the heavy oak door, and found the headmistress standing by the window, grey-faced. Said, "Rules are not for *my* safety, Miss Stone." She talked of trust, discipline. "I'd expected better behaviour from a scholarship girl." A fortnight of detentions for Moira, after that. In the cold ground-floor room with one small window, where the spare chairs were kept.

She thought, *Heather did this.* For Heather wore a green facemask in the evening, filed her nails as she revised. Did not look at Moira.

Moira did not see Ray for seventeen days. Over two weeks. But then, there were worse things. Far worse. A gill, thick with oil. Miscarriages in wintery lanes.

She thought of Til, too, who had written to her. *I've seen it with my own eyes. Love, it is bad. But imagine it will mend . . .*

Wise enough, maybe. But Til was on the edge of madness, she said. Still troubled, sometimes, by the pilot—she'd returned to Heathrow several times over, and had now taken to sitting for hours in prominent London places—Covent Garden, a café in Oxford Circus, leaning against Eros in Piccadilly Circus in the rain—just in case he should walk past, see her there. She wore her best lipstick. Drank in the day. *Of course, I won't see him.*

He probably gives his hotel number out to all the girls.

So yes, there were worse things than detentions. Oils slicks, but this, too.

Moira replied to Aunt Til. She placed kisses at the end of her letter, in blue ink—three neat *x*'s, in a row, underlined.

*M*AYBE *I LOVE HIM.*

She didn't say this. She thought it, only. In the library, in her old chair, across the mahogany table she wondered this. Did not revise, for her final exams. It wasn't Maths that she wanted to know more about, or excel in. She'd had enough of books.

• • •

HE WANTED TO KNOW all the things that made her cry. He wanted a list, so that he would know, and so perhaps never hurt her. She brought her knees to her chest, looked over to him. They were parked at Blakeney Quay. Dark outside. She could see his hair, and part of his face.

It was hard to answer this. Or easy—for he knew of the oil, and how she'd been. But what else? The old boatyard at Pembroke—its dry dock, and the missing sea. She was sad when she thought of the Bannisters, who'd blamed themselves for the spilt candles and the loss of the unborn baby, in the half-dark, by the field of horses.

"Who?"

She spoke of the lily-ponds. Their washing line. His neat, starched bowling whites, and his green knee.

Ray smiled. "What else?"

It was so hard. What else made her unhappy? What was safe enough to retrieve? She had seen an old woman crying over a dropped bottle of brandy once. She'd watched a hostage plead for his life on the news, and she'd left the room, been haunted by his blue eyes. Moira did not like migration. A girl had fallen at Sports Day, cut her leg, and Moira's own leg had ached, at that. She did not like passing the fishmonger's stall, with its gleaming display of dead bodies, which always seemed to watch her with their jellied eyes and say, *Don't*

look at us, we're ugly. That made her weak. She always wanted to grieve
for them. She wanted to pick the fish up, run back to the sea with
them in her arms.

In the gloom of the car, Ray watched her. She could feel his
breath on the top of her arm. There was no reason, she thought, for
him to understand any of this—the sadness of fish laid out on ice,
or Moira's odd resentment of boatyards. But he seemed to. He
offered up his own list—cities, cowardice, dishonesty.

"You're very different," he said, as he drove.

Which could have meant anything at all.

• • •

HE HAD HIS FATHER'S EYES. "And his colouring. He had a mop of
hair like this, too. Never brushed it, never went bald . . ."

And he'd died when Ray was ten years old—on a night of ice, a
week before Christmas. A gritting lorry on the wrong side of the
road, and Mr Cole died there—on the tarmac, near Diss. "The
police told my grandmother. She came round, told us—my brother
and I. And I remember Stephen stood up, went into the kitchen, and
made us orange squash." He exhaled slowly at this.

Moira listened. Stephen, the solemn, practical elder brother. The
father whose ashes were scattered at Lord's cricket ground. The
mother who had survived it, the crash, although her legs were taken
from her—or rather, her walking was. She might, once, have fought
it. But she chose not to, was wheeled through life, now—Ray said
that. In a house with lowered sinks and light switches, and no stairs.

• • •

AND IT WAS in May that he began to list all her beautiful things. Or
he'd try to sketch them down—the prominent bones in her ankle, or
how she wrapped her school scarf around her ears to keep them warm,
in the sea winds. He spoke as a man far older, really, than twenty. Perhaps it was the travel in him, or the other shadowy women she did not

doubt had existed, for it can't have just been Moira. The other bras he'd slipped off. But he spoke like a poet to her—too sincerely, perhaps, too wide-eyed. She tried to believe it. *You are . . . Like a cave. Like a mermaid, with such hair.* "I didn't see this coming," he said, on the fire escape, not quite touching her. Moira did not read poems or fiction, but she felt such lines came straight out of them. He pressed paper in the palm of her hand, sometimes, which she'd unfold, later, to find the curve of her lower back and bottom in her school skirt, as she'd lain on the grass. Or her frown. He loved her ladylike ways with her peppermint tea. Even her retorts—like, *Just you try.*

He never seemed to want such compliments back. He didn't give them, hoping to receive. Perhaps he knew Moira, already. Once, only, did she try to say something to him, about him, and them, and this. She pushed her thumb against his arm. Opened her mouth to speak, but what words were there? Not the right ones. She dealt with chemicals, and the physical parts of the bodies, and he was the artist, the one with a soul, not her. So she said very little. And he'd written such things as, *I miss you. I carry you with me, I think.*

· · ·

SHE LEFT THEM ALL revising for their A-levels in their rooms, or out on the lawn, and walked, instead, through Holt—with its war memorial, and boys' school, and the dragonflies in the churchyard. He took her to a gallery with landscapes on the walls—windmills, storm clouds, geese in flight—and said, "I'll have my pictures in here, one day."

Ice creams in the High Street, and the tearoom where, once, she'd unwrapped a nightdress from Til, and pints of stout in pubs that were hidden away in small, silent villages where walls were cobbled, and chickens crept over the road. They looked at their hands, over the wooden tables. Songs on the jukebox that they listened to, knowing it was a different song for them both, now. Sipping their drinks. He listed his favourite colours to her—vermillion, aquamarine, lapis lazuli. "When I'm famous . . ." he said, in the Lord Nelson, at Burnham Thorpe, and she thought, then, if a time would come when she'd say, *I knew Raymond Cole, once*, so that people would stare, not quite believe her.

She glanced at his profile, on the way home.

• • •

By June, the weather was warmer. Lapwings in the lanes, and she found him sitting on the bonnet of his car, smiling, arms folded, saying, "To the coast, I think."

Yes. She agreed. Five years since she had made her way to Sheringham, sat on its seafront, felt tearful, lost. Since she had thought, *This is not the sea.* But maybe it was, now, because it was his—his childhood sea, and his meaning of water. She stood on the shingle ridge at Cley-next-the-Sea, and taught him how to skim stones. Watched the birds in the Cley marshes with him, and on a Sunday he drove her east to Happisburgh, where the lighthouse stood—red-and-white, and Ray said, "This is my first memory. Seeing this."

At Cromer, they played in the penny arcades, and she lost every game, sulked, which he liked, revelled in. Over ice creams, he said, "An ex-girlfriend of mine lost her keys in the sand, here. Blamed me—of course." And Moira said nothing.

Kissed him, at Blakeney. A hard kiss, and the mud of the tidal beds were thick, buttery, marked with small webbed feet. He emerged, surprised. As if she'd tried to enter him.

She kissed him again, later, outside a cottage with a yellow front door. A brass door knocker. *To Let*, it said. Hollyhocks taller than her.

• • •

On Blakeney seafront, he said, "My dad was a surgeon. Hearts, mainly. He'd sit on the stairs, take off his shoes, and tell us stories. That he'd opened up a woman and a blackbird had flown out. Or that when he removed tonsils, or an appendix, he'd hang them up on a washing line to dry. Dad said he left a man on a ward for five minutes, and when he returned there was a light. Next to the bed. Gold-coloured."

She thought, *He'd died?*

Ray didn't know what he believed. He shrugged, said, "I know his body is gone, but Dad could sing 'La Vie en Rose,' and say words backwards, and knew the batting averages of every England cricketer since 1962 when he'd queued but failed to get into Old Trafford and caught May's ball when he hit it out of the grounds, into the street." He turned to Moira, squinted. "Where does all that go?"

She moved a strand of his hair. Ray's father—young and not yet married, fair-haired, good teeth, out in the street looking skyward, the leather ball fitting, apple-like, into his hand. A polished fruit. Plucked from the air, carried home, and placed on his desk for the rest of his life. He'd have felt its seam whilst he was thinking—she decided this. His dog learnt not to chew this ball; his sons grew up reflected in it.

• • •

THIS, THEN, IS THE SEA. *How it is now.* No white breakers. No caves to step into, but she still skimmed stones, and tucked her school skirt into her underwear, waded out into it. Ray showed her the place he'd found his metal treasure, fifteen years before—in the soft, pale sand under the pine trees, near Holkham Bay. It was there, too, that, mid-kiss, he found a chunk of her hair was missing, by the nape of her neck, and he frowned. "What . . . ?"

Chewing gum, she said. A few weeks before, and she'd had to cut it out.

He fingered her hair, shrugged.

• • •

ALSO, A DRAWING of her. Chalk on black card. Half-turned away, so that he'd drawn her cheekbone, her firm Celtic jaw. The fringe she was growing out.

I wish I could let you feel the paper, smell its chalk. But it is the only lost thing of mine. My fault—I left it on the table by my bed, so Heather found it, and it was torn. A dozen black pieces when I came back from the bathroom, with one piece taken—she was always sly—so that even if I tried to mend it, it could not be.

$\mathcal{T}$HE THINGS WE DID, Amy.

Love. How many years since Annie first said the word? Before she broke her arm? *Love*—which I'd stepped over, dived under, ignored— was here, or I felt it was, and I had never been as bold as this, before. I could say, *Five months of him,* and you would think this were no time at all—as most people did. What is five months? A season, perhaps, or a little more. Six full moons, and five star signs. I did not grow taller, for all my physical growing was done, by then.

I walked down the fire escape every night. I let homework lie unanswered. Messages and letters from Stackpole everywhere, which I did not reply to, so that our mother called the headmistress in June and said, *Is she well? Working too hard?* Even Miss Burke couldn't order a girl to write to her parents, or phone.

All the things. I sat in a darkened room in Holt as a middle-aged man lifted my eyelids, shined a light in them. And I walked outside, met Ray, who stepped back, blew out his cheeks at the sight of me. Four glasses of rum mixed with cola, later—a fierce, dark drink— and he said, *I see your face better.* I couldn't see his—not clearly. It took a while. On the balls of my eyes, the two thin discs slipped in their water, shifted themselves. I felt bare, cool-skinned.

I said, *Yes.* I wanted this.

Moira without spectacles. Like an unmoored boat. Only Annie mentioned it. Looking up from her textbooks, tired, and said, Wow.

It was strange, for a long time. To not have that extra weight on her. She'd still push her glasses back up her nose, or try to, and push nothing but air.

• • •

BRAVE RAYMOND. *Raymond the Brave.* He called himself this, patting his chest, reassuringly, because in the summer evenings, he'd take her to the quieter, overgrown country lanes further inland, away from Holt, climb out of the car, and she'd take his place behind the steering wheel. "Remember," he'd say—and then a list: the clutch, neutral, first gear. Mirror positioning. Handbrake. She was poor, at first. The engine stalled, or they jolted forwards, into hedges. "The paintwork . . ."

She couldn't, for weeks. The car jumped its way under the lime trees, and she lost her temper, and when she glanced over to Ray, fire-eyed, she found him laughing behind his hand. She resented this. She pulled on the handbrake, threw the key at him. "Ouch . . ." He reasoned, still smiling. He told her she was so close, now. She had all the principles. "Gentle," he said, "with the left foot . . ."

She relented. She tried this again, lifting her foot up slowly, feeling the car move itself.

"This is it! Keep going!"

Stalled again. A song thrush darted out of the hedgerow, screaming alarms. Ray laughed. He leant back in his seat, hands loose, and laughed. For a moment, Moira was indignant. She wanted to leave the car and walk back to school. But it caught her somehow—he did, or the car did, or perhaps it was the thrush. At any rate, she pressed her forehead against the wheel, breathed.

Others lessons, too—but all better ones. And she'd pass her test quickly, in the end, in her first few weeks at Blakeney. But he'd always call her a poor driver, would ask who'd she'd scared off the road that day. *Endearing*—so he called her three-point turns, knowing it would make her scowl. He'd catch her wrists, laugh.

•   •   •

SO FIVE MONTHS. Five drawings of her—charcoal, pencil, and pen-and-ink. One of her on Holkham, burying her feet in the sand.

He said it was Providence. Not Fate, or destiny—which were cheap words. Even Moira knew this. Clichés, and as hollow as drum. But *Providence* was different, somehow. It had an adventurer's breath to it—earth, a realness, and when he said *Providence* it seemed to echo in her, or near her, as if she had heard the word, in this sense, before. She hadn't, of course. But Ray would hold up a feather, or see a patch of blue sky in the distance and hold up a finger, philosopher-like, saying, *Ah, Providence . . .* This could be seen as one of two things, she thought—a foible (he also loved this word—he seemed to keep a list of hers in his head; her peppermint tea, or how she pressed her lips together when she was thinking. Her sleeves pulled down over her hands, too), or it was an annoyance. Aunt Matilda, of course, would claim it was the former. A lovely, suitable foible. If Moira were to telephone her, tell her of him and all of this, she would nod sagely, guess his star sign.

"Leo," Ray told Moira, when she asked. "Why?"

No reason. And she pressed her lips together. And Ray drove on. Not talking of Providence, at that moment, but Moira was sure he was thinking of it. He'd said it so often. And she supposed she was knowing him now, too—his foibles. (He walked purposefully; he invented songs; he tugged the bristles on his chin when thinking; he wrote on his leg, once, when he was drunk, so that he woke in the morning to find the words *Ray you are drunk* in biro.) And this worried her, at night.

● ● ●

HIS HAND moved over hers, and under. She watched how they looked together—his fingers, and hers.

He talked to her of love one night. So openly and unafraid that she could not look at him at all. She stood in the bathroom, later. The world was turning, and she was in it. *At last.*

It was early June.

• • •

THE FINAL EXAMS. The polished gym floor, again, and the red second hand on the clock. The lawnmower bouncing over the running track, and she could smell it. Casually wrote down the answers in ink.

And elsewhere in the world, hummingbirds were migrating, sipping from the same flowering plant as they had six months before; magma was inching under the earth; Amy was seven, and had learnt why cats were not to be pulled by the tail, or held near the face. Rita was in Sri Lanka, rinsing her hands, maybe; somewhere in Yorkshire, a man in his late thirties was missing his mixed-doubles partner.

As for Til, nothing was very different, yet. In the evenings, she was Madame Ranevsky in *The Cherry Orchard*, and by day she'd sleep, or buy huge African jewellery from Camden Market. Once, she took the tube out to Heathrow and sat all afternoon by passport control with a book in her lap, just in case. With her eyeliner on, and a wristful of gold.

But he wasn't there. She headed back to the city at five, and was back on stage at seven-thirty. She wrote, *Don't get like your crazed aunt, Moira. Just come and visit her, once in a while, when she's locked up and babbling . . .*

That small gem in her letter. Humour. In the dormitory's half-dark, it sparkled.

Moira smiled. Still, a sadness was in it.

She thought, *There is not one, wide happiness that reaches us all, at the same time.* No such luck as that. She wrote the word *Ray* in steam on glass, and had discovered contact lenses—whilst Matilda trailed her emptiness over the stage, like her skirts, like her citrus smell.

*Y*ou know this, because you asked for the story so many times. And it's late now, but I will tell you again:

The boardwalk, at Cley marshes. A wide, blue-sky day. Exams were over. I walked with Ray in the bird reserve there, not hand in hand, but close to him. Black-tailed godwits, and avocets. Ray talked of the time he had come here, as a boy, and seen a water-vole, swimming neatly, under the boards. Paws, and a lifted nose.

He asked me on the shingle beach at Cley-next-the-Sea, by the upturned boat. And I closed my eyes before answering. I felt the sun on my face, smelt the seaweed. The herring gulls called above me, and there was salt, and did it matter that I was only eighteen? That we had known each other for only a few months? Some would think so. Some would say to me, *You are still a child.*

He said to me, "Moira?"

So hard to imagine forever. So hard to imagine me as a wife, doing wifely things. I'd never thought to be asked, at all. And by Ray?

On the shingle, I thought, *A wife.*

It was simple enough. I loved him. I chose his life. I left the oil and caves and Stackpole behind me, nodded. Said, *Yes.*

We walked back down the boardwalk, passing the same people, the same wading birds. It was all laid out before me now. *Ray.* A new surname.

I wore a ring with a proper sapphire on it.

13

Beacons

It's a dark-blue evening sky across this city.

Your window faces east, so there isn't a sunset from here. But I can see the clouds, and the city's silhouette. Steeples, and trees, and homes; offices. All the lives. The cars move, and the streetlights are as orange as fire, or more so, and I am standing here now, two days after I last came, with my arms folded, listing all these things to you: the streetlights, and the stray dog in the car park, with its low, sideways movement. If we were down there with it, you and I, we'd hear its claws on the ground.

I will always admit to Heather's beauty. I did, even then. She was not kind to me—I do not talk, here, of kindness. But her face alone was beautiful, and is probably more so as the years pass—although I have no idea where she is now. I'm more forgiving, perhaps. For once, her looks were poison-cold, but I have the talent of seeing her twice, these days: with my teenage eyes, and also with these older, slower ones. She was brazen, cruel; or she was just a girl who wanted to feel better than she did, inside. A creature to like, then. To feel for. She had a sharp, silvery tongue, and she filled my bed with grass cuttings, but I broke her heart, I suppose—if you can ever imagine that. Or Ray broke it. Or we both did.

Me. As a breaker of hearts. Even Til missed that, in her cards.

Either way, Heather had the mouth that Egyptians would have painted on urns, or the Greeks would have named a god after. She knew this, too. All that pink gloss.

There are other people that I think of far more often than her— Annie, for example. Miss Bailey's parents, whom I never met, but I saw, once, sitting on their daughter's bench—elderly, soft-bodied, holding hands and wiping their noses. I do think of Heather, sometimes, though. *Beanpole. Chicken tits.*

Still. He chose me. I don't know why. Maybe because I didn't wear lip gloss, or try too hard, or give in too easily. Or because I threw back my hair, and then hid behind it. Or it was my brain. Or it was my eyes, which he saw his reflection in. I was a challenge, I know that much. Or maybe we were fated. Providence.

Anyway, he chose me—by the upturned boat called the *Mary-Jane.* My pockets full of flat stones.

The *Sea Empress?* You'd know better than me. You still found oil on rocks, years on. Even now, perhaps, although Ray was right—life does recover. And had that tanker run aground two weeks later, there'd be no birds on Skomer at all, now. Very hard to see any good in it—but truthfully, it could have been worse.

The city is drawing its curtains, and lighting its fires. Its fat, hearthside cats are settling down, licking their paws and dozing. You sleep, too. As tiny as a mouse.

I've known this view for years, yet I don't often stand by it, watch it, as I'm doing now. I like my views—you've learnt that, I think.

A ball of starlings rolls across the sky.

· · ·

YOU WERE SEVEN YEARS OLD, in the summer I left Locke Hall. Demanding. Our parents kept you away from the oil, but you knew enough. You'd heard the stories in Stackpole school, and wailed. Stayed away from the beaches, and lay, instead, in the garden in the afternoons, in the hope that the rabbits would think you were furze, and hop over you. Nibble the grass by your ear. Which they didn't, of course.

And know this, too: you were not shocked. The only person, Amy, who did not hold their breath, and say, *What?* "Moira's getting married!"—you chanted it. This was how our parents heard the news, so that they were all air and mouth at the end of the phone—grappling with words such as *Really?* and *No . . .* George said, "How has this happened?" Because I was the strange daughter; because I'd never breathed a word of a man, till now. He asked if I was sure. And I was the cool, indignant, unreachable voice. I said, *Love*, which was not a lie. That was my answer, and I put down the phone.

Even Aunt Til was surprised. She surveyed her niece over a table in The Plough, through her thickened eyelashes. Blue half-moons under her eyes. No questions in her, or none that she asked. But she smiled—wide, delighted. Said yes, it was right. Said, "This makes sense, actually."

At Locke, Annie found out. The last week of term, and she caught a blue flash, in the dormitory. She said nothing, but stretched out, reached through the darkness for Moira's left hand. She took her wrist.

Later, Annie tried the ring. Side by side on Moira's bed, she took it and pushed it down onto her third finger. It did not fit. It sat above the first knuckle, glinting. She held out her hand, fingers splayed.

Annie thought of him, then, or so Moira supposed. *Him.* A faceless man. Impassioned, and brave. The man who would, one day, push Annie's own ring onto her finger, say the words to her. Or at least, Annie hoped he would.

•   •   •

RAY MET HER in the entrance hall, as he had done a few months before. Said, "Look at you . . ."

She was nervous. Caught her reflection in the glass doors as she walked through them—neat, she supposed, with a navy skirt, a white blouse. School cardigan over her arm. She did not look like herself at all. She had no swimmer in her, as she climbed into his car, folded her legs in their rough, strange tights. She thought of the blue nylon rope.

They drove east, to Norwich, and he explained the music on the radio. "Listen to this part"—and she did. Turned it up. He told her that he'd first heard this music—drumming, and bells—in Thailand, of all places. Incense and frangipani.

I am engaged. Ray beside her—all words and energy, fingers tapping in time. Norwich cathedral in front of her, pale in the sunlight.

June—the month of early roses, dandelion clocks. Pink-edged water-lilies at Stackpole's pools. Sports Day at Locke Hall, with orange squash and applause. Wimbledon.

Also, it was her name—Ray's mother. *June*—who liked bone china teacups, and whose feet rested tidily on the step of her wheel-chair. No hint of her son in her—so Ray said. Moira saw this. She supposed he was more his father's child. A man who'd cut bodies open, clamped tissues. Swabbed blood.

She lived in a white bungalow in a quiet street. Red geraniums by the door. She was dark-haired, with hands as quick as birds, and she said to Moira, "So. We meet at last." Clear, grey eyes. June smiled without showing her teeth, and she eyed every part and gesture—the glasses, the long fringe, the blue veins on her wrist. She asked about Stackpole. George's job. Moira thought, *She is handsome.* The doctor's wife with the challenging eyes. An elegant figure at her old cocktail parties.

"I hear you're a scientist, Moira?"

It was hard to imagine this woman wiping crayon from the walls, or approving of drunken words on her son's leg. She drank her tea. The crossword lay beside her. Photographs of two boys in every room, in silver frames—one dark, one white-haired. When she kissed Raymond goodbye, she kept her eyes on Moira, and smelt of violets when Moira leant down to her cheek.

• • •

THERE WERE TIMES when she wanted to bring him into her small dormitory bed with her, to sleep with her head on the groove that ran down from his chest to his navel, and one arm underneath him, even if it meant that her blood slowed, and her arm would feel lost in the morning. Only four days until she left Locke for good. She wanted to walk its corridors and gravel paths with Ray. Her days were empty, and so she packed her clothes and books away. She sat on the roof with the smokers. Looked up into the walnut tree.

But then, sometimes, she was glad he was not. *Seven years of my life have been spent in here.* So perhaps it was right that she walked it alone, saying goodbyes. To the tiled floor of the changing rooms. To the metal trays in the dining hall, and the shrill bell, and the forlorn, eyeless girl of stone in the courtyard, with her empty jug.

She knocked on the infirmary door, left a farewell note on the desk. Polished the plaque on Miss Bailey's bench with her breath, and her sleeve. Wrote down Annie's home address inside *Further Mathematics.*

"I didn't think I'd ever miss here, but I will," said Jo.

Moira watched her. Thought, *I will never see you again.* She decided she would always remember Jo as she was at this moment—on the path, crouching, tying her shoelace, with a bruise on her left hand from a stray tennis ball.

• • •

ON THE THURSDAY AFTERNOON, she walked through the midges on the gravel path, pushed the door, climbed the science block's stairs, and knocked quietly on the Biology door. Mr Hodge looked up, a watering can in his hand. "Ah," he said.

She sat on a desk, sat on her hands, watched him feed the rubber plant. Then she followed him through the laboratory, past the fish. He talked of her skill, her good science brain. "Don't waste it," he said, over his glasses. "Think of university, won't you? Next year, perhaps?" With a click of his tongue, he added, "One of my best."

She reached in her pocket, then, and handed a small gift to him, wrapped in brown paper. He paused. Blinked. Put down the watering can, and unwrapped it gingerly. A tie with skeletons on it. He bunched his lips, smiled. Eyes shining.

Goodbye to the science room. To the three goldfish, her overall, and the plastic bones hanging by the door, which she touched, briefly, on her way out.

• • •

THREE NEAT RINGS. They called out in the hallway of a house in South Wales, where herring gulls hunched on the roof. Moira sat in the corridor, and saw this. Smelt the furze through the kitchen window. Then, on the fourth ring, her mother answered the phone.

"Love," she said. Slow, breathy. She sighed it, as if grateful. *Love . . .*

Moira looked at the wall. Talked of Ray, and their plans. Of the cottage with the yellow door in Blakeney, and its brass knocker, and his mother. She picked at the hem of her skirt. Didn't they see that Stackpole was too far—hundreds of miles—to go? Ray was busy. Painting hard. And she was busy, too. No time.

"We could come to you, then? Meet him in Norfolk?"

They'd marry soon, anyway. Why didn't they just wait for that?

• • •

MOIRA TURNED HER BACK on all the words she did not like: *income, young, university.* She didn't want to hear them. Instead, on a night in July, when she was newly engaged, Moira watched the Knox cousins crouch out on the running track, and light a rocket they had bought from Holt. It burst—a soft, silvery pop, and the school was lit up by it. The windows, and the clock tower. All of the Sixth Formers—whooping, dancing on the grass, and Moira thought of the younger, homesick girls watching this from their dormitories. Thinking, *One day* . . .

She decided this: fireworks smelt of the future, as cherries had done, as tennis made her think of a blonde, dead woman, and airmail paper led her to Ray. These things always would. It faded, the firework, and fell away beyond the poplar trees.

• • •

I SAID GOODBYE. To the sundial, and the poplar trees. The silhouette of the school from the village, in summer evenings. The bats, in the wall.

And the leavers' party? I'm sure you would like to know about that. My dress? What I drank? If I danced? If Ray came? Let it go. Because if you were to wake, go to a computer, and trawl through Locke's records in search of the photograph from that year, you'd see dozens of girls in thigh-length black dresses (save for Heather—she was in red, with a gold underskirt)—but you'd not see my face there. I didn't go. I had better places. I doubt I was missed, and I didn't miss being there at all. Can you really see that Moira at a party? In the school hall? Paper stars and lemonade?

She was in the orange car, of course. On the quayside at Brancaster Staithe, with her husband-to-be, and the sound of ducks settling for the night.

*T*HEY PUSHED THEIR KEY into the yellow front door. *Ready?*
He watched her, as she wandered through the rooms, feeling the
beams and the flagstones, opening windows. Breathing. Moving her
hand down the wooden bedstead. She liked it.

"Enough?"

Yes, enough. It was small, warm. There was a silence to it. It had
a deep bath, and a greenhouse for Raymond to draw in. A view from
their bedroom of Blakeney's rooftops, the masts of boats, and tidal
creeks. A wooden drying rack above the bath, so that as Moira lay
beneath it in the evenings, their clothes dripped quietly into the
water, onto her head, and knees.

• • •

BLAKENEY VILLAGE lay to the west of Cley-next-the-Sea, on the
coast road, by the salt marshes. Its two streets were small, narrow.
There were cobbled houses, hollyhocks, a gift shop in the summer
months. A tearoom, two pubs. She leant back against the railings on
the quayside, looked at the hotel. She imagined the view from its top
room.

This is home, now. White railings, and white quayside benches. At
high tide, the boats clinked on their moorings, and the crab-fishers
came; at low tide, its mud was dark-coloured, firm, and birds stalked
over it, sifting for lugworms.

And a wide, low sky. She walked beneath it when she walked
along the coastal path. Cley windmill to the east, and sea lavender
underfoot, and she said *home*, over and over. It would be. Her third
home, perhaps, and like the others, she wanted to walk through it. So
in the early summer evenings, when the tourists were drifting back to
their holiday homes, and as Ray painted, or stood in the kitchen with

coloured hands, she wandered the two streets on her own—past the
terraced cottages with shells on their walls, their tiny front gardens.
The slight smell of the dustbins, after a week of sun. Drainpipes
creaked. She read the menus of the pubs, sat on benches, viewed the
village from the coastal path. Moira, in a white blouse and a linen
skirt to the knee.

"Well?" he'd say, as she came in. "What did you see?"

The church on the hill had two towers to it, and children sat on
the quayside in the sunshine, with buckets of crabs beside them. Out
on the main road, in Cley, there was a shop that sold spices, fresh
apple juice, Norfolk wine and samphire, rosemary bread and quail
eggs, and she'd wander down there sometimes, in the years to come,
buy a new, strange thing to eat, with her husband, or on her own. A
month into their married life, Ray came indoors to find his wife in
her pyjamas, eating gorse honey out of the jar with a spoon.

• • •

HAPPY NEW HOME. She opened the card to see three names written
there. A note, too, from her mother, in which she said the hamster
had died. A sad, peaceful demise—found stiff as a spoon in his food
bowl, a dried pea in his paw. *The tears* . . . she'd written. Amy in black.
Crying at school. Leaving sunflower seeds by his grave, just in case.

• • •

SHE DIDN'T always walk the coast alone. Not in the first, few weeks,
for although Ray sketched in the greenhouse, and the bedroom, he
never did for long. "You," he said, sternly, "are a distraction." And the
pencil or paintbrush would be laid down.

Too much was new. Too many things were still to be learnt, and
explored—the pub's beer selection; the wading birds; the man called
Gordy who sailed out, to the seals, and who remembered Ray from
his childhood. She learnt about Ray's dramatic sneezes. How it was
to lie in bed with somebody else—even that, for when had she ever

done this before? To wake, and see him. Also, to watch his back, and
the shape of it, as he led the way along the sea wall—past the bones
of a boat. "I hid in there, once," he said. As a boy. Patches on knees.

Summer evenings on mudflats. The birds coming in, and Ray, to
hear them with. Locke was a thousand years ago, and she felt she
viewed him differently, now. She didn't have to glance, quickly, at the
mark on his collarbone, where he'd fallen on scissors; she could study
it. Bring a lamp over, as if she were a scientist, peer over her glasses
at the scar. Memorise it. Its shape, and texture. And he did this with
her, too—seizing her ankle as she sat on a bench to look for the prick
that the weaver fish made, all those years ago.

He'd cook—for she was poor at it. Felt the heat too much, par-
ticularly this summer month, so she'd lean against the fridge and
watch him. Raymond. Sieves and butter, and a recipe book held open
with stones from the shingle ridge.

"A masterpiece . . ."

And he did not smoke very much, but when he did, it was on the
back step of the cottage, barefoot. And he kept a handkerchief in his
back pocket—a white, cotton one—which surprised her, and which
she thought of, for a while, because it seemed . . . What? Safe. Old-
fashioned. *Practical?* he asked, feigning offence. He only used soap in
his hair. Strands of it, in her hairbrush.

Moira, you are . . .

This, still. But more things, now—*a well. A thing to drink.* He loved
her hair, and grasped it, breathed it in. Singled out a coot picking over
the mud and said, *That. That's you.* Because of her big ungainly feet. And
she sulked, next to him, which he smiled at, head back. The sun on
him. The coot, and the white bench, and a blue stone on her ring.

• • •

THEY HAD TO TALK of money, sooner or later.

"If there are to be weddings and honeymoons. Food. Baths for
you . . ."

Eighteen and twenty-one, and they had sat at the kitchen table one night with wine, a pen and notepad, worked it out as if they were middle-aged. Moira the accountant—her savings, his savings, and the money left to Ray by his dead father.

"I'll sell a painting," he said. Tapped his forehead. "Positive thinking . . ."

She nodded.

And so two weeks after moving into the cottage with hollyhocks as tall as her, he moved out into the greenhouse. His radio, his pencil tucked behind his ear. And she'd leave him there, walk the coastal path alone, again. Or she'd stand by the kitchen sink and watch him—his light-blue shirt, wild-haired. How he pulled his lower lip, when thinking. Sometimes, too, she'd join him—slide the door open, sit on the stool, and watch. *Dawn—East Africa. Hervey Bay.* How the jars of tap water turned to mushroom-grey.

• • •

WIFE. OR I will be.

Moira took a job in Cley, in the shop that sold fresh apple juice and eggs. Wore a white apron, and her hair pinned back. Came back home to her painter with a single plum, or a slice of cake.

And as she cut Binham Blue cheese, or weighed strawberries, he painted on. Faster, and deeper—as if he was full, and his seams were undoing themselves. So that she'd lean against the door of his house of glass, and say nothing at all, but in her head she'd think, *Come inside.* Or *It's late.* And mostly, he'd know she was thinking this. Lock it all up, and follow her indoors, talking of paint. Of colours.

A month, now, since Locke.

"I love you," he said. Late at night, she surfaced from the bath to find him crouching there. Socks drying above their heads. A smell of turpentine.

• • •

MOIRA CARRIED a shoulder bag of leaflets and posters that said *Raymond Cole. Local artist.* A photograph of him, and *Dawn—East Africa,* and his telephone number, prices—*commissions taken.* Reddish stubble on his jaw.

She pushed shop doors so that bells rang. Placed leaflets on counters, pressed them into windows, talked of Ray, or tried to. Curled her hair behind her ear.

Cafés, pubs, the pottery in Cley, guesthouses. She did her best. She clipped leaflets under windscreen wipers. Left them in phone boxes. Taped them onto telegraph poles, handed them out on Blakeney Quay, thinking all the time, *He is mine,* and she walked west along the coast to Morston village, left them in the seafood shop. In church porches. Through letterboxes.

She caught the sun on her scalp, so that her head ached, later.

"My errand boy," he said, as she walked inside with an empty bag. Winced, when he saw the reddened skin under hair. Said, "Moira . . ." She thought of standing under a cold shower, so that her scalp hissed, and the heat was gone. But, then, she heard a noise. Out in the garden. *Who?*

He grinned. "We have a guest." Took her by the hand.

A taller man. Not white-haired, like Ray was. But there was grey by his temples. Dark eyes. Not yet thirty.

June is in him. She saw this, in the way he held his glass, nodded. Fanned away a wasp, listened to his brother with his head on one side.

He said, "So how are you liking it, Moira?" She didn't know what he meant by this—life on this coastline? Or with Ray? Or the weather? "We used to catch boats out to the seals from here. One time . . ."

Stephen's hair was dark, thinning at the crown. Smaller hands than his brother—neater, too, with no charcoal on them. He kept these hands in his pockets as he followed Ray through the house, exploring it, bending to look out of windows. Two brothers. She saw no likeness. Never saw likenesses anywhere. Tried to imagine them

fighting, or digging a hole on a beach. Waking on Christmas mornings. Stephen making orange squash.

He worked with numbers; he lived in a flat above Norwich market, and worked by its railway station. He picked the label of his beer
bottle. Looked at Moira sideways, as Heather used to do. Said that
Venice's water was meant to be green, and pungent, which Ray shook
his head at.

"No—not true."

Moira left them, and showered. Filled her hair with water.

Later, once Stephen had gone, she said to Ray that they weren't
alike, that she couldn't tell they were brothers.

Ray nodded. He'd heard that before. "He said yes, though."

•   •   •

YES? TO WHAT? I didn't understand that.

Ray's idea, then—so you know. For the day after Ray asked his
brother to be his best man at our wedding, you sent an ugly, useless
thing in the post—dried pasta, and wool, glued onto a card, and a photograph of you, in new shoes. Pink, with a buckle. Ray had never seen
you before. He'd only heard my few, small stories—worm-coloured,
short. He'd called you *lovely*. "Will she be bridesmaid?" he said.

And what else could I have replied, to that? You, too, were hoping for this, and our parents were expecting it, and what reason, could
I give, for turning it down? How could I tell the truth to them, and
you—that I was still bitter? Still wished you were gone, or hadn't
been made? So jealous of you, I suppose. But not even I could say
that. Besides—who else would I have had, as bridesmaid? So I asked.
You said nothing at all to me, but you dropped the phone. I heard it
bang against the wall, and far away, out in the Stackpole garden,
maybe, I heard you shout it. *Guess what!*

You shouted this, too, when I telephoned Stackpole with my A-level
results, a week later. *Guess what!* Five A-grades, without even trying, so
that Miriam said, "Oh my love . . . !"

"You could go to any university you wanted to . . ." Ray said, head to one side, feeling a strand of my hair. But I wanted nothing like that. No desks or libraries. No more turning of pages, or ink pens, or looking over the tops of books, out of windows.

This, also, was the summer in which two children—your age; seven—were washed away at Brancaster, stolen off the beach by a quick, unseen wave. Currents and undertows. It was on the radio, and Ray and I stood on the quay at Blakeney, shielding our eyes, watching the helicopter pass overhead.

I confess this: I knew they had gone. Torches swept the water, but inside me, in the deepest part, I thought of a dead seagull I had seen, long ago, and oil, and the crumbled earth at Happisburgh. And I wondered where they would end up. If, at low tide, I'd see a yellow swimsuit half-buried in the mud.

So I walked the coastal path with them in mind—siblings, their shoes left high on the beach with their socks tucked inside them. And it was their vanishing that took me into St Nicholas's church at Blakeney, for the first time. A strange act, for me. But I chose it, and I sat in the half-dark of it, with a pigeon flapping in the eaves, and a tray of geranium seedlings for sale, by the door.

I didn't pray, or write my name neatly in the prayer book—I knew they had drowned, were dead. But I sat in a pew, all the same.

Later, that night, I said, *OK*.

He put down his book, propped himself up on his elbow. He said, "Are you sure? Really sure?"

It felt right, to marry there. Where else was there? Stackpole was gone; Lockham Thorpe had always been a lonely, overcast place. At least there was a view, here. An octagonal font, and red geraniums. The ghost of Raymond, squirming as a baby, being christened, as I once had been. His father's coffin, its polished wood.

*T*IL CAME. Left the diesel fumes and drove north, parked her car on the quayside, by the coastal path, next to the hut that said *Cockles for Sale*. She wore a scarf over her hair. Her lipstick as dark as a heart.

He said his name, shook her hand. *Ray.*

"Well done," Til whispered to me, later. Winking.

· · ·

THEY DROVE to Titchwell, as they always did—but three of them, now. Two women, with hair past their shoulder blades, and a blond-haired man with his bare arm resting on the car door, talking of legends, old truths. Of the glass-blowing, and the phantom of a black dog that stalked the shoreline, between Cromer and Overstrand. The disgraced reverend who became a lion tamer, and was eaten, later, by the lion. Til was shocked, delighted at this. "Eaten?" She thought of this story all day.

Avocets, eider ducks, redshanks. A cream tea, afterwards, in a hotel on the main road. Til's turn to talk—she listed her plays, shrugged. "I knew of a girl—an understudy—who put laxative in the leading lady's camomile tea. Got her role."

"There's a story," Ray said, stirring the pot of tea.

And Moira wondered if there had ever been a pilot at all, or a Hamlet, or she'd imagined both of them, because Til seemed bright, and happy, and it was hard to think that she was over forty, now—leaning over the teapot, with her rose quartz necklace swinging, and her eye make-up on. Laughing with Ray. Talking of art, and his sea air.

Dinner in The Sticky Prawn, in Wells. A view of the harbour from it, and Ray in a brown shirt which caught the reddishness in the hair on his jaw. His favourite painting? His ambitions? Til asked him these things, and Moira thought, *I have never asked this.*

That night, in the spare room, amongst the canvasses and science books, Til unpacked her bag. Placed her boots at the end of her bed. "Moira—he looks at you as if you're a *queen* . . ." Holding her hands up in the air. Also, she counted things off, on her fingers—his humour, talent, the kindness in him. How, in the kitchen, they had moved around each other like dancers, or trees. In time to a music she couldn't hear herself, but hoped to. Or she had heard it before, and lost it, somewhere in Miami.

She will pass all of this on. To the three people in Stackpole, who still ate their meals at a table meant for four. Amy had told Moira this. How she sat opposite the empty chair and her legs were long enough, now, to reach it with the tips of her toes.

•   •   •

SHE CHOSE an off-white dress, from a shop in Norwich. Off-white shoes. And, since it was to be an autumn wedding, she'd hold a bunch of sea aster. June frowned at this. "Sea aster?"

I'm here. Standing in the kitchen. Sitting in the tearoom, looking over the reeds. Ray hung his paintings in a shop window, booked a weekend in Venice with money from his dead father, and Moira sat in the bath or pulled up her fur-lined hood, on the coast. *Six months ago . . . Last July . . .* The quiet school infirmary, and the snow-globe in her pocket as she stepped onto the scales, and the sundial, and the pheasants that slunk under the boundary fence. She unfolded her air-mail letters, in the room. She imagined these words as they had been, for the first time, in her dormitory—*cassowary, Malibu*—and she thought, too, of the other Moira, the studious one, who'd cried in the shower, and marked her arms, talked to a red-inked monkey on a light bulb, and who'd had such a proud, stubborn soul in her that she'd found herself, stranded. No real friends. Confiding in a skeleton, and a pumpkin field.

I will be married.

Clutched him, in bed. Gripped him, with her fingernails, or what short nails she had.

• • •

"MARRIED . . ." her mother said. "I can't believe it. You didn't cry when you were born. You just slipped out, and . . . Well. Now, you're getting *married*."

And on the telephone, in October, Miriam talked of love. She talked of the man who'd helped her onto a red London bus, two decades ago, and who she had married, and how she had never regretted a second of it. "Not once!"

Said, too, how the happiest moment in her life had not been her wedding day, or meeting George on a London bus. But it was Moira. "Your birth. And that's the truth of it."

• • •

As FOR JUNE, she seemed less sure. "Impulsive Raymond," she said, smiling, her hand on her collarbone. Maybe it was because her own love had been broken up by a gritting lorry. But she sat in her chair by the garden, eyed the foxgloves, and said, "I have always loved my sons, Moira. With every breath in me. I would walk over fire, cut my own wrists, or cut someone else's, for my sons."

HAT NEEDS TO BE TOLD, of the day itself? You were there. Pink-dressed, with a white sash. Saving confetti from drains. I gave you my bouquet of sea aster, and you walked under the trees with it. *One. And two. And . . .* Remember?

I see it as if I was not there. Is this how it is, with brides? I see our mother, crouching down to her shoe. The vicar catching his gown on a nail. Til cried, and there were strangers by the church gate, watching, and Ray called me his wife, as we stood there, pressed the word into my palm like a jewel. *Wife.* A very certain word. Or I can tell you of the fishing boat, and how blue the lifeboat station seemed to be, in the sunlight, on Blakeney Point.

We stood on grass cuttings, in the evening. The hotel grounds were lit with torches, staked into the earth. Our father took my hand, danced with me, and Stephen drank too much, crossed the room at midnight, spoke to me as he shouldn't have done. Touched my inner arm. Said, *Remember I told you that.* The second tower of the church was lit up, as it always was, and Ray drew me down on a white paper napkin, which I still have—in a box, with his letters, and his lake of flamingos—and you, Amy, fell asleep on the grass, hidden by a tablecloth, so that no one found you until you wandered inside, cold, sleepy, past midnight, with damp confetti in your hand.

14

The House of Glass

"You have," he decided, "Italian blood in you."

No.

It was all Scottish and Welsh, and she told him this. She'd told him it before. But three days after their marriage, and for the first time in her life, her skin darkened. She didn't notice until she peeled off her dress that night, to find white marks on her. Thin, white lines. She turned slowly. She pressed her browner skin, testing it. "See?" Ray said, behind her. This was what he meant, then—that despite her whiteness, she did not always burn. Moira had grown to look as if she could live there, in Venice, but he, of course, hadn't done. Not with his blond hair, and the reddish eyelashes, and the new freckles on his forearms and knees.

• • •

They walked. When they weren't lying down, they were walking—along the Calle dei Fabbri, through *campi*, to Piazza San Marco. They explored the Frari, where Titian was buried; they spent a whole morning in the market in Rialto, buying silk and oil and a huge, yellow artichoke that they ate, later, in their room. There were eels, too, in jars. And on the bridge Ray said, "Even you must think this is beautiful . . ." She looked down the Grand Canal, at the sunlight on it.

This was Venice, as she'd imagined it. The quiet mornings, the whitish stone. Casanova's town. Where Cardano solved cubic equations, lived his sad life. Painters, too—so Ray said. "Lots of them! Veronese, Leonardo . . ." Titian's plump, bright-haired women that she'd seen, in his dark-red book. It was here, she thought, in these alleyways. Ray was always glancing up, and Stephen was wrong, because there were not many tourists here, in late October, and no green water.

The streets were empty, at night. Only sleepless people, cats, and Moira and Ray walked down them. Full of thoughts, and yet they talked of the unimportant things—wine, and handwriting; the best sport. She held his hand. They heard their voices on the walls, those cats, and the knocking of canal water against the walls. Ray paused, when he saw light on the water, or the shadows in it. Said, "Look . . ." Ever the painter. And she'd see such things, too, but in her own, different way. Ray saw the moss on the corner of buildings, the blue of her wrist; she saw angles of brickwork.

Ray teased her. A brain of maths, and Latin names.

One night, after a dinner over a bottle of wine and white napkins in San Polo, they rose, walked away. He paused at a bridge, and she did not. So Moira found herself in an alleyway, without her husband. He called out for her. Somewhere in the streets behind her she heard him say, *Moira . . . ?* Coaxing, like an adult to a child. She felt alive, then. Different. Married, in Venice, and darting into backwaters. Once, he stepped right past her. She could smell his skin. She flattened herself into the shadows, holding her breath.

It took him an hour to find her. Sitting by the fountain in a silent square, unflustered, with her legs crossed. Two in the morning. He approached her slyly. "That," he said, smiling, "is an unfair sport."

She moved, but he shook his head, caught her by the belt. They walked back to their hotel together.

Music, too, at night. They undressed in their room, and it came to her—guitars, and a soft voice of some kind. It intrigued her. She'd lean over their balcony in her underwear, looking for café lights, or the musicians. A cellar bar. In the morning, she asked the hotelier if he knew this music, where it came from. But he blinked at her. A popping of the lips, a wide shrug. *I do not know . . .*

Candlelit dinners, browsing in shops. Shared baths in a porcelain tub with copper-stained taps and glasses of wine. She tried to draw him once. He read in a chair, his left ankle resting across his right knee, one arm loose by his side, and she sat childishly on the bed, drew. But it was poor. She didn't see shadows, as he did. She lost her patience, tore the paper up.

"Does it really matter?" he said.

It mattered—because Venice was for drawing, for painters, and it was impossible for her husband (she tried that word so many times, there, as if it were a country. *Husband.* On the water taxis, and in churches) to spend an hour in that city and not want to pause, sketch something down. His sentences tailed away. He'd hold Moira back on a bridge, or a corner. By the Ca' d'Oro on Sunday he took a pencil from his bag and said, "Just give me five minutes . . ." But those five minutes were nearly two hours, in the end. She shifted, closed her eyes; she looked down at her shoes, pushed her toes up against their laces. Two hours. He apologised to her. Made it up to her later. And it would prove worth it, in the following year, for his wide, sunlit painting of the House of Gold, with gondolas, would be one of his best, and quickly sold to a man whose heart was cracked open there, by an Italian woman he wouldn't name.

• • •

THEY SENT POSTCARDS from Venice. They wrote to everyone who'd come to their wedding—thanking them, writing *Love Ray and Moira*, and adding kisses, as married couples do. This was done on terraces, over cappuccinos. She wrote to her parents that she was sitting in front of the basilica; to Til, she mentioned pigeons. *People drop seed on their heads, and so wear flapping pigeon hats* . . . She knew that Til would like this.

As for Amy, she was told about the alley-cats. Ray then added the Lido's sandy beaches, chocolate cakes, and that gondoliers really did sing, puffed up, in black waistcoats. He also wrote, *Well done.* For she had not stumbled in church, or giggled, or cried.

Her parents were told of the hotel, and the food. Ray wrote three pages to Stephen, in real ink. Brotherly love, she supposed; a groom indebted to his best man. She drank her coffee, watched the pigeons on the rooftops, felt the length of her hair.

Ray said to her, over the coffee cups, "You know, it is far better, the second time around."

He meant being here—Venice. He meant, he said, that to be here with Moira was a thousand times better than being on his own. Eighteen months ago, with a rucksack, and a leaking pen.

"It was a different city, then," he said.

She'd been different too, then. In her world of head-lice checks and frog dissection. On her own, in her single dormitory bed.

• • •

ON THEIR LAST NIGHT, she asked to stay there. To not go home.

They had both drunk too much. They were in a restaurant in the Castello, where the tablecloth was dark-green and there were lights in the trees above them—coloured bulbs, tied to branches. She leant back in her chair. Their fourth night, and she wore a grey dress that revealed the thin white lines on her shoulders, the nape of her neck. He'd put his hand there, as they'd walked over bridges.

He replied, "Home?"

To their Blakeney house. With the yellow door.

The sideways smile. He considered this, rolled his wine around in his glass. "And what would we do? Serve coffee? Blow glass?"

Ray would paint. Moira, she told him, would knead pizza dough.

He thought she was joking, which she was, of course. This couldn't be done. There was his mother to think of. Money, visas, the shop in Cley. She was a poor cook, too. But she imagined it: a Venetian apartment. Window shutters. An apron, and yeasty smells. Maybe much later, a sun-tanned child. She knew Ray would soak the language up, through his pores, because he was so full of words—but she was not, so that she'd have no choice but to buy things with gestures, alone. And he would paint—using cobalt blue and azure and vermillion. His titles would be *Accademia by Night. San Marco Viewed from Salute. Ghetto.*

She drained her glass.

Ray said, *"L'amo. Andiamo a letto."*

She paused, uncoded this. She found the words *bed*, and *Let's*, in the phrasebook. Blushed.

She woke early on their last morning. Moved out on the balcony wrapped in a sheet. Venice, before the lovers and artists and gondoliers. Sun on the rooftops. A man swept slowly beneath her. There were starlings drinking from a gutter of the house across the street, and she watched this.

She told no one. But she would think of it in the years to come, as she walked over shingle or waited in the cloisters—believing she'd always have woken to such quietness had they chosen differently over a dark-green tablecloth, and stayed in Venice, kneaded dough. No family, or trouble. Them, only—Ray, and his Venetian wife.

He grasped her hair in his fist at the airport. Kissed her.

Venice left them. She watched it creep away beneath, grow smaller. No more pigeon hats, or bridges.

• • •

THEY DROVE BACK to the Norfolk coast, across the flat, ploughed land, where autumn had plucked the leaves from the trees and blown them over the fields, under their front door. She scuffed through them, as she stepped inside. She held one—brown, as dry as a wing. Ray drew the curtains, opened the post. Boiled the kettle for tea.

*O*N CAME A COLD, SLOW AUTUMN. It shook itself open, brought
a darker sky and geese that arrowed over their houses, calling—but
otherwise, their lives returned to what they'd been before Venice, and
their marriage vows. The halyards still sang. In the mornings, she
placed the ash from the fire grate into newspaper, folded it up, threw
it away.

And Ray ran an electric cable down to the greenhouse, filled it
with warmth and light. He worked at night, now. Every hour, it
seemed. He was the artist—partly for money, but also, for him.
Because he had not truly painted for three months, and missed it.

She stood at the white porcelain kitchen sink and saw him there—
bent, thick-haired, colour on his arms. She carried food to him.
Sweetened tea. Wore his jumper, which fell off her shoulder as she
bent down. In the evening, when he turned on the light, he became a
painting himself—a man in a house of glass, its yellow light falling
into the dark garden. Like an old dream. Or something she had really
seen, somewhere. In a book, or on Miss Bailey's wall. She wished she
could mark it down, or talk of it to him, but she didn't know enough.
How could she describe it? All the sketches he'd made on bridges, or
in restaurants, or on the water taxi, or in the lobby of their hotel as he
waited for her, were laid down again. Coloured.

He works.

I love him.

And, on the telephone, Aunt Til said, "Of course he works . . .
And anyway—this was part of him, when you met. Wasn't it?"

Yes. It had been. This life in him, this art and appetite had caught
her, from the start. Those letters. He'd dared to write these things to
a girl he barely knew; he'd noticed the sap in trees, and how wasps

soften wood with their little insect mouths. He'd sketched pink birds, sent them.

I can see you out here. The only white-skinned thing.

A flat autumn sea, and spaces.

• • •

THE CHRISTMAS LIGHTS were strung up along the quayside, and a brace of partridges hung outside the wooden shop in Cley. Inside it, there was quince jelly, and chestnuts, cheese, spices for mulled wine, and she'd walked back along the main road with these things in her arms.

He painted. And as he painted, Moira chose, mainly, to be outdoors. So she'd drive east to Salthouse, where the sea defences were tall, hard to walk on in the wind, and the bones of a ruined house lay deep in its sand. Skimmed stones there. Or she walked on the vast, empty Holkham beach, with its rivulets and plovers, and she'd push her heels into the wet sand. Stood under the pines where Ray, once, had found boyish treasure. Shillings, and a rusty nail.

Mrs Cole. Which sounded old. Firm, like a thumbprint. The barmaid in The Red Lion, and salesmen, and Ray himself called her this. "Mrs Cole . . ." And Ray said it teasingly, his head on one side.

Moira, too, was the quiet, dutiful daughter-in-law, and as the rains came in, and flooded the fields to the south of them, she drove to Norwich in Ray's car. Knocked on the frosted glass of the door. Handed a jar of quince jelly down into June's small hands.

"How is my son? Happy, I hope." This, and other questions. About Blakeney, and the house. Money. Family. June was fragrant and soft-skinned, and afterwards, Moira wrapped her scarf around herself, and walked down the drive towards her car. Didn't look back, but knew that June was watching her—her big feet, perhaps, or the back of her head.

She thought of Heather, driving home. She passed a line of trees, and the sun fell behind them, and Heather said, *I saw you fall in the mud.* She'd rinsed her skirt. Tried to.

Where is she now? Sipping a clear, fierce drink in a student bar. Or dancing. A huntress, of sorts. She'd have brought more than a pot of quince jelly, and a false smile.

•   •   •

CA' D'ORO, which he worked on with his nose close to the canvas. Excited by it. Came inside with paint on his earlobe saying, "It's looking good!" And he'd drink a glass of water, kiss her twice, three times, and head back out to his greenhouse.

She sold olives in a jar, and cider. Lavender bread.

And she found Binham Priory, which lay inland. In ruins, now, but she walked through them in the afternoon, with her hood up and her glasses on. Mossy stones, and woodpigeons. Cloisters of air, and it was cold, here. She warmed her hands from a lone horse in the next field—its head over the wire fence, its breath warm, and wet.

I love him. And he had said it to her, too, once, under the clothes rack, by the bath. Told her in Venice.

She always thought that if it ever found her, if she was ever singled out and was lucky enough, or foolish enough, to say the word herself, that it would stay. Not leave. Other loves left, perhaps—but not this kind. Surely they didn't. She'd believed this, and hadn't sought out the pin of fishes, with its sharpness, for nearly a year, and so it lay, tarnishing. But here she was, now—newly married. Walking around a ruined church in December, on her own, picking at her nails as she used to, at Locke, in the weeks and months before Ray.

•   •   •

A GIRL OF *ball-and-socket joints.*

But he was hers again at night. He washed off his paint. He forgot about painting, and looked at her as if she were new again. They were together—his hands as warm as they ever were. Or they slept.

Or when they were too tired to sleep, and too tired for anything except it, they'd lie on their sides, look at each other. Say nothing at all, or, if they spoke, it was Ray—talking of his travels, but now they were stories she knew, too. Stories she could tell herself, as if she had been there. How he'd shouted his name into Vesuvius to hear it echoed back.

She confessed to him, in a whisper, that she used to sit in the library at night, open an atlas. Look for his countries, and their crops, their poisonous insects and life expectancy. How she'd thought, *Don't swim in Africa.* Or *Wear sunscreen*, and *Peel fruit.*

He smiled. "You did? Really?"

I am lucky. To have this.

Lucky, to sleep like commas, around each other. To have the yellow front door. The birds winging out in the dark. She told herself this, so it would not matter at all when he rose, in the mornings, rubbed his hand over his hair, picked up a paintbrush, and left.

• • •

AMY SAID, on the telephone, "I wish you were here, Moira. It *is* Christmas, after all . . ."

They had hung, she said, the red velvet stocking on the porch door, and bacon rind was left out for the birds. A dark, sad Atlantic. Moira said, *Merry Christmas*, before replacing the telephone.

But Moira's first married Christmas was not in Stackpole. It was with Ray—and his mother, who wore a widow's dress, picked at the turkey, and with Stephen, who drank too much, and said her name three times, for no reason, as she washed the saucepans. *Moira, Moira, Moira* . . . Who talked with his brother out on the quay, and he telephoned a girl with his paper hat on.

Moira was in the kitchen, on her own, when the new year came in.

*H*OW DO YOU KNOW time is passing by? Or do you at all?
A question that's easy enough for us, who are walking around
with our eyes open, and our mirrors, and clock towers, and calendars
to tick days off by. God only knows how it is, for you. I've heard of
others who've been in comas for years, and then woken to say, *How's
the dog?* Or *Who won the football match?* As if they'd been sleeping a
minute or two. Not that we expect that from you, these days.

• • •

MANY MONTHS, now, since Locke. A river of them. And yet, I could
still recall exactly the old school clock above the courtyard—its
copper-green face, the rusted hands that creaked round. The bird
droppings on it. I could ever hear, still, its low-pitched, weary chime
so clearly that I'd turn my head, listen. I measured the days by different clocks, now. Ray's wristwatch, or the alarm clock, or the green
flashing numbers on the oven door.

By the people on the quayside, too. The dog-walkers, the pension-
ers, the bird-watchers—they were all year round, and meant little. Even
Gordy, with his seal trips, braved the sea in all weather. But when the
children came, Moira thought, *It is summer;* the crab-lines and ice
creams meant the season was here, and the money came in for them—
Ray had painted, and in The Sticky Prawn his pictures were hung above
diners' heads, and small red dots were pressed on them. *Sold.* A piece in
the local paper, on him—Ray smiling, arms folded, sunburnt.

Local artist takes off.

"Takes off . . . what?" he said. Smiling, one eye closed.

Her own face, too. Her body, and its tissues—new and old parts
of her. He'd drawn her feet in charcoal on white paper, as she dozed,

because he liked them—"Elegant!" Not elegant at all. *Joker*. She pulled on socks.

He shut himself in a room of glass, at night. Talked to colour, and brushes.

She placed an advertisement in the *Eastern Daily Press*.
Home tutor. A-level standard. Maths/Sciences. What else could she do?

• • •

TIME WAS PASSING for Til, too. At last. She was, she said, Lady Macbeth—on a wide, West End stage, so that posters of her—black eye make-up, arched eyebrows—would, by March, be on the sides of London buses, on escalators in the tube. "It's true," she said. "Lady *Macbeth!*" She was rehearsing constantly. Or she was in her flat, by her electric fire, reading books on the Scottish play, studying it. Saying her lines. "Although," she said, "there is a catch." Til had to undress in her madness scene. *Blood out, damn spot*, and she had to see blood on the rest of her, to untie her nightgown on stage. "So I'm doing aerobics. No more free croissants for me."

Happiness in her again, or a form of it. Til doing star jumps, practising her *Unsex me here*, making friends with the three witches. And if there was still a man of any kind, in her head, he was fainter, and his voice was less distinct these days. She forgot to read her horoscope, sometimes.

Miriam said, on the telephone, "Your aunt sounds well. She didn't for a while."

So did George, who had won money on the horses, and so Moira found a twenty-pound note in an envelope three days later. *A gift! Have fun with it.* She spent it on kitchen scissors and a bag of salts, for the bath.

• • •

RAY SAID, "HERE . . ." Handing her a piece of square, peach-coloured paper with his own writing on it. She unwrapped her scarf. It was a telephone number. A surname.

She rang it. A man with a neat, clipped accent talked of Maths, and his only child. "As soon as you can? He struggles." Which was this week, or tomorrow, even.

• • •

MOIRA WORE A GREY DRESS, with grey-heeled shoes she had found in a charity shop in Holt. Pinned back her hair. Contact lenses curling over themselves on her eyes.

Their name was Hannigan, and they lived in Burnham Market, with its Georgian buildings, and hat shop. Moira walked up the gravel path towards the red-bricked house, knocked twice on its front door. The boy she would tutor was Sam. Nervous. He sat in the dining room of his home, with his hands on the table, palms down. A wide bay window looked out onto the street, to the church and the sycamores, and as he worked she'd watch the trees drop their leaves, and the hedges shake with birds. A tree house, in the distance. Theirs was a silent, polished home. His father brought in coffee, cinnamon toast, more pens, clicked the door shut behind him.

He struggled with Maths. With Pythagoras, and decimals. His breath changed when she lay a fraction down. He gripped his pencil, frowned, and Moira looked at him, at his treacle-coloured hair, at the strands of white by his left ear. They glowed. An injury, maybe. A blow to the cranium. A fall from a tree house, or a golf ball, neatly struck.

Sam's father pressed eighteen pounds into her hand, at five-thirty. A thin, angular man. He stood so close to her, sometimes, that she could smell his aftershave, and shoe leather. Once, she looked back from the road, and saw Sam still sitting there, in the dining room, in his sea of numbers where he hung, treading water.

A sea baby, maybe. And dark-eyed, like her.

• • •

A DREAM, THAT NIGHT, of the blue nylon rope that she had not seen, or climbed, for years. That must be gone, or midnight-coloured, now, with oil. But, still, she dreamt of it. A cracked sky, and a mouth full of fish scales, so that her father said, *Spit, spit.* She spat.

Moira.

Ray said her name again. "Moira."

The bedroom came to her, as did his face, and there was no blue rope.

• • •

SHE PAID FOR new advertisements in all the local papers, and church magazines, and she left fliers in all of the secondary schools. And soon, it was not just Sam. She began to work most evenings, as Ray did—loading herself up with textbooks and encyclopaedias and pro-tractors, and she sat in hushed rooms with children whose eyes bore into their work, worked their bottom lips. Pieces of them missing, somehow. A girl in Fakenham struggled with all the sciences. On Tuesdays, she was in a rectory in the Fens, sitting beside a boy with a broken finger and a heavy cold, and she saw a sadness in him. She spent an hour a week in the city, a girl who talked to sums. Didn't understand them, said, *You're a hard sum,* and Moira watched this, wondered if she herself had ever talked to numbers, like that. The cathedral rose beyond the house, and Stephen's home was nearby, and she could have knocked on his door, if she'd wanted to. But she didn't. She chose to drive home to Ray, instead, to feel a hundred things in the dark space of the car—old, lost things that she hadn't felt since Locke, when she was left in the dormitory at night, or lost her sea bean. To close herself up as she walked through the door, to put her keys in the clay pot by the front door and call out, *I'm home.*

*Y*ou have flowers. New ones. Last time I sat here, three nights ago, I saw lilies—pink-mouthed, sexual-looking, full of hot breath. The nurse sneezed when she came in the room, but she didn't move them. Or rather, said she wouldn't. But anyway, they are gone now, and you have daffodils on your table instead. The first of the year. Simple, loud. Are you aware of this?

My last visit affected me. I didn't think it would, but I drove home over the toll bridge with Sam in my mind, and it wouldn't go. I can't explain it. It seems a strange thing to be haunted by, out of it all. Why not the stone, eyeless, fountain girl? Or Venice? I don't know—although they, too, cast their shadows on me from time to time, or more often than that, as all our past things do. You, too, must have them. Schoolgirls have cruelty in them, and I suspect words have been thrown out at you, like grit, and hurt. You are the hurting kind, or were. *Princess*, perhaps. Or *Little Miss* . . . what? Bossy? Indignant? You grew your own radishes in a tub, one summer, and brought one into school. This is the sort of thing they'd have picked on. *A radish? Please* . . .

So I have thought of Sam. He moved across my textbooks; he walked beside me as I climbed the library stairs. Last night, he floated on my sleep, like oil, and here I am, two days later, with him still with me, and his father, of course, and I don't understand why it is this way, when I haven't seen either of them for so many years, and probably won't ever again. I haven't thought of Sam since my Blakeney life. No doubt my brain, secretly, knows why. Somewhere amongst the hippocampus and hypothalamus and the little grey cells.

Those children, too, who were swept away from Brancaster in the week before I married Ray? They did drown—did I tell you that? You probably guessed, anyway. Water is hard to escape from. It wins, on the whole. Waterlilies and seals and pooh-sticks don't lessen the power of watery places, or their secrecy. They beguile, as a smile does. Although they say that drowning is not such a bad death, and I believe it—I've read of oxygen deprivation, and its effects. I've sat in lecture halls, seen what your mind's eye might see. But then, you know what I believe, these days. And you know the feeling of salt in the lungs far better than me.

Did you ever like daffodils? I don't remember seeing you with them, as I saw you with other plants. Pansies, or blowing a dandelion clock. Daffodils grew by the field of horses, and the school.

Anyway. Amy.

I will try to leave Sam behind, at least for now, and move onto the road kill, and you, as an eight-year-old, who bewitched every soul in Blakeney, and Ray sketched you in pastel-pink (your choice— remember? You refused charcoal, saying it was summer, and who wanted black, in summer?). *Amy with Beads.*

You marvelled at it.

•   •   •

A LETTER CAME. Ray tossed it over the breakfast table to her. She took it to the bathroom, opened it there.

Moira,

> *I'm going mad. I have to come and see you, please. I know you don't really want me to, because you keep saying you're busy, but it's horrible being here sometimes. There's nothing to do. Mum and Dad are being really annoying. They keep talking about homework. I saw them kissing in the hall the other day, etc, which was really bad, and embarrassing. Can I come for half-term? I could paint with Ray. I'm good at it at school. If you say no, I'll be really sad, and I'll cause trouble.*

> *Love Amy xx*

"Blackmail?" said Ray. "Clever girl."

· · ·

Is there a choice here?

She asked her parents this—sharply, unchecked. She had pupils, and things to do. The house was small, and why did she have to? Hard words. But she was filled with them, and she didn't want Amy in the house, with her handstands and chirpiness, and Ray had loved her so much at the wedding, in her bridesmaid's dress.

George said, "She is your sister, Moira. Be reasonable."

Reasonable. She muttered the word.

· · ·

"This will be a good thing," Ray said. Moving a canvass. The windmill with a storm cloud. "You barely see her. Or know her."

A long time, now, since the wedding. She'd not be the girl in the pink sash, with the silver horseshoe tied to her wrist, fistfuls of confetti. Pushing sticks into the grate outside the church.

So Amy was placed on a coach in Bristol, and told to stay put, to not leave her seat or not talk to strangers, for five hours, until she reached Norwich. A long journey. And Moira expected a tired, quiet thing. But Amy ran across the station, her buckled shoes clapping the ground. She stumbled a little. No greeting when she reached the bench. No handshake or sticky hug of the waist. Instead, Amy pulled down her lower lip, showing the thin blue veins of it, and the whitishness to her gums. "Look!"

With her finger she wobbled a tooth. It crunched in its socket. Back and forth, back and forth.

· · ·

It was a gunshot, or it was a weaver's spine in her heel, or a torch switched on—having Amy in the house. It was a noise, too—a yo-yo knocking on the slate floor, or humming, or a clatter on the stairs.

Amy bought toffee, left their wrappers on windowsills, and sucked them thoughtfully as she drew at the kitchen table. Toffee—to pull out her last milk-tooth. Not that it worked.

Til was in her. Or Miriam was. She was eight and a half years old, and bold, and pressed too hard with her felt-tipped pens so that their ends splayed, their ink dried up. A darker blonde than Ray. His was whitish, with red in his beard when he chose to grow one. Amy's hair was deeper—the colour of a honeycomb. Unbrushed, mainly—although she owned a red butterfly clip which she pushed into her hair, fastened next to her scalp. Moira watched all of this. "Do you want to wear it?" Amy asked, butterfly in her hand.

Amy believed in everything.

In fairies, chiefly. Hands on hips, she had real, fiery belief in tiny people with wings who lived inside flowers and could be brought back to life with a handclap. She lifted bricks, turned leaves over. Announced over breakfast, with a mouthful of toast, that, yes, there were fairies in the garden at Blakeney.

"You saw them?" Ray asked.

She nodded. "Three."

"Three?"

A carpet became a pond, and a cushion was a stepping-stone. She considered the chimney, from the street—not really wide enough for Father Christmas to climb down, so what did they do? Open windows? Miss out? "Cats," she said, "understand us." There was a snowy world to be found in the back of a wardrobe, if you believed in it. And she wanted to be a fairy herself, by eating pollen cakes and drinking dew—so toast and orange juice became such things. She smacked her lips, said, *Aah!*

"I see you in her, Moira," Ray said. Filling a glass with water.

Liar.

No boundaries. Amy walked on no lines at all. The real and the fictional held hands, fell into each other. She pried, asked questions, opened doors without knocking. Tried on Moira's clothes. Took a pair of Moira's socks to bed. When June came, Amy sucked a toffee, considered her, and said, "Why don't you walk anymore?" Which June loved. Laughed at. Talked of such innocence, and those huge blue eyes.

Ray said, "She's fun to have around. Don't you think?"

He knew what his wife thought. He moved a strand of her straight, black hair behind her ear, as he asked her this.

Also, on Sunday, the three of them headed out on a boat to Blakeney Point, to see the seals there. Moira's idea. She paid for them to go on *Gordy's Seal Safari*, sat at the stern, by the motor. Arctic terns, and the church towers on the land behind them, and there was sunshine which she closed her eyes in, felt on her face. Amy was sick for an hour. Holding the sides of the boat, grey-cheeked, wiping her nose on Ray's handkerchief, and saying *sorry* to Moira again and again. For spoiling their nice day out.

·   ·   ·

IT WASN'T JUST boat trips that made Amy sick. In time, so would long, stuffy car journeys, so that on a school trip to the Black Country, Amy hammered on the coach door, fell onto the pavement. Vomited on a lady's shoes.

Perhaps this sickness was Amy's first adult truth: that her body could not do all things. Or perhaps, it was this: meat. For she cried one night when Moira told her that sausages were made from pigs.

"Do they die of old age?" she asked. Shocked. Hoping so.

Moira did not want to lie. She felt it would not help things, and that Amy needed to learn the facts at some point. So she said no, they did not. She spoke of bolts in the temple. Of the battery chickens she'd smelt, at Locke, with a south-westerly wind. Said the word *abattoir*.

But above all, it was road kill Amy hated. This was the worst of all truths, the worst violation of her girlish theories. It was early summer, and the Norfolk lanes were full of it—small, lost lives spread out on the tarmac, or softening on the verge. There were dead birds on the main road: fledglings which had not yet learnt the danger of windscreens lay in the gutters, their feet outstretched. Amy failed to see them. They were too small for her, or maybe she saw their feathers shake and believed they were litter. But rabbits, squirrels, foxes— she saw these. She counted them. She kept a mournful list of deaths in her head. Her first glimpse of this was in Wells-next-the-Sea—a squirrel was smeared out across the road as she crossed it to buy an ice cream. She screamed, grabbed Moira's sleeve. Her world caved in, on that pavement. Everything altered, she refused her ice cream, and in every car journey she made that summer in Norfolk, Amy prayed. To not see a death. For nothing to be lying there. Sometimes she stuck the heels of her hands into her eyes, so that even if she passed a rabbit, she would not see it. "Drive slower," she pleaded, as they drove to Cromer pier. She feared hitting something. A bump in the road would sicken her.

Had there been no such deaths in Stackpole? On its roads? The deaths, perhaps, had all been oily, and on the black sand, whilst here, on the main road that ran from Hunstanton along the coast, through the crooked towns and staithes, the cars surprised the wildlife. Did not learn. And Amy mourned all of them.

Moira noted this. She glanced across at the girl in the passenger seat as they drove home—how she bit her bottom lip, tugged her thumbs. Moira noticed, too, that somehow it was not the messy deaths that upset Amy most of all. A mashed, flattened hedgehog did not cause such grief as an untouched rabbit did. The unmarked ones. The bunnies that look as if they are sleeping, or have died naturally. The squirrels that seem to be basking in the sun. The hare they passed in the early evening, freshly dead, maybe still warm, lying on his side with one brown ear still standing.

"I don't like it . . ." She wept as if her heart had been cracked open. She pulled at the skin on her arms. She wanted to help, to save

them, or bury them. To lay flowers at their little graves. Moira wanted
to talk of tumors, and blood clots, and rupturing things. But Ray sat
next to Amy, instead, and told her how such deaths were quick,
unfelt, unknown to them. He said, "Everything dies, my lovely." She
seemed smaller, when he said these things. She closed up, flower-like,
and sniffled. It was the wisdom, Moira supposed. The shaft of adult
light coming through her trees.

．　．　．

DRIVING BACK from the Fens, after tutoring. Late evening, with
midges, and she drove in silence—past the lavender farm, so that she
smelt it. Somewhere to the east of her, Locke Hall stood empty for
the summer break. Bats in its walls, and a skeleton sitting in dust
motes, waiting to be found.

She thought of this, and so didn't see it bumble into the road
ahead of her, near Hunstanton. Braked, but she hit it. Felt the tyres
jolt, and she breathed for a moment, stepped out of the car, walked
back to where it lay. Dead. A grey bulk of badger, with its jaws still
open. A shining eye. She could smell it—its life, still; its musk, and
earthiness. She knelt beside it, gripped its warm fur, hauled it across
to the grass verge.

On returning to the Blakeney house she found the sitting room
filled with light. Amy, on a wooden chair. Ray sat with his legs
crossed—his right ankle on his left knee—and had a sketchpad, a
pink pastel in hand. "I'm sketching your sister. On demand."

Moira poured herself wine and watched this. The lifted chin of
Amy, her restless toes, and the beads she wore around her neck. Ray
saying, *Perfect* . . .

The badger was in the room, too. The fact that only yesterday it
had trotted in the lanes, barked, sniffed the air. Suckled, even. She
thought of the sett in Caroline's Wood, in Stackpole, three hundred
miles away—her father, and the crunch of acorns under her heel.

Amy preened, so that Ray laughed.

· · ·

MOIRA TOOK AMY to the railway station at King's Lynn, four days later. Through Hunstanton, and she had forgotten, perhaps, about the road kill. Had only remembered it as it appeared, on the verge where she'd left it—smaller, now. Amy's eyes brimmed at the sight of it, and said, "No . . ." Tears which carried on, so that she climbed onto the train with red eyes, wet cheeks, and she pressed her forehead against the glass at them. Not wanting to leave. Wanting to stay in Blakeney, with them. A blocked nose—but she had Ray's handkerchief, so she twisted its corners into points, and used that.

· · ·

LATER, ON THE SOFA, I felt a push at my spine. Your yo-yo, without its string. Which I picked up, dropped in the kitchen bin.

Later still—a fortnight, maybe, after you'd been—I opened a drawer in the spare room to find this string, lying there, with a hard, white square tied to one end. A slight redness to it. What had you done? Ray knew. He shook his head, impressed at this. The old trick—string, a tooth, and a slammed door.

"Don't mess with the Stone girls," he said.

This would be a story to hold on to, in the future days—in the years ahead, when you were to lie in a hospital bed, eyes closed, held beneath the surface.

I told our parents of this—the tooth, and the string. It showed strength, in you, and stubbornness, and it was a thing to grasp onto. So after that, they felt more hopeful. They leant down to your wounded ear, said, *Fight, Amy. Fight.*

15

Migration

So you lie in this hospital in a city you'd never been to until you fell from the top of Church Rock, near Broad Haven, when you were twelve years old. Not by the sea, now. You are inland, and the nearest real water is only a river, the Severn, which has risen up many times since you slept here—the giant wave, the Bore, which has roared darkly upriver, away from the sea. Not that we've seen it. Or heard it. We sat—or rather, I sat and you lay, and I read of it later, in the newspaper. I read it out loud. *Yesterday* . . .

That, Amy, is water, and how it can be. It isn't made solely for paddling in. It isn't just the pool of mallards that you liked to sit by (or so I'm told), with bread, and an eye on the shallow water for an otter's sleek back. Water can rise up. It can carry away, or bring in. The children who died near Brancaster in my first year after marrying Ray were moved in a current for days on end, circling, side by side and face down. Their bodies were found at Weybourne, in the end. Don't trust it. Don't believe it is a calm, beguiling water, that you can see your reflection in.

Stephen had a girlfriend, once, who reminded me of you. Not to look at—you were ten, or younger, at the time. She was cello-shaped, in her thirties, with wild, curly hair and a green tattoo of a dragonfly on her anklebone. But she talked of things that you might have talked of, too, one day—the planet, and its rainforests. Over our Blakeney kitchen table, she made the shape of the world with her hands and talked of acid rain, of oil reserves, tigers, carbon, plastic bags. Stephen only looked at his wine. I looked at her, and saw you. Even though, at the time, you were ten years old, or younger.

Perhaps you can take this thought with you, or we can: that your world is breaking anyway. We try to pretend it is not. But there are polar bears who look down, sadly, at their melting ice; monkeys that fall with the timber; plants that need more rain. A hot, red Martian sky races over our heads, and the wind has grit in it—or I can imagine this, and suppose it will happen soon enough. And so can we console ourselves by believing that it is right you should not be here, when this is the forecast? The path ahead? You, of the flowerbeds, and the fossil in a rock. You'd cry. You'd not understand the state of the world, crack your knuckles at it. You'd recycle. Demonstrate. Save water, walk with a heavy heart.

So at least you'll be saved this, Amy. The world will stay rainy for you, with molehills and a vegetable patch. No bombs. No rising seas.

Is this a consolation? And if so, who for? I don't know. But we try. Our parents try anything to make sense of this. And you were part of Stephen's girlfriend that evening, in Blakeney, with her lively straw-blonde hair. I thought of you. I felt you inside me, as she talked, and, later, I saw you on our ceiling when I could not sleep—hanging, bat-like, from the pear tree, your hair nearly brushing the ground.

Anyway.

The Severn Bore was surfed this year. Did I tell you that part? Right up to Epney. Ray was sitting on the roof of his car, eating a banana, and saw it.

• • •

THE LONG, QUIET marsh evenings. The light faded, and the birds settled on the water, or the mud banks. Moira brushed through grasses, left her footprints behind. Her hood pulled up, so that every-thing she saw was framed with dark-grey fur.

The woman in the shop at Cley talked of snow in the winter months. She wrapped walnut bread and mustard jars, shook her head. *Can't you smell it?* The smell of snow? Moira tried to—but what would this smell be? Cold water, only? So she imagined. Yet when she did step outside onto the street, she thought—yes, there is more to it than that. An air with sourness, like metal, or blood, and she had never smelt it at Locke, or elsewhere.

She waited for it to come. Sat in the window at night, with pepper-mint tea. And the winds came in; the reeds moved themselves. In the afternoon, as she was driving home, she left the car in a gateway and stood, watched. Bean geese were loud, restless, and as she stood there, in a field near Langham, they rose up, one by one. Hundreds of them, lift-ing up, above the ploughed fields, and they called to each other, so that Moira's sky was full of noise, and feathers, and the draught of them, and they circled the field twice. Then, they moved elsewhere. To another field, or a waterway. Not long, she knew, before they flew north again, to places far colder than here. Gone. Creaking over ditches, and graves.

She kept this migration to herself. The sight of them; how they sounded. Once, she thought of Til, and nearly phoned her. But her aunt was a daytime sleeper, now. Acting all night. And how would she talk of the bean geese, flying? It had to be seen, and it had only been seen by her.

In the evenings, she sat at a polished cherry-wood table in a house in Burnham Market, whilst Sam wavered his pencil between two fin-gers, thinking hard. Algebra. She watched him. Sat with her legs crossed, her hair loose. Every week he seemed taller to her. Still a boy, but there were parts of him that had age in them, now—the scratch of the head, the sigh. She hadn't read many novels, or poetry, but she felt this streak of white hair by his ear was a thing to talk of, and that girls would love it first, in him. But not yet.

Eighteen pounds from Sam's tall, cool-handed father. "You're good," he said. "He's improving, I think." Another from the woman with a child on her hips whose daughter had cried over her textbooks so much that the pages had crinkled, stuck together. And on this girl, Moira saw the old, known things, of herself—frayed sleeves, chewed nails. They sat in a bedroom with no pictures of friends on the wall.

She tried to talk to Ray of her sadness—but he was blond-haired, talented, knew jokes. He'd hold a man's shoulder when he shook their hand, and what did he know of emptiness? He knew nothing of it, she was sure. He had too many friends, too much adventure. He always had new stories—of people, or a barley field, and she'd come back from serving local cheese or duck eggs or from tutoring to find an empty house—Ray in the greenhouse, or in the pub, with friends. The barmaid purring at him. So Moira said nothing, to Ray. Instead she lay beside her husband at night, wished she could go back to Venice, or to Locke, even, when she was new to him. When he wanted nothing but her—not art, not money.

George said, "You're a clever girl, remember. And it'd be lovely to see you, sometime. It's been so long . . ."

So they said. But they had another daughter to be concerned about. Amy had missed school, forged a sick note, tried to sign her mother's name.

She taught a theory to a girl with bad skin. Moira had been handed it at Locke, in a classroom with pi written along the walls: that pressure was transferred in a liquid. That pain didn't stay still; it spread out, like ink. A pinch on the arm would be felt by the toes. In theory, if she dropped a stone in the sea at Cley, a whale in the Antarctic would give a slow, mournful blink of its eye, and feel it.

*W*HEN HE TOWELLED HIMSELF DRY, it was casual, absent-minded. He didn't stay still. He wandered through the upstairs of the house, rubbing his hair dry, pausing to tug his towel around his back. He hummed sometimes. Then he would sit on a bed, or a chair, and dry between his toes. She watched him do this, over the top of her book—the attention to detail. Moira imagined his mother, or father, teaching him to do this, after bedtime baths or sea swimming. Ray, as a boy, with one leg raised, being told the importance of dry feet.

Also, he walked from room to room whilst cleaning his teeth. He looked out of windows. He tested the soil of houseplants, saw the cracks in the paintwork or pools of condensation whilst brushing. He'd go to the bathroom, spit, and return, still with his toothbrush in his hand, and say, "Shall we repaint this room? What do you think?" Or, "This floorboard—listen . . ."

Once, she found him changing a light bulb with his bath towel wrapped around his waist. No other clothes. He grinned, reasoned that this job couldn't wait. Light was light. No time like now. He did not want to dress, and forget, and have to change the light bulb later, in the dark. She watched him do this—her husband, with freckled shoulders, balancing on a chair in his towel.

Also, how he spread the horsehair bristles between his thumb and forefinger, as he rinsed his paintbrushes under the tap. The colour, running away. He'd press them, afterwards, with a paper towel. Leave them to dry, like soldiers.

Or how he shaved, which she'd watched, before now—leaning against the bathroom door. The lather, and the care of it. And the strange, brief smoothness of his chin that followed, for she knew her husband as a man with rough, reddish stubble on his chin. That was him—even at Locke, by that fire. So she'd feel his smoothness with the pad of her thumb, and wait for a day, for the Ray she knew best to return to her.

He pushed his tongue into his cheek, as he worked. He didn't understand the washing machine. He did not talk of Stackpole anymore.

Moira's mother had said, once, *There are moments. You will know them.* She knew them.

• • •

WHEN THE SNOW CAME, at last, it was thin, and did not stay. It only pinkened her face. Hissed against the glass on the greenhouse.

He said, *Done.* Wiping his hands.

It was fitting. *Cley Mill; Winter; West-facing.* This was real, lasting snow—with light on it, and jackdaws, and it was truthful, too, he said—for he'd seen the mill in snow when he was younger, in the days before Moira, when he was still kissing a redheaded girl who lost her keys in Cromer's sand. A widower bought it for three thousand pounds. Missing his wife, who'd walked with him there.

Ray waved the cheque, as if fanning her. It caught the tip of her nose. "This, love, is a second honeymoon."

And for a week or more, it was as it was. It was as it had been in their early days, for Moira sat, or lay, or walked beside him as he talked of foreign places. Waterfalls, volcanoes, the African worms that could burrow into the soles of your feet. He said, *In Tonga, you . . .* And she listened. Felt seventeen again. Felt the love stretch inside her, so that she wanted to bite down on his wrist, or earlobe, or run her wrist over his chin.

Her husband, again. *My husband.* She could think of him, once more, as she drove past Blakeney church, and they made dips in the shingle at Cley, sat there, sheltered by the *Mary-Jane.*

He said, "Where to, then? The moon?"

She didn't know. Didn't care. Ray—who'd written her name in

snow. Who also skimmed stones, and she looked at the lines by his ears, and the white paint in his hairline, and she wanted to lie on his back, trap him, press herself into him as they sat on the shingle, at Cley.

· · ·

HE LIFTED HIS ARM, held it out in front of him. Showing her the view. Moira thought, *Barley fields*. All she could see was barley. She squinted, shielded her eyes. They were not far from home. They'd walked here—along the sea wall to Cley, past the bird hides, and inland. Ray had known this path since childhood. They used to walk the dog here in the evenings, he said, when his mother could walk, and his father was still alive.

He walked on, led her alongside it, uphill. Ray, in his white shirt. Sun in his hair, and she felt it on her own hair, so that its blackness might look almost bluish. "I hid here, once," he called back to her. "I stepped into the field as carefully as I could, so I'd leave no tracks, and I sat down in the middle of it."

He stopped, then. Turned, with a stalk of barley in his hand.

"So. What do you think? Do I paint this next?"

Wife. She looked away. *Barley, near Cley*, or, *Fields, North Norfolk*. The wind stirred it all. Green barley, blue sky.

They had walked here for art—she saw that now. No other reason. Ray had wanted her to see it; he'd brought a pad and his tin of charcoal to sketch down the shape of the fields, and how the fields moved, and the skyline. That was all.

She took his hand, and they made their own shape in that barley, and he caught the sun on the backs of his hands, which turned red, and peeled a few days later. Moira found, in the bathroom, she'd left a button behind.

· · ·

DO YOU REMEMBER *Barley, near Cley*? You saw it, in its early days. You returned in the spring that followed, plaited a strand of your own hair as you stood by Ray, in the greenhouse. He excused it, called it, *The bones. Just wait a while . . .* But then it grew, as you did, and found colour, and shadows, and Ray was proud of it. And so it was taken from us.

No second honeymoon, then. For you had pestered our parents constantly—aching, they said, for Norfolk again. To eat ice creams, and for Ray to drive the orange car through the ford at Glandford. *Can I go? Please?* So there you were, on a Friday—tying your shoelace on Platform One. No taller, but your face had a shape to it now, and you beamed with a set of white, tidy adult teeth. No fairies, but you still shuddered at road kill. Smiled with your eyes at Raymond, that evening, over a glass of watered red wine.

It was Easter. I remember that. For a bag of chocolate eggs was brought across on the train from Stackpole, and *He Is Risen* was written on the church's notice board, at the top of the street. "Again," said Amy, exhaling. Shaking her head. "Hasn't He risen before?"

· · ·

NO TRIP TO THE SEALS this time. Moira suggested it—perhaps she had outgrown such sickness, now? But Amy blew out her cheeks, as if re-enacting it all. The retching, the sore head. She held her stomach. "Can we not?"

Where, then? She had seen Happisburgh lighthouse. She'd climbed its stairs, and stood on the bottom iron rung of its railings, peered in at the light. Fed apples to the horse at Binham Priory. Blown glass at Langham.

Now?

Amy was ten years and four months old. She read comics on her front, chin cupped in her hands. She twisted Moira's finger, eyeing the sapphire on it.

"Can we go shopping?" she asked.

Which Raymond laughed at, said, *Of course.* "Women . . ." As if he was all-knowing about this. As if this need for shops was a sign, of some kind. Moira arched an eyebrow at him, fierce. Left him with his coffee, and a vase of daffodils on the table, and the radio on.

She hummed. She wore blue cotton socks with pom-poms on. She opened the window of the car, stuck her feet and these blue socks out of it. Talked of best friends at Stackpole, and the naked old man she'd seen, swimming at Presipe. He'd thought no one would see him, but she did. "I spied on him!" She considered this. "He was *really* old."

Norwich. The cathedral spire held up a white-cloud sky. She moved through the market, shook an awning so that rainwater fell on an empty bench. Asked for cherryade, and money for a purple plastic ring. She put her feet where Moira's had been, as they walked down the arcade. Moira noticed this.

Lunch? she asked. Amy nodded. So Moira led them to the hog-roast by the clock tower, queued. A prod in the arm from Amy, who was nervous, grimacing, not wanting this. The pig, turning over and over.

"Moira."

On the Prince of Wales Road, she turned. He was wearing his suit and tie, he looked different. Older. She hadn't seen Stephen for months, and Amy nodded, said that, yes, she remembered him from the wedding. "A long time ago."

"It was."

The three of them, hanging on the corner of the road. In the way. He asked about her jobs—the shop, the teaching. Amy showed Stephen her purple ring, and he said, in turn, he was busy at work. Always busy. "Ray has it," he said. "The right job. No boss, no office. Something to show at the end of it all."

A silence.

"Well, I'd best get back."

She didn't watch him leave, and she didn't talk of him. But hours later, as they were leaving Norwich with a pair of red patent shoes, and the plastic ring, Amy said, "Ray is much nicer. Stephen looks at you funnily."

Her mouth full of caramel.

• • •

AND THIS: CROMER. Amy had asked for shopping, and, also, she asked for Cromer—because didn't they have penny arcades? So she walked through its streets with pocketfuls of bronze coins, jangling, ice cream in hand. Gulls eyeing it.

They stood on the pier in the afternoon, looked down. The mossy legs of it, and the foam in the water. And on the beach, there were donkeys lined up under canvasses, dozing, flicking their huge, soft ears. "Can I?" she asked. Hands clasped together.

No. Too late in the afternoon. Too long a queue.

"Please?" And the begging moved on to sulking, and the sulking passed over rocks to become anger, then. On the pier. She stamped her foot, said, "It's my *holiday! Why* can't I?" Talked of their parents. That Moira was mean. That everyone knew it—even Ray. That she wasn't having any fun anymore. "It's just a donkey ride . . ."

Her eyes were huge, in the moments after Moira's flung hand. Across her cheekbone. Amy stumbled, and her eyes brimmed. But she did not cry. She did not say a word. After a while, she reached for Moira, tried to take her thumb, but Moira swung her arms as she walked, back and forth, so Amy failed. She took her own thumb instead, tugged it.

• • •

I SENT YOU BACK with a mark, on the face—a small bleeding under the skin, so that I waited for the telephone call from our parents to say, *What have you done? You hit her?* The phone did ring. But it was all the usual words, from them. How they missed me. Hoped we were well. That Amy was chirping with stories of birds, and penny arcades.

You could have told. Said, *She hit me.* And pulled your sorrowful, doe-eyed face, and think of the power, in that. Think of the out-come. All sorts of shock and reprimands from the house with the line of gulls on the roof.

I'd send you back again, with damage to you—remember? Over a year later, when you were almost twelve years old, you tore at your scalp in a tearoom at Sheringham. Tugged your fingernails so fierce over your skin that I heard a rasp, and saw the red marks on you. Under your hair. A bellow of anger, from you. So I sat you in the bath that night and scrubbed you with lotion that burned, and I pulled a comb through your hair to kill the head lice, break their legs. You cried. I threw out the pillows you'd been sleeping on.

• • •

TIL BELIEVED—or still does—in karma. In the returning of will. Kindness comes back in the shape of more kindness, she says, and so if this is true, my hitting of you would have rolled back to me. A slap, in one form or another. A pain, in the head.

So maybe I caused the illness that was to come by hurting you. Or perhaps—and more sensibly—I fell into a fever because I had paddled for too long at Holkham, with my trousers rolled up, or I'd lain down on the grass at Binham Priory until it grew dark, and the dew came on me. I drove home shivering. He said, "What's happened?" I suppose we'll never know which it was.

Moira's dreams were vivid when she was well, and sober. But they were worse when she was ill. Her skin flushed, at first. She believed it hissed, when she touched it, yet on touching it she felt cold. Ray said, "Your eyes . . . They are . . ." Small. Sore. She had to feel the wall as she climbed the stairs. What was it? The heat of her. The bed sheets caught themselves in her legs, and she dreamt of ropes, pulling her.

Ray's face came to her—roughened, the lines on his forehead, and the mosquito bites he'd had in Thailand were back, or she thought so. He put water by her bed. Said, "Drink, if you can."

Birds flying south. A sea bean in her hand.

Oil, and the shape of Annie as she fell, from the roof of the school, and she talked in her sleep, he said. Talked, and fought, and so he slept in the spare room for three days. Afraid of taking up her space. Or to scare her, in her lucid moments. But it was his absence that scared her, in the end. She woke, tangled, and saw the empty space, as cool as her own skin seemed to be, and thought, *He is gone.*

At twenty-two, this is how Moira looked: tall, with large hands and feet, and—so—long limbs. Her knees faced inward. She had hollows by her clavicle which filled with water in the bath, and her hair was longer than ever before—past her shoulder blades, so that when she looked down, it swung around her. Or she could throw it back, when wet, in an arc. Spray out water. Her eyebrows were thin. She'd plucked them into high, neat surprises, and she had cheekbones—or so Ray said, and dark, deep-set eyes. Her glasses, when she wore them, were frameless, rectangular. Mostly she used her contact lenses, and her face felt bare, and lighter, but they were hard to remove in the evenings—she'd redden her eyes, by trying, and Ray with the perfect eyesight didn't understand this. Would lean against the bathroom door, say, "Aren't glasses fine?"

On her left arm, a vaccination scar. Puckered, oval-shaped. Other marks, too, from old, childish wounds—on her knees, and the insides of her arms.

I love you, he'd said, once. A long time ago.

• • •

The world turned, again. She cut through her hand in the shop, in Cley. Slicing a ginger cake, and the base of the knife had nicked her skin. A blue plaster on her. When she showed it to Ray, he frowned at her. Said, "Ginger cake?"

Aunt Matilda came in the summer. A new colour to her hair—a deep chestnut, with the slightest hint of red to it when she walked on the quayside. And she said, "Who'd have thought my career would take off like this, at forty-five? A late bloomer. Still . . ."

She had lost weight. From the sit-ups and non-pastry diet, and from many months of taking her clothes off on stage every night.

"And it doesn't get easier. Trust me—all those eyes . . . Anyway—married life? And when are you going to go back to Stackpole?"

Til said the oil was long gone, and the birds were back, and Amy was at the best age of all.

"They miss you. And you could do with something," she said.

• • •

SHE DROVE HOME from a farmhouse in the Fens to find Stephen's car parked outside the White Horse pub. She put her key in the lock. A note on the floor in Ray's hand, saying *We're in the pub! Join us!* A small, smiling face, in blue ink.

She found them there, with pints of ale. The barmaid smiling at Ray. Stephen did not look up. Ray turned, whistled between his teeth, like he used to by the sundial, or from the boundary fence, and said, "Over here!"

Maybe there was a lucky moon—she thought of asking Lady Macbeth. But good news had wrapped itself around Ray, and he leant across, took her wrist, said, "Do you remember the gallery in Norwich? I showed it to you?"

A white-painted place, with a glass vase in the window; she remembered it. And they had offered him a room, there, all to himself. *Raymond Cole*, in black typeface, and then his work on the walls, under lamps, next to prices. He imagined it. He ran his hand through the air in the pub, said, "I can see it now . . . This, Moira, changes it all."

And it would, too.

No longer a man who painted in a greenhouse for tourists, a shop, and The Sticky Prawn alone. Now it truly began. His name would be spoken by others, and he'd be sought out in a room, and she'd stand by the kitchen sink to see a glass house with no Ray in it—for he'd be elsewhere.

Brushes will lie on their newspaper. Clean.
"Good news," Stephen said. Raising his glass.

She kissed her husband. Clambered over him that night, and a spring in the bed uncoiled itself, so that Ray laughed, and she didn't want him to stand up, stretch, in the morning, leave.

• • •

UPPER ST GILES STREET, near the other cathedral, and a pub she'd drunk stout in, with her aunt, years before. She stood outside with her hood pulled up. When Ray pushed the door, a bell rang.

"You must be Mr Cole?"

He was. And she was in her early thirties, with large teeth, and ironed hair, and a blouse with some buttons undone, too many, and she shook his hand without looking at it, or at Moira. "I'm thrilled," she said. "We loved your work. All of us."

Moira waited outside. On a bench, where there were pigeons. The clouds were blown over her, and litter skittered towards the market, and offices. She saw him beyond the coloured vases, his arms held up. His hair, and the back he'd scraped on wire, by an icehouse, once.

"You could have come in, too," he said, afterwards, bemused.

Said she'd needed air. Would have been in the way. Looked at his profile on the drive home, memorising it.

*H*EATHER HAD POURED WATER from the bathroom tap into the tooth-mug, carried the tooth-mug to my drawer, and filled it up. Soaked my clothes. She found a chalk drawing of me, which I'd left out on purpose, to say, *Look. I have him.* And Heather had torn the picture up. Of course. And stolen a piece.

Serves you right.

As for me, I did this: I pushed a stone into the wing mirror of the barmaid's car—casually, as I walked by. One quick movement, and then I carried on. Dropped the stone ten paces away, in a flowerbed. Easy.

And this new, red-haired curator with her keen eyes, and big teeth, probably thought she half recognised the woman who stood opposite her shop, in the fur-lined hood, staring. Retreated to the back of the shop. Used the telephone.

Moira at night. *I am his dark-eyed wife. I am a witch. A cave. A mineshaft.*

And she heard the sound of his skin on the sheets, as he turned over, and she slipped out of bed, knowing there was a moon outside. Downstairs, she went. Out into the night-time garden, and she found the key to the greenhouse underneath the garden gnome.

Perhaps it was wrong. Perhaps in the future, a different Moira would look back at this one and shake her head, feel sad. But this Moira moved through canvasses, lifted the pages of sketchpads, uncurled waste paper. All eyes. Hands under the table, over his char-coal tin. *Moira with Wine; Wells Dusk; Moira, Reading; Basilica. Cattle, Out-lined.* She was certain, and quick, and she only thought, *Who?* It could be many. More than one.

She knew there would be something. She was sure. And she

found it, in his drawer. Watercolour. A woman's back—smooth, long, and not hers, for the skin was pink-coloured. Tanned, even. And there was a left hand. Balled into a fist, with no gold ring on it, no sapphire.

She stood, stared.

. . .

I THINK OF YOU CONSTANTLY. He'd written this, once. He'd bought her a bracelet of shells that she'd worn in secret, felt on her wrist, heard other seas in their clinking sound. Once, perhaps he had thought of her. For a second or two. For as long as it took him to write down those words. Pay the Thai bahts for a string of shells.

Now, he slept upstairs, and his wife stood, half-naked, in a green-house, at night. Not surprised. Holding the proof, and empty.

. . .

MOIRA DIDN'T SEEK the brooch of fishes her aunt had, once, given her, or the red ribbons. Instead, in the house in Burnham Market, where the boy with the white streak of hair lived with his father, and a tree house, and Moira found herself in the kitchen with him—the father, his suit, his cool hands, a view of a hydrangea bush.

Quick, and strange. She banged her hipbone against the kitchen table, and he shook when it was done, filled a glass with water. They buttoned themselves back up.

She drove back empty. A skin stretched over bones. Found Ray uncorking a bottle of wine when she returned, paint in his hair, humming to the radio, not yet aware of his wife standing there.

16

Moira in Red

OUR WHITE HOUSE ON THE DEVON COAST SINGS IN THE WIND. IT is its wires, I think. Or the tiling, or the shape of the house itself, its angle to the sea. Or it has a soul to it, of some kind. At any rate, it sings.

And we stood together, Ray and I, in the garden two days ago, wrapped up, looking out—choppy, dark-iron water. No wading birds here, for him—or hardly any. Only a few, dabbling. Nor are there marshes, or reed-beds, or Cromer crabs, and the sky does not weigh down on us, as it did, east of here. Does he miss it? He hasn't said so, although there is a map of the North Norfolk coast pinned up in his studio—from Hunstanton to Great Yarmouth, with all its straight beaches in between. He must miss it a little, I think—after all, we moved here four years ago, after you fell, to be nearer to you— and four years is a long time. But perhaps he, too, needed to leave Norfolk behind. Ray has a strength, or pulse, in him. I saw it, at the start. Perhaps it is an artist's streak, or the boldness of the younger child, or just him—but he is so rarely afraid of things, Amy. He likes to venture out, to put his feet down on new earth. *The challenge*—for I must have been one. He says *yes*. Turns off the path into the jungle, pushes locked doors. Tries out new words.

Me? I have been afraid. But, also, perhaps, I've been restless. Hard, I think, for anyone to stand on a coastline and not think of other countries—of deltas, wars, pine forests, deserts, distant tribes. The sea is too wide. Ray calls it *sublime*, knowingly—and it does something to me, as it affects him, even. A sad heart is saddened further by big water, or it is comforted—one of the two. I suppose like most things in life, it's how you perceive it, or want it to be. After all, I've walked out across the tidal creeks at Blakeney and seen its darkness, and mud, and the steel sky, and felt lonely; also, I've stood there with my hands in my pockets and seen the tiny roots that push up through that mud, and the light on it, and it's been beautiful. The same birds; the same tidal creeks—just a different me. A different heart, perhaps. It is all in us, maybe—happiness. So was Til always right?

There is something in the sea—sublime, or not. And when I swim in the Atlantic in the warmer months, I think of the fish that have moved through this exact water, the boats that it's held, the legs, the weed, the spit, the blue icebergs that creak in bays to the north. The Atlantic must have strands of my hair in it—and if so, where are they now? On an African beach? Stuck to a squid's neat beak?

I thought all of this, or a form of it, for the first time with Matilda. Standing on Stackpole Head, after my mother's second lost child. I don't know what she wrote on her white paper, placed into her glass bottle. But I wrote: *Moira Stone, from Stackpole. August 1987.* Our phone number. I threw it with all my body's strength. And the sea became a deeper, stranger thing after that. I followed her home, thinking, for the first time, of all the other beaches. Although I always thought those beaches would have sand, and caves.

No phone call came. So perhaps the bottle still bobs in the Atlantic, or water crept in, so it bumps the seabed now. Or maybe it washed up on Manorbier the next day, scared of the open water.

Here's a joke, for you: at Locke Hall, in my early teens, I dared to dream in the night-time rooms that this bottle would be found by a boy, years on; that he'd call the house and ask for me. That, by then,

I might be beautiful—curved, freckled, good eyesight—and we'd meet, and it would lead elsewhere. This was my only hope, Amy. I saw no other way of it. It could only happen this way, and this dream was as the bottle was—tiny, and far away, but still, it was *out there*. Possible, in the way a snowfall can be. I know I have been far too spiteful and bitter to you, in your lifetime, and to others; but I wonder, too, sometimes, if I've been too hard on me.

Ray and I both want to draw up anchor, one day, and will. And if he misses Blakeney, these days, and its light, and the low beams in The Red Lion inn, he doesn't show it. But he was always better than me, that way. He doesn't count losses; his glass is half-full. He has never been one for quiet, backward glances.

·

• • •

I KNOW WHAT YOU'D SAY, if you could talk. With your little, pink cat's mouth.

That's not love, then. Or *How could you cheat on him, Moira?* Wouldn't you?

Not love, you'd say—not if such a thing can take place. Such a lie, as that. I know. Do you think I'm not aware of the depth and width of such an act, and of the acts that were yet to come? We can know what is wrong, and still do it. That's a truth for you. Add it to your list. Look at the mud inside my shoes, or the grass in my bed. Look at Heather, and tell me she knew no better as she did these things. She did know—although our eyes glance up to the right when we lie, so I saw it—those mirror-eyes looking up, past me. And I thought, *A lie.*

I know this, too: that there are, in fact, many different loves, and different stages of them. And as fierce as I've been, I believe I've always had love in me, in one form or another—for Ray, and the sound of Stackpole Quay, and for you, of course. *Sister*—try that, for a word. And I fought it, ignored it, but if I hoped for a telephone call from a man on a distant beach, bottle in hand, isn't that the proof? That I carried a love, from the start? And not a parental or filial love—or not only. And then, one night, at last, we met. Ray and I. On leaf mulch.

But I'm not the one to analyse love. Far from it. There are much better people to ask—our parents, Miss Bailey, you, Til, June, Mr Hodge. Heather, even. All I know is that I felt what I felt, I wanted what I'd come to want, and Ray said, once, half-joking, *Have we met before?* Had we? As for Til, she said that as she sat in our kitchen, with a glass of wine and wistfulness, she watched us—and that we made a strange sense to her. We wove between ourselves as we put the saucepans away. I didn't know what that meant, then. And I don't now. Here's another truth: adults don't know everything, and there will always be such dark, shapeless mysteries in the world, in us.

Still.

I've heard people say: *Love is just oxytocin and dopamine and hormones, inside us*; a drug; a cocktail, of sorts. If I hadn't walked to the icehouse, one night, I bet I'd now be the cynical woman who dismissed love, called it science, chemicals, and nothing more—and then, secretly, craved it. But I did walk to the icehouse.

I miss Ray when he isn't there. I look at his boots, his reading glasses. And I still ask myself, from time to time, what would have happened if I hadn't knocked back Jo's secret vodka, been bold. If I'd never gone to Locke at all. And then there are our mother's tiny dead children, three of them, to think of. All girls, in my head. All small, gentle, incomplete, white-skinned versions of you.

• • •

SHE HELD THE BROOCH in her hand.

It was coin-sized. Heavy—real silver, with small false crystals for the fishes' eyes. These fish curved, so that the brooch was almost coin-shaped, too. Their mouths were open; their scales were etched into the silver, so that it was rough under her thumb. She'd feel the scales, with her fingernail. Hear them. Feel the cool, glass eyes.

And the clasp itself was small, old-fashioned, with a silver-plated

cog that turned, to release the pin. The pin was tarnished. Darker, at
its point. It used to be sharper than this—sharper, and cleaner, for
she hadn't polished it in twelve years, and the brooch was no longer
moon-coloured. Once, it shone in the palm of her hand. Winked by
the field of horses. But she was older now, and the silver was grey,
and her hand was not smooth, or unlined anymore. A woman's hand.
And a woman's arm.

A bad dream, he said. Leaning over. Ray had turned his lamp on, and
was looking at her. Reddish lashes. A frown. "Moira? All right?"

If it had been a bad dream, she'd lost it. It had skittered, shaken
its tail, and sunk away inside her. She blinked. Took the water he was
offering her, in the pink toothbrush-mug.

· · ·

SPRING, WHEN THE SCURVYGRASS was in full bloom on the mudflats—white, and hopeful—and a pair of bitterns were spotted at
Cley, so there were cars parked on the verges, the glint of glass in the
reeds. Stephen dated the woman with a dragonfly inked on her left
ankle, which seemed, when she walked, to fly. A vegan, too; Ray
cooked her lentils, which she only half ate. Talking all evening of
wind farms, and fish stocks. Oil.

"Won't last," Ray said, undressing for bed. "Surely."

Moira thought, *Which?* Oil? The vegan?

He worked on a view from a bird hide at Cley, where the bitterns
were seen. Not a large painting—but there was a wall in the gallery
he'd seen, and considered. It needed, he said, a small picture. Rectangular. And who'd painted the inside of a hide, before?

"I'm off," he said. Pulling a rucksack onto his back. Kissing her,
before setting off on foot to Cley marshes. She chewed her thumbnail, watched him leave. The wind moved his hair in the same way it
moved the reeds, to his right.

But when he returned, he showered, and she unzipped his bag and turned each page of his sketchbook, looking for something that was not birds, or flat water. A wrist. Or a small, delicate foot. Anything. She found nothing, though. And there was a sweet, sawdust smell to the elbows of his jumper, where he'd rested them on the wooden shelf in the hide, watching.

· · ·

PERHAPS I *imagined it.*

She tried this—just as she'd tried to imagine the girls leaving, on fire escapes, and Amy. She'd sit beside the glossy, combed hair of other children, watch their fingers whiten with their pressure, on their pen, and she'd breathe. In, and out. She had proof of her own doing—the bruise on her hip, from the kitchen table in Burnham Market, which she'd blamed on the bedroom door, was blooming through all its colours—from a strange mint-green, to yellow, to mauve. She'd wake, think, *Did I?* Pad through to the bathroom, and in its mirror she'd see the answer, written. Fist-sized, and on the bone. Belts hurt her, for a time. She walked through her days and nights, cave-painted.

Then, as further proof, this:

A letter, addressed *Ms. M. Cole,* and a postmark not from Wales. Tight, angled handwriting, in black ink. *It is with regret that . . .* She sat by the window, looked out into the street, and knew she would not walk up the drive of the house in Burnham Market again. No more tree house or cinnamon toast. No Sam. Moira had been unfaithful; Sam's father had stopped the lessons out of shame, or fear, or embarrassment, and so he—Sam—would walk through his life with a white streak of hair, and only a vague grasp of algebra.

She folded the letter. Binned it.

· · ·

HE RINSED BRUSHES under the tap until the water ran clear, and Moira tried to call her aunt. She pulled on her denim jacket one evening, walked up the street past the hanging baskets, and from the telephone box by the church she dialled the London flat. Thought, *Pick up.* Listened to the rings, and to Til's bright, hopeful recorded voice four times, before leaving a message for her. *Nothing important. Just a chat.*

What was she, now? Hermione? Lady Bracknell? Someone.

· · ·

THE TOURISTS CAME; her bruise went. The foxgloves and sunflowers in June's garden rose up, swayed, and June wheeled herself over the paving stones with her scissors, picking them. Said, "These were Robert's favourite. Foxgloves. Said that as a boy, he thought that's what they truly were. Gloves—for foxes." She laughed at this.

Gordy's sign was set up again on the quayside. His boat knocked against the wall, with its blue cabin, and pirate's wheel, and she stood with her hands in her pockets, watched him rub the boat's sides with a cloth. He talked of seasons to her. Of the arctic terns. "There are less this year," he said. Sucking his teeth.

Also, he said, "Saw a painting in the window, in a shop in Holt. The lighthouse, over at Happisburgh. Your husband's name in the corner."

She nodded. Thought of the time Amy had hung over the side of Gordy's boat, grey-cheeked, wet-eyed, vomiting. Wiping her mouth with Ray's handkerchief, saying, *I'm really really sorry.* The seals watching her, bemused.

· · ·

MOIRA ALMOST PHONED Stackpole. No—*almost* is wrong. But she thought of it. For one, silvery moment she thought of it all, as she had done in Locke: of the patchwork rug, and the smell inside the airing cupboard, and what would happen if she took her mother to one side, said, *He is not mine anymore. Of course not.* Somebody else's. Somebody so beautiful she is worth drawing, naked, in pastels. But Moira didn't call.

In the long, drowsy, last summer of the millennium, she passed the open windows in Blakeney's streets and heard tennis sounds—back and forth. Polite applause.

And her work was less, since the term was over, now. Only one pupil—the blistered girl, who curled her hair with a finger as she thought. Out in the Broads, so that Moira's drive home was into the sun. A car full of light, and poplar seeds in the lane, and rapeseed in the fields. So yellow it hurt. She passed the line of trees near Stiffkey and the sun flickered behind them. Red, black, red.

So quieter, in her teaching. But the shop in Cley was busy, and she sliced ham, weighed cheese. The owner bustled, chatted, squeezed her bulk behind Moira, and as she brushed past, Moira wondered if it was her—her, with her shape. Perhaps he was starved of flesh, and so came here. But her left hand had a ring on it.

And she knelt on the flagstone floors, and scrubbed them. She washed every part of the house, dusted, cleaned the greenhouse windows. Lifted a rope of her old, black hair out of the plughole—slippery with soap, tongue-like. Ray would come to her from behind, arms around her waist, surprising her. Call her a washerwoman, or a scullery maid.

Ray of the words. Who knew nothing of an element's properties, or the body's way, but who told her beautiful, iridescent things on the evenings on their walks. *You are . . .* Regal. Helen-like. Words like spun glass, in his hands, which he passed over to her. She said nothing back. Her husband painted, drank, listened to cricket on the radio, drove his pictures over to Norwich, walked with her, and he might not look at his wife for a while. But then a yawn, or a trip on a tree-root on the path, would make him look up, see her, and say, *You are . . .*

A cheat, as you are. She believed none of it. Had she ever? All those letters. All those letters he'd written from foreign countries, with their stamps of flowers, or hummingbirds, and with praise in them—he hadn't even known her. He'd talked to her once. And what was that? A shifting of feet and a kiss by the games shed. All he'd known was how she looked, and wasn't that the worst part of her? Those glasses. The awkward joints. He had written of love, written as lovers were meant to, when they were still strangers. So no—she hadn't believed it. Had wanted to more than anything else, but hadn't quite. For years, she'd been fooling herself. *Stupid Moira,* all over again. She was serious, and practical, and in Venice, she'd worn sunglasses on top of her normal pair, because the water glinted, and he couldn't have loved that at all.

• • •

I SHOULD HAVE SEEN this coming, she thought. Moira mourned her loss. She mourned it inside her, when he waved at strangers, finished telephone calls with, *Good to hear from you.* He hummed in the shower. He took hours to drive to Norwich and back. He painted a naked woman with a pink flush to her skin, and then he'd smile at Moira, spin out lies. She nodded at this. Whenever she passed another woman, of whatever age, she glanced back to see the shoulders— their width, the backs of her hands.

• • •

IN AUGUST, she cut her hair. Or, rather, a girl with false nails did. Moira's long, mermaid's hair was left on the white-tiled floor of a room in Wells-next-the-Sea, and she walked out into the sunshine with a cool neck, bare ears. Hair that flopped over her eyes. Bristles that had fallen under her blouse, and made her itch. She scratched, on the way home.

Ray leant back against the oven. Ate a yoghurt, considering her. He blinked, and raised his spoon, asking her to turn around for him. She did. And the word he chose for his wife in the end, with her new hair, was *elfin.*

• • •

LOW TIDE, WELLS was laid down in the back of the orange car, and driven east, to the white-painted gallery and the woman whose blouse was unbuttoned too much. Moira leant against their front door, watched him leave. Two hours and thirteen minutes later, he returned. Rubbing his hands, saying, "Three weeks to go . . ."

And *Venice from the Lido*, and *The Grand Canal*. Leaving the house, as his friends might. One by one. Propped up on the sitting room, and then lifted out, under a sheet. Out to the car, and tourists watched this. She fanned away flies, counted the seconds, minutes, hours before he'd come back. Long enough for anything. And one afternoon, she drank. Brandy—and she thought of his freckled arms, the narrow hips, how he'd held the underside of her arm as she climbed over the boundary fence and thought, *What are you doing at this minute? Right now?* Just as she'd thought it at Locke, whilst he was away. Time zones and palm trees. He was gone, yet he was everywhere, too—in his socks, and razor, and the fork that had been pulled along his teeth, and his handwriting on the telephone pad. She drank too much, and saw a song thrush, an artichoke, her name in snow. The brooch of fishes, and the bones in her feet. The sapphire, blue as an eye.

· · ·

SHE COULD NOT FOLLOW her husband to Norwich, for there was no second car. No way of doing it. But at midday, as the swifts darted through the streets, over the top of their heads, he kissed her, set off for a pub in Cley. A business meeting, he said. "A commission," he said. "Or maybe one. We'll see."

She waited nine minutes, until he was almost out of sight. Then, in a grey shirt, jeans, and with her new, shorter hair, she set off, too—along the path, past the rotting boat. Ray paused, to talk to people. Or to shield his eyes, stare. And so she'd bend down to tie her shoelace, pick a flower.

He walked to The Three Swallows. Sat outside on a bench, with his sleeves rolled up, and a pint of lager next to him. And a red, roofless car parked on the grass opposite. She waited. Standing behind an oak tree, with white paint on its bark.

The woman from the gallery. Her red hair loose, and curled at the ends, and she kept her hand on her wine glass. Nodded.

"I'll have a proper launch," he told his wife, later, as he brushed his teeth. Was truthful.

Moira was sunburnt from spying on her husband in August. She thought, *It is deserved.* Ray questioned it, later. "What were you doing, to burn like this?" Touching her. She blamed the water. Out to the seals, with Gordy, and she could not lie on her back, that night, for her neck was scarlet, needled with sun. All her life, a bluish-black curtain had hidden her neck from sight; but now it had gone. She'd forgotten it, and so her moon skin was burnt, and he cracked a stick of aloe vera, moved its thick, clear sap over her neck, so that she winced, and he said, "There."

• • •

A WEEK LATER, he discovered her—against the hotel wall, eyeing Ray as he talked to the teenage girl from the tearoom.

"Moira?" he asked. Seeing her there. "What are you doing?" Bemused. His forearm raised up to his head, shielding his eyes. She lied to him—talked of the need for fresh air, and shade. Which he believed, of course.

• • •

HER PARENTS CALLED. Listed all the good things they could—surf, gorse, seagull chicks. The orchids. The soft booms from the army range, like the slow closing of a door. Amy's last day at the village school, so she'd be off to Tenby in the autumn. Not bright enough for a scholarship—although nobody said so much. Amy—with a shoulder bag, new shoes. "She looks the business," George said.

Til rang, too.

"I'm sorry, I'm sorry, I'm sorry . . ." So busy, she said. "All work and no play—or too many plays!" She smoked; she said a love letter was thrown onto the stage the night before last. She'd never had that. Never thought she would, in a million years.

She sounded happy. "Well, I am . . ." At last.

Moira invited Til to the gallery's opening night of Ray's exhibition, with its silver trays of wine and low lighting, and journalists. She waited. Wanted to hear *yes*—for her aunt to stand in the room with her, with her thumb-ring, her flower juice. But instead, she heard her aunt's finger moving down her diary page, reading the pink ink scribbled on the date. Imagined Til's face. Heard her say, "I'm so sorry, love. I just can't."

O F COURSE HE BELIEVED ME. I said many things at this time—that I was just going to the shop, or the church at Morston, or to see a man about a second-hand chair. And Ray smiled, accepted this. Not the doubting kind.

I knew this from the start. He lost money in Nairobi—from a card game he was pestered into, which was rigged. One hundred Kenyan shillings, and he'd shrugged, walked away. *Fair's fair*—even though it wasn't. He did not question the hostel owner who kept his deposit, citing a lost key. In New York, Ray had seen a homeless man biting his hand in a doorway, so that he bled, and Ray hailed a taxi, took him to hospital. Not thinking, once, that he might have diseases, or injection marks, or be murderous, or all of these things. He didn't understand, either, how people distrusted him—the restaurant owner who said Ray'd left without paying. The official who said, *You lie to me, I think,* holding out his hand for a bribe. This was the world, but he did not resent it. Brave, and trusting, too, and the sceptical brain is not part of Ray, as it is part of me.

Yet no one is perfect, and no one walks on this earth without making errors, now and again. If he was so trusting of others, so sure that others would trust him, would this not lend itself to deceit? *She will never know.* He never thought I'd follow him, or time his journeys, or that there was a reason why I did not teach Sam anymore, or that when he said he was going to his brother's flat, I'd call Stephen the next day, to check this. Hear the surprise in Stephen's voice, the searching for words.

"Yes, he was here. Why?"

This was Moira, in her early twenties. My hair. You never saw her hair at its shortest. You stepped forward nearly a year later—in the summer before you fell—quizzical, one hand out, to feel it. It was on my shoulders again, by then, and you were twelve—determined, and fearless, and full of jokes, and—like Ray—you were faithful. Wide-eyed, believing me.

•   •   •

SEE THIS, if you can:

Moira, in a black dress—velvet, to the knee, with a high neck, and it was backless, so that when she bent down she was sure her verte-brae stuck out, like knuckles, or pebbles under her skin. Shoes with a heel, so that was tall. Taller than Ray, but he didn't mind. She wore contact lenses. A small, nervous smear of red on her lips.

She leant back against a wall, and saw it—how the auburn-haired woman led Ray, her hand in the small of his back. Introduced him. Men shook Ray's hand, and he was smart, for only the second time in Moira's knowing of him. A tie, and brushed hair. He'd shaved, so that there was no reddishness to his jaw, and she missed that. Pre-ferred it there.

My husband. It felt hollow, now. Her husband's paintings on the walls. Terracotta, ultramarine, ochre. The curator, in yellow, called him *honest and modern.* "An artist with a classic yet distinctive style." Moira drank beside Venice, with the streets she'd walked down with him; the barley field; a grey night-time African plain she'd never walked on, but heard of; a gateway, near Walsingham; his own face, for he said all artists should paint themselves, at some point. *Artist, aged twenty-five.* "He's incredibly young, to be doing this. At this stan-dard." So a man said. "Really . . ."

Perhaps his mistress is here, now, in this room.

Stephen came to her. One hand in his pocket, one holding a glass of red wine. "What do you think?"

Eighteen paintings by her husband, in a gallery, and he was young, and far away from her, and it had all been a matter of time. She said she was proud.

"I know. Talented . . . He's come a long way from crayon stick men on the bedroom wall."

They did not look at each other, but at *St Mark's Square*. At its pigeons, and neat, painted waiter with a tray held in the air. The puddles.

Moira drank. She saw herself—reflected in a glass door. A black-and-white creature, long-legged, a flash of red, awkward. On her own in a room full of people, a glass of wine in her hand.

• • •

STEPHEN DROVE her home. She was not drunk, but had drunk too much to drive herself. So Stephen did it. Pushed her key in the lock, for her, and I could talk of alcohol, of brazenness, and that it was not her fault, as such. It was not her doing, exactly. Or I could talk of moons and stars, Scorpios, how a wind feels. But I understand blame, and I place it at my own feet, with their unpainted nails, and the black heeled shoes that did not quite fit. He moved forwards, Amy, because he was not happy, as I had not been happy, and because he, too, listed all the sounds at night, and so he paused, at the door. Dark-eyed, thin mouth. Count the seconds between a thunderclap, and the lightning, and it was like that. *One, two* . . . She knew it would come. She did nothing at all.

His hands were fast, and clumsy, and the clay pot on the table broke, and somewhere her husband was nodding, smiling to show his crooked tooth, thinking, *She is like* . . . Not his wife. But some other woman.

• • •

YOU WOULDN'T have climbed Church Rock if you'd known, would you? That your sister was such a bad person. So far away from what you, and Ray, and our parents imagined me to be.

No daisies and forget-me-not picked from the lane, placed in an eggcup, beside my Stackpole bed.

*S*HE HAD HEARD about men in affairs. She'd seen a film, listened to tales. They could flail, as if drunk—hunt the woman out as she walked through markets or stood beside her husband, or sat in an empty church. Catch her by her clothing, say, *I need to see you.* Those such things. Poetry. Flowers with no note in them.

She did not think this was Stephen. Didn't think she was the woman to make a man, any man, like that. He added up, and polished his shoes; he did not say much, at parties. Nor was she passionate enough—at least, she didn't think so. She had drawn blood from Ray's shoulder once, with her teeth. But Moira was cool, mostly, and mute, and she did not count the hours. It was not a need for him that kept her awake.

Still, there was a change. She saw it, in the days that followed—a tightness to his face, how he studied his drink before draining it. Stephen did not speak to her in company, anymore. Talked to his brother, or strangers, instead, and the girl with the dragonfly faded away, caught a strange breeze, and was gone. Ray asked after her. "What happened to her, then?" A shrug, from Stephen, and a shake of the head. *No.*

Did he have dreams, as she did? Not of her, surely. When she slept, or wrapped warm bread up in the shop, Moira did not see Stephen, or anyone—instead, she saw places, and past things, and she decided this, too, was surely Stephen's way of it. No flailing, in him. Of course not. She doubted that he looked at the dip she'd left behind in the bed, or that when he smelt the skin on her wrist, he wanted to tear it, keep it with him, as Ray had once said he did, in the early days.

• • •

HIS FLAT was in the city. Three floors up, and a floorboard on the landing that sighed when she trod on it. Footsteps on the pavement below, a dripping tap in a corner bath, and the slow hum of the fridge, and his neighbour's door, shutting. Traffic. A delivery van, reversing. These were the sounds of Stephen's flat, in Norwich, near the close.

He always wore shirts. Ironed, buttoned, and he did not write in pencil, or ballpoint pen—it was ink, on his notepads. Neat, blue-inked reminders: *Send tax letter* or *Golf at noon.* An exclamation mark, sometimes. The boy in him, who'd made orange squash when his father died on a wintery road. She did not touch his notes. Felt that if she had been another girl, seeking love, she might have found it there, in those words. *Dentist!* And, *NB: M.*

An orderly, masculine place. Leather furniture. Blinds at the window. She was detached. The scholarship girl, again, who'd found solace in a red-inked ape on a bulb, and who now kept the sound of his wristwatch in her, or who looked for comfort in the screws on his shelves, in the chip on a mug. As he showered, she lay on her side, watched the light from the street outside move across the ceiling, and thought of nothing at all. A dog barked; she was warm, beneath the sheets. This was her—but Stephen was jealous, at times. Didn't want to share.

"What am I doing?" he asked. Himself, more than her. He sat on the edge of the bed, his elbows on his knees. Head down.

She gave a blunt answer.

So they did not talk very much. For what was there to say? But he asked her this, sometimes, and, *What are you thinking?* He knew the answer—of course, he must have done. But she lied to him, gave him a smoother, better reply than, *Ray. The weather,* or *Food,* for she was always hungry in his flat, and he went outside to buy her fresh bread, or meat, or fruit, which she'd eat with her hands, leaving crumbs in the bed, and seeds in her teeth, so that she'd run her tongue over them in the car, find them, driving home.

•   •   •

A SILVER NECKLACE from him, for Christmas. A small bird, on it. In flight, with spread wings. She wore it once, in his flat.

From Ray, there was a dark-red, silk dressing gown that reached down to the floor, and which whispered behind her as she came down the wooden stairs. And in the sitting room, she heard water—not a running tap, but something like it. A sheet draped over a box, in the corner.

She lifted the sheet. A fish tank—with fish in it she'd never seen before. Not goldfish—but iridescent, thin, huge-tailed fish that had been in no book she'd read, and no rock pools. They picked through the stones, looking for food. Clung to the glass with their mouths.

"Because you've never had a pet," he said. Then—"I nearly got tadpoles . . ."

He remembered her story of them. Retold it, to her, there by the Christmas tree—how she kept them in a jam jar. Fed them with her father's corned beef sandwiches.

•   •   •

FLORENCE, TOO, was a gift.

A new pupil: nine years old, with ears reddened from new, gold studs, who found Maths hard, but who sang like a grasshopper, and drew flowers on each page. Wrote the numbers out in rainbow colours in her first hours, made shapes from them. Basic. But they were not dark, fearsome things on a page, anymore.

Florence, with the smile and the sore ears. And she lived to the west of the city, so Moira would be with her on Tuesdays evenings, walk on to Stephen's flat, spend an hour there. A routine. Like an appointment. If she had a diary, she'd put his name in it. Perhaps he wrote it down in ink—M! 7–8.

Or at least, this was how it began. His flat near the market, with few words. But he asked, once, to meet elsewhere, outside. The railways station, or she'd wait for him in the cloisters of Norwich cathedral, where the light striped the stone floor, and she walked it, monk-like. Blackbirds dug for worms in the lawn. Stephen walked with her, not touching her. Spoke.

"Moira, if you could go anywhere, where would you go . . . ?"

He favoured the rain, too. For it meant umbrellas, and they could wander, then, for a time, beneath one—only legs, to a passer-by. Their faces were hidden, so he'd try to find her mouth with his, with the sound of rain on the black canvas above their heads, and he liked it. He told her so. But she didn't. Moira thought, *There are two dangers.* Discovery; but also, in walking by the river, or sitting in the cool silence of the cloisters with him, they made a false world. They were a false pair in it. Pretending this was allowed and normal, imagining this as their other lives. Yet there was something in the way he looked at her, under those umbrellas, as if he believed it was real enough.

Safer, by far—or so she felt—to be back in his flat, and wordless.

•   •   •

THE PLAIN ADULT EXCHANGES. The practicalities. He did not ring, or if he did, and Ray answered the telephone, he had a reason in his mouth. A list of them, perhaps—help with a crossword clue; the wrong number.

"Senility," Ray told her, rolling his eyes, "as well as a bald patch."

And Ray painted, and drank in The Red Lion, and towelled himself, and threw a jumper into the washing machine after one wearing of it, which annoyed her, for this was a waste of water, and she told him so. Threw the jumper back at him. Flashed her eyes. Gave him enough to take to his painted, unmarried mistress, and complain of. *My wife is so solemn.*

No similarities in the Cole men. Or, she did not look for them. *No one is alike*—although there were moments when she'd wake beside one or the other and, briefly, be lost. Which? And it was almost laughable, almost beyond belief. Ask any girl from Locke Hall, say her name to them, and they would never have guessed this.

Moira Stone? Unmarried, they'd say. *Surely.*

• • •

It would be wonderful to have you both, this summer. There are no signs at all that there was ever oil here, now. Amy is worth knowing, as ever—a chatter-box, and a handful. Maybe July?

Moira—it's been years. We are your family, however much you might like to think otherwise.

Ray saw this on the bedside table, said, "Are you still against this?"

She considered how it would be to walk with him over Broad Haven, or inland, over the tree roots and duck feathers on the path, by the lily-ponds. What he'd pause at, sketch down. What Amy would make of his army boots, left in the hallway.

"Or if not there, let's go somewhere else. Anywhere."

That second honeymoon. She lay in the bath one evening, with crystals of salt shifting beneath her, and he sat beside her, dipped his hands into the water. Listed places for her: Norwegian fjords, Paris, west Ireland, a trip on the Nile.

"Which?" he asked.

She didn't know. Dropping leaves over a bridge into the Seine, and he'd think of *her*, whoever she was. Call her, maybe, from the hotel phone as his skinny dull wife showered, or went down the cor-ridor for ice.

• • •

HOTELS? I KNEW OF THEM only once, with Stephen. Brancaster, on the coast, so that I opened the curtains to see the curlews, and the sea pies, and the marshes were yellow in the sunlight, and Ray was far away in London, at galleries, or so he said. I stood in the window. Morning light on me. Stephen said my name, as if he had a right to.

*H*OW LONG? You'd ask me that, too, I suppose. As if time has a bearing on it—the longer it existed, the worse it came to be. But we think that with most things. With Ray, they said, *you've only known him for five months!* And had you come into existence in my first few years, instead of eleven years on, I'd have bore you with a far better grace, I'm sure of that. Might have enjoyed you. Stayed in Wales. Not said in my head, over and over, *Betrayal! Betrayal!* But I did think that, because I thought it would always be just us three—me, our parents—and you ruined it, you changed it all. You, the cuckoo's egg. And you know what I think of your lying here: four pumpkins, one leap year. Amy, it has changed us all far more than a month would have done, or six months, or a year.

Time matters, then. Didn't it at Locke? Those days and nights when I felt the sky was racing, and whiskery roots of plants were pushing themselves deeper into the earth with every breath I took, on my own, and I thought I could see—actually *see*—the lines on my face appearing. All the heartbeats were a thrum. Hands on a clock twirled.

Ten months.

That's your answer. Ten months of another man. And were there others? It's hard to understand it, I know—to treat him as I did. A husband who mourns, briefly, for those spiders who creep across his paint, and get stuck in it. Legs glued together. He winces. He says, *I'm very sorry.* And the dead, coloured knot is laid out on a stone in the garden. Hard, to walk away from that.

But *he* walked—didn't he? Whoever she was. Curves to her, I assumed—that my husband would crave a real, female shape, and would lie on his back, and pluck at her, cello-like. That he saw no warrior, as he saw in me. No witch, or cave, or sorceress, or well— none of these dark things, for she would have been light, as he is. She would have been a lit match, a comet, a glow-worm, or a porch light, shining. A beacon. A candle. A phosphorescent sea.

I assumed all of this.

I gave her a laugh, a fragrance.

And let me tell you this, too, before I go home tonight: that I believe the world is as we choose to view it. Simple as that. Our happiness is, in the end, up to us, and no one else. I looked for the mud, the falsities; Ray saw a beauty in the tracks of birds, and my big feet, and he memorised the exact shade of grey of aircraft trays. Imagine that. I try, these days, to be like this. I do try.

Anyway. I am not excusing those ten months with Stephen. How can I do that? I rarely make sense to myself, let alone others. But I think if we want unhappiness, we can make it for ourselves. If we want to be alone, we are, sooner or later.

· · ·

MOIRA—SITTING ON THE BED, with her feet on the floor, and a man beside her. A dark room, but she could see his profile, the line of his shoulder blade. His left arm was bent, so that there were shadows on it, the mark of his muscles. Bones in it. Tissues. Veins.

Three in the morning. How many other nights had she done this? Seen this hour click upon a clock? A fistful of nights, like dark-blue beads, like weed. At school, she'd retrieved her glasses from her nightstand to see the time better. In Wales, the sea said things to her, and this room was too quiet. No real sound.

He stirred. The left arm reached out, moved across the empty space until he found her, her hips, sitting there. She looked at the hand. Browner than her own skin. Half-moon nails.

And then she lay back down, onto the sheets, into the dip. Pulled the sheets up to her armpits. Moira, with her red-framed spectacles and her cloudy tadpole jar.

· · ·

GUILT? THAT, TOO. A sharp, black heart of it. She contained it, kept it down, but still, it was there. In the hotel room she thought of Ray's hand, how he'd brought it up to her own face at Cromer, to shield her eyes from the sun. She rose from the bed, locked herself inside the bathroom, and sat on the edge of the bathtub.

· · ·

EARLY JUNE, MAYBE. The swifts raced down the streets in Blakeney. Moira drove to Sheringham, to the only cliff she knew, which was small, and had no sea spray at the base of it. But it was a cliff, and she slipped off her shoes, moved to its edge, and pushed her toes into the thin grass that grew there, and looked out, to the far-out sea, and the tanker that moved, and she thought, *One small slip of earth, one push of wind, and I'll fall.* Wash up at Weybourne. Bump the hull of Gordy's boat.

And the seals would twist themselves around her, and there was a story once, of a cod with a man's skull in its belly, how it burped it out onto the deck. She'd think of this, now. The sound of a cod, burping. The smell.

But there was no fall. Moira crouched, instead. Pulled on her shoes, went home.

· · ·

ALSO, SHE DROVE to the gallery in Upper St Giles Street and moved around it, on her own. Pretended she'd never seen these pictures before. Tried to see shapes in them, messages. Bought a postcard of *In Water*, kept it in her bag.

Banged her head on Stephen's bedside table—the corner of it, which was sharp, and it nicked her skin, and with all head wounds there is blood, because so much is needed to nourish the brain—Mr Hodge told her that—so that she sat on his floor, a cloth to her head. Stephen talked of stitches. A new lie was conjured, and she told Ray, later, as he picked through her hairline, that she had risen up into an open cupboard door. "Do you need stitches?" Ray asked.

It throbbed. Her pulse was in her scalp. A scab formed, as thick as meat, and she fingered it. Broke it early. Made it heal all over again.

．　．　．

RAY LOOKED for his wife, and found her—sitting on the shingle at Cley-next-the-Sea, beside the *Mary-Jane*. Her knees to her chest. He lowered himself down, sat beside her. They looked out to sea, at a fishing buoy rocking on its own. She could smell his turpentine.

"I know," he said, "that there's something."

She pressed a flat stone into her palm, tried to talk. Wanted to lie against him, for him, to put his arm across her shoulders, and for them to sit in silence, watch the sea for a while. So bad at words, and he nudged her, said her name.

"I'll tell you this," he said. "We're going to Stackpole."

An order. A fact of life.

*H*ERE AGAIN. IN THIS ROOM.

Hard, last night, to sleep beside Ray when I'd been talking of what I talked of, with you. Our heads were so close to each other's, and I thought, *What if my thoughts are like water itself?* So that they might leak into him, and he'd learn the truth. Dreamt it.

There it was, all over again. Floating up to the surface of me. We bury what we can, but the mound of earth is still there, the foam on the water, from where it has sunk. All things leave traces.

Speaking of which. They have removed the bandage on your head, so that I can see all the old wounds, the shorter hair, where they shaved you. Sometimes you wear it; sometimes you don't. Tonight, you don't, and in the past I've pressed against your scalp, hoping you might swipe a hand, grumble, wake, say, *Ow!*

You were taller, still. Not Moira's height, or Ray's, but if you hung upside down from the apple tree, your fingertips could touch the ground, which was new. Still a flat, boyish frame. Still, a hop at the start of each run, and your voice had always been low, bear-like, although I can't remember it now—but I know you sounded older than nearly twelve years old.

•   •   •

AMY CAME DOWN the drive, arms out. Stopped just short of them, paused. Then embraced them. Beamed.

"You're *here* . . ." To herself, it seemed, although Ray nodded, said, *Yes.*

And her husband was stolen away by the thin, fair-haired girl, dragged inside by the wrist, so that he glanced back at Moira, widened his eyes as all victims would, and George patted her shoulder as he held her, as if checking her bones, her existence. "Hello, love," he said. And the green front door shone behind him, and a seagull cleaned its feathers on the chimneypot, and there was sea, and no oil, none that she could see, and the last time Moira had seen her father, he'd worn a pink tie, and had drunk too much in the evening, and had told Raymond all about love. Fifty-seven months ago.

*   *   *

"I DON'T KNOW what's changed, really."

Her mother's hair was greyer. Her forefinger on the teapot's lid as she poured it, in the garden. The house was the same—brown-bricked, and uneven, and the bank of gorse bloomed to the south of the garden, with cobwebs in it. The boot-scraper that Amy had sliced her gums on. The rusted swing by the compost heap. Moira had stood, for a moment, on her own in the garden, and breathed. Old traces of home were still there. She thought of what the mind forgets—the sound of air, or shapes of trees. Closed her eyes, smelt the sea—salt, and weed, and old wood. The fishes in it.

"And the beaches are as they were, now. But you'd not have believed it. How it was to the north of here. Angle Bay was covered. There were sea birds . . ."

They drank their tea. The two of them. Moira and her mother, whose face was older, and whose hair had silver strands by her ears. Older hands. Eyes with a sadness in them, or a loss, at least. She offered biscuits, shifted in the silences. Said,

"We've missed you, Moira. Do you understand that?"

On this lawn, once, Moira had sat on her mother's hips as she'd hung out the washing, held on to her shirt. And now she was here, thinner. Wiser.

Miriam took her hand. Called her *firstborn*.

*   *   *

AMY SHOWED Raymond everything—the gorse, the swing, the compost heap, and she clamoured to haul him down the lane, past the dairy farm, to Stackpole Quay. "Tomorrow," said George. She sulked at that.

She showed him the stubborn bathroom tap, and the lavender cushion, and where the firewoods were kept, and she led him outside in the evening, through a cloud of midges, showed him—and Moira—a red primula, under the apple tree.

"This is . . . ?" Ray asked.

A place for very sombre thoughts. For under the flower, and the soil, and the pebble which, once, had words written on it, but which had been washed clean by the rain, lay a bundle of animal bones—tiny, as thin as china lines. Amy was sage, respectful. Tutted at a dead leaf, removed it.

"This," he whispered to his wife, "is one guided tour."

But Amy did not show Ray into the smallest bedroom. Moira did. She said, *my room*—pushed the black iron handle, opened the door, and it smelt of sunlight in there. The slanting roof, and the same blue paint. The faded candle, and the wooden boat. The yellow pillowcase, and patchwork rug, and the last time she'd slept here, in this bed, she'd been seventeen, and unmarried, and she felt tearful. Put the heels of her hands under her glasses. Ray said, "Hey." Felt the curtains, gazed at the map of Pembrokeshire she had pinned up on her wall. On her desk, a puffin that sang.

She told him how long it had been.

"Before you met me." A slow whistle between his teeth.

· · ·

AND SHE TUCKED UP her knees in her bedroom, that night. Ray asleep downstairs, for there were no other double beds, and her room was a cloth around her, she needed it, and said, *It's fine*. The creak of the pipes and the sea noises came to her if she opened her window a little. The smell—for don't all things have a smell, to them? An eggcup, by her bedside lamp—ox-eye daisies, and forget-me-not from the lane.

And she woke in the morning to a feeling of eyes on her, or breath on her face, and she thought, at first, *It is Ray.* Or it was his brother. But she opened her eyes in her old, blue bedroom, to find Amy sitting on the chair in the corner, cross-legged, cradling a mug of tea. Said, "Morning!"

She might have just sat down there, or been there for hours. Either way, Moira said, *Go.* Threw a pillow.

• • •

AMY PRESSED HERSELF against doors, peered through their hinges. An old trick, George said. He used to look up from a newspaper to see a single, blueberry-eye pressed to the keyhole, blinking once in a while. *Nosy Rosy,* he called her. To which she wrinkled one side of her nose, said, "No . . . *Amy.*"

But that was years ago. "Thought she'd outgrown it," he said.

Amy the spy, then. Belly on the floor, like an assassin. Holding her breath, or trying to, so that if Moira suspected this, she'd wait, and—in time—hear the burst of lungs, and the new hauling-in of air.

"A-ha," said Ray, playing the game.

But Moira had the raised brow, the sharpness. Had to say, *Get off*, for Amy was all hands.

"She's only doing what younger siblings do."

He shrugged. Atlantic winds in his hair, on the coastal path. "Don't be so hard on her."

• • •

RAYMOND AND MOIRA again. Just them.

Take me to . . . Her best beach. The lily-ponds. *Ray*—whom she loved, and who had loved her once, perhaps half loved her now. They walked where she thought she'd never walk, again. All the coves and rocks and broken fence-posts that she knew. Over molehills. Down the mossy steps to Presipe, where he looked back up to the path and said, "I see what you mean. About cliffs."

On Broad Haven he took her hand. She showed him Church Rock, how she'd climbed it, and they wandered inland to the lily-ponds, walked home through the Stackpole Estate. And on Barafun-dle they skimmed stones, and he lifted her up, briefly, without warning, and at Freshwater East she showed him a cave. Dank, salt-mouthed. The green cracks, the driftwood. The view from the cave was ridged sand, and the fulmars and gulls were calling out.

Moira leant her head against him. And she felt his shirt underneath her, and the wet cave wall was against her back, again. A long time, in the cave. In its darkness, with the daylight and the sea outside.

· · ·

"I saw you," Amy said. *I saw you!* Singing it. Sidling by the back door, half a sandwich in her hand. "On the beach! Were you kissing?"

· · ·

In the evening, the telephone rang. Amy answered.

"For you," she said. Holding out the telephone.

The voice at the far end of it was low, quick, and it lived in another world, so that Moira did not blink, or flinch, or say a word. She stood. Replaced the receiver.

"Who was it?" Ray asked. Playing chess with George.

Til.

"Matilda? Why didn't she want to talk to the rest of us?" Miriam bristled. And Amy pursed her lips—wise, and fierce. She stared at Moira. Followed her all the more, after that, knowing this was a lie, that it hadn't been Til, because when had Til's voice been deep, like a man's?

In the lane, Moira turned, thought, *Bitch.*

· · ·

OUT TO CHURCH ROCK. Under the white water, in the salt and roar of it, and then she surfaced, carved the water with her arms, headed towards the sea stack with its mussels, and the blue rope, and the weed she slipped on, and she was taller and stronger than the last time she climbed it, and she hauled herself up, tugged on the rope, emerged wet, dripping, with her shorter hair in her face, so that she had to throw her head back. Up the rock. No oil, but the weeds were slick. She grazed her knee, became breathless. The old footholds. The balls of her feet remembered them, and she heaved her body over the last point of it. On top of Church Rock again. A good knot, she thought, in the rope. A decade, now, and it was still strong. She was high up, in her black swimsuit. Covered in salt and weed and her own blood on her left knee, which tasted of metal, as the railings on the fire escape did, on her hands, afterwards. Broad Haven beach. Lundy Island behind her, as it always had been. She thought, *What if things had been different to this?* And she blinked three times, until her lenses had centred themselves. The shape on the sand became a person—in a blue sundress, sandals in her hand.

Moira did not jump. She lowered herself down the rock, into the water, which rose up to take her. And as she came up onto the beach, Amy tilted her head. Frowned. The single freckle under her eye.

"Look at you," she said.

Three words. They stood in silence. Walked back to the house without a sound between them, to find George and Ray playing chess again, and Moira would expect, in the days to come, her parents to say something of it—of this real, huge skinniness in her, which she kept under clothes, or of the marks on her that she'd made, herself, sometimes, on her inner arms, and legs. But they didn't. So Amy must have kept it to herself, murmured about the collarbone, and the shoulder blades, and the thinness and the red scratches, to no one at all, and nothing, except perhaps to her toy cloth cat, or the soil beneath the primula, or to her own pink arms in bed, or in the bath.

17

Wake

YOU THINK OUR ONLY LANGUAGE IS IN WORDS? I SUSPECT SO. A sixteen-year-old's body, but you are nearly twelve, inside, and too young to know that there are other ways of speaking, or of calling out loud. Take an example: your eyelids. The way our father, ever the fixer of things, tried, at first, to understand you through the flickering of your eyes. *One for yes, love. Two for no. Go on!* And you did, for a while, raise their hopes. The famous day in 2001 when Miriam asked, casually, if the click of knitting needles was annoying you, and a firm single blink came back.

See? Language came in the twitching of nerves for you, for a time. Also, your little finger curled up once, as I read a weather report from the newspaper. What was that? I could choose a message from you, or a spasm you did not control, and I have chosen both over the years. Both have brought comfort, and then, not.

We all have our ways. I see that. I used to think language was in a girl's mouth, nowhere else, and so wasn't I lacking? Quiet Moira. *Freak.* But, now? Look at Raymond, with his paintbrush, and the stories that came out of them. People pay money for his pictures because they *say* something, not simply because they match the carpet in their front room, or fill up a troublesome space on a wall. Love is in them, or sadness, or peace, or whatever the viewer wants to find there. And Ray manages this—to reach through the skin and press the heart with the tip of his horsehair brush.

Or how about Til—who knows every gesture there is, and what it conveys to people sitting in the dark; the power in a single raised eyebrow, or the movement of the hips? Or June, whose eyes said a thousand things, or Annie, who made it with her French horn, or Stephen, whose language was strange, uncertain—words, but also, silences? I heard them. And I came to know what his silences meant, in those ten months of undressing him—anger, or guilt, or hunger. I think I, too, was like that—back in my early days with Ray. Solemn, with my chin pressed down into my neck when he said a kind thing, to me. *I like you, Moira.* And I was mute. Shut, like a clam. Still, he uncoded me.

And so, Amy, the body does not need words at all, and can live without them, and I know this because I have peeled back the skin of a person—a real, dead human being—and seen into them, and I have studied a brain on a table in the university laboratory, cut it open, seen diagrams of it, and from birth we learn to read a face when it is set before us: smiles, frowns, anxiousness. We blush when ashamed; we perspire when nervous; our skin is a message board, and so isn't there sense in what I did? My language. My words. My calling out loud.

Too much for you, perhaps. I see your little face, on the beach, when I came ashore that one time. All this talk. Ray thought I was naturally thin; he thinks I've been marked from the rocks that I've climbed, or the fences I've ducked under with him—at least, I've said this. Perhaps he knows better. He probably does. I know, too, that it's safer and kinder to choose art, or music, or words to talk in—and I am better at that, now. Because for more than four years I've talked to you—read headlines, and letters from Til. Prattled, even. I've talked to a woman who *counsels*—that's her word. And in the last two months I've made this confession; leant down to your sore ear, said, *Wake.*

Wake.

The sea, too, is wordless, yet it speaks of things—I believe this. I do. Colours, mists, winds, tides. Doesn't our father still predict each storm? And I have heard many of its stories, as I've walked along the edge of it—of fish with their own lanterns, whales that fall in love with the hulls of boats, rock against them, and so crewmen have died from this whale love. Plankton that glows like a sad, green moon. The lone albatross who skims the water with his wings, and the widows who stand on quaysides, and there is a creature whose call is so strange that if you hear it, you think your death is near. Or so our father says.

Wistful, then, tonight. To talk this way—of language, water, the soul—takes a wistful mind, and I could say it's the full moon, but that, too, would be wistful, and it can be tiresome to listen to. All sorrow and hope. Til used to fall into thoughts, like this. In pubs, or on Titchwell's benches.

· · ·

HE TOLD HER, "You said nothing. You hung up the telephone, and didn't say a word."

Moira eyed him. In the cloisters, as it rained, and he shifted from foot to foot. Looking older. Hands on his waist. A striped tie.

He'd called to hear her. Nothing more than that. And Stephen sighed, turned away. Fingers to the bridge of his nose. Thinking, *How did I get here?* Or something like that.

And I remember my dreams, in the weeks that followed Stackpole—how they all came back to me; old, creaking dreams that I'd wake from, think, *Have I dreamt that before?* Sometimes I knew I had done; other times, I wasn't sure, for dreams and the truth can be the same, or nearly the same, or a single dream can be so strong that you think you've had it a thousand times, carried it in you. The rope, or tentacles, which curl around my legs. Mrs Bannister, squealing. All the gulls dropping down out of the sky.

My first dream of Stephen. As he was in the cloisters—angry, pacing. In that striped tie.

As for Raymond, he came back from Wales with a slowness in him, a half-smile, and he did not paint as much, although he still spent time in the greenhouse—cleaning his brushes, placing the paint jars in a line. Leaning against his worktop, mug in hand, watching the garden. Thinking.

He was haunted too, maybe. The cliffs, and the caves, and the gulls that didn't squabble for food, bark on their posts, but that moved silently, in the bays beneath his feet. He'd said, in Stackpole, *You grew up here?* Knowing it was true, but surprised by it, or not surprised by it at all. Maybe it all made sense to him. Fulmars roosted at Broad Haven, on its western cliffs, and Moira had sat with him above them, on the grass. Two coloured, unknown things in anoraks at first, holding hands. The fulmars drifted up, eyeing them. But, slowly, the birds saw them less, or trusted them more, and she watched their bills, their hanging legs, their round, glassy eyes. Ray said, *Look.* And so maybe, in his greenhouse, five hundred miles east of there, he still felt the draught from a fulmar's wing.

Or, Moira thought, *He thinks of her.*

Perhaps he'd watched the fulmars, sat with his wife by the coastguard's house at Tenby, and thought of her—the other woman, the beautiful one. Whoever she was. Moira caught him, in Blakeney, twirling a sycamore seed between his thumb and forefinger, thinking. Guilt in him, then. Or regret. Or he was just missing her.

Moira dreamt of Stackpole, and of a faceless woman with no rings on her hand, and Ray woke before her, now. Brushed his teeth by windows. Watched his wife.

• • •

A DREAM OF HORSES in a field, biting their necks, with a red dust under their feet, blowing. Of birds flying backwards.

Til rang, in a strange mood. Twisting her silver ring as she spoke. She wondered what her life meant, if she actually wanted to act anymore, and there was the hauled breath of a smoker, the breathing-out. "I'm tired," she said. Forty-six years old. Perhaps she'd come to visit. Get her pointed heel stuck in the boardwalk again.

Florence was hit by a car. She'd seen a soft toy lying on the far pavement, run for it. She wasn't hit hard, but still hard enough—pins in her hip, as if she were old. Maths was left behind, for a time.

And Stephen rang twice more. Stood in the street in Blakeney in his woollen coat, with his hands in his pockets, and hard eyes, and what was there to do? *What?* She asked him this. What could he expect from this? Where could it go? She'd had her reasons for what they had done—although she kept them to herself. Deep, deep. Under her spleen, or in her stomach so that it hurt, and, sometimes, she'd taste it. Guilt, and fear, too, and she shook him away, so that Stephen hissed her name, said he loved her, and she walked uphill, away from him. Not wanting anything.

She sat in the church she'd married in.

And then, later, I came indoors, went upstairs. Ray was sleeping there—on his front, with his hands under the pillow, where it was cool. I laid myself down on his back, as I used to, as I had done in the barley field, and he felt my hair on his shoulders, shifted his head, turned.

"You smell of the outdoors," he said.

• • •

WHAT ELSE? A full moon. A rabbit, under my wheels, as I drove north from Glandford, my windows down, so that I'm sure I heard it cry out. Clouds and mist and wading birds, and the brooch of fishes, and the small wrinkles in the skin by my husband's ears, and his air-mail letters which I opened again, smelt Locke on, and dust, and all his old words. *Am I mad to be writing to you?*

Madness. A border country. I walked, perhaps, on the edge of it, as you now walk on your own straight line. Arms held out.

Did I ever, once, say, *Amy* . . . And talk of love?

*I*T WAS 20 SEPTEMBER 2001. Early evening. I half slept on the sofa, a glass of water in my hand. Woke. Wide-eyed.

I grappled for the telephone, said, *Yes?*

"Love?"

Our father's voice. And maybe we do know, when a change is coming—maybe we can sense it, as birds can, and Til was right, and her tarot cards were, and I think this because I felt, then, what had happened. On the sofa, I think I almost saw it—the mussel that pushed its way into you. His voice had a difference in it. He said my name twice, then, other words: *head. Water. Amy.*

· · ·

IT ISN'T MONEY or wisdom that changes lives. I know this now, because I've been told, and because, too, I've imagined it, as we all imagine accidents: you'd left your school uniform on the drier sand. Popped your socks inside your shoes, and put sun cream on your arms. Worn goggles for it. Stretched, for the swim. And probably dithered a little, in the shallows, because you were never too sure of water. And also, it felt very cold.

A helicopter came to you, half an hour later. You swung in mid-air, for a time, wrapped in foil, locked in a brace.

· · ·

RAY FOUND ME, and said, *You didn't do this. You aren't to blame.* And I said I was, and I fought him, and I took his jumper in my fists, because he knew me, Raymond, my husband. He always has done. Even in his foreign countries. Even in trees, by an icehouse, when I was sixteen. Over that fire.

You aren't to blame.

But maybe I am.

18

Oystercatchers

THEY ARE THE PIED, RED-LEGGED BIRDS THAT STALKED ALL THE shorelines I have ever stood on—east, or west; the shingle spits or the coves, or the wide surf beaches. Red-beaked birds, with a low, straight flight, and their call is mournful, or it always sounded so to me. My mother used to sigh, say, *Look—sea pies* . . . For she called them that. Puffins were *sea clowns*. In Norfolk, a long-tailed tit is called a *bumbarrel*—Ray told her this. So she, too, used the word, still does. *There are bumbarrels in the furze* . . . So that I would blink, say, *Sorry?*

I thought of them, as we drove to you. I pictured the eight oystercatchers that lived in a cove near Manorbier, and that stood, one-legged, in a line at high tide, and watched the waves unfolding. Or the pair of birds that said *kleep!* in the tidal marshes at Brancaster Staithe, as Ray and I sat there, late in the day. Or the flock of them that lifted themselves up from the sand at Holkham. I know the sound, Amy. Perhaps they were calling out as I was born, or maybe they just talked to themselves in the background and I soaked this up, as I soaked up the guns on the army range or the wind sounds of Stackpole without knowing it. They always make me think of home. It was sea pies I thought of first of all, when the tanker ran aground—their white patches turning black, and their red beaks sealed. Always in pairs, too—have you noticed that? And there is no migration for the oystercatcher—no leaving for warmer weather. Every season I'd expect them to rise up, leave me. But they stayed. They are happy with this life here, on these beaches, and they dabbled at Titchwell all year round, so that Til said to them, *Hello, again,* and their neat red legs were enough to make you think of clowns, of stilted men, or woollen leg-warmers.

• • •

WE DROVE INTO the night to reach you. Ray at the wheel. As the sun slid away, and the evening came in, we saw all the soft shadows of things—houses and trees and churches sinking into their dark-blue sleep. A bridge swooped over us like a night-time bird, was gone, and I knew I'd never see it again—not like that. Driving to you.

Oystercatchers and, also, a baby, with a face like dough. Or a bridesmaid—how, when you saw the dress, with its pink sash, its flowers, its underskirt, you gasped. Strawberry-mouthed. You'd pressed your hands together, said, *This is for me?*

Or, at Stackpole, after a glass of lemonade you had burped—a huge, bellowing noise, and you'd laughed. Laughed till you'd needed the toilet. Five years old, maybe.

I thought this: *If she dies, what wouldn't change?* All of it would. Each part of life. Everything changes, and I'd never have imagined it to be this way, but in the car, believing you would die, I was sure your death would shift the whole world, so that the tides altered, the winds changed direction, and birds forgot their roosts, and their breeding grounds. And I thought, *Where would your absence be the strongest?* In the places where you walked, snapping branches, or in the places you never made it to? Would you haunt the hockey fields, because I never let you see them? Or would I find you in a wooden bird-watcher's hide because I denied them to you—said they were pointless, that you'd be too loud inside them, and all the birds would fly away?

Or you'd be clutching the sides of boats, saying, *I'm really really sorry* . . .

Or on a pier, wordless, with a hand-mark on your face.

• • •

I FOUND OUR mother standing there, on the fifth floor. Stooped. Thin, even. Motionless, with her eyes on the floor, and I thought, *She will be like this, when she is old.* When I stood beside her, she held my coat, and leant against me. Made a sound into my collarbone. A frail, child's sound.

George's forehead was pressed against your hand. And you, Amy, were tubes. You were a green heartbeat on a screen, and false breath. Red skin, black stitches, and a white gauze. Huge white gloves. A blue mussel had been plucked away.

And we waited.

We counted the minutes that passed. And then the hours. Then the days.

*F*OUR YEARS HAVE PASSED BY. More, now—four and a half, because it is March. I will be twenty-eight, and you have rolled through another birthday of your own. Sixteen, Amy. There were roses in your room, and a silver balloon. Think of what you should be doing. What you should be like.

And I am here, tonight, as ever. On a chair with a plastic cushion that wheezes when I sit on it, and a sour smell in the room, and all the floors in this hospital seem to be exactly the same—blue and beige tiles, scuffed from shoes and trolley wheels. The man with thick glasses mops the corridor, and I wonder if I've had more words from him, in my lifetime, than I've had from you. My fault, if so. For walking away from you, as you spoke them.

. . .

YOU KNOW IT ALL, now. Or most of it. I've forgotten parts, I'm sure—but the bones are all there. Enough of the truth for you to know it, and fill in the rest. The city outside lies in darkness, and beyond your heart, and your breathing, I can hear the light outside in the corridor—it hums.

I have seen you so often, and so closely, and I have studied every part of you for a sign of life, or understanding, that it's hard to believe I will ever forget what you look like—the pores on your face, or your downy earlobes, or the freckle under your eye. The fronds of hair, by your temples. Or the way your lips are—pink, and their pinkness seeps a little over the edges of them, as if you have pressed your thumb into colour, rubbed it on, thoughtlessly. As sixteen-year-olds do. And there are all your old injuries, which I can list as Ray lists countries, or colours, and as Til can talk of star signs. I've always been able to list them. People would say, *How is Amy?* And so I'd begin. From the torn fingernails to the collarbone to the lifted chunk of your scalp.

We've all aged, I suppose. How can we not have done? But I can say honestly that you are the same as you were, when I saw you last. Waving as we drove away. Thinking, perhaps, *Til hasn't got a man's voice. Has she?* Or, *Why is she as thin as this?*

I wish I'd stopped the car. Walked back to you.

*L*IFE RECOVERS, Ray said. When the oil seeped into lungs and gills. It did. You wouldn't know there had ever been such a thing as that, now, as the *Sea Empress*. Scoter ducks are many, again. In the final days before our parents sold End House and moved away, I walked with them on Freshwater West, for the last time. Huge surf, and my mother talked of how it had been, with the oil—as black as a mine. Sad to its core, with its dead fish, and birds. A seal pup, mewling. But all Freshwater West was to us, that afternoon, was foam and light, and a wide sky, and the rock pools with their crabs and sea anemones, and the three sets of footprints we left behind, on the beach. Sand dunes, and choppy water. And sea pies, standing on the water's edge, with their wise, private dreams.

Our parents live, now, on the Gower peninsular, where it is still quiet, and salty-aired, and there are cliffs they can stand on. Gulls that wheel beneath them. But it has no memories of you in it, and this is what they wanted—because how can they walk on Broad Haven, now? Or sit in a room you crawled in? Their hearts hurt so much they could barely stand it—so our mother said. So they left the hamster grave and blackthorn bushes and the horses, and Lundy Island, and the old, abandoned Bannister house, and they drove east. This new house of theirs is by a stream. They have painted its spare room a pale pink, filled it with your horse magazines, and hair ties, and your white towelling slippers with their two flattened circles, made by your heels. They say, *when you come home . . .*—but even they must doubt this, now. Our mother sits in this spare room daily, humming, smelling your unwashed pillows, dusting the bookcase, and she smoothes the shape of her bottom out of the duvet, when she stands up. But I can't believe that truly, she expects you to ever be in that room. Maybe once, but not these days.

We live our lives, and we grieve, and we hope, and we live our lives, and Miriam laughed at a novel, once, and pressed her hand against her mouth, ashamed of it, of laughing. And George still twirls his spanners, still walks on beaches, buttoned up, and I have told him a little of all these things I have told you—the fire escape, and Miss Bailey. The airmail letters. I've linked my arm through his. Til once said, *It is the simple things that make us happy*. And he patted my arm, then. Walking on a new Welsh beach that didn't have you in it, but, also, it did.

• • •

So YES. Life recovers, in a certain way. It goes on, and in truth, Amy, it's hard to sit beside you and not think of all the other people I have watched, and liked, or disliked, and how they might be, now. If they're still here, breathing. Morbid, I agree with that—but I could still describe, exactly, the shape of Mr Hodge's head, with his thinning hair, and his spoon-like ears, and yet I have no idea where, or how, he is. He was kind to me. He hummed like this: *doo-be-doo*. And because of him alone I looked for Locke Hall's web site, a year or so ago—typed in its name, scrolled down. But it is gone. Abandoned. It was broken up, sold into flats, and there is another part of my life taken away, so that there is no trace, anymore, of beanbags or piano lessons, or mustard cress on paper towels, and I can only hope that Miss Bailey's bench is still there—shiny from behinds that have sat on it. Mr Hodge? Retired. Tending to his vegetable patch, and wearing his skeleton tie on Sundays. Or I hope this, anyway.

Heather—well, who's to say? She'd have blossomed further, or lost her shine. Forgotten me, or spat my name in the years to come, measured all deceit or ungainliness against my own. Stood on a netball court at university, aware of her legs, and the boys that watched from the football field.

As for Annie, I doubt her hair is still orange, but I see it as such.

She plays her French horn. She's either changing the world for the better, or she's left it already. Choked on her own tongue.

. . .

Two weeks after your fall, Ray and I drove back to Norfolk, gave our notice on the Blakeney house. Packed our boxes. Moved our hands over each other, in the evenings, and sat on the white benches at Blakeney, as the old people did. Saying goodbye to it.

The last time I saw my brother-in-law was in the cloisters. We didn't say much, of course. He knew, from Ray, that we were leaving, and that nothing ever stays the same—that daily, things are gained and lost. He looked as if he had nothing left inside him, or more than ever before—both—and I know that look well, and how it feels to have it. I think most people do. But I watched him walk away, through the cathedral close, through pigeons and a soft, autumnal watercolour sky, and I knew he'd be fine, in a day or so. I was ten months of rain, that's all. A slow rain, too. A drizzle.

He still adds and subtracts. He phones his brother weekly, and asks after you—I hear this from the stairs, or as I fold sheets in the spare bedroom. He is a lost dream, in that he kissed an old, buried Moira, not this one, and I'm sure he feels the same way—that he frowns at my name, as if he half remembers it, but can't quite place how, or why.

I hear he will marry. There is a girl who lives in his flat now, who plays the flute, and her hair is in ringlets—or so Ray says. I can see her in the corner bath. Under the same cracked ceiling. Or leaving the empty milk bottles on the front step. So one day I will be back there, in Norfolk—back on its dark-brown earth. There will be godwits and other birds out on the marshes, I'm sure of that. I'll think of them, sifting. And I'll sit in the church and watch him, my husband: how he moves, how he strokes his hair forwards, how he takes photographs of the small, private, overlooked things—rain on the hem of the bride's dress, or a cobweb, or the linking of their little fingers behind her white back. I'll see these things, too. And I will read his airmail letters in the days afterwards—*I miss you, Moira. I carry you in me.* Amy, I know what love is.

There is an elephant shrine, in the hills . . . We are going there. He has bought it already—a small porcelain elephant, deep-blue, pocket-sized, with its trunk raised up. We talk of Thailand in the afternoons, when we skim stones—how hot it will be, or how cool. We will go there. But for now, we wait here, for you.

• • •

AND ONE more thing worth knowing? The pastel sketch? Of a woman's back, and an unmarried hand?

I never thought to turn it over. I was too fierce for such a clear thought, as that. But when I saw it again, months later, as we packed our things up for the westward move, I held it. Looked at the back of it, where there was no drawing. But there was a word: *Moira.* From Mary. A name like an attic map.

He said, *Ah . . .* Said that, in my fever, my skin had flushed, and in my bad dreams of oil and birds falling down from the sky I'd flailed, scratched the side of my face with the ring he'd pushed onto my finger on the shingle beach at Cley-next-the-Sea. So he eased it off, left it on the bedside table, with water, and aspirin, and my spectacles.

I know what this means. It was always me.

My husband said to me, once, that he couldn't believe he ever saw some places—an evening river with a platypus in it, or game parks. He showed me his hand, said, *This hand has actually picked a coconut. How strange is that?*

And I am like that, daily. I have him, and this is what makes me think, *How strange . . .* Me with the scholarship. Me with the over-sized feet.

• • •

AS FOR OUR AUNT, maybe the strangest story of all is hers to tell, not mine. What did she deserve? All the best things. *Matilda.* Violet eyes and a jewellery box. I think, now, that she walked the stage because it was a safe place for her. She had lines to say. A dress to wear. Knew what the ending was.

Perhaps I'm wrong. I know I have been a hundred times over, or more. But she is not an actress, anymore. She's left the theatre, and the underground mice, and the almond croissants, behind her. She lives in the countryside now. Because every year, at Christmas-time, she'd sit in a café at Heathrow and watch the pilots click across the floor in their polished shoes, with their leather bags and coffee cups, with a seed of hope in her, or nostalgia, and I always thought *pointless*, and even *desperate.* Every year, she did this. On the same date, at the same time. She marked the anniversary of seeing a man—just one man. And I was wrong to say *pointless*—because as she sat there, at Heathrow, on a Friday morning three years ago, in a floor-length skirt, with a herbal tea and a newspaper, a man with flecks of grey in his hair walked past her. Glanced across, and slowed. A decade, after they'd met.

He said, *You probably don't remember me, but . . .*

Til always talked of *The One*—as novels do. I have no idea if there are such things. Nor do I know if there is a god, or if there are real, absolute truths in crystals, or flower juice, or stars. I can only answer *maybe*, to all of it—because how are they proved, or disproved? I've turned towards them all, at some point, like fish turn to moonlight, or a plant turns towards the windowpane. I've read my horoscope. I've read yours. I've prayed, or my version of it, here, by your bed.

Anyway: I don't know if this was Til's doing, or the world's, or luck, on its own. She sat there, waiting; but did she actually think he would walk by? *Him?* Did she really believe it? He did, all the same. The pilot who'd flown from London to Miami ten years ago; who'd written his number on square, pale-yellow paper. Who'd eyed his hotel phone for two nights, years ago, waiting for the woman who smelt of oranges, and whose smile had bewitched him, to ring.

What do you think of that? Do you even believe it? I didn't. I blinked. I shook my head, and when I told Ray, in the kitchen, as he peeled potatoes with the radio on, he widened his eyes as if I were singing in tune. Said, *You're joking. You're joking, aren't you?*

At any rate, she lives in a leafy market town, now. Aunt Til, and him. They have squirrels in the garden that dart over the lawn, steal bread, and drop acorns on their kitchen roof. He retired early, because of her. At night, there are tawny owls; she hears them, in her sleep.

*H*AIL AGAINST THE WINDOWS, so that any other sleeping person would raise their head, rub their eyes at the noise. Say, *What's that?* What else is there to tell you? I have picked up many small, sharp things, put them down again. There was a boy—do you know this? Dark-haired, long limbs, and he'd hang, nervously, outside your room. I spoke to him; he shook his head. Enough, for him, to just look through the glass at you, perhaps, and I saw him as often as I saw the cleaner, or your doctor with the slow hands. But his visits dropped away. He no longer comes to you; his life has moved on. He is sixteen, too, now. He'll have a girlfriend. A story in him of a girl he once knew who fell from a rock, hit her head. Died, or as good as.

. . .

I HAVE WALKED on boundaries all my life. From the first, dark-blue evening when I was born—I had two worlds, beckoning. And I chose this one. I chose, in the end, to stretch my mouth open, and howl.

And I walked on the edge of friendships, of marriage, of sisterhood, and of being a daughter as if these things were wires, or fenceposts, or shorelines, and I have imagined a simpler life, where there are no boundaries at all—just one, plain life, with no choices in it, and a life at sea would be like that. Just water, for mile after mile, like the bottle with my name in it, or a lost piece of wood. Bumping into nothing at all. And that's the pirate in me, perhaps. The mermaid, which Ray claimed to see, for the first time, by the icehouse.

But now, it is you who lies there—ash-skinned, mute, with a blue vein in your forehead, and a catheter, and needles, and a half-life, a half-death. You are the person now, I suppose, who treads the fine line, who stalks the water's edge, and I have never yet said to you, *I am sorry.* I've never said it.

But I am. I say it now, and not as if I've knocked into you on a street, or trodden on your toes as I passed you. It is a deeper word, than that. Deep as the sea, or deeper.

• • •

AND AMY, it has taken me all of this, too, to be able to see that not everyone hates glasses, or that quiet does not always mean dull, and that large feet and hands don't always make you clumsy. Truthfully? He sat me down, in the weeks after your fall from Church Rock, and made me believe it. That I am his best colour; I am the wildest foreign land he's been to; that I'm all his words—all of them, from his letters, to his stories, or to the words he does not say but shows, in a movement. I am the woman in the street who turns his head, and that, for a moment, he thinks, *Who is . . . ?* Then, *It is Moira. And she is mine.*

Strange? Yes, I am. We all are.

We dream what we dream; we believe what we believe. And if ever you were the proof of something, it's that we love what we love. We can't help it.

*A*MY, YOU SURVIVED.

You live on. Not as we live—not in a way that I can touch, or hear your voice again. But you do live. You are more in this world than you ever were.

Six months on, since our mother knelt in the early evening, and felt your name on the small stone plaque that lies above what's left of you—a soft, grey powder, in a wooden box. Six months since I walked out of the sea, towelling myself, to see Raymond standing on our lawn, his hair unbrushed, waiting for me.

Amy, I still dream of water. I still feel I'll be in it, one day—as a pilchard, flashing. Or a sea bean. Or whale song.

But I see you, in the daytime. I see you as I walk in countries I knew nothing of, before Ray. You dangle from branches. You lie on your belly by a spider's web, watching it, stick in hand. I've seen a red rock turned redder, as the sun goes down, and I thought of many things—but mostly, I thought of you.

You're this: an onion bulb. The glint of a rabbit's eye. The clicking of beetle's legs on a leaf; the leaf's brown edge; dandelions; a pebble; windfall fruit. You're a camel's long eyelashes. You're the smell of hibiscus tea, and you're the first few drops of rain, in the canopies, and when I hear a hedgehog's evening bustle I say, *Ssh!* Because you are in it, and because I miss you, and so I want to hear this hedgehog as much as I can, before it potters into its leaves, and is gone. You are in my own movements—in my own, small pout. I caught a bee, once, and let it go, and Ray said he'd seen you do that, too. Long ago.

I think this, as my comfort: that you existed. And by existing, there will always be traces of you, blowing over the earth.

•   •   •

I HAVE THOUGHT THIS in a hundred different places. In snow. In a dark wood.

I think it now.

I think it, as I follow my husband down a track to a small hut, in a clearing, after a day of sun. His shirt is damp on his back, and his left arm is behind him, his hand open, asking for my hand to be placed in his. I do this. His hand closes round it, tightens, and in that one gesture, I think of you.

Acknowledgments

Many thanks to Bert Jones; Helen Ryan and Rosemary Philpot; Ian and Claudine Causer; Naomi Wyatt; Sarah Bower; Ross Peat; Matt Colahan and Ben Youdan.

Thanks, too, as always to Christy Fletcher and Jill Bialosky; Viv Schuster and Clare Reihill; and to my parents, to Michael, my friends and family who make it feel like I never write alone.